Glimpse the Promised Land

AN AMERICAN TALE
OUT OF THE CAROLINAS

Glimpse the Promised Land

—⟫⟪—

HOUSTON L. CRUMPLER, JR.

CHAPEL HILL

FULL-SERVICE   BOOK-MAKERS
ESTD.   1999

PRESS

Contents

Chapter One

Midnight September 11, 2001, This Tale Begins

September 11, 2001, 12:01 a.m. Eastern Daylight Time,
September 10, 2001, 11:01 p.m. Central Daylight Time
Lambert–St. Louis International Airport

And the Voice said, "Let there be . . . Light."
And suddenly there was light reaching far beyond the Voice, and e did equal mc²,
and the present Eon, as we know it, began according to the Word of the Good Book.
> —*"Preamble to the Beginning," Chaplain Wesley Wyatt, U.S. Army*
> *The Coosa Valley Boarding School for Boys, ca. 1954–55*

I

"MRS. PENNY, I REACHED PEM and told him we're stranded. He said call from Denver to-morrow to let him know our airborne Santa Fe stagecoach hasn't been hijacked by more mechanical problems. Then he laughed, and said, 'I sure hope Jesse James won't hijack you either as you fly over the Arch to the West.'"

"Did Pem's great-granddad know Jesse James, too, Melody?"

"Pem was only joking. His forebear, Croatan Joe, never knew Jesse James, just Billy the Kid, Johnny Ringo, Ike Clanton, and the Apache Chiefs Victorio and Geronimo before he migrated into the Navajo Four Corners.

"But never mind Pem's family history. I'm still amazed at your leg's healthy color after Duke Hospital's hyperbaric treatments. Bessie Mae said that pressurized oxygen would help you!

"And I'm glad you could meet her husband, too. I've known Bessie Mae and Donald since we worked catering college fraternity parties at Duke and Chapel Hill. My friend Desmond Printce, 'Dizzy,' also worked with us back in the early seventies. That job was fun because we got to know the band members who played at those parties."

"Melody, Donald and Bessie Mae talked about this past weekend's Sunrise Acres barbeque reunion as joyously as you did on our Santa Fe flight to North Carolina. We've nothing to do tonight but wait for tomorrow's flight home—tell me about it."

"Mine's a long story if you want to understand it all, Mrs. Penny. I know so many background stories besides what I witnessed or participated in."

"Melody, Pem's dad, Silver Hawk, and his Navajo World War II code-talker connection with my Billy centers our relationship, certainly. Silver Hawk was Billy's best man at our wedding after the war, too. But this trip has made me feel even closer to your family—like you and I are family soulmates. So tell me about those folks—Brick, Junebug, Marsh, Chaplain Wesley, your dad, Mingo, and the others."

"Well, Mrs. Penny, Bessie Mae's Donald told how it began with Sunrise Acres."

II

A rising moon appeared through the clouds that half-hid the fading sunset of a cold November sky in eastern North Carolina—a complicated sky, Mrs. Penny. Mr. Malcolm Marshall MacKoy looked up from his office desk and out the window at the treetops on the skyline. Donald continued cleaning up, waiting to take Mr. Malcolm home after his last cancer treatments in 1970. Donald remembered it because it was his last day of chauffeuring and the day he first spoke with Mr. Malcolm's nephew, Brick.

Recalling similar sunsets, Mr. Malcolm told Donald about boyhood quail hunts near his Sampsons Landing hometown with Donald's mama's daddy, Lester. Granddaddy Lester had lived on Mr. Malcolm's parents' farm, and Lester's mama was their maid. Donald's mama's brothers, Luke and Tyrone, had worked for Mr. Malcolm's brother, Mr. Lee, and his Aunt Wixie still worked for Mr. Malcolm's family. Donald had worked part-time for Mr. Malcolm's sister, Dot, and at the Pineland Springs Resort Club that Mr. Malcolm and his brother, Lee, had an interest in at Pineland Springs. The club was generally referred to as the PSR Club.

The wall clock read six. Donald's Aunt Wixie had said that Mr. Malcolm's wife wanted him home by six-thirty because his daughter, Diane, and family would be there for his postponed sixty-fourth birthday dinner party. His first cancer treatments had taken place on his birth-date weeks before. But Donald just kept on cleaning and dusting while Mr. Malcolm viewed a subdivision plat named Sunrise Acres.

Donald dusted the picture frame holding Mr. Malcolm's 1930 law license. Then he moved to the frame holding a 1933 photo of Mr. Malcolm with his parents, brother Lee, and sister Dot in front of the Sampsons Landing house his parents lost during the Depression. Donald's granddaddy's mother also lost her job then as Mr. Malcolm's parents' maid.

Next Donald dusted off the photograph of Mr. Malcolm and his wife, Mrs. Colleen, standing in front of his old law office about 1938 because Mrs. Colleen was holding baby Diane. The next one showed a four- or five-year-old blond girl standing beside her mother, with Mr. Malcolm in a naval uniform and holding his baby boy, Malcolm Marshall, Jr., called Marsh. Soon after, in 1943, Mr. Malcolm went to the South Pacific as a Naval Supply Officer.

Mr. Malcolm watched Donald dust off the photo of the house Mr. Malcolm had built for his family just after the war. He had never occupied it, however, because he received an offer for it that gave him more money than he had ever had, and that money started him on a career as a builder and real estate developer.

Beside it was a photo of Mr. Malcolm and Mr. Lee with their Sampsons Landing boyhood friend, Holden Rollins, and the Lazlo brothers at the PSR Club they had all partnered to build in the fifties. Another photo showed the same men looking at Donald's distant cousin, Shank Poe, admiring a gold pocket watch the club had given Shank upon his retirement as the club's bartender. Retired Brigadier General Eisner, the club's board chairman, was presenting the watch.

On the adjacent wall hung a photo of Mr. Malcolm's sister, Dot, and her army-doctor husband who died in Korea like Donald's own daddy. Next to that, Mrs. Dot stood in her Pineland Springs Antique Furniture and Interior Art Decor Shop, where Donald did part-time furniture refinishing. Beside it, Diane and husband, Austin, each held one of their twin boys born prematurely at Duke Hospital. The couple had met at Duke and had worked in France with the Foreign Business Service upon graduation. When pregnancy problems forced them home, Mr. Malcolm hired Austin, and he eventually became Mr. Malcolm's General Manager.

On other office walls were housing-project photos taken in Raleigh, Fayetteville, Greensboro, Charlotte, Durham, Chapel Hill, and other communities near the Wisdom Station and Pineland Springs area, where the MacKoys lived.

I already knew quite a bit about Mr. Malcolm's numerous building operations because Dad had worked on many of them while also being a customer of Mr. Malcolm's lumber and hardware company. But I knew little about his wife, Mrs. Colleen, then, except that she came from Evabay, near the coast and New Holland where numerous attempts since colonial times had failed to drain Lake Mattamuskeet for farming its rich lake bottom. Her father had been a school principal and her mother a teacher there. Her brother followed in their footsteps at Evabay's school. His only child was severely epileptic and had recently died at the advanced age of 30 for someone of his disability level. Donald had driven Mrs. Colleen and Mr. Malcolm to the funeral.

"Melody, rest his poor soul. But go on."

Well, Mrs. Penny, when Donald dusted off the newest photo, showing Marsh just back from Vietnam and still in uniform, Mr. Malcolm said, "Donald, before my prostate kills me, I hope to pass something onto Marshall like I'm doing for Diane and Austin. Austin's done well here and given me handsome twin grandsons. I want the same for Marshall. I'm hopeful his new wife can finally settle him down.

"Speaking of romance, Donald, your Aunt Wixie says you've been seeing Malachi Owens' daughter. What's her name—and where does she work?"

"Bessie Mae," Donald replied. "She's studying nursing at N.C. Central, in Durham. We've talked about marriage when she graduates and I find steady work. She'd rather work at the hospital in Durham than the one in Fayetteville because the pay is better. 'Course, if we live here, we'll be as close to Durham as to Fayetteville. If we live in Pineland Springs, we'll be closer to Fayetteville, and that drive's cheaper."

"Well," Mr. Malcolm said, "I might find you work here next year if I can put this building project together for Marsh and my nephew, Brick, you were re-introduced to this afternoon.

"Brother Lee is selling his Pinestate Foundry in Pineland Springs to Amalgamated Industries and retiring. Brick is remaining briefly to help his dad with the ownership transition. Afterward, he'd like to try building houses. This Sunrise Acres property is just the project if I can get this old set of plans approved. I drafted it for another Sunrise Acres partnership that didn't work out.

"Donald, I do appreciate your coming here from Pineland Springs to chauffeur me around. Mrs. Colleen and I couldn't have gotten along without you and your Aunt Wixie, especially last week going to Evabay for her nephew's funeral.

"Now, I don't want to take you away from your cousin Thomas at the PSR Club, or your Pineland Springs family, but if you are thinking of living here in Wisdom Station, we may spot you a construction job with my son and nephew. Sister Dot says you're good at light sanding of furniture for refinishing. That's a good skill for finish carpentry work. If you don't like that, we might put you on driving a truck for the lumber company. Last week, you backed that hay trailer into the cow barn like a professional."

Donald smiled about these job possibilities before Mr. Malcolm said, "Well, let's go—or Colleen and your Aunt Wixie will think something's wrong."

III

Walking to Mr. Malcolm's sedan, they sensed lumber and plywood smells permeating the air, a forklift roaring near the dry kiln, and the contented lowing of Mr. Malcolm's cows milling about to feed nearby. Donald said, "I appreciate your thinking about a job for me here, Mr. Malcolm. Seems my family's worked with you MacKoys for over a hundred years, going back to Sampsons Landing and that long-ago life on the old Negrohead Road."

Before Mr. Malcolm could respond, a sheriff's patrol car eased into the parking lot. The car's window was down, and an arm, sleeved in a deputy sheriff's uniform, stuck out holding a brown paper bag.

"I killed these quail this afternoon and thought you'd like a taste of bird since you've not hunted this season, Mr. Malcolm. You haven't even been able to touch the old Ghost Dog, Bentonville Blue, for good shooting luck. Iris said you'd still be here."

"Carley Ray!" exclaimed Mr. Malcolm. "I haven't been through a fall, except for my Navy years, when I didn't taste quail. And that goes back to my Sampsons Landing boyhood when I bird-hunted with Donald's granddaddy, Lester."

"Well, gotta go," Carley Ray came back. "The high-sheriff made me the night watch commander since that Ronald Moore was caught stealing drugs from the evidence room. It's a shame, too, with us being looked over by the Feds so much. These new equal-opportunity rules! They'll just stop processing those grants we need to start our rescue squad.

"Moore was likable—seemed sensible! It's a shame 'cause we don't get many chances to hire ex-Bragg MPs who want to move back here rather than onto big-city pay."

"So I've heard. Thanks for the birds, Carley Ray!" exclaimed Mr. Malcolm. "Oh, Mrs. Iris told me that the 'Mingo Kid' is out of prison. I suppose he'll have to work to abide by his parole terms?"

"Yes," answered Carley Ray. "But he's not the Mingo Kid anymore. He's the big, filled-out 'Mingo Man.' I wouldn't want to arrest him today if he wanted to get troublesome! I was glad his daddy and Deacon were there when I arrested his skinny butt. Although he'd voluntarily returned after running off with his stepbrother, Juan, and Juan's Crow Indian roommate from Pembroke, Deacon and Mingo's daddy still had to encourage him to go with me.

"But Mingo seems more sensible now that his rough times in Montana and prison life have aged him some. Iris and I hope such common sense will sink into her late sister's boy, Ollie. I haven't caught Ollie with drugs since last summer 'cause Ollie knows I'll send him back to his daddy, stationed in Germany, and that stepmother Ollie despises. Hope Ollie matures like Mingo."

"If Mingo'll work with Deacon," said Mr. Malcolm, "it'll help Deacon get back on his feet enough so I might get my money back on the judgment I'm holding for his building materials."

"Well, I got to go to work myself, or I won't get paid!" said Carley Ray as he eased off.

Watching the patrol car leave, Donald asked, "The deputy is your secretary's husband?"

"Yes—Carley Ray! I got him that deputy's job after the war. Iris was my law-office secretary. I knew back then that the best way to keep her from going to Fayetteville or Raleigh-Durham was to have her husband well-employed locally. My courthouse contacts helped me get Carley Ray the deputy's job. Then Iris came with me when I quit practicing law to take on the lumber company.

"Over the years, Carley Ray's come to know every lawman, lawyer, and judge in the surrounding counties. I know that because they go to our annual dove hunt in Sampsons Landing. Carley Ray's my guest every year, but his contacts make him more like the unofficial host. He'll retire in a couple of years."

IV

On the trip home they spoke again of the long-ago Negrohead Road.

"Mr. Malcolm, I often think of our forefathers standing naked in the rain, looking at that skittish horse about to jump away from a stump by the cart path."

"Donald, that Negrohead incident reminds us of our connection, but it reminds me, too, of how Brick's name comes from the Brickman part of my family tree. It's funny how the passing down of family names connects families to their forebears. Brother Lee's retirement shows me it's time now for my generation to pass something on. I hope I can pass on more than my dad was able to.

"Dad and his Uncle Tobe lost their car dealership in the Depression but both held onto their farms. Lee had just graduated in Engineering from State College and was working for the foundry. I was just entering law school and waiting tables for room and board. Thankfully, Lee saved enough money for seed and fertilizer so our folks could farm that first year after losing the auto business. Sister Dot was still a teenager.

"Since Dad needed more income for Dot's college, he started building a house for a man on the Cape Fear–Sampsons Landing Road beside our farm. But he caught pneumonia in the middle of the project. That was my first homebuilding experience.

"It happened after I started practicing law in Wisdom Station with Mr. June

Willingham, Sr., who's ten years my senior. Lee couldn't help because he had dropped a foundry mold on his leg, leaving him with his limp. Fortunately, the pre-sold house only needed contract work by plumbers, electricians, and painters to be finished. I arranged my law work to go to Sampsons Landing weekly to supervise the finish.

"When the Depression eased, Colleen and I married and had Diane in 1938. A year later Mr. Willingham and his wife produced their only child, June, Jr., called Junebug, who's about to be discharged from the Army's Judge Advocate General's Corps. Junebug's returning home to work with his dad.

"Brother Lee married at the outbreak of World War II, and that union produced Brick. I was drafted, but Lee wasn't because of his leg injury. When Vietnam started, Lee's limp justified General Eisner arranging a Compassionate Army Duty assignment for Brick to serve at Fort Bragg so Brick could be close by to assist his dad at the foundry. Eisner could not do the same for Marsh because I had no disabilities.

"World War II gave Lee his break. He bought the foundry on payment terms from the retiring owner with a loan from our Great-Uncle Tobe, who had no heirs because his son was killed in an auto accident before the war. That's when Lee got your granddaddy Lester to move to Pineland Springs to help at the foundry because the younger workers were involved in the war effort. Construction of Fort Bragg, Camp Lejeune, and other nearby bases provided enough profits for payments to the retiring owner until the war ended. At the war's end, Lee got a small business loan to pay off the previous owner and Great-Uncle Tobe. That loan was paid off in four years, thanks to the postwar building boom."

"Yes," noted Donald. "Granddaddy Lester and Aunt Wixie told me how lucky Mr. Lee and you were."

"Well, after my naval discharge, my business experience did mirror Lee's," Mr. Malcolm responded. "I got a GI loan and built a house, but Colleen and I never moved in because I sold it for a nice profit. The experience told me that there was more money in building up real estate than in defending poor criminals.

"Over several years I eased out of my law practice to become a full-time builder–real estate developer. After doing a twenty-five-house project near the Lazlo Brothers' new textile plant between Wisdom Station and Pineland Springs, I realized I needed a lumber-hardware store to help control my material costs. Through my law contacts I knew the elderly Wisdom Station lumber operator and copied Brother Lee's pattern of buying out a retiring owner. The Veterans Home Loan Administration would lend money to all credit-worthy veterans, and this whole scenario fueled the building boom that helped Lee and me to pay off all our debts by the early fifties. We were truly blessed.

"Then Lee and I enticed our boyhood friend, Holden Rollins, to join us in building the PSR Club on three hundred acres of timber property my mill had cut. Holden had done well in insurance sales to Fort Bragg troops. We expanded the club into a small convention and meeting retreat for small businesses when the Lazlo brothers became partners. Their textile wealth assured the club's financial foundation, and they also hired O.B. Cannon to be the club's manager and golf pro. Later Holden persuaded General Eisner to join and become our chairman."

"Your sister, Mrs. Dot, and my cousin, Thomas, kept me up on Mr. Brick's comings and goings to Georgia, and being in the Army and all," Donald said. "But I'll tell you: Today's the first time I ever saw him with any clothes on! That other time he was butt-naked except for that shotgun he was holding onto trying to cover his own self up."

"Oh, that old skinny-dipping, swimming-hole story of him and my Marshall as kids!" Mr. Malcolm laughed. "That happened as we were building the PSR Club."

Chapter Two

A Southern Dinner Sets a Table for the Tale

I

DRIVING UP TO MR. MALCOLM'S HOUSE, Donald saw his Aunt Wixie at the kitchen door. Entering the kitchen, Mr. Malcolm passed off Carley Ray's quail to Wixie before saying to his wife, "Colleen, the meeting with Brick went well. I know a partnership with Brick has a better chance of helping Marsh get into business than our previous attempt with Cy Turner."

"I'm eager to hear about it," replied Mrs. Colleen, "and I know that Austin and Diane are, too. Let's wait until they arrive to hear your report. Meanwhile, ask Donald to bring in extra firewood for the weekend."

Donald followed Mr. Malcolm to the den and began moving in the firewood, while Mr. Malcolm looked at the television weather report until identical twin boys bounced in. These were Austin Winship, II, called Kit, and Nash Winship. Kit was named for his father, and Nash was named in honor of Mrs. Colleen's family.

Nash pleaded, "Granddaddy, we're old enough now to hunt this Thanksgiving. We'll touch Bentonville Blue's picture for good luck before the hunt."

Donald smiled as Diane arrived to save her dad from the badgering boys. The firewood stored, all returned to the kitchen.

"Malcolm Marshall!" Austin toasted, raising his drink to his father-in-law.

"Greetings, Austin," said Mr. Malcolm. "I hope you're ready for some tender Sampsons Landing field peas. I've been looking forward to those delicate little peas since Wixie and Colleen froze them last summer."

Not paying any attention to her husband's jolly remarks, Mrs. Colleen looked at Donald and said, "Wixie, go get Malcolm's dress shoes for Donald to polish for Sunday. Malcolm hasn't been to church in weeks."

"Donald has polished many a shoe at the PSR Club locker room, my dear," said Mr. Malcolm as he sat down at the kitchen table with Austin. Wixie returned shortly, and Donald carried the shoes into the laundry room.

Mr. Malcolm breathed in the kitchen aroma. "Yes, I remember the first time Colleen went to meet my family. Mother's big Sunday dinner included a large pot of Sampson snap field peas. We each ate three or four servings of peas before I detected that Colleen hadn't eaten any. I implored her to try some, and she did. After a couple of forkfuls, she announced that they were unusually good.

"I couldn't tell if she was just being agreeable or if she really liked them. Driving back to Wisdom Station, my lawyer instincts obliged me to cross-examine her.

"Colleen said the peas were surprising. She said the Evabay soils grew only large field peas that were mealy, like a black-eyed pea. Those larger peas were so mealy that the Evabay farmers fed them to the hogs as a food supplement, and only ate field peas when they were penniless and starving. One had to be as poor as those souls who suffered through the New Holland Farm project failure near Lake Mattamuskeet in the thirties, or those first Europeans who left Sir Walter Raleigh's Lost Colony to move inland with the Indians for food. 'Hungry people will eat anything, including large mealy peas without seasoning!' she said in female authority."

Amid laughter, Mrs. Colleen added, "Yes, the Lost Colony and New Holland failure stories of looking for some promised land were ingrained in all Evabay children. The unpalatable thought of eating a mealy pea, cooked without salt or meat, stuck with me! It concerned me that I had made a courting mistake with Malcolm's family. Such minor-seeming culinary differences have ended more than one courtship and even marriages in North Carolina.

"Yes, our Old North State is several states within a state: the Coast, the Coastal Plain, the Piedmont, and the Blue Ridge–Smoky Mountains. Each geographical niche has its own localized customs, food tastes, and a resulting view of the world influenced by those regional customs. Our different ways of speaking English from region to region influence these worldly views, too, my schoolteacher parents always said; from High-Tider, Old-English brogue on the coast to Scots-Irish dialects in the mountains. Field peas from region to region is but one food difference—barbeque is most certainly another. Chopped in the east, ladled in a vinegar and red-pepper sauce; or sliced or pulled off the pig and put in a tomato sauce in the west."

"Yes," interjected Austin, "it's like the different French wine regions. The meat, vegetables, and wine all blend together for better taste if they come from the same soil. It's the one culinary insight I gleaned in France before returning here for the births of Kit and Nash.

"In fact, Malcolm said something similar to Junebug Willingham at his wedding last weekend. Malcolm congratulated Junebug on marrying Kay and noted that this marriage should have a better survival chance than his first because Kay knows what a tasty Sampsons Landing field pea is. He even asked Junebug if proper field-pea cooking was written up in their vows."

"Humorous wisdom and advice for an old law partner's lovelorn son," said Mrs. Colleen. "You Southern men of the legal profession! You spiritualize everything, from food aromas to the Ghost Hounds of Bentonville Battlefield bringing good shooting luck to hunters! Dinner's ready."

II

Donald finished the shoe-shining as the MacKoys began eating. During dinner, the door to the dining room remained open and Donald heard them all talk.

"Daddy," Diane said at one point, "we discussed this when you tried to get Marsh established with the Cy Turner partnership. We appreciate that starting Marsh out on that old rattlesnake-infested dairy site left over from our General Electric sale takes the remainder of that land off our property-tax expense. Of course, we all have more faith in cousin Brick's stability than in Cy's because Brick's work around Atlanta was largely responsible for Amalgamated's generous buyout of Uncle Lee. But still, Brick and Marsh have ways of getting into adventures with their friends. And I say that even though Brick did assist Wesley at the Bragg chaplaincy post.

"Brick has settled down from his Army motorcycle-winning, poker-playing days, and won't run off on a dope binge like Cy, but there's still Dutch Lazlo and the others. Gosh, Dutch is supposed to be the group's intellectual powerhouse because he nearly aced the college entrance exam at the Georgia Coosa Valley School. But he's already been married three times. So much for brains! Yesterday Dutch offered Aunt Dot a half-dozen of his newest negligee designs as a donation for this spring's PSR Club rescue squad fundraiser. Dot thanked him but told Dutch his new business, spun off from the rest of Lazlo Industries, shouldn't contribute until profitable.

"Of course, Marsh's second marriage to his bathing-suit beauty queen came on a whim after his Vietnam return, thanks to an introduction from Dutch's negligee-consulting lady friend. I hear she's been talking with Eisner's nursing daughter, Nicole, about new, combat-fatigue, mood-stabilizing medicines being offered at Bragg's Womack Hospital Veterans' Outreach program. That indicates she has Marsh's best interests at heart. But I still don't know if I should call my new sister-in-law Sue or Sue Anne because they've been living at the beach since the Cy Turner partnership debacle. Marsh, I fear, would still rather be an Ocean Drive–Myrtle Beach dance band set-up man and bus driver than settle down."

"Your concerns have merit," Mr. Malcolm acknowledged. "However, this time, with John T. retiring from the cattle operation next fall, I plan to give the cow division to Marsh. It'll equal my gift to you of my vacant PSR Club building lots. With Brick mostly running a Sunrise Acres construction operation, I'll have more opportunity to share practical business philosophy with Marsh this time around. You really learn by doing, and also by discussing problems when they occur. This partnership will help Marshall and me to get along better."

Austin said, "Malcolm, you're the senior partner in every decision, and we all appreciate your feeling obligated to help Marsh learn to fish for his living. It can be good for Marsh and for Diane and me. But we can't swing both a Sunrise Acres building attempt and the railroad-tie operation we've wanted to start. I mean, along with all the other projects going on through the mill and the supply store, the bank will say enough is enough, especially with your cancer scare. We shouldn't rock the boat requesting too many loans at once."

"I concur, Austin," Mr. Malcolm answered. "I know you'd do well producing railroad ties, but I need to establish Marshall while I still have time. We MacKoys have struggled with issues like this ever since 1746 when the first of the family came here looking for a better life after Bonnie Prince Charlie lost the Battle of Culloden.

"There were terrible struggles to carve a life out of the Carolina pines and even family disagreements when our direct forebears married into the English Brickmans family of prosperous blacksmiths who furnished tooling to the turpentine trade. Our MacKoys opposed the King's colonial tax policies by the time the Scots' inspirational leader Flora McDonald and her military husband, Allen, arrived near the beginning of America's Revolution. In fact, the MacKoys and Brickmans spied on Highland Scot loyalist troops, leading to their defeat at Moores Creek on the old Negrohead Road from Wilmington to Campbellton, now Fayetteville.

"After the Revolution, Brickman MacKoy married the only child of the slave-holding Butler family of rice farmers. Brickman and his heirs continued the marginally profitable rice farming until it began to take time from their more lucrative wholesale business of turpentine and general merchandise trading. That's when they gambled to free their few slaves to be sharecroppers in the mid-1840s. That worked out better for us as well as for Wixie, Donald, and Shank Poe's forefathers. But that bet wasn't guaranteed beforehand any more than mine or Lee's or Dot's after our dad and Uncle Tobe lost their car dealership in the Depression."

"You just have to try with what you've got to work with," inserted Mrs. Colleen. "Yes, North Carolina is first in many things, like the Wright brothers' first flight. But failed efforts are one of our many firsts, too. From Sir Walter Raleigh's Lost Colony to my childhood memories of the New Holland–Lake Mattamuskeet drainage failures, I witnessed ruined dreams long before Rachel Carson learned of them here and became inspired to write *Silent Spring*. Yes, I know all kinds of failure stories! But doing nothing is not an option for Malcolm and me at our age. We can't delay any longer trying to establish Marshall."

III

"Wixie, we're finished," Mrs. Colleen announced. "Please take the teapot and pound cake to the kitchen. Diane and I'll clean up the rest."

When Donald and Wixie left, the family was still discussing Sunrise Acres. Donald remarked as his truck picked up speed, "Aunt Wixie, you know how Grandmamma and Granddaddy took me in after Mama died. They were good as gold to me, but I've never known feelings like I've seen Mrs. Colleen and Mr. Malcolm express to each other. I guess I feel that way because my daddy got killed in Korea before I was born and he won't even married to my mama! I want my own family-feeling, where I feel accepted for being me. I hope me and Bessie Mae can do that because I don't want to create no throwaway child."

"Donald, life's a struggle," Wixie said. "But if you'll stay out of trouble, you won't make your struggles worse. Mr. Malcolm and Mrs. Colleen have had to struggle to make it, like anybody. Of course, their struggles are bigger 'cause their good education gave them bigger dreams to tackle.

"Mrs. Colleen met Mr. Malcolm at a dance. He got his rhythm from his daddy, who was good at the Virginia Reel, the dance of his youth. Pop MacKoy also fiddled and called dances while doing a little Pigeon Wing step himself to put more sashay into the dancers. Mr. Malcolm's a Foxtrot man, says Mrs. Colleen and Mrs. Dot. They used to do that at the White June Germans over to that Rocky Mount tobacco warehouse. We did the Black June Germans right after them. According to what I'm told, Marsh and Brick inherited some of that white man's rhythm, too. They dance to rhythm and blues, and call it the Beach Boogie; slippin-slidin-tryin to dance like us blacks, hoping to find a groove!"

Wixie cackled. "That albino, 'Chalky' Newton, he's the one they say taught Marsh the steps. Don't know how Brick learnt.

"Now Mr. Malcolm and Mrs. Colleen want to help their children take what they've done and build on it better like the first MacKoys did in looking for a better life here.

"Austin and Diane are following in those footsteps, but Marsh worries them. He was always a fidgety child. Once they thought he might be like his Evabay cousin but with a milder form of epilepsy, but Dr. Street said no. When Marsh got older he went off to that Georgia private school they all went to, but he got kicked out. Then he was booted out of a military school. He married once, for a month, just out of high school.

"Marsh went to a half-dozen colleges, while working in between at beer joints in Myrtle Beach or as a bus driver for rock-and-roll bands. Diane called him 'Marsh' when he was born because she couldn't say Marshall. The name stuck with everybody, even though his parents mostly call him Marshall.

"Marsh had to go to Vietnam 'cause he wasn't in school and his daddy's not crippled like Brick's. The Lazlo boy also got stateside duty because of his daddy's heart problems. But Marsh's bus-driving license got him a motor-pool job. He was lucky not to see real shooting; just took on some fire in a back-bunker supply area. He won't say much about it. What he did see, I believe, was lots of drugs, according to what's said about Vietnam. Marsh could be easily trapped into that.

"After Vietnam, they wanted to start Marsh in home building and took on the Cy Turner partnership to help get him started. Cy's the younger brother of Mr. John Turner, the lumber foreman. John T's solid, but, honey, Cy's trash! I believe Cy and Marsh got into drugs the day Marsh went to Chapel Hill to see what that building project was about. He left Cy, headed to Myrtle Beach, and married that Sue Anne girl. She's a former beauty queen and suntan-oil saleswoman who now judges beauty contests. She's never been married before.

"If Mr. Malcolm offers you a job, take it, Donald. We go way back with these Mac-Koys, to Old John with Micajah; them two standing naked on a rainy farm path, with nobody to trust but each other. I've seen Mr. Malcolm have success and setbacks. If Mr. Malcolm and Austin aren't around, you consider Brick's advice. Marsh is good-hearted, but I'd hate to see you paying the price for his shaky advice."

I had known that Donald's family had come from some MacKoy-freed slaves, but didn't know *how* until Donald told me, Mrs. Penny. However, I still didn't know the more sinister history of the old Negrohead Road and how that tied Donald's family to the MacKoys far more closely than most Southern blacks were ever tied to whites.

Chapter Three

The Rescue Squad Fundraiser

I

DONALD CAUGHT UP WITH THE SUNRISE ACRES STORY AGAIN, Mrs. Penny, at the PSR Club's rescue squad fundraiser on a spring Friday night before the old Stoneybrook Steeplechase in 1971. This event attracted an overflow crowd, and Donald was called into duty to help serve.

The fundraising committee held this event the Friday night before the nearby Southern Pines Steeplechase because the area's college students and out-of-town relatives returned for the horse racing. The MacKoy brothers and their PSR Club partners relished hosting the event because it promoted the club's value to the area.

A dance was the main draw for attending a silent auction, a raffle, and an open-bid auction for items donated by local businesses. Sister Dot, who organized the money-raising raffles and auctions, donated several items from her antique shop, and sold items to industries that did not produce products suitable for general-auction appeal. The funds raised were going to establish a rescue squad. Add to that the fact that a well-known beach music band would perform with a special guest appearance by Sonny Turner, former lead singer of the world-famous Platters, and they had a sellout.

Donald and his cousin Thomas were lowering the American flag and PSR Club colors when Brick's black convertible appeared through a dark cave of pines bordering the club's driveway. Thomas advised Donald: "I know you want to work on Brick and Marsh's new project so you can develop the carpentry skills for someday working with Mrs. Dot's interior décor remodeling group. But you need carpentry skills already even to work for them. I know Aunt Wixie done told you that everybody at Mr. Malcolm's lumber company says you're only a sandpaper man, all thumbs with hammers and saws. I bet Mr. Brick's already been told plenty about your sandpaper thumbs."

"Well, I bought carpentry tools while I was chauffeuring Mr. Malcolm last fall," Donald returned. "And I'm asking Brick for work tonight because I've been practicing."

"Thomas, my favorite bartender! Well, after old Shank Poe," said Brick, approaching them. "Is that Dutch Lazlo's new car in the parking lot I've heard so much about?"

"Yes, sir," replied Thomas. "And since your daddy now has his retirement money, you should hit him up for a foreign car, too."

Brick mused, "Dad didn't sell out for big bucks like Mr. Duncan Lazlo. They sold for enough to spin off part of their business into Dutch's lingerie operation. Now, Dutch chauffeurs around his female models. You must need a foreign car for work like that. It's foreign to a poor construction-products man like me, anyway."

Thomas laughed. "Speaking of Dutch, he and Mr. Stan Cannon are waiting for you in the bar along with your old poker buddy, Monroe Hill."

"Really?" Brick asked.

"It's been two years since Mr. Stan qualified for Augusta's Masters," Thomas continued. "This week he's helping his dad at the Pro Shop entertain the Southeastern Coastal Plains Telephone Managers Association by giving tips to their golfers because they're the club's biggest customer group.

"Oh, and your Aunt Dot wants you to stop by the bar's card room nook. She and others are having a light dinner before everything begins."

II

The three found Brick's Aunt Dot socializing with the Holden Rollins family. Rollins' wife, daughter, and another college-aged girl made up the group.

A movable sideboard serving station was near the diners, and Donald took its coffee pot to refill Mrs. Dot's cup. As he poured, he reflected on her coffee addiction he'd observed from having worked in her antique shop.

Mrs. Dot almost dropped her hot coffee when she spotted her nephew. "Brick, tell us, has your daddy's retirement made you miss those Georgia belles? Now, don't worry! I'll introduce you to two charming young ladies who'll make you forget all about those Georgia peaches.

"Of course, you know the father of one of them, Holden Rollins. He and his family moved over from Fayetteville recently to their new home at the club.

"Do you remember back in the mid-fifties when we all went to Myrtle Beach for a week, and your dad and Malcolm sold Holden on partnering with them to start the club? Cousin Diane was a college freshman, and you and Marsh, eleven or twelve.

"There was a little girl on that trip that followed you and Marsh around, and now look at her today, all grown up as a college junior. Becky Rollins, if you don't recall her name. And this is her college roommate from our Sampsons Landing hometown, Wendy Granger."

"I know Mr. Rollins well," answered Brick, "because I write checks to his insurance agency. I also recall the discussions on that Myrtle Beach trip about forming the club. And I remember a six-year-oldish, bluish-green-eyed blonde in a ponytail, but I can say that I've never met the dazzling adult beauty you're reintroducing me to now!"

"Well said, Nephew!" Mrs. Dot remarked, looking over the rims of her glasses. "Where did you learn to compliment ladies like that? Your serious-minded Daddy or Uncle Malcolm don't even know how to sweet-talk a puppy or a kitten!"

"What Brick recalls is an annoying, tagalong little girl, interrupting all the fun he and Marsh were having," put in Becky.

"That's too long ago to remember," Brick nodded toward Becky. "Are you here for the races?"

"Yes," returned Becky. "Wendy's heard about the steeplechase all during college. So we came now that Mom and Dad live here. It's a free place to stay for girls on a budget who can't afford an Ocean Drive–Myrtle Beach trip."

"What are your majors?" Brick inquired.

"Wendy's is social work, and mine is art history," Becky answered.

"In other words, Brick," put in Mr. Rollins, "Becky's in an educational field that'll take as long to graduate from as that of our second son, Bob, who's still in medical school at Atlanta's Emory. I may have turned over much of the business to Holden, Jr., who's managing our Fayetteville headquarters, but I still have enough need for income that I continue to work daily at our branch office here."

"Becky," Mrs. Dot chimed in, "remind Daddy of your part-time job at my shop. That income will keep his wallet fat. You are like my own New York City-certified art curator!"

"Well, it's nice to see you folks again," Brick said. "It's been years since that beach weekend. I know of brother Bob's Emory education through Holden, Jr., but I never ran into Bob in Georgia.

"Changing the subject, Aunt Dot, do you know if Uncle Malcolm will be here tonight?"

"Yes, and they've invited the Willinghams. So Junebug and his new wife, Kay, are coming, too. Your uncle and aunt won't spend the night at their cottage, however. An architect-engineer Malcolm invited from Raleigh will be staying there. Vann and Lisa Hutton are a husband-wife architect team that Austin and Diane met at the New Orleans Building

Products Show last fall. They've begun advising Malcolm and Austin on their building projects, and Malcolm is showing them around now to lay the ground floor for club renovation
work. They're also looking at Malcolm's remaining vacant building lots for future home-
construction ideas. Diane and Austin have sickly twins tonight, so they're missing. And
Marsh and his new wife, Sue Anne, are moving back to Wisdom Station from the beach."

"Thanks for the rundown, Aunt Dot," said Brick. "Oh, I see my friends by the bar,
looking this way. Better join them now that your meals are arriving. See you later!"

III

Still at the sideboard, Donald heard Mr. Rollins say, "Dot, Brick and Marsh going into
business remind me of starting the insurance business before the war. As an N.C. State
chemistry graduate, I found employment easily as a high-school teacher in the Depression, but the pay was poor. For summer income I sold insurance and did well because
of Fort Bragg's population growth in preparation for the war. I quit teaching once I was
too old for the draft, but my first years were hard even with many angels of good luck
shepherding me from above."

"Brick and Marsh are like two peas in a pod, and will read each other's minds,"
Becky said. "They'll do fine together. I recall that Myrtle Beach trip, just before I started
first grade. They cannonballed off the diving board, then squirted each other and me
with water pistols. Marsh also squirted a couple of football jocks hassling Diane as we
returned from an arcade."

"I recall your telling me that story at the shop," Mrs. Dot remarked. "I hope that
enthusiasm and eternal hope will carry my nephews through their rite-of-passage challenges into the real, adult world they're about to embark on."

IV

Then Mrs. Dot saw people approaching, and announced, "It's Brick's parents, Lee and
Loraine," before Holden interjected, "The ladies outnumber us, Lee. Let's retire to the bar."

"Lee," put in Mrs. Dot with a wink, "you're retired and have no business to talk with
Holden about, not even Brick's motorcycle insurance! Don't leave."

"Motorcycles!" Mrs. Loraine sighed. "Thankfully, Brick's over that. Girls, Brick was
stationed at Bragg as a chaplain's assistant to my deceased brother's son, Wesley Wyatt.
Brick made arrangements for films to be shown to the post children. Dutch Lazlo, who
was a corporal like Brick, allocated the films through the Post Recreation Office.

"Naturally, card games occur at military posts, and Brick and Dutch began inviting their superiors to cookout–poker nights at the Sampson Hunt Club cabin. The sergeants were avid hunters. The hunt club appealed to them because they could shoot skeet and trap before dinner and playing poker. That routine kept Brick and Dutch off KP duty. Monroe Hill—see him standing by Brick and Stan Cannon at the bar? Those boys, plus fellow Hunt Club member Brewer Melvin, always helped Brick and Dutch entertain.

"One evening, a sergeant bet his motorcycle, and Monroe won it. Brick, however, had loaned Monroe money to stay in the game, and thus it became Brick's bike."

"Oh, Brewer and his wife, Nicole, she's a General's daughter!" exclaimed Wendy. "I went to a Super Bowl party at that hunt club last January. It's quite a place, with a wonderful old jukebox, television, fireplace, and all the comforts of home. They even have a picture of a deceased hound dog called Bentonville Blue. They say the dog brings good hunting luck and has other spooky qualities. The Melvins are older than I, so I don't know them well, but I recall going to their wedding. I'd just entered high school and had no marital thoughts. But I remember being moved by the words of some Arab poet the Army chaplain quoted: 'the white wings of death,' and so on. It was most romantic."

"That Army chaplain is my nephew, Wesley Wyatt," responded Mrs. Loraine. "He'll be here soon with Nicole's father, General Eisner, who's retired now."

"You know, Lee, I never knew Monroe Hill held the winning poker hand for that motorcycle," put in Rollins. "Brick just showed me a clear title for his insurance. I only later learned he got it playing cards. I suspect Monroe's Uncle Charlie 'Circus' Hill, who ran away with a circus side-show game of chance, must have given Monroe his poker-playing moxie rather than passing it to Monroe's dad, Mitchell. And I suspect that same instinct made Monroe risk consuming two pounds of salt-cured country ham plus salt-loaded tomato juice the morning of his military draft exam so he could fail with high blood-pressure readings. I imagine his frequent heavy drinking added to his critically high hypertension readings. Mitchell and Madge would be retired for health reasons now were it not for trying to establish Monroe in their pawn shop/washerette operation on Madge's Harnett/Wake County property."

Then Mr. Lee and Mr. Rollins saw Mr. Malcolm coming toward them with another man.

v

"Lee, Holden," said Mr. Malcolm, "meet Vann Hutton. Vann and his wife are the Raleigh architect-engineers that Austin and Diane met last fall in New Orleans. They're now advising us on our building projects.

"They'll be spending the weekend at our cottage. Colleen is settling in Lisa and her sister, and they'll be along shortly.

"Lisa's from Québec, and she and Diane have bonded like sisters because of Diane and Austin's stay in France years back. Diane says the Huttons have been a tonic for their sparse Wisdom Station social life. Anyway, Vann swears we have lots to be proud of here because it requires extra to compete with the big Pinehurst resorts."

"You do have lots to be proud of," inserted Hutton. "Hello, Lee, I've heard your brother speak of you and your son, Brick. I believe your son is to start the Sunrise Acres project with Malcolm next week. We expect to work with Brick, too."

"Vann," said Mr. Malcolm, "Lee and I always say that Holden is the PSR Club's secret to success because of his insurance connections at Bragg and Pope Air Force Base. He's the one who brought in General Eisner to be our chairman."

"Malcolm's too kind," commented Rollins. "Speaking of the General, he's been inquiring about your stamina, Malcolm."

"Yes," answered Mr. Malcolm, "Lee told me. I am already counting the fifths of his special Pennsylvania rye to be consumed at the nineteenth hole. We always had drinks before returning to our bungalows on Friday and Saturday afternoons. I miss his wife because we would all gather here every Saturday night for dinner. After her passing, the General dropped out of our informal dinner club."

"Vann," inquired Mr. Lee, "your wife's being French Canadian makes her an interesting match for a born-and-bred North Carolina boy!"

Hutton smiled. "It began when I did graduate work at N.C. State, and Lisa, like her younger sister, came as a scholarship exchange student. They're from a little town near Montréal, called Pointe de Castor, which translates as Point de Beaver, as it's an old beaver shipping point off the St. Lawrence. The English noted it on maps as Point de Beaver after the French and Indian War and it's been called that since, to the irritation of Francophone purists, like Lisa's mother, Madame Émilie.

"While Lisa's people speak both French and English, she had difficulty understanding North Carolina colloquialisms and it affected her grades. I did tutoring work, and she was assigned to me. Later I married my student!

"Their father perished in a Seaway accident when Lisa was eighteen. Lisa's sister, Marina, followed her to State College and has lived with us for the past two and a half years. She's graduated, and her apprentice work has broadened our firm's client services. We hope she'll remain with us, but her Green Card expires in two years. She'll have to decide if she wants to become a U.S. citizen, or return to something in Québec."

Then Mr. Lee announced, "Oh, there's General Eisner with Loraine's nephew. Loraine said Eisner wanted to invite Wesley before he makes his second Vietnam tour. Excuse me while I give Wes the family welcome."

VI

As Mr. Lee departed, Mr. Malcolm said, "Vann, General Eisner looks as fit in civilian clothes as he did in uniform when Holden introduced him to us.

"Loraine grew up in the township of State Line, where the main street is the borderline between North and South Carolina. Her family lived on the North Carolina side. When her brother began his ministry, his first assignment was on the South Carolina side. Wesley was born there, well before Diane or Junebug.

"Later, the church transferred Wesley's parents to North Augusta, South Carolina, where they were killed in an auto accident. Wesley was fourteen, but his grandparents were too old to care for him. So, the church, through contacts with Georgia Methodist, arranged for Wesley to be educated on a scholarship at the non-denominational Coosa Valley Boarding School for Boys, west of Atlanta. The school practically raised Wes, as he attended the regular term and worked there during the summer sessions, too.

"When Wesley came home, he stayed at Lee and Loraine's house here in Pineland Springs because of his grandparents' poor health. Wesley entered Duke on a divinity scholarship, just as his grandparents passed away, leaving Loraine as his only effective family support. Wes and Brick became like brothers.

"After Wesley's graduation in the early fifties, he accepted the Methodist calling to preach, but never connected with his parishioners. I believe his detached attitude probably resulted from the combination of his moving with his parents from parish to parish as a child and then their untimely deaths. He confessed to Loraine that although he was a preacher, he couldn't develop the warmth for individual souls that makes a preacher a minister.

"So he returned to the Coosa School as a history and Bible teacher for several years. During Wesley's tenure there I recommended to my old law partner, June Willingham, that he send his son, Junebug, there. Junebug said recently that Wesley's teachings were more helpful to his legal insights than any college ethics course he ever took. Brick, Marshall, Dutch Lazlo, and Stan Cannon all went there later.

"But Wesley left before their arrival. Academic life didn't satisfy him. Somehow, the spirit led him to the Army Chaplain Corps. That was before Vietnam heated up. He studied and affiliated himself with the Episcopalians because he felt that the Episcopal outlook was non-denominationally better for the troops, who come from wide faith backgrounds.

"In Vietnam, he met Eisner, and the General became Wesley's father-figure. I guess for Eisner, Wesley is like the son Eisner never had. Although Eisner was only a Colonel then, it was always known that he was at the top of the Brigadier General's nomination list because he had served on MacArthur's staff in Korea. The need of military professionals to please a future General is a strong power card. Eisner used that to promote Wesley and himself. After Eisner made Brigadier at the Pentagon, he supported Wesley's career move.

"When Eisner transferred to Bragg, he had Wesley assigned here. A year later, Eisner had Wesley officiate at his daughter's wedding when she married a Sampsons Landing friend's son, Brewer Melvin. Their ties are strong, and that friendship played a big part in Brick's becoming Wesley's chaplain's assistant and avoiding a Vietnam tour."

"Vann, Brewer Melvin's dad grew up with Malcolm, Lee, and me," observed Rollins. "At his daughter's wedding, we were still in shock over Eisner's pending retirement following a swift rise in rank. But Eisner was often like his mentor, MacArthur. Not going along with the new limited-war philosophy kept him from moving up the promotional ladder.

"On the other hand, Eisner says any deep-thinking geopolitical military analyst has to admire the thinking of MacArthur's superior, General George C. Marshall, who, of course, influenced much of President Truman's outlook on trying to corral the North Koreans without blowing up the world in the process. No one wanted to facilitate another Hitler's rise to bullyhood with the peace-at-any-price policy of post–World War I Europe. But with today's Communist intrigues, our country is continually faced with that confusing moral problem of having to decide between a need-to-win strategy versus a need-to-restrain.

"Eisner says he stuck out this hair-splitting pressure between battlefield winning and geopolitical military restraint because of his admiration for General Marshall. He says he wishes he could have been assigned to Bragg sooner so he could have had Marshall's tutoring while Marshall was still living nearby at Pinehurst.

"While Eisner says that no one can argue sensibly with Truman's undisputed authority and good reasons for firing MacArthur, carrying the burden of restrained combat confusion under armed fire is an exasperating waste of well-trained people that's unbearable for a commander's soul. Like Korea, he hates Vietnam. That's how his appreciation for Wesley's Chaplain Corps grew to a passion.

"Of course, as a consultant to that munitions company, Eisner says he still gets frontline briefings that allow him to keep his fingers in the pie."

VII

The three approached Wesley and Eisner in time to hear Mrs. Dot say, "Yes, General, like you, we are proud of Wesley's promotion to Major, and we pray for his safety over there."

"It's unfortunate," grunted Eisner, "that our well-intentioned need to oppose communism has led to this commitment level. I don't know why we think that our Vietnamization campaign can win the Vietnamese mind over to our modern democracy ideals when those illiterate Stone Age souls are incapable of putting to use any concepts of it. Most peasants can't even define communism or capitalism, much less know the difference between the two.

"We might as well be trying to teach them nuclear physics. You know, the English weren't too successful trying to colonize India. They stayed there over two hundred years, and India remains about as stuck in the Stone Age today as ever. It's just hard for a Westerner to comprehend a people who drink their own urine and worship cows. Oh, India will join the modern age someday, but we should recognize that they have to do it at a pace their cultural mind-set allows.

"Really, it took us from the Lost Colony in 1587 to the surrender of Geronimo in 1886 to pacify Native Americans. Hell's bells! Two hundred and ninety-nine years! America's best diplomatic weapons are probably Coca-Cola and Mickey Mouse. I expect they've won us more friends than all our foreign-aid programs.

"When I visit my son-in-law's farming operation in Sampsons Landing, I see the difference between his farming methods and the ancient Vietnamese methods. It makes me shiver at the knowledge gap between our societies. American know-how can't be easily transferred to cultures that aren't able to read and write even in their own language—much less in English."

Hutton smiled at Rollins and the MacKoys while Eisner caught his breath.

"But we're in there now, and we just can't risk sending the wrong message to our enemies by pulling out. It'll show weakness to brutes. I just hope that President Nixon and Kissinger can figure out how to disengage. We don't need any more Lieutenant William Calley massacre incidents.

"From an ideal organizational-responsibility perspective, our President should be dealing only with the larger issues that affect nearly everybody in the world. But now, Nixon's got to stop to deal with every minor detail of this Calley personnel matter. You know, the other day, I heard there's been lots of high-level talk about our ending the Bretton Woods agreement. Just think of the many unforeseeable economic consequences a decision like that might have worldwide! Going off the gold standard could create clouds of trading uncertainties for our many complex, international trading arrangements. Looks to me like a financial train wreck is coming, but our President has to spend much of his thoughtful day on—Calley!

"It'll work out somehow, but you can always expect Calley-like incidents amid guerrilla-war battlefield confusion. That's why we should all be proud of Wesley's wading back into the fray. Our troops need all the spiritual support they can get in their hour of confusion."

VIII

"I appreciate the General's kind words," Wesley put in. "Chaplains are just camp follow-ers back at the hospital when the nightmares begin over dreams no longer available to a trooper. Blindness and loss of limb are tough encounters when a soldier awakens from anesthesia. But the thing I most witness there—and here—is loneliness, and the numer-ous unhappy marriages between the Vietnamese and our troops.

"You may recall that I used the words of the Lebanese American poet Kahlil Gibran on marriage at Nicole and Brewer's wedding. Gibran's words are something like: 'And together you shall be forevermore. You shall be together when the white wings of death scatter your days,' and so forth. I often use Gibran's line in my counseling, along with our traditional 'I plight thee my troth for better, for worse, till death us do part.' But loneli-ness seems to have the upper hand on young men far from home, in the middle of hell, being shot at with real bullets."

"Mr. Hutton," said the General, "speaking of young men's needs to act on unlimited dreams, I understand that you'll be working on Malcolm's new building project with Brick and Marsh?

"Those boys were in my daughter's wedding to Brewer. I'd love to be in their shoes as they embark on Malcolm's housing venture. It'll be like continuing America's multiple Homestead Acts. Those laws broadened our tax base and gave our country extra muscle by encouraging stable, self-reliant family formations beyond the Mississippi.

"As these gentlemen have often heard me say over drinks, America was founded on the idea of being able to pursue opportunity for the peculiar happiness it brings to each individual's soul. The French political thinker Alexis de Tocqueville was the first of many who defined this image of hope that America gives the world. Old soldiers know that better than most. We fought in two world wars because we didn't want to see our own future opportunities cut off.

"However, that's not the clear situation in Vietnam. It's so murky. Our governmental tradition goes back to King John's Magna Carta signing in 1215. It was only intended to apply to royal barons, but shopkeepers saw in it a hope of their greater personal fulfill-ment, too. The Magna Carta became a foundation stone of both our Declaration of Independence and Constitution. Even slaves and their descendants saw hope in these documents. Although they were written by slave-owning masters and not intended for blacks, the purity of the promise was so evident that Dr. Martin Luther King's 'I Have a Dream' speech connected with today's blacks and whites. However, that long European–American trail of promise has a history unfamiliar to the Far East.

"But I'm carrying on like a silly old man trying to solve the world's problems—and without a drink, Lee! Let's see if Loraine's good Episcopalian nephew will allow us to invite these gentlemen into the bar where we can really have prayerful conversation about all the world's ailments. Hell, after a couple of stiff rye sazeracs or martinis we might be able to get the ideas of Manifest Destiny and that 'Don't-Tread-on-Me' Gadsden Flag notion to accommodate one another. I can almost visualize it being like some new Bretton Woods policy! Heavenly clarity and transparency for souls to find faith to pursue their inalienable right—manifesting their best and highest dreams."

"General," laughed Mr. Lee as the group moved toward the bar, "Wesley says he's a 'Whiskey-Palian,' not an Episcopalian. I imagine we'll need all of his Whiskey-Palian theological insights if we're to reconcile the Manifest Destiny ideal with the 'Don't-Tread-on-Me' Rattlesnake Flag of Independence. Those ideals can be contrary."

Walking along, Eisner said: "Malcolm, at the board meetings, your old law partner Willingham has helped Lee, Holden, and me keep our club solvent. And you seem mended, too!"

"Yes," answered Malcolm, "there are no guarantees, as you know from your late wife's cancer battle, but I have confidence in the treatment program that Dr. Street referred me to at Duke. I think it will get me back to touch Bentonville Blue's picture for several more hunting seasons. Who knows, maybe Blue's ghost will cure my cancer, too."

"That Ghost Dog may, indeed," Eisner noted. "He's improved my shooting eye. I sense that on the practice range during my Vietnam junkets for the munitions firm."

IX

While the men assembled at the bar, Donald cleared the dinner tables before opening the louvered doors to the dining-ballroom area where band members were assembling. Milling around the musicians were partygoers of all ages. About that time, Mrs. Dot announced, "Here come June and Martha with Junebug and Kay. Donald, please bring more chairs for the Willinghams—and the Hutton ladies, who'll soon arrive with Colleen."

"Martha," said Mrs. Dot, "you and Kay join us. The men have abandoned us for the bar's mystique and the geopolitical opinions of General Eisner. Perhaps your menfolk will feel more comfortable there, too.

"Malcolm said Colleen's coming late with the Hutton women. Vann Hutton is that man standing between Malcolm and the General. He's the architect Malcolm wants Junebug to meet. Besides, I'm sure Junebug doesn't need to hear Kay give another report on their honeymoon."

"Acapulco will live in my memory forever," began Kay Willingham as she and her mother-in-law shooed off their husbands and sat. "It catered to American tourist expectations, but we got off the beaten tourists' path when June rented a Piper Cub. Easy in Mexico! He only had to show his pilot's license and the money.

"We flew over to a little Pacific coast fishing village on the Baja Peninsula to meander around. It's the first time I'd ever flown with him, and I'll have to admit that I had second thoughts about following my husband's lead even though I knew he had often flown to Duck on the Outer Banks.

"We wanted to rent a plane for our trip home but couldn't. And that turned out O.K. because we visited the Grand Canyon for a sleepover on the Canyon floor. It made us want to visit the Canyon de Chelly cliff dwellings in northeast Arizona, but we didn't have time."

Kay paused, watching her husband and father-in-law move toward the bar. Then she announced that she was expecting in December and charmed her companions with the possible names of the couple's offspring.

x

Donald helped his cousin Thomas at the bar where the Willingham men were conversing with the others. Junebug Willingham renewed his acquaintance with Wesley and was introduced to Vann Hutton by Mr. Malcolm. Then Dutch reentered the bar with touring pro Stan Cannon, closely followed by Brick and Monroe Hill. The younger Willingham smiled as he shook hands with Brick, Dutch, and Cannon and acknowledged Monroe.

"Look, Wesley, the three prep-school musketeers and speed-demon intellectuals have graced us with their presence!"

"Speedy intellect Brick," said Wesley as he put his left arm about his cousin's shoulder and shook hands with Dutch and Stan. "A boarding-school reunion, indeed!"

As conversation turned to Stan Cannon's professional golf career, the band began to play. Becky Rollins, Wendy Granger, and the college-age crowd swayed to the rhythm and blues flooding the room with musical reveries of Myrtle Beach, Ocean Drive, and Cherry Grove, all barely a hundred miles east.

When the first set ended, most went to view the auction items. Mrs. Dot wove among the tables answering questions about the items she had donated or sold. Spotting Brick, Mrs. Dot made her way to him and his friends at the bar.

Mrs. Dot said, "Monroe, I understand that your Ginger is due any day now, and that Junebug's Kay is also expecting."

"Junebug and I were comparing notes," Monroe replied. "Ginger's due next weekend. Her mother is with us until the big event to share the grandmother's workload."

"Wonderful!" Mrs. Dot exclaimed, smiling. "And now that you're about to become a respectable married man with children, please encourage my nephew to reactivate his dancing feet tonight with Miss Becky Rollins."

"Indeed!" returned Monroe. "I remember her being a tot, hanging around her dad's insurance office. She's become a beauty, and Junebug thinks her poise exudes a charming mystique."

"Exactly, Monroe," replied Mrs. Dot. "And Brick can dance with a good-looker even if this function is not like the wild parties you boys had at the hunt club, or at Lazlo's Ocean Drive beach house cabana after the dance halls closed."

"Mrs. Dot, those were wild times," laughed Monroe. "And Stan and Dutch and I can testify that we've not seen Brick dance with a good-looker since he brought that Georgia girl to the Camden, South Carolina, steeplechase in '66 before he entered the Army. I asked Brick why he didn't marry her. He said that relationship was blooming about the time our old hunt club friend, Johnny Bell, lost both his legs and most of his privates to a mine in Vietnam. Johnny could fast-dance a doorknob to death, in practice, or a girl to death on the dance floor with true cool-cat aplomb.

"Brick said no girl deserved the uncertainty of such war wounds in the 'better-or-worse' part of a marriage vow. So yes, Ma'am! I'll encourage dead-foot Brick to dance with Becky the way he used to at OD, Cherry Grove, and our hunt club."

"Monroe, I've heard you mention Johnny Bell at our Raleigh poker games," put in Hutton.

Monroe shook his head. "Yes, Johnny died recently of liver cirrhosis. The doctors said he didn't move about enough to stimulate water passage. But he also drank a quart of vodka daily to hasten his demise."

"Oh, Mr. Hutton, I see that the band's returning, and here comes Colleen with your wife and her sister, I presume," interrupted Mrs. Dot.

"Yes," said Hutton. "My wife was looking forward to being here with Diane and Austin, but I'm having a good time with my new acquaintances, Brick and Junebug. Monroe and I see each other in Raleigh often, so his being here helps me fit right in. I'm sure my Lisa and her sister will enjoy meeting a new group of women, too! I'll get Lisa a cocktail. Her sister, Marina, is not feeling well. Let's get her a club soda."

Mrs. Dot then asked Donald to bring her a club soda, too.

XI

Hutton and Mrs. Dot made their way to Lisa and Marina, sitting with Mrs. Dot's sisters-in-law and the other ladies. When Donald arrived with the drinks, the band began its second set with the evening's featured artist, Sonny Turner, singing the old beach-music favorites "Washed Ashore" and "I Love You a Thousand Times" from his days with The Platters.

At the serving station, Donald observed Mrs. Dot and Vann Hutton surveying the dance floor where Brick and Becky danced to the music's up-tempo backbeat. Their backs were fairly straight, with only shoulder tilts toward and away from each other in a mirror-image response to the gliding shuffle of their feet. Their turns and reverse twirl drags were executed tightly to miss other dancers.

"This music encourages a smoother dance than that of my 1940s Jitterbug days when we traveled to June Germans in Rocky Mount," Mrs. Dot said to Hutton. "These dancers are so smooth that they seem more like ice skaters, gliding, than dancers. The motion's as natural as ocean waves breaking onto a Carolina beach at an incoming mid-tide. I guess it's that concept of refined dance movement that I like, although I'm too old to participate like I used to."

"The movements are fluid," replied Hutton. "Having come along a few years after your Jitterbug time, and just before the age of these dancers, I believe I was nearly around at this dance style's creation during the last days of World War II up through the Korean War. It's been a favorite in our Tidewater coastal plain and Low Country ever since.

"Mrs. Dot, the White Man's Soft-Shuffle, Sugar Footing Fast Dance, Sand-Shuffle, Carolina Beach Boogie, or whatever you want to call it, has no one birthplace. Recently, some have started calling it the 'Shag.' This dance evolved in the boardwalk pavilions at Carolina Beach, North Carolina, and the Ocean Drive–Myrtle Beach area of South Carolina. Like the rock and roll of the mid-fifties Elvis Presley era, many church groups campaigned against Beach Music because it was also known as race music. The Ku Klux Klan even stormed a black Myrtle Beach dance club, often patronized by whites in the early fifties. But neither the Klan nor the churches could snuff out the rhythms that seemed to appeal to some great eternal tempo, luring kids from the cotton mill and furniture towns beside the tobacco patches back then. And it still appeals today."

As Brick and Becky continued dancing, Hutton asked his wife if Marina would like another club soda. When told that she would, he gave Donald a five-dollar bill and asked that he fetch one.

XII

Returning with Marina's club soda, Donald found the women engaged in the story of Lisa and Marina's Francophone heritage, and how they came to be in North Carolina. All agreed that Lisa and Vann Hutton's love story was most romantic and that Marina's future employment was dicey as it depended on her Green Card renewal.

When Brick and Becky returned from the dance floor, Brick seated Becky beside Marina, and commented to Hutton that he looked forward to working with him on Sunrise Acres. Brick then went to the bar along with Donald. At the bar, Donald washed glasses for his Cousin Thomas and overheard Brick say to Junebug: "Well, my speedy Jewish friend of Episcopal persuasion, I know you and Kay are excited to be joining Monroe and his Ginger in the parental parade by Christmas."

"Yes," replied Junebug. "Kay and I were engaged once, you know, but went our separate ways, with me entering into a marriage that ended in irreconcilable differences. When I came home last fall on military leave, we met again at the church homecoming. Although Kay had avoided marriage failure, she had experienced relationship disappointments. At first sight, it was evident that we accepted one another in a non-judgmental way. Our spirits blossomed, and we married practically on the spot. I had enough leave time to squeeze in an Acapulco honeymoon."

"Man," gleamed Brick, "you exhibited speedy insight! Our old Coosa Valley professor couldn't harangue you for any lack of intellectual acuity over Kay the way he used to over students missing the point in Latin class."

"No, the old professor couldn't say I left my thinking cap off concerning Kay," Junebug smiled, agreeably.

"The Junebug-Speedbug!" hailed Dutch as he approached with Cannon. "I hear you've married again. Stan pointed her out. If you marry once more, you'll catch up with me. In fact, speaking of marital relations, perhaps you're the one to advise me about my pending divorce number three."

"See me Monday. We'll review the matter," said Junebug, rolling his eyes.

Then General Eisner called out to Dutch, who glowed, "Excuse me, men, while I visit with our real intellectual leader, who has the grace not to reprimand me with the Coosa School epithet of Speed! And that's no matter how slowly my brain cells fire."

XIII

"Stan," said Junebug, "when are you returning to the tour? I always appreciated you getting me those tournament passes when we were both in California."

"I'll go to the New Orleans tournament after the Masters," said Stan as all gazed at Hutton dancing with his Lisa. "The last two years I've had no wins, making just enough money to get by. If I'm to do anything in golf, I have to refocus—winning again and now! Dutch and his family sponsored me until I got a win and picked up other sponsors. But my endorsement contracts will end soon if I can't perform better. Of course, now that the Lazlos have sold out their bigger operations, I don't have endorsement opportunities with them. So my future's now, which means winning.

"I always knew real-world difficulties would be out there for me to grow through. But the degree of focused fortitude needed to cope with adult difficulties is not what I imagined. It's something they didn't teach us on the blackboard or from a book at the Coosa School. No, maturity must have been implied between the lines, somewhere, and I didn't make the speedy connections. Life pangs are wising me up now, though.

"Brick, after our Monkey Island trip last Christmas, my black-and-blue shotgun shoulder took a long time to heal. That made something click in my head about my lifestyle, and I wondered: 'What else am I bruising?' Changing from vodka to club soda hasn't paid dividends yet, but it should. Partying is a luxury I can't afford because my athletic future is now, while I still have youthful body strength. I guess you could say I can't afford black-and-blue arms from hunting with Dutch or a black-and-blue brain from absorbing his cowboy movies that become drunken stupors. But the old gunslingers of our childhood Saturday afternoon movie days were great fun, as was all the beach-dancing it morphed into.

"That Monkey Island trip showed me I need to stretch myself to a new level of maturity. I expect you'll have to do the same, Brick, in your new building venture. It'll be a whole new way of life for you. How are you going to sell these houses, anyway?"

"Uncle Malcolm has a fellow who owes him money from a failed construction venture," replied Brick. "His name is Deacon Buckhorn. I've never met him, but Uncle Malcolm says he's a real salesman."

"Oh, Deacon Buckhorn," Donald's cousin Thomas put in from behind the bar. "I know him. He's called the Black Indian."

Chapter Four

Construction Plans Take Shape

I

THE NEXT NIGHT, MRS. PENNY, Donald told me about Mr. Malcolm's plans to restart Sunrise Acres as we catered an event after the Southern Pines Steeplechase. On the previous effort that Cy Turner considered building, Dad had said some of his sales commission could be withheld to retire his debts to Mr. Malcolm. I hoped a similar deal could be worked out now.

Until now, my Sunrise Acres information had come only from Dad and Donald. From here on, others also confided in me—Marsh's wife, Sue Anne; Mr. Malcolm's secretary, Iris Craft; Junebug Willingham; his wife, Kay; Brick; and Cousin Mingo. Eventually, I participated in Sunrise Acres events, too. Then a few years ago, long after the project was finished, Kay told me her perspective plus details I had totally missed. This refreshed my young-adult memories.

The Monday after the rescue squad charity dance, I was home on college break when Dad told me he was going to Mr. Malcolm's lumber company to discuss the Sunrise Acres project, so I went along.

Entering Mr. Malcolm's office, we saw two young men. I knew Marsh, and the other I assumed to be his cousin, Brick, because of their family conversation. Mrs. Iris was on the phone, talking to her deputy sheriff–husband about her nephew Ollie's skipping school. It was also a hectic morning for the lumber company's delivery schedule, as several drivers had quit for higher wages at the local concrete ready-mix company, and Mr. Malcolm and Austin were monitoring deliveries.

Soon, Mr. Malcolm and Austin arrived. "It always amazes me, Malcolm!" Austin exclaimed. "We borrow money all winter for staff payroll, and then, suddenly, BAM! They leave just when the good building weather returns and we need them! I pulled

Cotton Roberts from the drafting office to drive materials to Raleigh because he's the only one left qualified to operate our boom-lift trucks."

"Austin, Wixie can contact her nephew, Donald. He backed the hay trailer into the cow barn to get it out of the rain while chauffeuring me around last fall. If he can back a tractor-trailer rig, he can certainly handle our short trucks. He wants a job here. If we hire him, it won't take Cotton Roberts long to train a couple of our other drivers."

As Austin and Mrs. Iris calculated Dad's debt, Mr. Malcolm phoned Mrs. Wixie about hiring Donald. Then Austin and Mr. Malcolm explained Dad's repayment plan from future Sunrise Acres home-sales commissions. As the three were agreeing to terms, Vann Hutton entered.

After introductions, Hutton noted that he had missed Austin and Diane at the rescue squad fundraiser, then asked, "What's first for our Sunrise Acres discussion?"

"Vann, this subdivision's property is left over from an old dairy farm," Mr. Malcolm said. "I sold the portion served by sewer on the city side of the river to General Electric. The land we retain beyond the river—city limits has no sewer, but it has water. So, it's ideal for septic-tank sewers since city drinking water will eliminate septic sewage contamination issues that might accompany well water for human consumption.

"Now, Deacon here is a Native American whose family comes from a long-forgotten local Indian band. Deacon's deceased wife was a Lumbee Indian from the Robeson County–Pembroke area, and his daughter Melody's a sophomore at N.C. Central.

"Deacon attended school with blacks in the segregation era, and thus has a good entrée to the black community which facilitated his building houses for them. This in turn gave Deacon a good relationship with the local Farm Home administrator, Wilbert O'Cain, also black.

"The O'Cain relationship led Deacon to build some apartments for a Farm Home Rental Assistance program the government previously offered. Unwed mothers, however, primarily occupied these units, and drug users chased the women. This rowdy element damaged Deacon's apartments until repair bills became larger than his monthly mortgage payments and it broke him. Deacon now hopes his Sunrise Acres commissions can pay his debts to me and leave him extra money to start again as an independent contractor. For now, he's returned to being a brick mason with his brothers.

"Vann, we have starter house plans in our drafting office library for the first houses I built after World War II. I also have a Sunrise Acres street draft."

"Good! Let's see your old house plans first," said Hutton as we all followed Mr. Malcolm to the drafting office, where they reviewed plans for a half-hour.

Finally Hutton said, "These plans are like all low-profit, starter-home plans where the house's small size badly influences the home-loan valuation-price formula. This fact means that you must build as big a small house as the home valuation formula of Farm Home and the Federal Housing–Veterans Administration programs allow.

"I always advise builders doing low-profit homes to use that old architectural trick called a profit-expansion ladder in the floor's middle. It creates extra square feet for little lumber cost, which creates some profit opportunity.

"Marina can draw up expansion-ladder scenarios that Cotton Roberts can refit into your existing house plans here. Then you should be O.K. But as we know, low-profit houses must be built fast. Delays will run up your construction-loan interest charges. When that happens, things get unprofitable fast, and a host of architectural tricks can't save any starter-home project.

"As to the subdivision's street and water-line layout, I'll have to take your draft plat back to our survey group. It'll take a couple of months to verify this plat's street layout. We also must obtain a general county septic inspection approval so you can get a construction permit.

"Realistically, our planning, plus the lot and street-grading work, will take six months before home building can begin. There'll be some coordination work for Brick and Marsh to do, but they still need to learn something about house construction. Driving here, I realized that you need Marsh and Brick to gain day-to-day construction experience. You should let them finish up Cy Turner's abandoned job in Chapel Hill. If they're serious about building, there's no way they'll screw up things like Cy did, so long as Cotton, Austin, and I are offering guidance. That way they won't be greenhorns going into this hundred-house monster project.

"If you'll give me that street draft, I can be on my way. I'll have Lisa and Marina determine when we can get to Chapel Hill to figure out how to proceed there. They'll work out a meeting day when Cotton Roberts can be there for better all-round communication. I appreciate Cotton's value in keeping your costs down."

Hutton left, and Mr. Malcolm said to Dad, "Deacon, go see Mr. O'Cain. Advise him we'll soon have a hundred-house subdivision project ready for him and his Raleigh supervisors to review."

"I'll see him today," Dad said.

As we left, Donald entered, smiling about his new job. Later, Donald said as he was filling out his job-application form, he overheard Mr. Malcolm tell Brick about the cattle partnership for Marsh. "Brick, I'm sure you know my business style of having multiple partners on our projects. Austin's my Senior Partner, and it's his responsibility to keep our building sites supplied with materials. Our individual site partners keep the subdivisions on schedule without wasted labor or stolen lumber. That's essentially what you and Marshall will do at Sunrise Acres.

"I look at my cattle operation the same way. The manager is just another partner, and I want Marshall to take it over now that John Turner is retiring. John's the older brother of the infamous Cy Turner, but John T's a reliable man. I hope you understand this'll help me pass on some fatherly insights to Marshall."

"Sounds sensible to me," Brick replied.

II

For two months the MacKoys met in person and by phone with Hutton's firm, Will O'Cain, and his Raleigh supervisors before the final house plans and the subdivision plat layouts were ready for review.

Near the end of my school year, the MacKoys, Hutton, Dad, and Mr. O'Cain's Farm Home superiors met at the Sunrise Acres site. Also along were Jeffery Mack and his son Jeff, Jr. The Macks contracted for the grading, paving, and waterline installation because they had done such work on Mr. Malcolm's other projects.

The son, recently out of the Army Corps of Engineers after his Vietnam tour, was preparing to take over his dad's business. Jeff, Jr., had also played Junior Varsity football with Marsh. All the men carried long sticks to protect themselves from snakes on the site. Jeff, Jr., carried a shotgun.

Walking along, Hutton pointed out land features and explained why certain lots were shaped the way they were on the plat drawings. Marsh and Jeff, Jr., swapped football stories, but most of their conversation centered on Vietnam.

At the old dairy barn, Mr. Mack stopped and exclaimed, "Now this is the kind of land-clearing surprise I can't bid on: here where you say the snakes are! All these rocks have to be cleared, and $450 a lot won't be enough for such extra-heavy work."

"That's why I made the two lots here bigger, Mr. Mack," Hutton said as Jeff, Jr., and Marsh stepped off the footage from the approximate road location to the rock outcropping, carefully looking for snakes as they went. "I've made them larger for easier septic-tank placement to reduce extra land-clearing expense. There's three more septic-quirky lots at the property's rear, but rocks aren't an issue there for your grading-cost estimates."

Mr. Mack nodded grudgingly before all continued down the path to an aged concrete pipe exposed at a drainage swale. Stopping, Mr. Mack noted, "Your plan says a thirty-six-inch culvert here, Mr. Hutton. You can't ever tell about these highway engineers. One day they'll say this spot needs a thirty-six-inch pipe, the next day another man will say it needs a forty-eight-inch pipe. Whatever, Malcolm, you'll have to pay for the pipe."

Mr. Malcolm nodded. Then O'Cain looked at Dad, and then at his Raleigh supervisors to say, "This gully where the new pipe must go is the place Deacon told me about. That gully appears to drain these top ten lots. And those ten lots follow that old log road that returns to the main road at the development's back corner.

"I think we all know this subdivision will be sold primarily to blacks, but government-housing finance programs can't appear to discriminate. This second entry point and the natural barrier of those higher elevation lots could be used for establishing the white section we need to incorporate into this project to avoid overt reverse-discrimination issues."

"O'Cain, that higher elevation should provide an obvious, but delicate separation boundary that'll allow for a racial harmony secure from worry," one of his Raleigh supervisors said. No one commented further, and the group hurried to complete their review. Dad said the fear of snakes seemed to speed up the inspection.

III

Once the Macks began the grading work, Brick and Marsh started their education by finishing Cy Turner's Chapel Hill project. Here Hutton put Marina in the lead consulting role after outlining how the project should be completed.

Cousin Mingo began as the trim carpenter and cabinet installer for Brick and Marsh as well as their all-around handyman. Because Mingo had been out of prison less than a year, he was financially forced to ride his old Indian motorcycle to work daily. The motorcycle wasn't constructed for carrying his full-set toolbox, though. At first Dad transported Mingo's toolbox to the job and later Marsh did it. The toolbox and its tools were all initialed "MT" for Mingo Turnbull, to reduce the chance they'd be mixed in with the tools of other workers and lost.

Mingo, Brick, and Marsh were nearly the same age and became friends quickly. Brick talked to Mingo about motorcycles and Marsh about trim carpentry. While Mingo's skill level was good as a result of his prison carpentry classes, he learned some new techniques from Marsh, too. Dad always said that for all Marsh's faults, he was a real trim artisan doing miter-saw cuts, and joked that Marsh was good enough to have been in prison, too.

I first met Marina in early September of 1971 on the day the Chapel Hill houses were finished. She was there for a preliminary inspection in preparation for the official bank inspection. It was my second week as a junior at N.C. Central in nearby Durham. I had forgotten some school items, and Dad brought them to me.

When Dad arrived, my last class, American Music Appreciation, had just ended. He said he wanted me to see the Chapel Hill houses. Generally, I would not have wanted to endure one of Dad's side trips, but with Aaron Copland's *Appalachian Spring* still dancing in my head from music class, I didn't object.

Dad was excited that afternoon. "These three houses were far more complicated to finish up than anything we'll build at Sunrise Acres, Melody.

"Marina, the Canadian architect I've told you about, is doing a pre-inspection tour to make sure that all is in order before the bank's official inspection. Her approval will tell me that these two white boys have learned how to do quality work. If they pass this, I know they'll do well building small, three-bedroom homes at Sunrise Acres. Good workmanship will make those starter homes easy to sell.

"I wanted you to come along to see the possibility of better times. If I can pay off Mr. Malcolm, you won't have to work at those catering jobs with that Desmond Printice boy to make it through school. He's not nicknamed Dizzy for nothing! He's dizzy in the head about himself, life, and everything else. We promised Mama on her deathbed that you'd get a college degree. Now that we can both see there'll be money for the tuition, the rest will be up to you, and I want you to see this project for reassurance."

"I won't fail at that promise, Daddy," I replied. I could see now why it was important to him that I was along, although I had not cared for his rude reference to Desmond's nickname. Dad's commanding tone abruptly ended Copland's master-melodies in my mind's ear.

IV

Cousin Mingo and Cotton Roberts were standing outside the first house, with a young woman and the MacKoy cousins. I could hear Cotton telling Mingo about his previous weekend hunting with Brick, Marsh, and Mr. Malcolm at the Sampsons Landing Hunt Club. The ghost dog had given shooting luck to all, evidently.

Then Marina came over to me. "I'm Marina LaGraves, the project's architectural advisor, and I assume you are Deacon's daughter, Melody, whom I've heard about."

I shook her hand while noticing her olive skin, similar to my own. I admired how her skin tone and auburn hair blended into her clothing. Her appearance was as artfully planned as a painting. However, when her eyes looked out of that painting, you knew she was very much alive by the way her eyes engaged you from the depth of her soul.

Inspecting the unit's interior, Marina found a bedroom closet door not functioning because the sliding door had come off its rail. Dad, Mingo, and Cotton remained to fix this, as I continued on with Marina, Brick, and Marsh. Momentarily we heard an outside door open, and a female voice calling, "Hello, hello?"

"That's my wife," said Marsh. "Sue Anne came along to check out fall, bargain-priced swimwear at the mall. We're going to the beach tomorrow after our bank inspection. She's a former beach swimsuit queen, and this weekend she'll review girls for next year's contest."

This was the first time I had met Sue Anne, whose long, black hair nearly covered the straps holding up her mini-skirted sundress. "I've heard so much about how great these houses look, Marina, that I pestered Marsh into bringing me," Sue Anne cooed. "You've turned the cousins into real builders."

"I didn't train—only suggested! And they executed my suggestions well."

"It's more correct to say that Mingo's good carpentry is what did the trick," interjected Brick. "Marsh's supervision of Mingo's miter cuts helped get the job done right the first time, without repair expense."

We toured the house, eventually coming to the back door. The two women talked about their past and how they had come to this moment of introduction. The ease of their conversation would have made strangers think that they had known each other for years. They ignored Brick and Marsh totally, seeming like true friends from the start. Even today, I don't believe either ever had a hard feeling toward the other. At the back door, both turned, and looked at me as if to say, "We're sorry to have left you out of our conversation."

"Melody," said Sue Anne, "Marsh says you're studying social services with an Indian heritage minor."

"Yes," I replied, "my family's observance of Indian customs encouraged my study. This rawhide holds my birthstone. I got it from a jewelry booth at the Pembroke powwow. We Wisdom Station Indians are beginning to acknowledge our Indian roots since North Carolina recognized the Columbus County Waccamaw Siouans and the Sampson County Coharie tribe this year. State-government recognition of those tribes gives us hope that we'll be recognized someday. Today we can't prove our blood connection to known tribes, but improved blood-testing should establish that someday.

"Grandfather bought the necklace for me after first suggesting a dream catcher to hang over my bed so its webbing could capture good dreams while filtering out bad ones. Looking at the dream catchers, I saw my birthstone necklace, and he purchased it for me."

"Interesting," put in Marina. "What else have you learned?"

"Well, even though the Pembroke Lumbee Indians on my mother's side are the largest grouping of Native Americans east of the Mississippi River, most North Carolina people are rarely conscious of Lumbees because they don't live on a reservation. You see, there were no reservations during colonial times, when European diseases and wars had killed off or dispersed most eastern tribes.

"That was especially true in eastern North Carolina after the Great Tuscarora War of the early 1700s at an Indian compound on Contentnea Creek, between modern-day Goldsboro and Greenville. About five hundred Tuscarora were killed and four hundred taken prisoner. Like the prisoners of other Indian wars, many were sold into slavery. This pleased many smaller Indian bands that were friendly with the Europeans. One thing that prompted some Indians to join the white militia was the inter-tribal hate and mistrust caused by Indian language differences. The Tuscarora spoke Iroquois but most Atlantic seaboard Indians spoke Algonquin.

"After the Tuscarora defeat, some of that tribe remained here, but others migrated to the Iroquois lands of New York. The Tuscarora that remained here did like many small tribes of the area and began coexisting with the Europeans. Besides the Tuscarora, some of the other local tribes adopting European ways were the Coharie, the Waccamaw, the Occaneechi, the Meherrin, and the Haliwa-Saponi.

"But many small Indian groupings or bands vanished completely, like Cousin Mingo's forebears. While his family has lived in the Wisdom Station area for over two centuries, his family tales say that the Turnbulls came from east of the Cape Fear River after the Tuscarora War. The Turnbull forefathers lived in and around Big Mingo Swamp over where the Sampson, Cumberland, and Harnett County lines merge.

"Their legends say that Mingo's forebears fished and hunted there, and would sometimes steal a few animals from the whites. You must appreciate that fences were put around the gardens and fields in colonial times to keep the animals out. The stock ran free, but knew where to come at feeding time. So if a few animals were missed, it wasn't unusual. Of course, one couldn't steal many, or it'd arouse suspicion. These Turnbull forebears stole some animals for food, and some for slaughter to sell along the Greenpath Road that ran from modern-day Fayetteville up to Virginia.

"This Indian hunting-and-stealing life didn't last long because much of the land was cleared for rice fields. The swampy area suited rice farming. So when their woodland cover vanished, the Turnbulls moved west of the Cape Fear to unclaimed lands. When they moved into this area, they were called Turnbulls because of the rumors of their cow-stealing. The name Mingo came down through the generations, too.

"My Grandfather Buckhorn's sister, Star, married into the Turnbull family before World War II. Her husband, John Turnbull, was a tobacco farmer, and they named Dad's first cousin Mingo. After Mingo's mama died, Uncle John married a widowed Indian named Eunice Ingros from Durham. She was a Cuban of the Taíno tribe that Columbus encountered when he discovered Cuba after Hispaniola on his first voyage.

"Her first husband was a high-yellow Cuban mulatto cigarette-factory worker, and they had a child named Juan. At first Granddad didn't much like Uncle John marrying Eunice and taking in Juan. But he tolerated it for the family's sake at church and such. Then when Granddad saw Juan following his mother's Taíno Indian ways, he took to her son. I think Mingo and Juan have always been closer than real brothers because our entire family accepted Juan.

"Probably one thing that helped that acceptance was my mother's Pembroke legend. Mama's birth name was Winnie Oxendare, and she claimed kin through her family tree to the American-born English white, Virginia Dare of Sir Walter Raleigh's Lost Colony. That's the Dare part of her maiden name. But there's no proving that; too many lost people. Also, there were not just the Lost Colony people and the lost tribes of the Colonial era, but runaway black and Indian slaves along with whites escaping debtor's jail or trial. Lots of mixing up in those days of 99 percent illiteracy and poor record-keeping.

"Mama's family story partly explains that. It goes that a Spanish seaman raped a slave girl when the Spanish invaded the southeast North Carolina coast during the War of Jenkins' Ear in the 1740s. They raided the slave girl's plantation, and the confusion of that enabled her to escape into the surrounding swamps, but the rape made her pregnant, too. Indians befriended her before she had a baby girl. Later these Indians migrated west into what became Bladen County and then into Robeson County.

"That's where my Mama's family picked up the story. The child of this rape was called Pale-Face-Black-Dove because she was issued of a black but had pale red skin. She's an example of mixed-up heritage."

Dead silence came when I finished, but in that moment, a dozen flashbulbs of insight went off in my head. Why, Why, Why in my deepest thoughts did I always feel so alone, and why on Earth did I feel so comfortable expressing myself to total strangers? I felt like I had said too much, but Sue Anne's and Marina's friendliness had loosened my tongue without fear of judgment. I was glad that Dad was in another room, and not there to frown at me.

"Well, your family is proud of you, and I know your mother would be, too," said Brick. Then, still looking at me, Brick asked Marsh: "So, you're headed to the beach on Friday and not to Saturday's UNC-VPI football game with Dutch and the crowd?"

"Oh," replied Marsh, "there'll be plenty of time later for football tailgate partying. Hey, I'll bet Marina's French touch could really spruce up somebody's picnic basket."

"I'll bet Marina could!" exclaimed Sue Anne. "Brick must bring her sometime so we can test her culinary talents."

"I imagine Marina would do well," smiled Brick, looking at her. "Maybe we can find a good weekend for that. As for me, I've got a weekend date with my sister. But know that I'd like a rain check."

"Sounds interesting," smiled Marina, "but it'll have to be before or after my early-October Canadian Thanksgiving."

With that, Brick nodded, and left as Dad, Cousin Mingo, and Cotton Roberts rejoined us. Cotton teased, "So Brick's going to beat everyone out of town this weekend. He must have a hot date."

"With his sister!" smiled Sue Anne. "It's Mary Lee's debutante weekend, and Brick is escorting her because of his dad's leg injury."

Chapter Five

Building Begins

I

MONDAY AFTER THE CHAPEL HILL HOUSE INSPECTIONS, Dad, Brick, and Marsh were in Mr. Malcolm's office to discuss starting Sunrise Acres.

"Dad, we need to start fast," Marsh said.

"Uncle Malcolm," pleaded Brick, "Deacon has several homes pre-sold, but we've lost two customers to Cy Turner. Cy took customers we had worked to get an approved status for over to the next county and signed them up on lots there. These customers said they couldn't wait for us to start, when they can see Cy getting them into a house before the holidays. We gotta start before Cy steals more."

"Well, everything's in place to begin!" returned Mr. Malcolm. "And we should start as many of the first fifteen as we can find the labor to support a fast building schedule. Lumber prices are predicted to increase. Remember, the government's pricing data reports lag a month behind. We can stay ahead of the pricing curve if we lock in lumber prices on as many units as you can start in a month, and then submit the following month's house prices for the higher prices the government reports will certify."

After more discussion, only Marsh, Brick, and Mrs. Iris remained. Mr. Malcolm asked, "Brick, did Mary Lee receive our roses before her debutante presentation?"

"She did!" answered Brick. "And she said thanks again for the party you and the Rollins family gave her at the PSR Club last month. Her thank-you notes should go out soon."

Then Brick and Marsh left to notify the Macks to begin digging the foundations.

II

The next day Cotton Roberts said the cousins could meet for lunch with the framing contractor, Bobby Jack Johnson, who was finishing a remodeling job at Uncle Henry's, the local pool hall and hamburger joint. Bobby Jack examined the floor plans amid the noise of breaking pool balls while the jukebox turned out Carl Perkins' twangy "Blue Suede Shoes." Bobby Jack had served prison time for shooting a neighbor over a barking dog, Mrs. Penny, and he made me nervous because I always saw the outline of a pistol concealed in his back pocket.

Signing on, Bobby Jack said, "I've built starter houses, but I want to do bigger houses because their pay's better. I know you MacKoys ain't ordinary white boys 'cause you got a chance to go places. Maybe I can go onto the bigger houses with you. Anyway, building another set of starter houses beats prison time. I'm like Mingo—ain't never going back to prison unless they kill me and tote me in."

The following day, the Macks prepared footings for three houses. A week later, Dad and my uncles laid the brick foundations, and the following Monday, Bobby Jack began the first unit.

As Bobby Jack's crew started, they were cheered by the promising sight of more foundations in front of them, with more lots cleared beyond. The whole construction site had so much energy that not one man missed a hammer lick at a nail or at the striking of a brick mortar line. The workplace hummed like a sewing machine.

After starting the fifth foundation, the Macks began paving by the first fifteen lots. That really shaped things up, and Dad began showing houses to the first customers already approved by the Farm Home Administration.

On the day of the first customer house-tour, Dad learned that things were progressing for Brick elsewhere, too. Cotton Roberts had come to check on roof vents and remarked that he had learned about a football game the cousins had attended the past weekend. Cotton said Marsh had praised Marina's tailgate picnic basket as having been a hit with Brewer, Monroe, Dutch, and their ladies.

"Yes," Brick responded, "Marina's French twist sent her basket home empty. But those chilled bottles of white wine might be the secret of her success. I'd like to be a connoisseur like her and know my wine-way around any food. But she won't improve my culinary sophistication this weekend because she and Lisa are at their mother's for Canadian Thanksgiving. I never knew it, but Canadians celebrate Thanksgiving the second Monday in October. Say, let's lunch at Uncle Henry's so we can return in time for our first customer appointment."

Suddenly a large, old black man, with a tattered copy of the weekly newspaper *Grit*, stood in the doorway. Dad said the newspaper looked like his only possession. "What do you want, Rufus?"

"Ain't talking to you, Buckhorn. Mrs. Wixie says MacKoy's the one running things here. You's just talk!" grumbled Rufus.

"I can't help a man like you with no job, just living on Social Security," Dad quipped.

"Aw, pshaw and shit, Deacon!" huffed Rufus. "Look here, white boy, I needs a house 'cause I lives in a shanty by the junkyard. I ain't even got a place to sit down and take a shit! All these people talking 'bout getting these government houses. It ain't fair for me not to have one too. Can't a poor WWII black ass get a place to shit in this here U.S. of A.? Shoulda stayed for retirement benefits. This here *Grit* newspaper's always telling about our American opportunities."

Brick gave Rufus a long look. "Wixie and Deacon say you're Rufus Timms and retired with just Social Security income. I'm sure that won't be enough income to qualify you for a house. But bring me a Social Security check stub and we'll ask Mr. O'Cain at the Farm Home office."

III

At Uncle Henry's, Dad related the first customers' backgrounds. Two sisters were married to ex-paratroopers. The younger sister, Celestine, was married to Allen Lamb, who drew total disability from a Korean War head wound that had not bothered him until just before he retired. Allen's head wound was more contaminated than first realized. It made his brain swell years later.

The older sister, Bertha, was married to Henry Moore. He received partial disability for a leg wound. O'Cain, an ex-Army man, liked the two men because they had been a part of the old Triple Nickels or 555th, an all-black Airborne Battalion in the days before President Truman desegregated the military. The Triple Nickels' legacy came out of how heroically the Buffalo Soldiers of the Old West had fought in the Indian Wars. So, O'Cain believed Allen and Henry's spit-and-polish manner would be good for the community's stability.

"But Henry and Bertha Moore are a sad pair," Dad went on. "Bertha's not mentally right because her son died in prison. That's why the two sisters want to live beside each other—for moral support. Celestine says Bertha takes lots of pills."

"Moore? Moore?" asked Cotton. "Was that the black deputy sheriff who was sent to prison for drug trafficking last year? Mrs. Iris and Carley Ray sure go on about him!"

"Right," answered Dad. "He was in all the papers, this time last year. Bertha's son, Ronald, followed his stepfather's military life, but served as an Army military policeman. When he got out in 1968, he was the first black deputy hired by the sheriff's department. He had gained insight into the drug trade as an MP in Fayetteville. At our sheriff's department, he was responsible for sending several drug pushers to prison.

"But somehow he turned bad and was sent to prison with the very ones he had sent off, and revenge against him was inevitable.

"Carley Ray says the story along the lawmen's grapevine was that Ronald was given the ultimatum to turn prison-queer or die. He put up a good fight for two months, and then he was found hanged. But there was something funny about it since it happened in the prison workshop, not in his own cell, and at night, under lockdown. Carley Ray says most suicides are in private, but they couldn't prove anything otherwise, even though the suspected crime took place in confinement, with all kinds of security."

"Strange," Brick remarked, "but I don't doubt it, the world being the way it is."

IV

When the two sisters arrived with their husbands, Dad and Brick took them on a tour of the houses under construction to show them the various building sequences, before taking them into the houses they would purchase.

At the tour's end Allen said, "This is the cleanest, neatest housing project I've seen since being out of Army-base housing. Henry, this is where we'll rest our bones."

With that, Dad escorted the first customers to their car, and waved them off. Celestine blew her car horn at Mingo, who was walking toward the construction office.

"Boss, Jeff says come to the rocky snake den," Mingo called out to Brick. "He's about to set fire to some brush he's pushed up. Maybe you can shoot a few escaping the heat.

"But first, I gotta say that I need steady help if I'm to do the trim carpentry any faster. At first, Marsh helped me set those kitchen cabinets and sliding closet doors. Now he's more interested in his cows, and hardly around. And Donald is not reliable on a part-time basis because he still hasn't done enough carpentry work yet to know how to be careful.

"I keep tearing down Donald's trim and putting up new. He's still just a sandpaper man because of driving lumber company trucks. If he was here regular, he could learn how not to be all thumbs.

"I know this older white man everybody calls 'Hogbear.' His real name is Oscar Waley. He only wants to work two or three days a week because he's on Social Security. But he'll work when we need him because he doesn't have other jobs that would interfere like Donald does."

Brick said, "I know we've promised Donald fill-in carpentry work, but if he hasn't developed beyond a sandpaper man, we'll have to try somebody else."

"Hogbear would love this job," Mingo noted. "His wife gives him a bad time over having to sell off her family farm piece by piece when they hit hard times."

"O.K., try him," said Brick. "As for Donald, maybe we can work out a contract job for him to clean up the brick work and the final housecleaning. Those are two things he can do in the late evening or on the weekends that won't conflict with his truck-driving."

v

Brick pulled a Colt .45 pistol from his car seat and they walked to the old Dairy Barn rock pile where Jeff Mack had bulldozed up underbrush. The three climbed into the bed of Jeff's pick-up truck. Jeff stayed safely on his bulldozer and used a small Army hand shovel to throw a flaming rag into the debris pile.

As the flame began, some snakes managed to escape through the rubbish before the fire grew too hot. The few Carolina pigmy rattlesnakes that did emerge were about a foot and a half long, and Brick picked them off from the safety of the pick-up truck bed. Only in two instances did Brick fire more than once. Dad and Mingo marveled at his marksmanship.

"Well, here comes my albino friend already," Mingo said, looking past Dad. "And your two sister-customers are hardly out of sight. Reckon he's your buddy now, Deacon, and not mine since he couldn't help me stay out of prison."

"He's come to see if I got any finder's fees for him since he put me on to the sisters," said Dad. "No use in you coming, Mingo! He might think you'll get a shot of ass-whipping courage once he sees Brick killing these snakes."

Brick asked if the albino was Chalky, and Mingo answered, "Yes. He's the one my step-brother Juan cut but I went to prison for. He was messing with Juan over a woman. I only slapped Chalky to get him off Juan. But then Juan choked down on his switchblade so it wouldn't go too deep and pricked Chalky several times just to let the albino know he'd better not mess with Juan. My lawyer said Juan's choking down on the knife showed no intent to kill and it was self-evident that Chalky's wounds were not life-threatening. It was the lowest class of a deadly weapon assault that could be charged and would have carried no jail time for Juan and especially me as a bystanding accomplice. I should have just walked away and dragged Juan along. Chalky told the Judge I didn't cut him, but I went to jail anyway.

"Boy, them courthouse prosecutor pricks screwed me extra good over running off to the Crow Reservation with Juan's Pembroke College roommate who came from there. Damn, those were some poor-assed Indians in Montana. I 'bout starved! When I returned, I thought I'd get off with probation. But they threw the book at me for being an accessory and taking flight. I got a three-year sentence but did just one. I may have only been an accessory, but I pulled the time. So, I'm like Bobby Jack and won't be doing that no more; even if jail is the only place I can eat regular.

"His real name is James Newton. He's a black, but chalk white and that's why he's called Chalky. His mama and daddy were as coal-black as a brand-new asphalt highway, they say. Chalky thinks he's a businessman. He just pimps, hustles drugs is all."

Brick and Mingo saw Chalky give Dad a piece of paper. When Dad returned waving the paper, he said, "Brick, I guess Mingo's told you about Chalky. He's a shady dude who does some scouting for me of customer prospects. If his prospects become real buyers, I'll pay him a fifty-dollar finder's fee like I did when I used to build houses. That'll come out of my commission fee, so you and Marsh won't have that expense. I got the tip on Celestine and Bertha from him. But we need to keep him away from the Lambs and the Moores, and especially Bertha. She still believes it was Chalky that got her son in drug trouble and sent to prison to be killed."

"Whatever works," said Brick as Jeff Mack arrived.

Jeff asked, laughing, "Is Chalky buying a house or selling pot? He's put me on some that's better than any I ever had in Vietnam. Was potent, right, Mingo?"

Mingo nodded before Jeff added, "Yeah, Marsh said it reminded him of Vietnam pot, too, but he didn't want to be around it on Monday morning near a SKILSAW; might lose a finger. Brick, you ought to try some. It'll mellow up that stick you got stuck up your Army preacher's ass right fast."

"Nothing wrong with being sociable, occasionally, if you've got nothing to do but watch paint dry," Brick replied, showing no concern over Jeff's snide remark. "But monopolizing your time with it could hinder thoughts from fermenting in your mind that help you deal with the real world as it is. Some restraint might help you save more than your fingers."

Later, Donald delivered some material. After unloading, Brick and Dad explained the work they had in mind. Donald seemed hurt that masonry and house-cleaning were all that they wanted him to do. However, when Brick explained to Donald that his truck-driving job would offer more steady pay than the spurts and stops of construction, he seemed to understand, and cleaned every house ever built there.

VI

The first two houses were ready for final inspection after Donald's cleaning. Prior to that, Brick had inspected and made notes on what remained to be done or repaired in each room. The correction notes were made on pocket-sized notepads printed by the Virginia-Carolina Fertilizer Company as an advertising tool. Hogbear furnished the notepads left over from his farming until the project ended.

After the two sisters' move-in, two more houses were ready for inspection. However, one failed because the painting contractor left early to go fishing at Topsail Beach, and the inspector wouldn't wait for Brick to fix the errors before the inspection tour ended. This approval delay also meant paying another week's interest on the construction loan, and less profit for Brick and Marsh because the homebuyer could not take ownership.

Mr. Malcolm raised holy hell about this delay, and soon located a painter he had known for years, Bill Thornbo, whom Brick and Marsh arranged to meet. Marsh had purchased small cans of paint and painted the door tops and bottoms of the house himself, and thus the house was ready for a second inspection. They agreed that this completed house would be ideal to show Thornbo what was required. As this house had running water, Donald was also using the outside spigots to mix his brick-cleaning recipe of chemicals.

Because of the heat and the need for ventilation, Marsh left the unit's windows and doors open while doing his touch-up work. The windows and doors would be closed once Thornbo left. This would give the paint ample drying time. As a result, Donald heard most of what was said at the Thornbo meeting.

As the MacKoys toured Thornbo through the house, all was quiet in the absence of SKILSAWs and hammers. Only the conversation among the three men and Donald grunting from carrying pails of liquid brick cleaner to adjacent houses interrupted the evening's peace. At the tour's end Brick explained the painting contract.

Then there was a pause, and Thornbo said, out of nowhere, "I'll declare! You boys are doing a real good job for these here Uncle Tom chillens! Reckon I could sell 'em some lightning rods?"

"Our black Farm Home Administrator, Mr. O'Cain, isn't too fond of lightning rods," answered Brick. "We think they're tacky, too."

"And we can't be using that kind of racy language here," Marsh said in an alarmed whisper. "These people are our customers. I'm not saying Brick and I are perfect with our language, but I know our Grandmother MacKoy couldn't stand the word 'Darky' or even the proper word 'Negro' as both reminded her of that other word which hurt her maid's feelings. Her old black maid was the great-grandmother to that fellow cleaning up the bricks on the houses next door."

"Didn't mean to offend you, and most certainly wouldn't offend your customers,"

Thornbo replied. "I guess I come from a different era, and I've worked around blacks more than you two combined. Hell, they call each other the "N" word more than whites do. They're always speaking to us whites about some brother or sister, with an odd, peculiar attitude they can't tolerate themselves. It's just people."

"I know what you mean," replied Marsh. "It's not much different from those comedians Redd Foxx and Richard Pryor using it for a laugh line. But that's for the sisters and brothers, as they say in the real world—not us. Times are changing. I know. I've ridden around with my share of black musicians as a roadie working out of Myrtle Beach."

"Marsh is right," Brick said. "Times have changed. The word is in the Mark Twain books on Huck Finn and Tom Sawyer that blacks read in school just like us. But I gather from Mr. Twain's writing tone that he probably wouldn't use the word today."

"Oh, you boys are right! I just said something I shouldn't have," replied Thornbo. "You know, I come from down near the Sampsons Landing way, too, and once upon a time I knew your daddies' bootlegger and old bartender, Shank Poe of Mudhole Alley. I did some painting in the PSR Club lobby when old Shank was still around."

"Oh," said Brick, "we knew about Shank's Mudhole Alley bootleg-liquor joint in Sampsons Landing. We rode through there once on horseback going to an old swimming hole. The fellow cleaning the bricks outside is a distant relative of Shank's, too."

"Damn, I sure hate I got off on the wrong foot here, and I certainly don't want to get on the wrong side of your daddies or their sister Dot. I know 'em all. Besides, I got a barracks repaint job coming up at Fort Bragg. That'll be my priority. You fellows need someone who'll make your project his first priority. Sorry for the misunderstandings."

With that Brick and Marsh looked on as Thornbo left. Then Marsh said: "I'll shut the windows. Everything should be dry by now, and damn that Thornbo. I guess I pissed him off."

"Screw him," returned Brick. "Like he said, we need a full-time painter. He was just looking for fill-in work to keep his crew together until that Bragg job begins. And I sure as hell don't want to hear any careless language or see tacky lightning rods!

"No, Marsh, don't apologize for what you said about us catering to our customers. All our contractors must be committed to giving our customers as good a job as they would anybody else because our customers' money's just as good as anybody's."

Suddenly Donald walked around the corner of the house and said, "So Thornbo's not taking the job? I couldn't help but hear through the open windows. But I won't spying."

"Well, things do happen beyond our control, Donald," said Brick. "We're just doing the best we can."

"I understand," Donald answered. "By the way, there's a new guy managing the lumber company's paint-mixing department. He's from Southern Pines, and they say he's brought a couple of new customers with him that live halfway between here and there. He might know somebody who can do your painting."

"Great tip, Donald," said Marsh. "I'll check it out tomorrow after cow-feeding, Brick."

VII

The next day the cousins met Riley Carlisle. With one helper, Riley started the next day and remained for the project's duration. Sometimes he was called Riley, sometimes Carlisle, and at other times by his initials, RC, which could mutate into RC Cola, in lighthearted moments.

Within days, Marina came to Sunrise Acres for the first time.

"You are really progressing here, Brick!"

"We moved our first customers in during your Canadian Thanksgiving," he said, holding up a sharp-pointed, spindle note-holder full of customer application forms. "Thankfully, Deacon has more customers here. We're trying to get ahead of the winter rains so we won't lose more customers to Cy Turner."

"That spindle nail looks dangerous," remarked Marina. "Is that your only paperwork filing system?"

"Dangerous is what Diane says about our filing system, too! Come on, I'll show you around," said Brick before escorting her through several houses. Later they were returning to the office when Mingo drove up on his motorcycle. He had purchased Cokes for Hogbear and himself at the country store by the General Electric plant.

As Mingo dismounted, Marina held up a Virginia-Carolina Fertilizer notepad, saying, "Mingo, this notepad and your good trim carpentry work are Brick's secrets to a quality house. I've never seen better craftsmanship, even in the expensive country-club homes we design."

Mingo thanked her before Brick said, "Mingo, let me borrow your bike. Since our lady architect has on slacks, I can give her a quick tour of the property. We'll be back shortly."

"OK," said Mingo, taking the Cokes from the saddlebags.

"I don't believe I should have told you about riding with my motorcycle friends to New Brunswick last summer," laughed Marina. "Have you done much riding since your Army days?"

"I'm steady enough for Diane and Austin to let me tour their twins around. Diane only objects to her sons' swordfighting with our spindle note-holders. She's more afraid one of them will put out an eye than get hurt with me on this bike."

They mounted the bike, and Brick drove away. Twenty minutes later, Brick circled around from the back of the property and drove into Allen and Celestine Lamb's driveway. Inside they found Donald's fiancée, Bessie Mae, with the sisters. Introducing Marina, Brick said, "This woman helped us design these houses, and wants to see what they look like, lived in. Could she look around?"

Marina smiled at Celestine and Bertha, saying: "I understand you two are sisters and help each other."

"They need a connecting walkway between them," laughed Bessie Mae. "And maybe a gazebo like I sat under when I went to Fayetteville State for a year."

"A gazebo sounds like the place to shell field peas on a summer's afternoon," laughed Brick.

"Yes," said Bessie Mae. "A gazebo would be good for that! Neighbors might come and help shell a few peas just for the company."

Brick added, "Well, Marina could draw you up plans for one."

Marina laughed before she and Brick returned Mingo's motorcycle to the construction office and departed in their separate cars.

Chapter Six

Cap-Gun Cowboys to Rock and Roll Boogie-Woogie Men

I

WHILE I KNOW NOTHING ABOUT the first football game that Brick, Marsh, Sue Anne, and Marina attended other than Marina's success as a Picnic Diva, I do know something about the second because Donald, Bessie Mae, Desmond Printice, and I helped cater a post-game party for a group of fraternity houses. Dutch Lazlo had briefly been a member of one of the fraternities co-sponsoring this public party.

Besides the MacKoy cousins, Sue Anne, Marina, and Dutch, the group included Dutch's girlfriend, Lonah Slueter; Monroe Hill and his wife, Ginger; and Brewer Melvin with wife, Nicole, General Eisner's daughter. Sue Anne and Lonah were acquainted through the bathing-suit contest circuit, through which Marsh met Sue Anne after his return from Vietnam.

The local rhythm-and-blues band, The Hot Nuts, a bawdy bunch, opened the party with the pulsating Cliff Nobles and Company instrumental, "The Horse." Just then I saw Brick and Marina crossing the grassy courtyard toward my drink station with Brewer and Nicole Melvin.

I half-filled their plastic cups with mixer and ice, and they spiked them with vodka. Marina said that Sue Anne, Marsh, and the others would be along soon. When they appeared, I overheard Ginger say to her husband: "Monroe, you look dazed. We shouldn't have stayed in Dutch's motor home. What if the cops had happened by? I don't fear partaking in secure circumstances, but taking an open risk is foolish."

"Hush, Ginger," Monroe giggled. "There's too much stuff going on here. The cops don't have time to bother with people who aren't showy about it."

Dutch, Lonah, Marsh, Sue Anne, and Monroe bobbed their heads to the music and smiled like loons. Soon a lanky man moved into the group and began shaking hands. Brick introduced him to Marina. "This is the Langdon Butler we've spoken of. He's called 'Salt-Dog' because he helps his uncle's family manage a charter fishing-boat fleet out of Ocean Drive, South Carolina."

I served Langdon while he and Brick talked. Marina interrupted them by pointing into the crowd, "There's your dance partner, Becky Rollins, and her friend I met at the PSR Club before the Stoneybrook Races."

"Wendy Granger of Sampsons Landing," noted Brick.

"Brick and Marina!" gleamed Becky, before introducing her escort and Wendy's.

"We're just reliving our college days," said Brick after the introductions.

"Ah, college days," put in Langdon. "Enjoy them while you can! Once out in the real world, you'll wish colleges had taught Practical Happy Life 101. Many a day you'll wish you had been a better student so you could have become a brain surgeon or somebody with a promising financial future.

"I should know. My degree and I both hang in Ocean Drive—that's OD! I'm considering moving to Nags Head to sell marine supply parts. That'll give me normal work hours and better pay than the charter-boat business, which rarely gives you days off. I don't get home to Fayetteville often. As close as I've been lately is Sampsons Landing—bird-hunted there last weekend with Brick, Marsh, and Brewer Melvin."

"Oh, I'm from there," put in Wendy. "I know Brewer and his wife, Nicole."

"Well," said Butler, pointing, "they're sitting on the far steps."

"Becky," said Wendy. "Come, meet the Melvins. Don't you remember their wedding by Brick's chaplain cousin, who quoted the poet Gibran's white wings of death verse?"

As Wendy and Becky's group approached Brewer and Nicole, Langdon asked, "Who's Wendy, Brick?"

Brick replied, "She's a senior here. But these college girls are too young for you salty-OD-beach-party dogs."

"I tried the party-hardy life when I first moved to OD. Now I'm feeling older, like Stan Cannon, and just wanting a good night's sleep," laughed Langdon.

Brick then noted Dutch Lazlo's Monkey Island hunting plans. "Dutch has the place rented out for New Year's week. His Puerto Rican lingerie associates come in first. Then we'll come to hunt the last part of the week and also do a New Year's hoe-down with the girls."

"He and Lonah better come up with some movies for the ladies," responded Langdon. "Dutch's John Wayne and Lash LaRue cowboy movies won't appeal to them on an island in the middle of Currituck Sound without shopping malls. But Dutch'll have some romantic films for the girls. He's stocked a library of all film types from his Army days."

"Brick, Marina!" called Ginger. "When the band finishes this set, we're leaving for the restaurant."

The rest of the group talked with Becky, Wendy, and their dates as Brick, Marina, and Langdon left my serving station. While the three meandered through the intoxicated crowd, The Hot Nuts belted out their most famous bawdy tune: "My Ding-a-Ling Is the Cutest Thing."

Thus ended the group's first wild party that I'm aware of. Later they had even more out-of-control, Wild West–type parties. But I soon learned that their rowdiness had begun long before, with a youthful visit to an old colored swimming hole at Sampsons Landing, just off the colonial Negrohead Road.

II

By Thanksgiving all the first section houses were under construction. A second crew that Bobby Jack Johnson had added sped the progress. Mrs. Iris' nephew, Ollie, was on it.

Because of good sales, the MacKoys were ready to begin the next section. My father's ties with the black community produced the first sales. But the news of high-quality workmanship broadcast by the first homebuyers gave later customers enough faith in two white boys to continue buying. Only a few withdrew their applications and went to other builders to avoid waiting, most to Cy Turner.

But there were other issues, like the customer wanting to change his name. This presented a potential house-closing delay, as Brick found out on Thanksgiving Eve before he went home. I was just in from school when Donald entered the construction office. "Mr. Deacon, is Mr. Brick ready to leave for Pineland Springs? My old pick-up truck broke down, and he promised he'd give me and Bessie Mae a ride."

Dad said, "He's with Jeff Mack, unloading pipe at that low spot below the top ten lots. The highway engineer's there, too, telling them how to reinforce the soft soil so the pavement won't crumble later.

"Sit tight. He'll be back soon because I've given him another problem to think about while he's down there. That Cecil Crisp at the twelfth house! We're supposed to close his house, but now Cecil wants to change his name. Says he's joined the Black Muslims but changing his name will legally stop his house sale from going forward."

"Oh, my," sighed Donald, rolling his eyes, "them Muslims is spooky!"

Dad grimaced, "I can near see my way now of paying Mr. Malcolm off, and having enough left to pay the rest of Melody's college. I hope Cecil don't bother that.

"Cecil wants to quit his job and start his own Black Muslim business selling fish out of Durham. Starting a business may disqualify him from getting a house loan because he'll have no income track-record. But he's free to do what he pleases, even if it don't make sense."

"That's a mess," Donald said. "Think you'll be talking about this Muslim stuff long? We're supposed to go by and pick up Bessie Mae at the hospital in Durham."

"We've got plenty of time before you'll need to go," Dad replied. Then we talked about Donald and Bessie Mae's Christmas Eve wedding until Brick came. At that point, Donald and I just listened as Brick and Dad discussed Cecil's job and name change.

Brick concluded, "If Cecil loves his wife, he'll want her to have this house. If he starts changing his name now, his loan will be delayed or denied, and the two will just continue paying rent. But if he's serious about this Muslim business venture, the idea of owning, rather than renting, should appeal to him.

"If he'll wait until he gets the house papers signed, he can do whatever he wants. Assure him that Junebug will help him get a name change after the house-closing sequence. After all, there's nothing we can do about a customer's religious choices or job changes."

"I sense his wife's not too keen about it," said Dad, "so maybe that approach will work."

"Good," smiled Brick as he and Donald left. Donald said that after picking up Bessie Mae, they talked about Donald and Bessie's wedding plans, and also the upcoming Fourth Annual Thanksgiving Day Ecumenical Service that all Pineland Springs churches participate in.

This year, the service would be at Brick's church. The previous year, the event had been at Donald's AME church. These services were mostly singing hymns of thanks, with the offering monies going to the rescue squad formation campaign.

"Don't worry, Donald. All us MacKoys will be there to see you and your Cousin Thomas in the multi-church choir," Brick assured him.

III

Now Mr. Malcolm, Mr. Lee, and Dutch Lazlo's father and uncle owned several bungalows fronting the PSR Club golf course. They had built these to rent to club guests when the resort's little inn became overbooked with the small-business association groups holding conferences there. As Mr. Lee and the Lazlo brothers lived in Pineland Springs, all their units were available for rent. Mr. Malcolm, however, kept one of his bungalows for personal use since he lived in Wisdom Station. He and Mrs. Colleen used their bungalow most weekends for their recreational and social outlet as well as for Mr. Malcolm to assist in the club's management.

Because the MacKoys' social life centered in Pineland Springs, that's where family holiday gatherings were held. The MacKoys also departed for the Sampsons Landing Hunt Club from Pineland Springs to hunt on Thanksgiving mornings. Mr. Malcolm and Mr. Lee had gone for years with Marsh and Brick on Thanksgiving morning to hunt the fields where the elders had hunted in their Sampsons Landing youth. In recent years, they had returned to Pineland Springs early for the Ecumenical Church Service before retiring to Mrs. Dot's or Mr. Lee's homes for Thanksgiving dinner.

This Thanksgiving hunting tradition had ended for the elder MacKoys when cancer sapped Mr. Malcolm's energy. Brick and Marsh, however, had enjoyed good hunting that fall, and wanted to make a Thanksgiving pilgrimage to hunt with their friend Brewer Melvin.

When the cousins learned that Brewer had farming duties and could not hunt, Marsh said he was going anyway so Sue Anne could see the hunt club. He had already scheduled a visit to the Tory Hole Revolutionary War battle site with General Eisner. Learning of this development, Brick altered his Thanksgiving Day plans, saying that the change offered him an opportunity to take Marina on a tour of old Fayetteville architectural highlights she had expressed an interest in since their first date.

"Marsh, Marina and I'll meet you and Sue Anne at the hunt club after our separate tours end," Brick said.

It was a wind-chilled day, not good for hunting, but perfect for sitting by the cabin's warm fireplace to savor the boys' childhood tales. Marsh, Brewer, and Langdon Butler were walking out the hunt club's front door with their shotguns to shoot skeet when Brick drove up with Marina. Learning they'd arrived, Sue Anne and Nicole went to the door and waved for Marina to join them.

As Marina got out of Brick's car, she stumbled and leaned into the open car door, holding her left hand to her side. Brick, sensing an illness, steadied her walk to the cabin.

When Brick released her to Sue Anne and Nicole, he teased, "Marina, what's wrong with your Canadian blood? Was the chilly walk around Fayetteville's Market House and the Carver's Ferry ride across the Cape Fear too much?"

"It's not from the choppy ferry ride or the cold walk," Marina said. "I'll be O.K. inside, where I can rest a few minutes. This happens occasionally. The last time was last spring before the Stoneybrook Steeplechase."

"Brick," interrupted Nicole, "remember! I'm a registered nurse. I can look after Marina! Why don't you go to the skeet range with the boys?"

Brick departed. Once inside, Nicole offered Marina a Coke and two aspirins as she sat on the couch nearest the fireplace. Marina refused the aspirin. "I appreciate your trying to help, Nicole, but aspirin gives me bad nosebleeds."

Both women continued to express concern for Marina until Nicole concluded, "Well, Marina, I'm only a nurse, but if you frequently experience such episodes, you should have them checked out. They may point to something serious that might affect your health as you age."

"I take something for it, but my doctor back home instructs me to skip taking it twice a year. This is one of those times," Marina responded.

Sue Anne and Nicole then discussed Marsh's trip with the General to Tory Hole until Marina's normal skin color returned. Sue Anne noted, "You're looking better, Marina. How was your tour in Fayetteville? I'm sure it was nothing like mine with Marsh and Nicole's dad to Elizabethtown this morning."

"Well, my Fayetteville tour didn't focus exclusively on Revolutionary War history, like your Elizabethtown tour, but was historical nevertheless," Marina said. "I had heard lots about Fayetteville's Colonial architecture in my N.C. State classes. Naturally, I wanted to visit there.

"On our trip down, Brick gave me the city's history. I knew Fayetteville had been named for the Revolutionary War hero, the Marquis de Lafayette. But I did not know the city was the westernmost point on the Cape Fear River open to Colonial river traffic because the waters became too shallow for commercial vessels to go farther west.

"I understand how river rapids made the Campbellton and Cross Creek towns into a trade center, from which Fayetteville evolved. Some of the Liberty Point and Bow Street buildings where that Colonial trading took place still stand. In fact, a sign there commemorates the Liberty Point Resolves that were signed in June of 1775, a year before the July 4, 1776, Declaration of Independence signing in Philadelphia.

"First, we saw the First Presbyterian Church on Bow and Ann Streets near Liberty Point. Its roof is supported by a truss system patented by a local architect, and the church still has its original whale-oil chandeliers hanging in the vestibule, though they now operate electrically.

"The Market House was our main focus. Its rounded French windows, cupola, and North African, Moorish-looking arches make it one of the most unusual structures in North America. It was designed in the English, town hall–market fashion, with an open-air, ground-floor market, and second-story government offices. Livestock and farm-to-market goods were sold there daily, as well as slaves occasionally as a part of estate liquidations.

"The current masonry structure replaced the original wooden version that hosted

North Carolina's first General Assembly meetings prior to establishing a state capital sixty miles northwest in what became Raleigh. In the original structure, the General Assembly ratified the U.S. Constitution and ceded the state's westernmost lands for the formation of Tennessee. So Fayetteville was a river town on the edge of the wild frontier. It reminds me of Montréal, near home, on the St. Lawrence. Montréal's rapids stopped upriver traffic, too, before our modern era of locks and pumps.

"An historical district has now been set aside to preserve old Montréal. It does people good to know their historical foundations. There's just something about walking history's holy ground! Fayetteville's inland seaport status of yesteryear is smaller than Montréal's, but its history should be preserved."

"Dad would agree, Marina," Nicole noted. "He says that Fayetteville still has an edge-of-the-frontier aura because of the transient military personnel going and coming at nearby Fort Bragg. Due to the unsettling nature of troop reassignments from Bragg to Vietnam, many have taken to calling Fayetteville by the nickname of Fayettenam. Dad says that if people want to call the city Fayettenam, O.K., but they need to say it with a smile.

"Lots of good people have gone onto the heavenly hereafter from Bragg trying to be frontiersmen for some idealistic new-world order. The rub, of course, is that soldiers get killed over fleeting visions divined by our political bureaucracy that too often promote goals that can't be understood by foreign cultures still stuck in an ancient era. But despite bureaucratic misconceptions and policy gaffes, the soldiers' well-intentioned deaths are holy."

IV

Then the men returned to the cabin's warmth. "Men, there's beer in the fridge," Brewer announced. "I'll abstain until I feed my pigs because my farm crew has the day off except for one helper. Nicole's abstaining, too, since she's working tonight at Womack. We'll do Thanksgiving with her dad at the PSR Club this weekend and hope to see you there!"

Nicole put in, "I changed my holiday work schedule so we can go to Dutch's Monkey Island hunt and New Year's Eve blast. At first, I didn't like the idea, but after talking to Ginger about Dutch and Lonah's plans, it sounded like a once-in-a-lifetime get-together! We've been trying to get Langdon to come, but he's begging off, even though he enjoyed last year. He says it's a couples' year and he doesn't currently have a chick to sport around."

"Marsh, you and Sue Anne should go," noted Langdon. "The guide we had last year said he once met your Granddaddy Nash with Rachel Carson. He's an old salt named Wayhab."

Brick removed his gun coat, saying the cabin's fireplace made him too warm. He took a set of keys from his pants pocket and opened a cabinet beneath the bar to produce a bottle of Scotch whiskey. He noted, "Winter is brown-liquor time, and Scotch is perfect."

"Brick," Marsh said as he opened his own locker, "instead of Scotch, let's try one of the General's Pennsylvania ryes. He gave me a fifth today after our Tory Hole tour. He says when he's not mixing sazeracs, he enjoys rye, just slow sipping it on ice like Scotch. Said it was the drink of Buffalo Bill Cody, Wild Bill Hickok, Doc Holliday, and most of the Founding Fathers. General Washington actually produced rye for sale."

Langdon left and returned with three Old-Fashioned tumblers full of ice, and Marsh filled them with rye. "Now this is going to be the real-deal Thanksgiving memorial drink. I hereby toast Washington and the Founding Fathers, along with Wild Bill Hickok and Holliday Doc."

"'To Wild Bill Hickok and Holliday Doc' is a real catchy, ass-backwards toast, Langdon!" laughed Marsh as all raised their tumblers. "We had some real cowboy-western wipeouts here—drunks, actually. It's the perfect toast for us."

"Sue Anne," remarked Nicole, "I remember the first time I came here with Brick and Marsh, and met Brewer. It was a wide-open crowd, especially for someone like me, who had been sheltered by military life. I thought I had found the true civilian life I had always dreamed of and had died and gone to heaven all in one flash. I miss those times. They're still in my blood, but I couldn't party now like we did then."

v

"So this place is where Aunt Dot says all of you began to wander from grace," Sue Anne said. "And that old jukebox in the corner, is that what led all of you astray, or was it the picture of Old Bentonville Blue, the Ghost Dog, hanging over it?"

"Ghost dog, arguably not, since he's their sure-shot, aiming spirit from some happy-hunting heaven. On the other hand, jukebox, arguably yes," answered Nicole.

"It's still the best jukebox I ever heard because it has the cherry pickings of the best beach boogie-woogie music anywhere outside the city limits of Ocean Drive. Now that our crowd has started families, we have to go elsewhere to find party action. But the party used to be right here. Not to mention Ocean Drive, Atlantic Beach, White Lake, Williams Lake, or even the dance floor at Faison's Pickle Warehouse."

"The good old days," said Brewer, "before bank-loan responsibilities."

"Well, I would have been too young to be hooked up with this crowd back then," Sue Anne said, "but I sure would have been a wannabe, waiting in the wings! Speaking of the beach, the land here reminds me of the beach with so much white sand."

"Local old timers say the Atlantic Ocean came this far inland billions of years ago. So, you see lots of beach-type sand hereabouts," Brewer replied.

"How do you farm such inert-looking soil?" Sue Anne pressed him.

"Mass-produced chemical fertilizers," said Brewer. "In Colonial times, there were no commercial fertilizers, so farmers used manure. There was never enough manure, so it was handled like a precious item by hand-placing small quantities in each plant hole for maximum plant growth without waste. The farmers here would take swamp mud, also called swamp bog, and blend it with the manure. Swamp bog was nutrient-rich and extended manure supplies.

"These Coastal Plains are full of swamps like Virginia's famous Great Dismal Swamp. Indians called them *pocosins*, meaning swamp on a hill. Bail jumpers, runaway slaves, even Revolutionary War heroes like the area's General Kenan or South Carolina's General Francis 'Swamp Fox' Marion hid in such isolated areas to avoid capture.

"Besides manure and swamp bog, the other fertilization method was the slash-and-burn method of clearing trees and burning them for potash. Due to the large King's Land Grants, timber-based potash was the most common fertilizer source of the Colonial and pre–Civil War eras. But the deforestation depleted the timber faster than the tree re-growth cycle could supply a sustainable potash supply. Consequently, succeeding generations looked for land farther south and west in Georgia, Alabama, Mississippi, Louisiana, Tennessee, Kentucky, and Texas.

"Everyone remembers Daniel Boone leaving North Carolina for Kentucky as being a part of this westward movement, and Andrew Jackson leaving for Tennessee. Their migration was about looking for free or cheap land, and the opportunity it afforded.

"This area also has a hero of that great westward movement. He was Micajah Autry, who died at the Alamo. A postmortem inspirational painting of him hangs there along with those of Davy Crockett, Colonel William Travis, Jim Bowie, and Santa Anna. These five paintings are the Alamo's only ones. Of the five portraits, Autry's is the only one with a byline under it, even though all the others are more famous: 'Hero of the Alamo.' He was a friend of Crockett and Andrew Jackson. Like the others, he died there looking for land and the freer opportunities its individual ownership promised. Like Bowie, Autry was a slave owner.

"Sue Anne, you've been married to Marsh long enough to hear his Mama's stories of failure at low-land farming in New Holland–Lake Mattamuskeet. Such marsh bogs are rich in nutrients, but they present numerous problems from out of nature's left field that make it hard for even large investor groups to ride out the setbacks.

"We all know that history from having hunted at Mattamuskeet, and I learned more about it in my State agricultural classes. This area is not fundamentally different from Mattamuskeet, but at least we have good field peas to eat here.

"The poor nutrient-holding capability of our sandy land was not the foundation for many big plantations, although where we are now was once part of a big plantation. Its outcome was like that of the large New Holland effort. In fact, this old slave cabin came from the place. The Island Fields Plantation is said to have had sixty-five slaves in its heyday, raising rice, cotton, tobacco, and indigo. It was a community unto itself since swamps and streams surrounded it. The old Negrohead Road that ran by here was the only path to Fayetteville or Wilmington. A hurricane-like storm destroyed it in the 1830s. Our forebears, as well as Monroe's, bought tracts of it before the Civil War for its timber and turpentine."

VI

"So, where does Old Bentonville Blue come in, Brewer?" Sue Anne asked.

"You must first appreciate the futility of the Civil War Battles of Averasboro and Bentonville to understand why a ghost-sighting event is reasonably connected to a hunting dog. I knew about Bentonville from my grandfather's ghost story, which prepared me for General Eisner's military-historical view later. It was all about Sherman's need of supplies.

"Sherman's march from Atlanta to Bentonville in 1864-65 took him through Fayetteville so he could destroy the arsenal. Unlike Savannah and Charleston, Fayetteville was seventy-five miles inland. Consequently, this march took the Yankees away from their sea-based, Navy Quartermaster re-supply sources. Sherman's sixty-thousand-man army thus had to seize chickens, hogs, hams, sausage, horses, mules, corn, honey, and any other thing they could from the local population. Because of their urgent need for re-supply, Sherman's marching progress was so rapid that the opposing Confederate General Joseph E. Johnston said that Sherman's force was like no other since Julius Caesar's Legions.

"Leaving Fayetteville, Sherman's destination was Goldsboro, North Carolina, the junction of two railroads that could provide him with reliable supplies from the Union Navy occupying the coastal towns of New Bern and Wilmington from which the railroads came into Goldsboro. Sherman split his force, sending Major General Oliver O. Howard's Army of Tennessee east to Faison to secure the midpoint of the railroad running from Wilmington to Goldsboro. Thus, General Howard's wing went through the Sampsons Landing-Negrohead Road area. Major General Henry Slocum's Army of Georgia was Sherman's West Wing.

"At Averasboro, the Cape Fear River and the South River might be two miles apart—a good place for a Confederate attack because the two tightly pinched, parallel rivers would prevent flanking movements by Sherman's larger force. Also, the heavy rains had flooded the South River drainage basin, making all the surrounding swamps too mushy for Howard's East Wing to reverse quickly and rescue the Slocum West Wing.

"The Battle of Averasboro took place on March 15-16, 1865, and resulted in 500 Rebel and 682 Yankee casualties. The significance of the Battles of Averasboro and Bentonville, according to Eisner, is that these two battles were the only time since Atlanta in early September of 1864 that the Confederates chose the battleground and initiated the attack. Really the Appomattox, Virginia, campaign was anti-climactic, with its two battles producing 500 total casualties.

"The Bentonville Battle was, in reality, the war's last battle, and resulted in more than 4,000 casualties for both sides. That's nothing compared to the more than 51,000 casualties at Gettysburg or the more than 34,000 at Chickamauga, but it's North Carolina's largest and bloodiest battle. It occurred outside modern-day Newton Grove near the Sampson and Johnston County line junction. The John and Amy Harper farmhouse served as a hospital where surgeons operated on the troops of both sides. Limbs, amputated to prevent gangrene deaths, were piled high just outside the first-floor farmhouse windows. The stench of blood and rotting flesh was all about, and it is said that even today the echoing screams of suffering still haunt the place nightly.

"Appomattox took place a few weeks later, followed by Confederate General Johnston's surrender of his Averasboro-Bentonville troops to Sherman at Bennett Place, near Durham. The Durham surrender was the Civil War's largest, and its true end.

"Averasboro and Bentonville wasted lives and changed nothing. I suppose the screams of those suffering troops echoing over the years still haunt us today because of such egregious waste. And that's where the bloodline of Old Bentonville Blue's ancestors comes in.

"Granddad's story goes that forty years later, about 1905, there was a Smithfield man with a weakness for possum hunting. He was also known to be a serious Christian man, who wouldn't lie and who also did not believe in possum hunting on Sunday.

"He had an English friend and took him possum hunting late one March Saturday night in the woods at Bentonville, where his family had a hunting cabin. When the hounds finally chased a possum up a tree, the two men worried that it might be after midnight, and officially Sunday because the moon was sinking out of sight. However, the local man wanted to catch a possum for the Englishman, and he grabbed his axe to chop down the tree.

"Now the Bentonville Battle took place in March of 1865 on about the same dates these two men were hunting in March of 1905. Whatever the date coincidence, when the axe hit the tree, blinding flashes of light illuminated everything in the woods. The two men saw ghostly figures of foot soldiers and cavalry fighting.

"In one spooky scene, they saw a deathly encounter as a Yank attempted to take a Confederate flag away from its bearer. A second Reb rushed to assist the Confederate flagbearer in the struggle but was killed by the Yank's bayonet. The flagbearer also suffered a knife wound to his shoulder. With the noise of bullets, screams of death, and charging cavalry going on about them, the possum hunters stood frozen in a time warp forty years before that foggy night!

"Scared out of their wits, they ran. Running past the Harpers' abandoned hospital farmhouse, they were running so hard that they did not consider the lights streaming from it until they reached their hunting cabin. You see, electricity wasn't available in the early 1900s for the rural Bentonville area. So what had caused the bright lights? Spooky!

"Later, when the possum hunter told this story to others, a veteran of the Bentonville battle happened to be present. At the end of the story, all scoffed except the old soldier. He said that he had been the flag bearer in the battle, and that his shoulder was still useless from its battle-knife wound. Also, it was his older brother who had died from the Yankee bayonet in an attempt to help him bear the Confederate flag.

"My dad was a baby then and Granddad went to the Wilson tobacco market, where the possum hunter of this 1905 ghost-sighting was present with his dogs. He related the whole story to Granddad, and then Granddad asked about buying a puppy for my dad from their litter. So that's where Old Bentonville Blue's blood line and namesake came from.

"Blue was our last dog from that blood line. He was a good hunter but was run over by a car before he was bred. Because he was so good in the field, hunters had a habit of touching his picture before they went out to hunt, no matter what they were hunting. Blue was a hound, not a bird dog, but his spirit seems to bring bird hunters good luck, too."

Sue Anne exclaimed, "I know all of you believe it because it's been a part of you for so long, but I find it extremely hard to—!"

"Believe it, Darling!" Marsh interrupted. "You should hear the other battlefield ghost stories that Nicole's dad tells about Gettysburg, Shiloh, Chancellorsville. Each has similarities of the dead seeking a way back into this world to take care of the business of their unmanifested dreams. The Tory Hole Revolutionary War site we visited with the General today is probably no different in that the ghosts wish they had done something else the day they died."

"Oh, I believe in such things, Marsh," Marina put in. "Montréal's Saint Joseph's Oratory is a shrine where many pilgrims have reportedly been healed by miracles or had life-changing experiences. We went there not long after Dad's passing. The place made me think that the spirit world is always close by even though we humans can't begin to comprehend how those metaphysical communications work. Such places are true holy grounds for the energy they send to us, the still-living."

"Yes, and for Old Bentonville Blue's ancestors, history's extraterrestrial holy ground was only one axe chop away," noted Brewer.

VII

"Bentonville Blue was a part of growing up around our grandparents like everything else in Sampsons Landing," reflected Brick. "As mid-fifties'-era kids, we could still ride horses over the mostly unpaved roads here. You felt like Tom Sawyer or some cowboy in a movie when you went fishing, swimming, or snake-hunting in the marshes near the river's run. There was a cart path that went through cornfields near Monroe's grandparents' house down to the river. A fence followed beside the path part of the way. We'd set cans on those fence posts and take turns riding by them at full gallop to shoot the cans off with our shotguns.

"I remember that first time we all drank beer. We were about twelve and had been to the Saturday afternoon Lash LaRue double feature. Dutch had come down with Marsh that weekend. Marsh complained about Dutch having to ride in back of him since Dutch had no horse. The rest of us took turns letting Dutch double on our horses.

"After the movie, Monroe and Brewer said let's go by the colored bootlegger's joint on the way to the swimming hole. That bootlegger was Shank Poe, who later bartended at the PSR Club. We rode up to the back, so no one would see us from the road. Brewer hollered out for this colored boy who had worked on his dad's farm. Little Richard's 'Long Tall Sally' played on the jukebox, visible inside the dilapidated screen door, before Joe Turner's 'Honey Hush.' It was the first time we had ever heard such music, and we really liked it.

"We had just over a dollar among us and gave that to the boy for our two bootleg beers. Brewer then came up with another nickel, which he gave to our barefooted, curbside waiter for playing another Little Richard tune, 'Ready Teddy,' that rang in our ears as we rode away. Truly we rode out of a little-boy, bad-assed Lash LaRue cowboy mentality, and straight into rock and roll in one collective epiphany while drinking our first of many illegal beers. Turner's 'Honey Hush' Lone Ranger ending line of 'hi-yo, hi-yo, Silver' seemed to reinforce the wild time vision our twelve-year-old gang had that day.

"Riding toward the river we did our usual thing of shooting cans off a fence post, except this time we got to shoot off our empty beer cans. Bentonville Blue would follow, barking at our horses, as we galloped by the fence post to shoot. Continuing on toward the swimming hole, we were still singing and humming Little Richard's 'Ready Teddy' when we came to a fork in the path. One led down to the white swimming hole and the other to the colored swimming hole. Of course, no sign designated this, like it was a law or something—it was just the custom. They had their place and we had ours, and it was expected that all would respect it, law or no law.

"Anyway, Monroe said let's take a dip in the colored swimming hole, and on a wild dare everybody agreed as long as nobody was using it because we didn't want to offend anybody. When we got there, it was empty, and as usual we yelled 'Last-man-in-is-a-rotten-egg.' Now, to be sure, all of our swimming in those days was nude. We got off our horses and stripped as fast as we could to keep from receiving the 'rotten-egg' appellation.

"Well, that's when I had to do my first beer pee. So I'm peeing beside my horse while still humming to Little Richard's 'Ready Teddy,' and the rest of the guys are about to take their first dive into the old colored swimming hole when someone exclaims in an urgent, but soft voice, 'Snake!' I could see from the corner of my eye that Old Bentonville Blue was looking at it, too, real still-like.

"I reached up and pulled out Granddad's old L.C. Smith from the saddle scabbard. It was loaded, so I was ready for the kill even if I was just as naked as the day I was born. Of course, singing and softly humming 'Ready Teddy' just took all the fear of God and Satan out of me after several swallows of beer. Hell, I was bulletproof, slipping up to the bank, where lay a big moccasin, curled up on a bunch of lily pads. Still humming to 'Ready Teddy,' I let the snake have it with both barrels! No more Mr. Snake!

"Then I jumped up in the air, private parts all flying, and turned around in midair to yell a victory shout of 'I'm READY, READY TEDDY TO ROCK 'N' ROLL!' When I did, all I could see was a bunch of black faces staring at our naked bodies from their position up by the last curve where the path straightened out for its final approach to the river. That was, of course, Donald or Little Donald, at the time, his grandma, and a slew of other blacks I didn't have time to recognize from my embarrassing position of mid-air nudity.

"Well, all of us, except Dutch, got our jeans on pronto and lit out of there. Dutch's fanny was still showing as he hung onto Marsh in the doubled-up, back-rider position. A young black man hollered as we galloped out of sight, 'GO SWIM IN YOUR OWN SWIMMING HOLE!' Another yelled, with a big-sounding belly laugh, 'THAT'S RIGHT, AND DON'T COME BACK, YOU LITTLE WHITE ASSES!'

"Well, we thought that was the last of that as we galloped off like Jesse James from a failed bank robbery, with Old Bentonville Blue following, but it wasn't. When we got home, after taking a dip in the white swimming hole, we were met with a big parental reception. Donald's Grandmamma had made phone calls all around, and we were the talk of the town by sundown. Boy, did our ears ever get scorched! I guess we were too big to get a whipping by then, but their words about respecting others hurt anyway. Later though, we all realized that it was a true victory of some kind, as we had all made a clean getaway with the real jewel of the afternoon, our first beers! They never did find out about that, even to this day."

"So, Sue Anne," Marsh interjected, "it wasn't the cabin jukebox or Bentonville Blue that led us astray, like Aunt Dot says, it was us just being Lash LaRue primed and ready for Little Richard's rock 'n' roll. And this hunting cabin became the headquarters of it all."

The cousins returned to their Aunt Dot's Pineland Springs home, where she hosted her brothers, sisters-in-law, and niece, Mary Lee. All enjoyed a few moments of conversation with Marina about the architectural aspects of her Fayetteville Market House tour before going to the Ecumenical Thanksgiving Church Service. There the overflow crowd heard Donald, his Cousin Thomas, and other choir members do the Shaker hymn "Simple Gifts," and General Eisner noted it was his late wife's favorite.

Chapter Seven

Holiday Barbeques and Outer Banks Duck Hunting

Then the Voice said: Let Knowledge go where it will, for
unlimited freedom is the only state in which it can function.
—*"Preamble to the Beginning," Chaplain Wesley Wyatt, U.S. Army*
The Coosa Valley Boarding School for Boys, ca. 1954–55

I

AFTER THANKSGIVING, MRS. PENNY, the usual winter rains slowed construction and
stopped Sunrise Acres' road work. Thus, some finished houses couldn't be sold until
paving was completed.

Jeff Mack's failure to install sixty feet of pipe near the top ten lots on the Friday after
Thanksgiving caused this delay. That day Jeff had an equipment failure and couldn't arrange
repairs until the following week. By then the rains had begun, stopping all road work.

Amid these dilemmas were the 1971 Christmas holiday functions. Lisa and Marina's
mother did spend three weeks at the Huttons' before going to Florida to be with her
sister, Joan, for New Year's and to winter there through February. The MacKoy families
also had their numerous holiday celebrations.

The biggest event was the annual lumber company barbeque for employees and cus-
tomers. I often attended these because Dad was a longtime customer. Vann Hutton and
Lisa came that day, along with Junebug, his father, and Mrs. Iris' husband, Deputy Carley
Ray Craft. Marina, however, remained behind to manage Hutton's office, her two nieces,
and her mother. Lisa Hutton asked Sue Anne about the pending Monkey Island trip as
Hutton, Brick, and Marsh discussed house designs. When Donald passed by, Marsh asked

about his Christmas Eve wedding. From our table, Hogbear said loudly, so all could hear at both tables: "He'll need one of my fertilizer pads to make notes for staying out of trouble!"

Hutton laughed, "That's a wise man! He even makes notes for avoiding troubles."

Lisa laughed at her husband. "Poor Vann is outnumbered these days with our two girls, Marina, and Mother all at home. He loves for men to drop in—even Cy Turner brings relief!"

Then Mr. Malcolm, Austin, Mrs. Colleen, and Diane came to greet us, but looked away as Mr. Malcolm announced, "The Willinghams." All turned to see the elder June Willingham and his son, Junebug. "I suppose Mrs. Martha and Kay's mother are eagerly awaiting the new arrival?" Diane Winship asked the men.

"If Kay doesn't deliver tomorrow," answered Junebug, "her doctors will do a Caesarean."

"I required one for our second," Lisa put in, looking down at her barbeque.

Junebug smiled at Lisa when she raised her head. Then he said, "Malcolm, here's your legal paperwork on the new MacKoy and MacKoy cattle partnership for you and Marsh. You're official now."

"Oh, Marsh," said the elder Willingham, "I understand you'll be hunting at Monkey Island around New Year's. If your party ventures south towards Duck, I'd appreciate your stopping by my beach cottage to check on any nor'easter winter-storm damage. You remember where it is, don't you?"

"Yes," answered Marsh. "Junebug has mentioned this to me, and I asked Brick about the possibilities, as I've never hunted there. Brick said that a man like Dutch who can arrange hunting trips and lingerie sales can likely arrange about anything."

All laughed before Mr. Malcolm and his former law partner turned to their late 1930s and early 1940s law-practice days. Eventually, Dad and I, along with Mingo and Hogbear, excused ourselves to attend to Sunrise Acres details before taking off for Christmas. Brick soon returned to talk with Dad before leaving for Pineland Springs.

As Brick and Dad talked, Cecil Crisp drove up, all smiles. He greeted everyone while his wife, Shasta, remained in the car, perhaps because she appeared uncomfortable in Muslim wear.

"Gentlemen," Cecil bubbled, "I want to thank you both. That young Willingham lawyer said he would assist me in legally changing my name after New Year's to reflect my religion.

"I'll then be Cecil X Crisp. So if I can help you, call. It'll be my way of saying thanks."

Brick said, "Well, there's something you can do for me, Cecil, since you're selling fish. I don't want to get you into any trouble with your new community of brothers. I'll be glad to pay you top price for a cooler of shrimp and scallops, as well as fresh clams and mussels. I'm hunting next week, and I need to bring seafood because we'll be stranded on a tiny island with no grocery store. I'll call you when I find out how many pounds of each I need, and I'll need to pick them up by Wednesday noon."

"Yes, it'll just be between us," Cecil answered, handing Brick a business card, reading "Shabazz Fisheries."

II

Between Christmas and New Year's, construction work was on hiatus, but before departing for Monkey Island, Brick and Dad showed four houses. Then Wednesday Cecil X delivered a plastic cooler of shrimp but no scallops, clams, or mussels. Brick paid Cecil and left for Marsh's house from which they departed.

I heard about that trip from nearly everybody, including Brick, Marsh, Marina, and Sue Anne. Then, a few years ago, I heard all the juicier details from Junebug's wife, Kay, as we toured Four Corners' Canyon de Chelly near my house.

Brick, Marsh, and Sue Anne traveled in Marsh's new sporty 4-wheel-drive utility truck to Raleigh to pick up Marina and purchased wines to complement the menus the group had planned for the next several days on Currituck Sound's isolated Monkey Island. The drive from Raleigh to the boat landing, thirty minutes east of Elizabeth City, put them arriving there in the dark.

Marsh parked near Duncan Lazlo's motor home. They spotted a small power launch moored beside a rickety pier, illuminated by a single light. Then two men, dressed in hunting waders and coats, emerged from the pier's storage shed. One greeted them with a doleful wave.

Getting out of Marsh's vehicle, Brick called out, "Your name is Wayhab Sully, right?"

"Aye," a man replied in an English brogue, common to old-time residents of the Virginia-Carolina coast. "And this is my mate, Charlie Durwood."

"I remember you from last year's hunt with Dutch's group. I'm Brick MacKoy. This is my cousin Marsh and his wife, Sue Anne, and my friend Marina LaGraves. This is their first hunting trip with Dutch.

"And Marsh is the grandson of the Evabay School Principal, Mr. Nash, who helped you guide Rachel Carson around Mattamuskeet after World War II."

"Aye," replied Wayhab, shaking Marsh's hand. "You're the last ones. We'll be taking you to the island once we haul your gear to the launch."

The men transferred the luggage, guns, and coolers of food, liquor, and wine while

Marina and Sue Anne carried their train cases and pocketbooks. As the water gurgled about the launch, Marina said, "These dark waters remind me of my father's drowning."

"Don't worry," Brick noted, patting her shoulders. "The Currituck Sound isn't deep. You can actually walk across the Sound in most places from here to the Outer Banks and the village of Corolla, due east."

Charlie removed the mooring ropes when the boat's engine started, producing a plume of smoke. As the smoke faded, the pier's light rays seemed as murky as the waters the craft traversed. After minutes of foggy darkness, an outline of Corolla's Currituck Lighthouse emerged to the east. Wayhab said the expensive French-made lens of the lighthouse's rotating beam no longer functioned and had not been replaced because satellites now guided ships. The boat made a turn toward the northwest, where lights flickered as the sight of trees and a pier came into focus. While the launch glided toward its mooring, Wayhab employed reverse-gear engagements to slow the vessel's forward motion to a crawl.

On docking, the outline of a house appeared through the trees. Then voices called out, and soon Dutch Lazlo, Lonah Slueter, Brewer Melvin, Nicole Melvin, and Monroe and Ginger Hill made their way down the pier to help unload.

III

After the new arrivals moved in, all convened by the lodge's clubroom fireplace. Once drinks were distributed, Brewer raised his glass. "In honor of our missing friend Salt-Dog Langdon, let's raise our glasses and repeat his newly phrased toast: 'To the Founding Fathers, Wild Bill Hickok, and Holliday Doc!' May our next few days be fondly memorable!"

"Well," laughed Ginger Hill, as Wayhab and Charlie placed more wood on the fire, "This is a toasty place! I mean, all the bedrooms, and those huge old bathtubs."

"They're big enough to fill to your neck without the water running out the overflow; truly late nineteenth-century," noted Lonah. "I've spoiled myself soaking daily while Dutch and his Puerto Rican guests hunted."

Marsh remarked, "Impressive, Brick! This exceeds all my expectations you built up from stories of your hunting here last year."

Dutch said, "Until 1886 the Pumonkey Indians inhabited the island. Then there were several ownerships by whites. In 1919, tobacco executives formed the Monkey Island Gunning Club. One of those men was George Washington Hill of the American Tobacco Company and Lucky Strike Cigarette fame. Mr. Hill arranged for the company's Vice President, Charles A. Penn of Reidsville, North Carolina, to become a member in 1927.

In 1931, Mr. Penn purchased all the stock, but American Tobacco executives continued entertaining major customers here. In fact, Mr. Hill was here when he crafted the 'Lucky Strike Goes to War' slogan of World War II.

"My grandfather, father, and uncle became friends with the Penns. Granddad came from New England looking for textile opportunities in the early World War I era. The Pinehurst area attracted him because it reminded him of New England villages. Being an avid hunter, he often practiced at the Pinehurst Annie Oakley Gun Club, where he encountered the late Mr. Penn and they became friends.

"Occasionally, Mr. Penn would invite friends here who had no tobacco industry connections, and Granddad—and later my father and uncle—would come. With age, the Penns used the place less, and rented it out once a year to my family to entertain our textile client-base. We are about the only ones who use it now because hunting for entertainment is becoming something of a long-ago lifestyle relic. In fact, the Penns' estate managers are advertising for a buyer."

"I'll bet Junebug would love waxing away on a philosophical idea here," said Marsh.

"Yes," mused Brick, "I can envision him nursing a Scotch or rye and gazing into that fireplace. But I expect he'd be musing about his new baby girl today, rather than sounding out lofty thoughts of how hunting connects spiritually to the great theories of jurisprudence."

"Yes, the Willingham babe," noted Nicole. "How's the expanded family?"

"Kay joined Junebug's mother's name with her own mother's to create the name Martha Sarah," Sue Anne related.

"Folks," Dutch announced, "sorry to interrupt, but Wayhab will be here to locate us in the hunting blinds before daybreak, and we've got a movie to see before bedtime.

"Wayhab's wife, Jharu, has prepared tonight's dinner, but tomorrow night we'll be on our own, cooking the foods that you ladies have discussed by phone since Thanksgiving. Let's finalize those culinary plans at dinner. Jharu is ready to serve now. Also, I've got several love-story movies the ladies can discuss viewing, while we men hunt the next two days.

"Saturday is New Year's. Wayhab can't spot us in duck blinds that day because he and Jharu must manage a store at Corolla for the owners who'll be away for New Year's. The two make their living doing odd jobs, as well as doing commercial fishing and hunting. Maybe Saturday will be the day to go view Mr. Willingham's cottage at Duck, Marsh. Wayhab's agreed to letting Charlie and you take his four-wheel-drive vehicle, which was formerly a twelve-passenger school bus especially designed to traverse the area's sandy beach roads.

"Brick, I told Wayhab and Jharu that after three nights of crab and lobster with my Puerto Rican friends, I'm ready for a steak. Did you bring any red wine?"

"Marina got wine today," Brick responded as all moved into the dining room. "But my seafood supplier is just getting his business started and doesn't yet have sources for fresh scallops, clams, or mussels. Can Wayhab find any?"

"Not in Corolla," Dutch replied. "We might purchase some at Duck or south of there at Manteo when we check out the Willingham cottage Saturday."

Sue Anne, Ginger, and Nicole began conversing about Junebug and Kay's baby, and Brick laughed. "Yeah! He'll cross-examine every suitor to determine if they're good enough for Martha Sarah, and his old Jewish genes will make him also ask if they have any real prospects for supporting her."

"I thought Junebug was an Episcopalian, like Wesley," said Nicole Melvin.

"Well, he is," replied Brick. "But ancient Willingham history says he's Jewish. Marsh knows more about that since Uncle Malcolm and old Mr. June were law partners."

"Yes," Marsh remarked as all sat down. "Mr. Willingham's grandfather was a Willingstein from Charleston, home to America's largest Jewish community before the Civil War. Mr. Willingham says Jews have been running from persecution throughout history. Before Hitler's Nazi era, there were the Catholic Inquisitions. One found Galileo guilty of heresy for writing about the Copernican System of universal heavenly order in the early 1600s, long after the 1492 discovery of America. Today we're prone to think of that era as one of unencumbered enlightenment, but it wasn't. Galileo suffered by having to recant his scientific truths and endure house arrest until death. Many Jews, however, were sentenced to death by inquisition trials, or forced to flee with few belongings.

"The Willingsteins, like many Charleston Jews, were merchants. They had come to South Carolina because its John Locke–influenced constitution offered religious tolerance and an equal opportunity to chase their dreams for fulfillment. Locke's thinking influenced both Carolina constitutions as well as Virginia's and Georgia's.

"Mr. Willingham's granddad was nearly twenty at the time of the Civil War. He became involved with the Underground Railroad, hiding runaway slaves before Sherman's march into Charleston. While doing this, the young Mr. Willingstein became involved with a Catholic girl, whom he married. Although the Willingsteins were of the Charleston Reform Jewish community, these reforms did not extend to marrying Christians or diluting the Jewish bloodline. The Catholics were just as staunch in believing all Catholic offspring must be adopted into the Catholic Church proper. Their families disinherited them both!

"Prior to Sherman's Charleston invasion, locals got wind of this cross-cultural marital ruckus, and how it had evolved from the lovers' anti-slavery connection. This in turn disclosed the group's hideout, and the Confederate civil authorities raided it.

"Young Willingstein and his bride escaped the foray by going to Fayetteville to hide with his mother's cousins. Store clerks were scarce during the war, and his cousin took him in quietly to help out. While young Willingstein was befriended by his Fayetteville family, they did not approve of his marital choice, or let anyone know about this interfaith marriage. They also did not inform their Charleston family of the couple's whereabouts.

"After the war, the Fayetteville hosts feared this cross-cultural marriage would be found out by word of mouth from traveling salespeople. Such in turn could affect future business support and loans between the Fayetteville and Charleston Jews. No use jeopardizing that business-support foundation, one can easily imagine the Fayetteville cousins' reasoning.

"Consequently, the Fayetteville cousins assisted the mixed-faith couple's move to Wisdom Station where there were no Jews or Catholics, and the couple's background could be hidden easily. Also, forecasts said the Wisdom Station area would revive economically once the war-torn railroad line was rebuilt, thus creating a new outlet for Jewish-financed merchandise.

"The couple changed their names to Willingham to avoid prejudicial inquiry into their past and took up the Episcopal belief, as many of their Charleston anti-slavery friends had been of this faith. Junebug's dad says his grandparents never saw Charleston or their families again, or even heard whether the Charleston Willingsteins survived the war. Only our family knows this story, even today."

"Marsh, your tale reminds me of my father taking Lisa and me out of the Catholic Church back home over a religious ruckus," Marina said as they began to eat. The blowing of the wind outside was a stimulant to their appetites, and all ate heartily.

After washing the dinner dishes, Wayhab, Jharu, and Charlie left. Dutch then began loading the movie projector with the 1946 Western *My Darling Clementine*, with Henry Fonda as Wyatt Earp and Victor Mature as Doc Holliday.

Marsh said, "I don't know if anyone's interested, but I made a pot buy yesterday from an albino black we call Chalky. Sue Anne and I did a joint last night and we still feel its effects. Would anyone like to do one before the movie?"

"Well," said Dutch, "do what you want, but smoke it outside, please. I don't want to get the inside of the house smoked up tonight. Our three caretaker-guides are next door at the caretaker's cottage. So they'll be in here early tomorrow before we'd have time to freshen up the air. We mustn't spook these folks because they're just stand-in caretakers. Wayhab is mostly a commercial hunter and fisherman. That makes him the best kind of guide, but he doesn't have a lot of personality flexibility, and neither does his wife or Charlie.

"Besides, my Puerto Rican friends left some pot behind that's probably better. Lonah and I did some last night with them on the back porch, while we were roasting oysters. Talk about feeling numb today! Wayhab boated us over to Corolla to check out a few blinds for tomorrow's hunting over by the Whalehead Hunt Club. It was cold, but not as cold as my body thought it was. I was on a cold-enhanced pot trip, for sure! Let's take a break. They'll all be at their homes in Corolla tomorrow night and New Year's Eve. Then it'll be easier to get away with what we want."

"O.K.," noted Marsh. "We must be temperate to stay on the good side of strangers."

When the film ended, Monroe Hill and Brewer Melvin stood arm in arm by the fireplace and sang their own intoxicated, construed lyrics of the tune "Clementine," as well as verses of the hymn "At the River," both of which had been featured in the movie. As this transpired, Dutch and Lonah set up the first reel of a movie the girls would view the next day.

IV

Before sunup Wayhab and Charlie had the men in the hunting blinds, so all would be quiet when the waterfowl flew in for daybreak feeding. It was windy and just above freezing with little ice in the marsh grass. To help the hunters fight the cold, Jharu had furnished each with a thermos of she-crab soup, her specialty, and spiked it with sherry.

Brick hunted alone, while Marsh was with Dutch, and Monroe with Brewer. When sunlight pierced the deep blue clouds on the horizon out to sea, Brick caught a glimpse of two teals inside the marsh grass, and in borderline range of his shotgun. Brick knew it was illegal to shoot ducks sitting on water. He also knew that if he missed a shot he might not see another duck the rest of the day in such windy conditions. But if he got off a lucky shot with the long-range left barrel of his double-barrel, he might get caught by some eager game warden, perhaps well hidden nearby. So he bided his time.

After over an hour, the teals swam from the marsh grass to circle on the water as if preparing to fly into the oncoming northeast wind. Now they were about ten feet away but showed no flight intention until Wayhab's noisy approaching skiff excited them into lift-off.

That's when Brick cut loose with his right barrel at the closer bird, and then with his left, long-range barrel at the bird farther away. The first bird dropped to the open water but the second fell inside the marsh grass. Wayhab retrieved the teal on the open water and recovered the second bird with the coaxing stroke of a boat paddle.

"Aye, good gunning," Wayhab said as he came up. "Brick, do ye need anything?" Brick said no. Then Wayhab added, "I'll tag your teals and have Charlie dress them for packing in ice to transport home."

Wayhab then reported a goose kill by Brewer Melvin and noted the windy conditions before saying, "I'll return before noon to take you all to the lodge for lunch."

After Wayhab left, Brick looked for additional shooting opportunities, and seeing none, set his shotgun aside to partake of Jharu's soup. For the next several hours he scanned the horizon but saw no birds. At 11:00 a.m., Wayhab returned to Brick's blind with all hunters aboard save Monroe Hill, who had returned to the lodge earlier to relieve himself from the cold and the she-crab soup. As for Marsh and Dutch, they had discharged shots at some birds beyond shotgun range to ease their monotony. Thus Brewer's goose and Brick's teals were the morning's only bounty.

For lunch the group ate grilled ham and cheese sandwiches, and more she-crab soup. Because the women were eating, too, it became evident that the soup was going to run out since Jharu had made it as usual only for the hunters. Marina volunteered to prepare a similar recipe with clams that her mother had prepared for her father's St. Lawrence Seaway trips. When a search of the lodge's pantry produced no clams, Wayhab offered to ferry Marina off the island to a store at Corolla after redeploying the hunters for the afternoon hunt. He promised to have her back for the screening of *Brigadoon*, with Gene Kelly.

That afternoon Wayhab repositioned the group to different blinds hoping to improve their shooting opportunities. Brewer Melvin was placed with Brick, while Marsh and Dutch were placed south of them. Monroe Hill, chilled in lighter-weight clothing, was placed to the north on the main barrier island in a one-man coffin blind on a grassy sand dune. Wayhab hoped that the sides of the coffin blind would protect Monroe from the cold, and Monroe also carried along a thermos of bourbon. Bird flight, however, was spotty and distant.

At sunset, two ducks flew near Marsh and Dutch's southern position, but upon seeing the flash of a thermos lid, they veered west, out of gun range. They continued a northerly flight out of range as they went by Brick and Brewer's center position. Then they veered back to the east, and conveniently over Monroe's northern coffin blind. He bagged both to end the first day's shooting. Seeing Monroe's kills, Wayhab pronounced them mainland wood ducks, probably en route to better feeding in the Backbay, Virginia, area, just north across the state line.

V

After the boat ride back, the men bathed and then gathered in the clubroom to snack on shrimp Brick had purchased from Cecil X. Ginger announced, "Marina's already made soup for tomorrow! She braved a chilly boat ride to Corolla in her long leather coat and toboggan. These Canadians know how to survive the cold."

Marina noted, "Brick, I saw a mansion there—delightful architecture. I wanted to tour it, but Wayhab says it's off-limits."

"It's an interesting place," Dutch said. "I'll tell you about it at dinner. Brewer and I have to grill the fish now."

Brick inquired about the evening meal, and Marina responded, "Flounder with a butter-lemon marinade, grilled in tin-foil wrap. Also some of your shrimp, skewered with tomatoes."

"When are you cooking the bouillabaisse everybody's been talking about?" Brick asked.

"The last night, so everybody will have a take-home culinary memory," said Marina. "Help me pour the wine. It's the same Loire Valley Fumé Blanc your Aunt Dot enjoyed with her Thanksgiving turkey. It'll do even better with seafood."

At dinner, Lonah said, "Dutch, this wine is perfect. It reminds me of that bottle we had in Puerto Rico, with fish, back at Thanksgiving."

"It does," remarked Dutch, dislodging a shrimp from a skewer. "Speaking of reminding, Marina, the mansion you saw is now called the Whalehead Club. It has an elevator in it, and a history, which should appeal to your architectural interest.

"It was built in the early twenties by a Northern gentleman, Edward Knight, a retired railroad and sugar company executive. He was also an architect and artist. He hunted here for years as a member of the old Lighthouse Club, founded by a group of New York hunters in the late 1800s. Knight bought out the other members because they wouldn't let his wife hunt. She was his second wife and like you, Marina, a French Canadian!

"It's a thirty-five-room, three-story house, but the roof line makes it look like a large story-and-a-half structure. The roof is copper, the floors cork, and the original wall covering was corduroy. Like this lodge, the building materials were barged in from nearby Norfolk, Virginia.

"My father and grandfather visited the place many times on trips with the Penns. It also had the first swimming pool on the Outer Banks. The property is well secured, as it sits on a man-made mini-island that Knight created by digging a canal around the property from the Currituck Sound side. So he called it Corolla Island, but retained the club's original title of the Lighthouse Club because it's beside the Corolla-Currituck Lighthouse. Two English-style wooden bridges cross the canal for access to the village of Corolla. The canal also has a large boathouse on it with slips that provided portage for boats ferrying hunters, visitors, and supplies from Elizabeth City on Carolina's mainland.

"The Knights treated the place as their primary home, but it was truly an entertainment enterprise for hire, and required many people to run it. Wayhab worked there briefly, when he moved here during the Depression.

"Wayhab says the Knights hosted Saturday-night dances at the mansion for the guests, and also invited everybody in Corolla. At Christmas, the Knights bought a Christmas tree for the local church and gave the church women enough money to buy every man, woman, and child a present, plus fruit, nuts, and candy. To this day, this noblesse oblige endeared the Knights to the locals still living, who remember their generosity during the Depression, when Outerbanker commercial fishermen and hunters didn't have two cents to rub together.

"Both Knights died in 1936. Then in 1940, a Washington, D.C. lobbyist, Ray Adams, purchased the property and changed the name from the Lighthouse Club to the Whalehead Club. He was a great entertainer of politicians, powerful industrialists, and celebrities. He often invited Jack Dempsey to hobnob with guests.

"During World War II, Adams leased the club to the Coast Guard for a training center. After the war, he tried to expand the property's appeal by building a small airstrip for flying in prospective cottage buyers. Adams' remote vacation-property idea was ahead of its time, though, and failed. He died in 1958.

"Since 1962 a secretive, quasi-governmental firm known as the Atlantic Research Corporation has owned it. That's why it's hard to get locals to talk about what's gone on there, even though there are rumors that the place may go up for sale again.

"Atlantic Research used the isolation of the place for a top-secret rocket test site. At Whalehead, engineers developed the gel-solid rocket fuel that landed man on the moon. They constructed concrete launch pads to which rockets were bolted for static firing. After firing, each fuel blend was measured to ascertain how its recipe had reacted.

"The northern Outer Banks' seclusion is perfect for such secretive stuff because there are no paved roads to the town of Corolla, even today in the modern-moon-travel 1970s. To go to Virginia Beach, Virginia, one has to drive on the beach. To go south to Duck, N.C., one has to drive eighteen miles on the beach and on the telephone-pole maintenance road. Such trips are very slow in low gear, and if an unlucky traveler gets stuck in the soft sand, an hour-and-a-half drive becomes an ordeal. Rusted-out cars litter these sandy roads, decaying in the salt air because they didn't have large flotation tires for traction like Wayhab's former school bus Jeep that carried kids to Corolla's school."

"Dutch, your story makes the Whalehead mansion all the more intriguing," said Marina. "I'd like to see it up close. The architecture is so out of place in these sparse-looking surroundings, which makes it an absolute jewel here, but it would be anywhere."

"It'll be tricky to see it," Dutch responded. "Now, Lonah and I toured around the mansion's outside before all of you arrived checking out blinds with Wayhab, but he was very nervous. Keeping a check on the place is one of his holiday odd jobs while the regular man's away. Perhaps Brick and I can talk him into giving you the outside tour like Lonah and I had."

"Sounds like the VIP spirit to me," Nicole added. "Dad is always getting permission to tour some classified military site through his old acquaintances, whether it be in the U.S. or Vietnam. I don't know how guys do it, but if anyone can get Marina onto the Whalehead property, it ought to be you, Dutch."

"What's tonight's movie?" asked Monroe.

"*The Searchers*, said by many to be John Ford's best Western, even better than his 1939 *Stagecoach*," replied Dutch.

"And, since Wayhab and crew aren't here tonight, you fellows had better bring in enough logs to keep the fire going tonight and also tomorrow for the women while we're hunting."

Once the men began storing up firewood, the women removed the tableware to the kitchen sink. Eventually, Sue Anne found herself in the big clubroom with Brick, Marsh, and Dutch, enjoying a brandy, awaiting the others to assemble for the movie. Dutch said to Brick, "Look, Speed, Lonah and I got our up-close Whalehead Club tour simply because Wayhab was checking nearby blinds and felt at ease because of his longtime relationship with my family. Outerbankers are secretive toward strangers about things that could affect their part-time income.

"Wayhab might allow you and Marina to tag along with him if you and Marsh could get him to talk about how he and Jharu got here. He loves reminiscing. Let his reminiscences morph into a conversation of how he and Marsh's granddaddy Nash met Rachel Carson over at Mattamuskeet just after the War. It'll be a trust builder.

"I'll get him to be with you and Marsh in the blinds tomorrow. After that it'll be up to your MacKoy charm to get the rest of the job done. Remember to remind him that Marsh and the rest of us will go to Duck to check out the Willingham Cottage, and that only you and Marina are going to the Whalehead Club with him. He'd be nervous with more than two impostor inspectors."

After the film ended, the men gathered about the fireplace, polishing off their drinks, while Dutch and Lonah spotted up the first reel of the film for the girls the next day, the 1957 *An Affair to Remember*, with Cary Grant and Deborah Kerr.

Brewer said, "Working alone on the farm, my mind wanders. I feel like I'm in an old western about to hum a Gene Autry-Roy Rogers tune or Tex Ritter's 'High Noon' ballad. The 'My Darling Clementine' song from last night's flick, or even the "At the River' hymn from both John Ford-directed movies appeal to my fancy.

"Ford captured that pioneer determination to conquer the land and establish civilization. Before our wedding, Wesley spoke about the farmer's creed deriving from the line in Genesis that says the Lord put man in the Garden of Eden to work it and take care of it. Those old Western movies about pioneer struggles always connect me to that Biblical legacy.

"Brick and Marsh might feel the same about building houses if you recall the General's Homestead Act speeches.

"Eisner's thoughts remind me of the movie *How the West Was Won*, which Ford co-directed with Henry Hathaway and George Marshall. You know, the Cinerama film. Its theme tune had a line that went something like 'the Promised Land where there's a dream for every mother's son.' Whether you're building a house or planting a field of grain, you're doing something that assists the potential fulfillment of the unalienable promise for yourself and also for your neighbors. The General's come to make me believe that doing something to help the rest of society's progress is the only thing that gives a person a sense of worth.

"Of course, the open struggles between right and wrong, like the Earps against the Clantons in *Clementine* at the O.K. Corral gunfight, are not something we worry about today. But we still have those mental struggles to define right and wrong within ourselves, like the John Wayne character does in tonight's *Searchers*. The Wayne character's hatred for Indians is as strong as his vision of some elusive, perfect love hammered out from his cradle beside the family hearth. Like all men, he seems to be struggling to recapture his vision of feeling and oneness he had with the universe prior to his birth and long before his return to that universe via his grave.

"I heard Nicole's dad tell Wesley once that film critics described John Wayne's character as the dark knight, searching for a lost paradise in which to redeposit his soul. As for me, I often feel like Don Quixote charging the windmills of modern mental confusion. As slow as I am, I don't know if I'll ever figure life out. I'll be like John Wayne's character, warped by too many hard realities requiring immediate solutions to find a greater peace of mind my insides are always seeking. Today's real-world obscurities makes it too easy to fantasize about living back then, when opportunity seemed simpler and closer to nature."

"Brewer, *How the West Was Won* was the last movie I ever saw with my father," chimed in Marina. "Mother wouldn't go to it because it was only in English. You must have been a real fan to remember the lyrics to the title tune. The phrase 'A dream for every mother's son' truly appeals to my architect's heart: being a can-do builder."

VI

The next morning the hunters filled their thermos bottles with Marina's soup.

Mrs. Penny, when I told Marina how they praised her soup, she laughed. "Melody, it was the cold weather and hunger on a hangover that made them praise it." She said she made it with minced clams and diced tomatoes, sautéed in olive oil with garlic. Prior to adding the clams, she drained and blanched them in water before soaking them in dry vermouth. Her mother used this trick so the clams would not taste canned. I make it now for Pem and me the same way.

The wind had died down, and at lunch, each man reported multiple kills, lifting their spirits. They ate and quickly returned to the blinds. Wayhab was delighted and said that he'd like to get home early to enjoy a New Year's Eve dinner with his wife and friends. Unlike the previous day, Wayhab separated everyone except for Brick and Marsh.

At 4:00 p.m., Wayhab arrived at the cousins' blind to announce that the others had begun an early New Year's celebration. Brick reported one kill that afternoon, a canvas-back, and Marsh a blue-winged teal. Both were hoping for another kill. However, being mindful of Wayhab's desire to retire early, and wishing to coax him into a tour of the Whalehead Club for Marina's benefit the next day, they said they would wait only a half hour. The bird flights had been active, and it seemed reasonable they'd get another shot.

Brick bided his time before thanking Wayhab for his guide service. Then as Dutch had suggested, Brick asked Wayhab about his life, hoping this would entice Wayhab to give him and Marina a Whalehead Club tour while the others were trekking down to Junebug's family's beach cottage at Duck and buying bouillabaisse ingredients. Wayhab talked about his and Jharu's family backgrounds and his early life as a guide until Brick felt that Wayhab trusted him enough to ask about visiting Whalehead.

Brick said that Marina was a French Canadian architect who was attracted to the place, and would keep her mouth shut. Just as Wayhab said, "Maybe so, if no one's around; but the grounds only, when I make my rounds tomorrow," a big mallard came into view. Brick brought him down with a frontal shot. The three then got into the skiff, retrieved the bird, and returned to the island compound, where Wayhab promised to see Brick and Marina the next day.

VII

Returning to the lodge, they had drinks along with some of Cecil X's shrimp dipped into cocktail sauce. The exception was Marina, who was still bathing. Once Marsh's initial hunger was satisfied, he said, "I want to know about your Puerto Rican pot, Dutch! I'm ready to party!"

"Brewer," said Dutch, "lay down some beach music on the record player while I get my stash. It'll be good to have a couple of tokes before we pop those two bushels of rock oysters. I've also got a little hash the Puerto Ricans left."

Now, Mrs. Penny, no one there ever told me about this part of the story. I learned of it only a few years ago from Kay, and this is how she told it.

The lodge was soon swaying with the sounds of smooth rhythm-and-blues. Marijuana aroma wafted, as did the earthy beach music. Even now, I sense both filtering up the big fireplace chimney, each the hallucinogenic agent of the other in a phantasmal, cosmic rhythm enjoyed by the stars above and the eternal spirits of the universe. At least that's the way it seemed at college fraternity parties. These folks were a little older but just as happy to be free for a while of society's restrictions.

The joint was making its second pass when Marina came in. Sue Anne offered the joint to her. Marina looked at Brick.

"Go ahead. You'll like it," he told her.

She nearly gagged exhaling the smoke.

"It's been a long time. We never had anything like this in Canada. Should be a power-ride. Brick, the tub is ready."

Brick smiled, "I might catch a cold outside shucking oysters. I'll bathe after dinner."

Then Marsh questioned Dutch about his sources, declaring that this pot was as good as Vietnam's. Dutch responded, "I pick it up when I'm in Puerto Rico bringing back finished lingerie on the company plane."

"I've never understood the Puerto Rican part of your lingerie business, Dutch," said Ginger.

"There's a little-known U.S. Internal Revenue tax rule that promotes Puerto Rico's economy because it's a U.S. Protectorate," Dutch said. "We pay little income tax on the goods we fabricate there. My main job is transferring the goods from there to market on the company plane. I also entertain our customer storeowners and supply them with catalogues full of items modeled by beautiful girls that Lonah finds in her bathing-suit contest work."

Later the men shucked oysters into bowls while the women heated bowls of butter and cocktail sauce. They also took a soup pot of corn on the cob that had been cooking in salted water, beer, and butter off the stove and set the steaming ears on a platter.

The table had two large mismatching plastic tablecloths for protection from oyster liquid and cocktail-sauce spills. When enough oysters had been shucked, a consumption orgy began.

After the first round, the women retired with drinks to the clubroom, but the men steamed more oysters and continued eating. At the end, Brick, Monroe, and Brewer polished off the leftovers amidst spatters of butter and cocktail sauce. Marsh and Dutch, meanwhile, had meandered to the clubroom to dance with their partners to the beach music tunes of "Te-Ta-Te-Ta-Ta" by Ernie K-Doe, "Sixty-Minute Man" by The Dominoes, "Shake, Rattle and Roll" by Joe Turner, "Walking Up a One-Way Street" by Willie Tee, "Money Honey" by The Drifters, "Sick and Tired" by Fats Domino, and "It Will Stand" by The Showmen.

When the last three men entered the clubroom, Monroe Hill sized up the dance scene, saying: "O.K., girls, I can tell by the smooth steps that you've been to Cherry Grove and Ocean Drive—more than once! But, realize now that this is not a public place where you are chaperoned by a crowd. You need to watch those smooth belly-roll dance turns tonight because both you and your dance partners have just partaken of a mess of oysters and pot."

"Right," Ginger laughed, "it can be warm-up time in a place like this with the type of guys you girls are dancing with!"

"Oh, Marsh," said Dutch, hanging onto Lonah while eyeing Marsh and Sue Anne's footwork, "I don't mind making it easy for a woman to take advantage of me. Let's try some hash. The Puerto Ricans say it's laced with a tad of opium. It puts you in dreamland without placing you in hibernation."

"Dutch, if you and Marsh did a joint this afternoon, one tonight, and now hash, you'll crash," cautioned Lonah. Dutch only smiled, went to his room, and returned to share the contents of his hash pipe. The pipe made one trip around the room when Brewer asked Brick if the ploy with Wayhab had resulted in success for a Whalehead tour. Brick said that it did, and that Wayhab had endured a lot that he would relate after his bath. However, on returning, he saw that Dutch and Marsh had faded to bed without their mates and the group was into other topics.

Wayhab's family legacy didn't come up again during the trip.

"So those two beach-boogie dance pros have retired," smiled Brick, as he sat beside Marina. "Dutch's pot is kick-ass—glad it's a long weekend. You can only do this type of thing when you've got several days to recover. Tomorrow I'll still be feeling this and that good music you brought off our Hunt Club's jukebox."

"Marina just wants to immerse herself in it like we did, growing up," said Nicole.

"Oh, yes," admitted Marina. "Back home we always talked about going to Myrtle Beach for Canadian Days like college students here talk about going to Fort Lauderdale for Spring Break. Myrtle Beach was our Fort Lauderdale. I'd never heard of Ocean Drive or OD, as you say. These records remind me of my conversations with our family friend, Henri, about his trips to Canadian Days. It's one danceable record after another, and I wish I could dance like you Carolinians. I asked Lisa to teach me, but it's no good. I must just be a snow skier."

VIII

The next morning, Marina made preparations for the bouillabaisse dinner even though some elements were missing. She pulled Brick from his clubroom couch to help her brainstorm, over coffee, on how to make substitutions. Fortunately, there were shrimp and four lobster tails Dutch had left over from entertaining the Puerto Ricans. But what was really missing were the fresh mussels, clams, and scallops that Brick had not been able to get from Cecil X.

As a backup plan, in case the Duck trip failed to produce the missing ingredients, Marina prepared her dry vermouth–enhanced clam-tomato soup for the bouillabaisse broth. While this simmered, she toasted several pieces of bread and oversaw Brick scrambling eggs for their breakfast. After breakfast, the soup had cooled enough to be refrigerated. The broth would be reheated with the addition of any other seafood ingredients the day trip might produce.

Then the others awoke and readied for the excursion to Duck. At noon, Wayhab ferried them to Corolla, where Charlie awaited with Wayhab's converted four-wheel-drive school bus.

Brick and Marina stood by Wayhab, waving as the oversized Jeep left the convenience store that he and Jharu were managing. Slow traveling on the beach and the road that followed the phone lines south would extend the round trip to conclude after dark. When the Jeep disappeared beyond the wild ponies feeding on the dune grasses, Wayhab said, "So, Missy, you want to see the Whalehead Club?"

"Oh, yes! But I understand your position, too," Marina replied.

"Aye," returned Wayhab. "You can be my assistants if neighbors happen by. There's not a lot to see now because most everything inside has been removed. We can only tour the outside, unless it's evident that something's amiss inside. I do have keys if I need to enter."

The three traversed a sandy path that wound through small trees and spots of wiry grass near Corolla's Currituck Lighthouse. Parts of the Whalehead Club were visible, but low, full-canopied, wind-blown trees blocked most of the view. The green tree canopy blended with the green tarnish of the copper roof to obscure the size of the house.

The shape of the roof came into full view when they left the wooded area. The story-and-a-half configuration muted the mansion's size, but its nine dormers testified to its massiveness.

Facing the house head-on, one would not see immediately a three-story structure until noticing the third-story windows in the gables at each end. Crossing over one of the English-style wooden bridges to the estate, Brick and Marina followed Wayhab around the house. On the south side, they counted nine dormers matching those on the north side facing the lighthouse. Wayhab allowed his two charges to peep through the windows, just as he did for inspection purposes, but they did not enter. The recessed window niches on the south porch overlooked the Currituck Sound, so Wayhab sat on a metal chair and lit a cigarette, as Brick and Marina peered through the windows.

"All's bare now but since you are an architect, I'm sure you still appreciate it. This was the place to be in the Depression for Jharu and me. We lived simple but had all we needed. Modern travel provides lots of entertainment now without the effort one exerts in hunting. I don't expect the place will ever be used as a hunting lodge again. But it was a beauty inside in its day."

They lingered after Wayhab finished his cigarette and before returning to the store. There, Jharu greeted them with a smile as she waited on an elderly woman. Also greeting them was an aromatic bazaar of crackers, sweets, cheeses, kerosene, fatback, and fish bait, along with the lingering fragrance of many a spilled grape soda.

When the customer left, Wayhab asked if there had been any calls from the Lazlo group, and Jharu said no.

"Marina, Brick, do you want a snack?" Wayhab asked.

"Let's try a grape soda with a slice of hoop cheese on a johnny cake," said Brick. "Haven't feasted on any country-store culinary items this hunting trip. Maybe that'll reenergize us after our walking through soft sand and tide us over until dinner."

Brick and Marina sat on a bench, sharing the snacks. Then Brick meandered around the store before suggesting to Marina that they walk down the beach to view the Atlantic and the wild ponies while waiting for their friends to call in. Wayhab assured them that he'd call out when word came. They rewrapped their scarves, buttoned their topcoats, and headed out. The day had not only been chilly, but also overcast, as rain clouds formed to the south. While they walked along, talking about their Whalehead tour, the wild pony herd continued grazing.

Up to this point, Mrs. Penny, you should understand that I was naïve about adult love. When you are a Native American minority living among whites and blacks, you don't have much opportunity to spiritually connect with other people similar to your own family members that you'd want to be with. The Wisdom Station area was not like the Pembroke area, flooded with Lumbee Indians, or the Cherokee Reservation area of western North Carolina, or even the vast Reservation areas of the American West where you and I now live.

Most people thought of Wisdom Station Indians as mulattos. Consequently, I had never been attracted to a man, and had no perceptions about love's physical attractions. My only male friend then, Desmond Printice, was a gay black and non-threatening.

Thus, I never had any sense of the intimate nature of Brick and Marina's relationship until years later when Kay told me about it. She said that Brick had confided these events to her husband and Wesley later at the Willinghams' cottage at Duck.

The couple strolled along observing the wandering ponies, which also appeared to be biding their time, as if there were nothing else pressing to do but be pleased with grazing and existing. But two ponies faced each other, neck across neck. Their manes, ruffling from the winds directly off the Atlantic, increased the sense of isolation.

Leaning into Brick with his hands around her waist, Marina said: "I hope you aren't sorry we didn't go with the others. I am sure that their trip will show the seashore's desolation. But nothing could make one feel any more isolated than this, as we look south and north along the beach at vast nothingness. The view is like the edge of eternity.

"That's why I am so enchanted by the Whalehead Club. It's so out of place, like Dutch says, and that's part of its spell. The mansion also makes me feel so 'in,' as your American slang says. I've always admired America's determination to start the grand project and stick it out through thick and thin until finished, like putting a man on the moon for all humanity. It's the great adventure! Man is here, but is going there, into the great cosmos, into the great unknown of our collective eternity.

"The isolation here, where the moon-rocket fuel was devised, gives me a sense that I have seen the grand plan at its inception. I don't know how else to verbalize the moment. It's also fitting that the Whalehead moon-rocket project is located so near the Wright Brothers Memorial, where man first flew. And isn't it ironic that the Lost Colony site at Manteo is also so close to these two sites of achievement?

"I can tell you are going to become a big, rich builder, Brick, while I'll be a poor little architect. Someday maybe I'll design someone a Whalehead-like mansion that you can build."

"It'd have to be for somebody else," Brick answered. "If Whalehead cost four hundred thousand to build in the 1920s, it'd cost four million now! If I ever had that kind of money, it'd take a lot of French persuasion to get me to turn loose such funds on a house."

"It's a fantasy, but we should enjoy the creative juices that fantasies nurture," Marina said as they smiled at the necking ponies. "We could do it together for somebody else. My designs corrected by your day-to-day practical building experiences. You could persuade me to the simplicity of seeing how building materials could be used more efficiently."

"I believe I especially like the persuading part of your fantasy," Brick remarked. "And big structures certainly would offer more profit opportunity than the small houses I'm building."

"I know what you're building are starter houses," said Marina. "And they'll not appreciate in value so you'll make money off any land-value gains that generally accrue to a builder as a project's property improvements add to the lot value even before completion. History shows that land-value growth occurs mostly on large, restricted-development homes.

"Although your houses are not big and grand, they are fulfilling the dream of owning a place of one's own. It's part of the promised-land dream; like Brewer said, 'A dream for every mother's son.' That makes your project worth more than anything because it builds and knits together the fabric of the country's hope and morale.

"You and Marsh are doing a good job, and those people trust you, too. I've never had an opportunity to tell you, but do you remember that day I came to Sunrise Acres but couldn't find you because you were at Will O'Cain's office? When you returned, you found me at Allen and Celestine's house with her sister, Bertha. We were talking about gazebos again.

"They also said many good things that day about you and Marsh. Most of it was about the Bill Thornbo interview for the house-painting contracts. Donald, of course, heard everything, racial slurs and all, through the open windows. He's related that event to everybody who has purchased a Sunrise Acres house. They have in turn related it to just about anybody who might be a buyer there. That's given you a good reputation and helped your sales volume."

"I didn't know that," Brick returned. "I worry that Deacon is overselling the repairs we must make for a year. That's in the house purchase contract. But after a year any repair is the customer's responsibility. We don't mind doing what we're supposed to do because it's also good for customer referrals, but we can't do free repairs forever.

"The black and white race relations environment of small Southern towns can be good if relationships between individuals have been built on trust from previous promises kept where circumstances allow. If impractical promises are made that fail, then, understandably, mistrust takes hold. When that happens, it can take a long time for the mistrustful feelings to heal, and in some cases they never heal. So I worry about others overpromising our responsibilities."

"But if they know they're going to get a fair shake in answer to their complaints, that's all you'll need for continued brisk sales," noted Marina.

Then a light rain began, and they returned to the store. Wayhab said that the safari party had called, saying they had found fresh mussels, clams, and scallops at Wanchese, near Manteo. In addition, Wayhab speculated that it would be a four-hour trip back, due to the intensifying rain. Then Brick and Marina accepted Wayhab's offer to return to Monkey Island before harder rain bands came in. An early return would at least give them time, Marina said, to reheat the bouillabaisse stock so the fresh seafood meats could be added near the dinner hour.

As the skiff crossed the Currituck Sound, two separate rain bands fell. Brick and Marina huddled, pulling their coat collars and scarves over their heads as much as possible. When the skiff docked, both gave Wayhab waves of thanks, then scurried to the lodge.

Inside, they found the fireplace flame barely aglow. Marina stoked the white ash-covered coals with a poker to expose the red-hot coals, while Brick fetched three dry logs from the porch. Soon the fire was ablaze, and they warmed their hands before removing their coats and boots.

"We'll catch a cold if we don't dry off soon," Brick remarked. "Better get a towel."

Marina turned her gaze from the flames to Brick and followed him down the hall. On the headboard of her unmade bed Brick found the towel he had used that morning while shaving. He ran the towel across his forehead, then hers. As he did this, she ran her fingers into his hair. They looked into each other's eyes and kissed while pressing so closely that they could feel each other's chill bumps form as hard rain fell again.

Brick reached out and shut the bedroom door, and they continued to delight in each other until their unclothed bodies met for the first time in the unmade bed. The rainfall gusted, and as the Biblical saying infers, the freedom of their spirits soared into each other, and each knew the other flowing to and fro until each and every cell in their bodies screamed to participate in a crescendo of affectionate release. They dozed briefly, but soon aroused from their slumbers to caress each other again.

Then Marina rose and crossed the darkened room to the bathroom, partially lit by the clouded sky's light coming through the small, head-high bath window. She turned on the huge bathtub's water, and beckoned Brick. Their bodies glistened amid the dim light from the small window as they lathered each other with soap. The only sounds were the occasional gurgles of water flowing out the tub's chest-high overflow. Each soul had returned to its own inner sanctum.

Dressed in fresh clothing, Marina said, "It's time to heat the bouillabaisse so it will be ready for cooking the seafood when the others return."

"They should be in Corolla soon," Brick replied, smiling at her. "I'm glad we stayed here rather than ride up and down the Outer Banks."

She embraced him. "I'm glad you are glad we lingered, but now let's get ready for them to return, famished."

In the kitchen Marina retrieved the stock from the refrigerator and set the soup kettle on the stove. She asked for a glass of white wine while Brick prepared himself a vodka martini on the rocks. They arranged the last of Cecil X's shrimp on a tray of ice around a serving bowl of cocktail sauce.

Then they went to the clubroom, and Brick turned the TV on to the 1972 New Year's Day Rose Bowl game, with Stanford hosting Michigan. The combination of the fire's warmth, their drinks, and a football game being played by two colleges far removed from North Carolina soon put them to sleep. And that is how the safari entourage found them.

After dinner, all partook of a last round of Dutch's pot on the back porch, and discussed the rusted-out, abandoned cars and shipwrecks they had seen on the Duck safari. Ultimately, all slipped away to bed, and Brick again visited Marina's bed, but Kay elaborated no further.

The next morning, Wayhab and Charlie ferried all to their vehicles on the mainland. As Wayhab handed Brick his dressed-out birds, Brick thanked him with a handshake-hidden tip of a hundred dollars. The others gave tip money, but nothing like Brick's. Brick's tip was perhaps extra payment for the private Whalehead Club tour and the joy it allowed.

Chapter Eight

Mysteries and Mountain Music

I

THE NEXT DAY IT RAINED AT SUNRISE ACRES, and no one did any outside work. About 10:30, Marsh called to say that he had caught a flu bug after checking on his cows in the downpour and was going home for the day.

At noon Mingo told Brick he and Hogbear needed finishing nails for cabinet installations. Brick called Cotton Roberts and offered to buy Cotton's lunch for delivering two dollars' worth of nails. He also offered to buy Mingo's, Dad's, and Hogbear's lunches, but only Dad accepted as the other two had home-packed lunches.

When Cotton arrived with nails and lunch, all ate around the office desk. Cotton opined that the Monkey Island hunting trip must have been a blast since Marsh showed up only briefly to check on a report that three of his cows were missing. Brick ignored the missing-cow comment, and gave Cotton a sanitized Monkey Island report that left out partying details.

Afterwards Cotton said, "The only excitement this rainy day at the lumber company is talk of Marsh's missing cows. No one can figure it out. The fence and back gate were secure. Donald noticed the missing cows when he counted them at feed-up time that first night you were away. That never happened to old John T. Mrs. Iris says Carley Ray tried following up a tip about a weird-looking man having three cows butchered at a wholesale meat shop in the next county, but it was a dead end."

Marsh didn't show up the next day either, and Donald continued feeding Marsh's cows. The following day Brick and Dad took new buyer applications to Will O'Cain and checked on the status of applications already in process. The subject of the old black widower, Rufus, came up again, causing Will O'Cain to comment, "Rufus can't get a loan now like he did before he and his wife retired. Their two incomes and his WWII service assured approval, but the wife died. So, Rufus became unqualified with only one Social Security check—not enough income.

"I've often been called a yellow-dog Democrat and liberal sympathizer. But old Rufus' circumstances go beyond the bounds of what this government program can do. You know, rules are rules for a reason. After all, the government does have the fiduciary responsibility of guaranteeing these mortgage loans to the individuals and institutions that buy the bonds to finance Sunrise Acres' home loans.

"Rufus might make one payment, but he'd likely miss the rest, forcing me to repossess his house. Then you and Marsh couldn't sell another house until I could get Rufus' repossessed unit sold first to a qualified customer you would have to furnish me with. That's how it works, and that process would result in you and Marsh competing against yourselves by having to sell a house twice but only being paid for it once."

"Speaking of credit-quality customers, Will," Dad put in, "we've got something that'll get us all around the race discrimination that concerned your Raleigh supervisors."

"Yes," said Brick. "You know we've got a problem getting the road paved by those houses we've already completed because this wet weather is holding up the pipe installation. We've built a few foundations beyond the missing culvert because we can deliver materials to them by that old log road where the top ten-lot section is that we were holding out for whites. Deacon has six white prospects we think will go in there now. Because that road is on high ground, the road-building process won't be stalled like on the low ground by the old dairy barn culvert trench. Uncle Malcolm's all for starting that section now."

O'Cain asked when he could get the applications, and Brick replied, "Soon."

II

The rest of January was chilly but dry enough for limited outside work to proceed except on the pipe installation. Seeing an opportunity to regain some construction momentum, Marsh urged Jeff Mack to grade the top-ten section.

At this time, I became involved with Sunrise Acres in a small way. Because of the good customer-application rate, Brick asked Dad if I could type up the customer-loan applications on my weekend school breaks. Dad and Brick would fill out applications in pencil and have the customer sign a blank form for my weekend typing. My typed applications were the ones sent to Will O'Cain.

While slow, careful typing was required for application forms, it nevertheless improved my typing skills to the point that I rarely made mistakes on the rapid typing I did for school term papers. The greatest job benefit, however, was not better typing skills, but the education I got from seeing Dad and Brick consult with applicants on issues like income, credit, and budgetary matters. That experience, more than my social-services degree, is what encouraged me to be in the profession today. My Sunrise Acres knowledge couldn't be learned from a college professor. The experience itself was the professor, and it gave me the faith that I could do a job that helped people.

This also led to another job with less prestige but better pay, one that began my life-long relationship with Junebug's wife, Kay. I became Martha Sarah's babysitter. Marsh suggested my services when he and Sue Anne hosted a Super Sunday Super Bowl party for Brick, Marina, Junebug, and Kay. Marsh's house and Junebug's were only two blocks apart in Wisdom Station.

The new parents were happy to have a social evening near home, in case they needed to return quickly to Martha Sarah.

I recall Sue Anne and Marina coming over with Kay during halftime to check on the baby and me. I also remember Marina watching Kay's motherly affection and holding the child briefly as Kay reviewed the feeding schedule with me. Marina had a deep contentment as she rocked the baby, saying she would like to see the babe in a few months to see her budding personality.

"Me, too," Kay said. "I can hardly wait to take Martha Sarah to our beach cottage. To see her eyes when she takes in the ocean for the first time and hears its roar! June wants to fly down, but I'm afraid the higher elevation will hurt her ears. He says he'll chart a low flight pattern to prevent that, but I think the first couple of times should be by car."

Two weeks later I got another real-world insight that's not taught in college. Brick was reviewing my office work before he went down to check out Jeff Mack's probing of the open trench to see whether it was dry enough to begin the culvert installation work on Monday, barring rain. Afterward Brick was going to dinner with Marina, Monroe, and Ginger in Raleigh. However, into the office stormed Celestine Lamb, with Allen following sheepishly.

"Deacon, damn your lying Indian ass!" screamed Celestine.

Of course, her language made the hairs on the back of my neck stand up so straight I thought they'd self-ignite in the heat of her fury.

"What's wrong?" Brick said, looking over my last typed application form before passing it off to Dad, adding, "This one's O.K., too."

"That damned Chalky Newton!" screamed Celestine. "He's down there with that Mack boy! You know how Bertha feels about that albino trash, and what he caused to be done to her son. She believes in her heart of hearts that Ronald didn't hang himself. She says that's just jailbird talk, and that Chalky's prison pals done it."

"We'll see what we can do," said Brick, looking over at Dad. "We can't guarantee you anything because our streets are public. But we can ask him to stay off our lots that remain private property. That's all we can do."

Dad added, "He'll be scarce here, but we can't guard him twenty-four hours a day."

That said, Celestine nodded and mumbled, "O.K. But keep him away from us, 'cause I'll kill him or try to if you can't make happen what you say."

"Now, now," said Allen, patting her back. "Losing a good person like you to right his wrongs ain't worth the effort. We've said our piece; let's hope these fellers can bluff him into staying away from here for our family peace."

When they left, Brick, Dad, and I went down to where Jeff was doing his culvert prep, but Chalky had gone. Jeff had installed a bed of gravel in the bottom of the trench like the highway department engineer had instructed. The engineer was to return Monday to inspect the gravel bed. If the rains didn't return, the culvert pipe would then be placed on top of this firm gravel bed, and the installation completed that day.

Then Brick brought up Celestine and Allen's concern about Chalky. Dad allowed that Chalky often gave him customer leads, and that this had contributed to good home sales, which in turn meant construction work for Mack Grading and Paving. Dad noted that it was Chalky, in fact, who had provided him with the lead on sisters Celestine and Bertha. All agreed that it was for everyone's benefit that this should remain secret, and that any additional contact with Chalky be done elsewhere. With that, we went our separate ways.

The following Monday the culvert pipe was installed, so paving could begin by the houses that sat beyond the culvert. Because the top-ten section had been started, its road paving was done, too. Having access to two paved roads upon which to construct houses, Brick continued his weekend work to keep crews, home sales, and building material coordinated.

Near the end of February, however, Brick was ready for a break. Closing on the first two houses beyond the newly installed culvert allowed for a less pressing schedule. For these closings, Marsh came to the construction office to go over last-minute details before all went to Willingham's law office. While there, I heard Marsh say that he and Brewer had discussed a Boone ski weekend during a tour of the Moores Creek Revolutionary

War Battlefield with General Eisner the past Sunday.

After Marsh made his ski-trip pitch, Brick said, "Great! It'll give Marina a chance to show off her skiing expertise. From the past few weekends out at Raleigh nightspots with her and Ginger and Monroe, I sense she'll never make it as a fast-dancing girl. She digs the music, but she just can't put it into her footsies. I think that's why she speaks so much about skiing. Everybody wants to be a show-off at something. Maybe this is her chance."

The ski trip took place the following weekend. That Friday, Marina drove to Wisdom Station and left her car at Marsh and Sue Anne's house. Brick and Marsh had wanted to leave by 3:00 p.m. so as to reach the Beech Mountain area by 6:00 p.m., like the rest of the group. All the Monkey Island gang went except for Dutch and Lonah. They were in Puerto Rico again for an airplane delivery of lingerie back to the U.S. mainland.

The cousins, however, were delayed by the late arrival of more shrimp from Cecil X. When Cecil arrived, his long face sent a signal that the cousins should remain and listen for a spell. Dad said that there were tears in Cecil's eyes.

Cecil moaned, "Shasta's getting cold feet about our religion. I know it's her old Aunt Swaniebelle in Winston-Salem that's turning her off. The aunt's a retired schoolteacher.

"Shasta and I met at an NAACP meeting at Winston-Salem State College when we were students there. Her aunt graduated from there and has lived in that area since.

"Well, there were some Black Muslims outside this NAACP meeting. They were talking about Black Pride and distributing copies of their newspaper *Muhammad Speaks*. I liked their term 'Black Pride' better than the word 'colored.' After that first Muslim encounter, we read *Muhammad Speaks* occasionally, but neither of us really ever thought about joining them.

"Upon graduation, Shasta got a job at the Durham Veterans Hospital beside Duke Hospital. She'd studied accounting, and they had an opening for that skill. But I never could find a good job with my business degree, so I worked in grocery stores as a stock boy, and at a car wash on weekends to help pay my part of our family bills.

"One Saturday at the car wash I read about Elijah Muhammad's work-for-self fish-selling business in the *Muhammad Speaks* newspaper and got started in the fish business. I'm doing pretty good. Others have failed because they don't see the need to get out of Durham to chase the business in the country on Thursdays and Fridays. I bring the product to the country people, who can't travel a city bus service route.

"At the mosque they say my success has come to the attention of the Honorable Elijah Muhammad, and that he may recognize me someday at a Savior Day Annual Convention by giving me a Holy Arabic name. Only a few people of distinction get a Holy Arabic name: people like Muhammad Ali. All the rest of us use the letter 'X' because our African surnames are lost in the history of slavery.

"When I put 'X' in my name, her Aunt Swaniebelle didn't approve. Now Shasta won't join the mosque or wear Muslim clothes to work. Says it'll hurt her job advancement opportunities."

After Cecil left with a hangdog look, Brick said, "We don't have the skills to advise him on marriage or their religious division. But I hope a divorce doesn't cause him to lose his house. If he does, O'Cain will stop approving our house sales until he manages to sell off Cecil's repossessed house. We don't want that, but anyone's religious choice and how it might affect his personal life are things we can't interfere with either. Our inexpert advice would confuse his situation more, but O'Cain may know of some way to help him, so you'd better inform him, Deacon."

III

Cecil's drama made the cousins arrive late at their ski chalet. After the group settled down to drinks and shrimp, Sue Anne said, "I'm hoping Marina will give me some skiing tips tomorrow."

"Me, too," Ginger Hill added. "However, the lodge manager said the temperature may be too warm. We should have come last weekend."

Marina moaned, "And I was looking forward to skiing since I can't do the Beach Boogie without Brick frowning.

"Durn-it-all, as you say, Nicole! Our last several Saturday nights out with Ginger and Monroe at Raleigh night spots, I felt like a dancing cripple. This was supposed to be my redemption weekend."

Nicole said, "Marina, I know the feeling. Having lived in Europe and Washington during Dad's military career, I had to adjust my worldly experiences to the ways of my small-town neighbors, who rarely travel. That makes for an acceptance complex. Sounds like you're suffering an acceptance complex, too, but over dancing."

"Seems so, Nicole," answered Marina. "It got especially vexing when Brick just gave up on me to dance with Becky Rollins, who came to the same clubs that the DJ, Rocky, played for. She flirted with Brick every night."

Brewer interjected, "We would have loved to have seen you folks and Rocky at those Raleigh night spots just to get the details on how Brick and Marsh convinced Wayhab to allow Marina's Whalehead tour. I missed that part because of farm duties."

"Well," said Brick, dipping a shrimp into the cocktail sauce, "Dutch suggested we get Wayhab to bond with us by encouraging his reminiscences about his past, and especially his connection to Marsh's Granddaddy Nash and Rachel Carson. Then Wayhab might feel like he could trust us more at Whalehead.

"Wayhab's family came from Salter Path near Morehead City. They moved to Salter Path from that Diamond City whaling community on the Shackleford Banks before Wayhab's birth. Two hurricanes destroyed Diamond City because salt water from ocean flooding ruined the town's freshwater wells.

"The family continued to live off the bounty of the waters and lands around Salter Path, and Wayhab was born into that professional fishing and hunting life. Unlike his forebears' lack of education at the isolated Diamond City, there was some schooling in Salter Path, and Wayhab's reading ability grew adequate for understanding short, simple motor-repair instructions and boat-hull construction manuals with diagrammed explanations. He developed the skills to keep family and neighbors' small commercial seafood boats repaired beginning when he was about twelve.

"The best thing about school, he said, was meeting Jharu. They married at sixteen in the worst of the Depression. One day he learned of the thriving fishing village, Wanchese, near Manteo. So he and Jharu went there seeking better opportunities.

"He found no work at Wanchese but learned of the Knights' Lighthouse Club at Corolla. Knight hired Wayhab because of his multiple skills as a boat repairman and a hunter-fisherman, so he worked for the Knights a short time before their deaths.

"Between the Knights' deaths in 1936 and the Whalehead name change by Adams in 1940, Wayhab took odd jobs. He sought work with the Civilian Conservation Corps charged with transforming the financially defunct Lake Mattamuskeet–New Holland and Evabay area agricultural drainage project into a hunting preserve. The Conservation Corps, however, took only single men, initially. So Wayhab went just north of the state line to take a job as a fishing and hunting guide at Lake Drummond, Virginia.

"The Lake Drummond Hotel had been built in the early 1800s to accommodate boat traffic off the adjoining Dismal Swamp Canal. Despite good intentions for the place, its isolation made it a perfect spot for lovers to meet or for fugitives to seek a more comfortable refuge than the nearby swamps that had always sheltered runaway slaves and remnant Indian bands.

"Numerous duels occurred there during this era, too. Edgar Allen Poe frequented the place, mostly under the influence of opiates. He, too, nearly had a duel over a woman, but several miles removed from the hotel.

"When Wayhab worked there a century later, only thirty cabins, built on stilts, surrounded the lake. Although it was advertised as a hunting and fishing outpost, its reputation as a lovers' hideaway remained. Wayhab witnessed numerous fights over women that could have resulted in death.

"This unnerved Wayhab and he gladly took employment with the Mattamuskeet Lodge as a guide, once married men were accepted as employees. In the off-seasons he still did boat repairs on the Outer Banks at Corolla. One of the things that still amuses Wayhab in a haunting way about Lake Drummond was the lovers' tale of a young Indian prince who had gone mad over the death of his Indian princess. He is said to be still paddling Lake Drummond today looking for her ghost. Wayhab wonders if the ghosts of these two Indian lovers enticed whites to flock to the place since illicit loves had been so much a part of Lake Drummond's history.

"When Ray Adams purchased the Whalehead Club in 1940, Wayhab found full-time employment with him, but this was short lived, as World War II began and Wayhab was inducted into the Coast Guard. In service, Wayhab received advanced formal training on motors as well as on small electrical systems like those used at isolated Coast Guard posts on the Outer Banks. After the war ended, he returned to work for Adams as a hunting guide and all-around maintenance man. With Adams' approval, he also did maintenance for others in addition to his commercial fishing and hunting. This moonlighting included occasional work at Mattamuskeet, which helped Wayhab substantially equip himself as a professional market fisherman. During this period just after the war, Wayhab came into contact with Marsh's Granddaddy Nash and researcher Rachel Carson.

"Carson came to Lake Mattamuskeet as a U.S. Fish and Wildlife Service employee to write reports on the lake's transformation from a failed agricultural drainage project into a wildlife hunting and fishing preserve. Mattamuskeet is over thirty thousand acres of water barely three feet deep, with a soil bottom said to be richer than the deltas of the Mississippi or Nile. So there have always been efforts to drain it for crops, much like the farm-rich polders of Holland.

"The submerged silt of the lake waters, however, could not provide the plant-feeding opportunities for the varieties of waterfowl that wintered in the area. The best feeding sites were in the surrounding marshes adjacent to the lake. Thus, many of the hunting blinds were on private lakefront property. As a part-time guide, Wayhab made the acquaintance of several farmers who leased their lands adjoining the lake for waterfowl hunting.

"A retired farmer-friend of Marsh's Granddaddy Nash owned one such spot, and Wayhab often overheard many a conversation of Mr. Nash and Miss Carson discussing the failed glories of the Mattamuskeet–New Holland Agricultural Drainage project. They spoke of how modern civilization would not be possible without mass-produced foods, capable of being preserved, and how irrigation-drainage water management systems were the agricultural foundation of all civilizations from Abraham's time forward.

"The water management project had failed, however, because the annual cost to dredge silt from the lake's drainage canals added more expense to the farmer's cost than he could profitably sell the crops for. Mr. Nash and Miss Carson often agreed that the Mattamuskeet project was like Sir Walter Raleigh's Lost Colony and the failure of Diamond City; it failed to survive nature's insurmountable forces over which man often has little management control.

"At that point, Marsh told Wayhab his mother's Evabay story of eating peas with no ham seasoning, and also our Bentonville Blue legacy. I believe Wayhab then recognized commonalities between our family struggles and hunting experiences which made him feel comfortable enough to let Marina and me tour the Whalehead grounds with him."

"Yes, we agricultural students studied the Mattamuskeet Project at N.C. State, where Carson was required reading," commented Brewer. "Although she studied the wildlife benefits of the area only as a managed waterfowl sanctuary, she always remarked what an impact the haunting musical calls of the birds had on her later works that dealt with DDT and other overkill uses of pesticides. In fact, the title of her book, *Silent Spring*, came from the idea that chemical overuse harmful to bird eggs would make for spring seasons silent of chirping chicks.

"Since Carson's death, her ideas on agricultural chemicals have influenced our growing concerns about prudent fertilizer use. Some even question the use of nitrogen, one of the most common elements in the universe. Researchers say that if you use too much, the excess that runs off kills the shrimp and oysters harvested downstream by people like Wayhab. If you use none, you have no modern food production and no modern civilization. Modern farming can't rely on the simple swamp bog and manure fertilization techniques used to feed the small populations of our colonial and frontier yesterdays. Today's massive population forces chemical fertilizer use, but we must adjust to understand its limitations, too."

IV

"Speaking of adjusting," Brewer continued, "I guess Dutch must be adjusting to good work habits since he's transferring goods this weekend from Puerto Rico to the mainland."

"I hope that's all he's transporting," replied Brick. "I saw a newspaper story recently about a planeload of dope being abandoned at some isolated air strip, its crew nowhere around. The plane's numbers were falsified so it couldn't be traced. Incidents like that will probably put the authorities to checking out all sorts of air traffic like Dutch does. I hope they don't catch him smuggling in some Acapulco Gold for personal use."

"Lonah wouldn't look good in a Lazlo negligee behind bars," laughed Marsh.

"Oh, you men wouldn't mind viewing Lonah behind bars, if that was the only way you could get a look at her!" Sue Anne exclaimed.

"Yes, Brewer," Nicole fumed. "Aren't we exciting enough for you and Marsh? Why do you always have to be staring at somebody else's girl?"

"Oh, it never hurts to give complimentary looks at a friend's woman," gleamed Brewer.

Nicole huffed, "I'm not seeing any gentlemanly looks. I'm seeing the thunderstruck stares she gets from you! In fact, all of you, except for Brick, and that's only because he's paying attention to Marina."

"Brick may be the honorary-colonel, Southern-gentleman type," wheezed Monroe as he rose to refresh his drink. "But Brick and all you women will have to admit that Lonah is about the most delightfully whorey-looking thing around."

"Monroe, hush," smiled Ginger, shaking her head in amusement.

"She's sexy today," continued Monroe, "but in about five years I bet her body will be dragging like that gal who used to come to the Sampsons Landing cabin with Johnny Bell. Everybody wanted to screw her, but the fast-dancing Mr. Bell kept her on a short leash."

Brewer said, "I don't recall her name. They barely left the backseat of his '62 Chevy all that summer. Her fallopian tubes were oozing with so much wetness that her vaginal ziz-wheel musta' been cranking out a climax every ten seconds. I bet Johnny still thought about her after he lost his legs and most of his privates in Vietnam. What happened to her?"

"I saw her at a Fayetteville pharmacy while getting prescription refills for my mother's heart condition," responded Monroe. "Miss Wanna Screw of '62 was waddling along with a paratrooper. They looked married. She was a pure-damn hog!

"That was before Johnny died. I told him about her condition when we went with Dutch to a Carolina-State football game in Chapel Hill. Johnny appreciated Dutch getting him out into the greater world, but it was the last time Johnny ever went anywhere. You see, he wet his pants with his war-short nub in the bathroom at Dutch's fraternity house post-game party. I had to step between Dutch and one of his fraternity brothers who laughed at Johnny wetting his pants at the urinal. Dutch nearly hit the guy!"

"Well, what can we do tomorrow besides talk about old floozies?" deadpanned Ginger.

Brick said, "Stan may be on TV tomorrow. He's only two shots off the lead in that

West Coast golf tournament and will get some TV exposure. Maybe it'll help out his endorsement income, especially since his high U.S. Open finish qualified him for this year's Masters."

The conversation then meandered into family members' health, like Monroe's ailing mother, Marsh's father's cancer check-ups, and Junebug and Kay's daughter. When the eleven o'clock news came on, all watched the weather report, but it offered little hope of lower temperatures for skiing.

v

The next morning Ginger announced, "The lodge says this unseasonably warm winter weather has caught them when their snowmaking equipment is down. They had to order the repair parts from out of town. So, no skiing."

"What do we do?" asked Nicole. "We can't go see the outdoor drama of *Horn in the West*. That's a summertime event."

"I've heard of that play. What's it about?" inquired Marina.

"We've talked of *The Lost Colony* at Manteo that depicts the first English attempt to colonize North America," Brick explained. "Well, there are two other North Carolina outdoor dramas. These plays cover other sequences in settling America, and both were written by Kermit Hunter. He was a student of Paul Green, *The Lost Colony*'s dramatist.

"The *Horn in the West* that's produced here tells the story of Daniel Boone and others who helped fight the British at Kings Mountain, near Charlotte, during the Revolutionary War. Many say this American-patriot victory was the turning point of the Revolution after many defeats in the more heavily British-occupied northern colonies. It's fitting, too, that it was an army of backwoods frontiersman who turned the tables because it was primarily their westward-advance mindset that the English Crown had opposed.

"The Crown's opposition to westward expansion rose out of the fear they'd have to impose even more hated taxes to keep British troops in place defending a larger territory. But alas, the American babe had already cut its umbilical cord from the mother country through the daily trials of living in the New World. The colonists no longer wanted Britain treading on their promised-land opportunities.

"Now Hunter's other play, *Unto These Hills*, is about the negatives of forging a New Jerusalem out of a Promised Land. It's about the Cherokee Indians' loss of their vast tribal lands in several states of the Appalachian Mountain area. The Cherokee, like other American Indians, lost their lands through numerous broken treaties with a long list of elected U.S. governments. The 1828 Cherokee Trail of Tears forced-march tragedy from the eastern states to Oklahoma is the drama's focus.

"*Unto These Hills* captures the story of those Indians who eluded the Army roundup by hiding out in the rugged mountains of southwestern North Carolina. Later elections produced a U.S. government more sympathetic to these remaining Cherokee and provided them with the reservation in Cherokee, North Carolina, several hours southwest of here."

"Nicole," Marsh said, "it's your dad's Manifest Destiny thing again, but different because it was politically driven by mob sentiment. Flora MacDonald's defeated Loyalist sympathies at Moores Creek were like the Elizabethtown Tory Hole Loyalist defeat, and other numerous Loyalist Revolutionary War defeats. These were visions of destiny being manifested by similar-thinking neighbors in the absence of government. Both sides tarred and feathered the opposition, and such events often turned into lynchings and property destruction. Thus our Revolution was also a bloody civil war of neighbor versus neighbor even more so than in the War Between the States.

"Your dad added that Flora probably always wondered why her thoughts were never manifested when her property was confiscated, and she returned to England in the early 1780s. Between 75,000 and 100,000 Loyalists escaped to Canada and other English colonies.

"Yes, we Europeans were hard on each other, but truly callous to the naïve, uneducated tribes of Eastern Indians. For the Indians, it was not about a John Locke–inspired governmental system that protected inalienable rights: it was get the hell out of the way, or I'll not just tread on you, I'll trample you to death!

"The General says his favorite example of social and spiritual contract abuse by the democratically elected Manifest Destiny–minded European ruling majority over the Indians is the tragic saga of Major Ridge, in northwest Georgia and Tennessee. Ridge and his Cherokee band fought with Andrew Jackson against the British and the Red Stick Creek Indians in the War of 1812. Later, in 1814, Ridge's group fought with Jackson at Alabama's Battle of Horseshoe Bend, where the Creeks were defeated. For his service, Jackson awarded Ridge the rank of Major, and the Cherokee used this rank as his first name thereafter.

"At some point Major Ridge moved his family to property near modern-day Rome, Georgia. There they had a trading post at a river-ferry landing as well as a multi-crop plantation with slaves. His family prospered so well that Ridge had his son formally educated in New England. However, in spite of Ridge's service to Andrew Jackson in times of war and his subsequent wealthy standing, he, too, lost his constitutionally sacred property rights, and had to move to Oklahoma during the Trail of Tears.

"Such was the frenzy of the educated white man's distrust of the native Indian at the time. So *Unto These Hills* is about that Manifest Destiny of an amoral majority that can democratically elect officials to steal, and also outright stab a helpless minority in the back, no matter the worth of their contributions to the common good."

VI

The group then caravanned to town where all wandered in and out of shops, enjoying the spontaneity. A gun shop captured the men's attention. A stop at a custom-made drapery and stained-glass store allowed Marina to entertain the group with her interior-design savvy. Another store was a combination antique-auctioneer emporium, where a woman auctioned carpets, lamps, artwork, and items of exceptional exotica. The most unusual item was a stuffed Bengal tiger, which bid off at $12,000. A dapper, sixtyish gentleman, attired in a tweed gun jacket-style sport coat claimed the tiger with his personal check. Smiling Marsh said, "Damn, that purchase would bust Dutch Lazlo's American Express limit and mine!"

Then Nicole suggested that they at least go by the ski lodge to check for early-evening skiing possibilities, however remote. When they were advised of no skiing for the balance of the weekend, Ginger asked the manager, "Is there any entertainment around here tonight?"

The manager directed her to a dinner-club nightspot near their chalet. The establishment was a BYOB place that served dinner and offered traditional American mountain music, and reservations could be made immediately. Ginger looked at Monroe. "Sounds like the only game in town. Do it," he said.

Back at the chalet, Brick turned on the TV, but the golf tournament had not yet come on. Meanwhile they looked at a basketball game in Chapel Hill between the University of North Carolina and Clemson. Clemson had never won there and was losing again by such a big margin that the group showed little interest as they mixed drinks and made their quirky toast in honor of Langdon: "To Wild Bill Hickok and Holliday Doc!"

Sipping his drink, Marsh said, "Someday, I hope I'm just like that suave, elderly gentleman who bought the tiger. Can you imagine stroking out a $12,000 check, then having no one question it? The sublime essence of having arrived as a self-made American man, with nothing to prove to a damn soul!"

"He reminded me of Stewart Granger or Clark Gable in some movie," said Brewer. "That worldly, self-assured look, no matter whether he's dressed in black tie and tails or ready-for-work clothes. Marsh, he's made his fortune, and now has nothing to prove to anybody."

When the golf tournament came on, Stan Cannon got some television exposure.

After his play ended, all expressed hopes of seeing him when the golf tour made its annual stop at the Greater Greensboro Open, held in that decade just before the Masters Golf Tournament.

VII

The recommended nightspot was on an overlook. A cashier collected the dinner charge at the door and informed the guests that if they wanted brown-bag set-ups, wine, or beer, it would be an extra charge when ordered from the waiters.

The room accommodated about a hundred, and a stage with musical instruments was at one end. Large glass windows exposed the valley below, where the sparkling lights of the valley's mountainside homes highlighted the winter's beauty.

A waitress informed the group that they would be treated to a family-style dinner with salad, medallions of beef tenderloin ladled with a port-wine sauce, dilled red potatoes, steamed carrots with onion, and bread.

Monroe then ordered two brown-bag set-ups of tonic and limes for the group's vodka. Marina suggested a Côtes-du-Rhône for the beef tenderloin, and Brick ordered two bottles.

As the staff scurried among the tables taking and delivering orders, the murmuring of the room rose to a soothing hum but subsided after the food was served. During dinner, Marina accepted praises on her wine selection.

After dessert, two female waitresses and several male waiters mounted the stage and began playing the instruments. No introductions were required as the audience collectively tapped its toe to the high, lonesome whine of a long-bow fiddle harmonizing with a banjo, harmonica, guitar, and mandolin to the tune of "Foggy Mountain Breakdown," by North Carolina native Earl Scruggs.

At the end of the tune, the leader announced that the performers were local college music students, here waiting tables and performing to pay a portion of their educational expenses. Most had worked in the summers with *Horn in the West.*

The group then did Appalachian Mountain songs that the area's frontier settlers had played. One was the classic "Hang Down Your Head, Tom Dooley." The band leader gave a history of the song's connection to the local area and that of the nearby Tennessee-Virginia border, adding extra significance to the presentation. The entertainment ended with the ballad "Shenandoah," and all complimented Ginger on how her inquiry at the ski lodge had produced this entertaining evening.

The next morning the group went their separate ways, hoping to meet again at the Greater Greensboro Open golf tournament to see Stan Cannon play.

Chapter Nine

Poker, GGO Golf, and 'Fass' Dancing at Ocean Drive

I

BETWEEN THE SKI TRIP AND THE GREATER GREENSBORO OPEN, buyers purchased the houses out beyond the belatedly installed culvert pipe. But these delayed sales resulted again in a customer loss to Cy Turner. The lost customer was replaced by the next approved application in line, Donald and Bessie Mae, who moved into their home in the early spring of 1972, on the Friday before the Greensboro golf tournament week.

That day, while I did my typing, Brick said he was going to spend the evening with Monroe and Ginger in Raleigh, while Marina and Lisa were at the High Point Spring Furniture Mart with their hometown Canadian friend Henri Parquette. His family owned several Montréal-area furniture stores. As Brick reviewed my work, Mingo waited for his Monday schedule.

Into the middle of this came a visitor I would soon adore, Miss Peaches Jones. She had a glitz that at first obscured her friendliness as she entered shaking her head against the chill. Her pearl-white teeth chattered, too. Moving directly over a heat vent, she cooed, "I got to come out of this coat. You've got it warm in here, baby!"

When she took off her topcoat, she wasn't naked, but might as well have been. Her body oozed sensuality from head to toe as I compared her sleekness to my own body that always concerned me back in my young adulthood days, Mrs. Penny. Thank goodness Peaches was wearing low pumps. If she'd had on spiked heels, she'd have seemed naked, clothes or not. Her attire's tan color and her skin tone seemed one, and with every movement, her breast line cut through the air like that on a statue of a noble but indifferent Greek goddess.

"I see my house is finished," Peaches said to Brick and Dad. "When can I move in?"

"Your loan package came into Will O'Cain's office yesterday," Dad answered. "It'll take Mr. O'Cain two days to check it out before sending it to June Willingham's law office for the signing and courthouse filing. Between Mr. Willingham's work schedule and O'Cain's, you can probably move in next Thursday or Friday."

"Why can't I move in now?" asked Peaches. "I got two dressers that need moving while my brother's in town to help."

"Against Mr. O'Cain's rules, Peaches," responded Brick. "A builder let a buyer move in once before the final closing papers were signed. The movers damaged the walls, and Mr. O'Cain couldn't release the government check until the damages were repaired. That created a two-week delay, and he's told us no exceptions.

"Mingo here is our repairman. He fixes our mistakes, but not a buyer's mistakes. Sorry, you'll have to wait."

Then Peaches walked, catlike, her hands on her hips, up to Cousin Mingo. "So, the 'Mingo Montana' man here is the fix-up man, huh? You gonna come and fix me up just anytime I squeal?"

Looking dead into her eyes, Cousin Mingo beamed until his gold bicuspid showed, and said, "I can fix anything you got wrong with you anytime, Peach."

Brick grinned, "We'll know by Tuesday when you can move."

Satisfied, Peaches left, saying she was going to see her friends Celestine and Allen.

II

Brick departed for his Raleigh night out with Monroe and Ginger but reported later that the couple's baby had a fever. So Monroe and Brick went out on the town by themselves to a downtown oyster bar and several nightspots. But things were slow, so Monroe suggested visiting a weekend poker game he frequented outside the city limits. There they found among the players Vann Hutton and Cy Turner, but clearly Hutton was not enjoying the game like Cy, who was betting big on every hand.

Liquor, beer, and platters of assorted deli items were set out in a kitchen nook adjoining the game room. As each hand finished, the winner tipped the house 10 percent of his winnings to pay for the drinks and food, as was the general custom. Brick and Monroe each drank a beer while watching the game from the kitchen area.

Eventually, Monroe asked a wheelchair-bound man where Rocky was. The man said Rocky was outside in a camper bus posted as a lookout. Monroe said, "Brick, let's go see the Rock."

Outside, Monroe called to Rocky, and the bus door opened. Rocky whispered a welcome. A seven-shot, police-style riot pump-shotgun lay across his lap.

"You're heavily armed, Rock," commented Monroe. "Expecting the law?"

Rocky replied, "No, if the law came up, I'd call on this walkie talkie to Uncle Blue inside to give them time to stash the cards and money. I'd unload the gun, and pretend to be asleep, or walk away through those woods if I felt I could get away unseen. No, the law raiding a poker game is about the last thing I'd expect.

"I'm looking out for robbers. There was a robbery last Friday night in Johnston County, and then Saturday they hit a game in Fuquay-Varina. These robbers must figure no one's going to call the law for robbing a poker game. A perfect-crime type thing!

"I help Uncle Blue with his poker games when I'm not doing my disc jockey gig. You've got all kinds of broke-assed dreamers coming here: contractors, car salesmen, Realtors, white-collar ex-convicts, and a lawyer or two. It's hard to spot the difference between the sporting man and financially desperate ex-cons. They all drink too much, work like hell during the week, scheming to get ahead on a big score, and those same mental wheels just keep humming into the weekend for good and bad."

Monroe responded, "Sounds like a free pass on crime for the poker-robbing mentality. Speaking of a perfect set-up for theft, looks like Cy Turner's got a big roll and is trying to buy every hand whether he has winning cards or not. His kind is always easy to beat, if you play it shrewd even on a small stake. I wish I could get into that game, but all the seats are occupied."

"Cy's playing with his construction crew's withholding money and what he still owes suppliers for a small apartment project," Rocky explained. "Hutton said Cy's got six thousand."

"Damn!" said Monroe. "I'd love to get in that game. You got any money, Brick?"

"A couple hundred," Brick replied.

"Give it to me," said Monroe. "With my four hundred, maybe I can sit in long enough to catch a big winning hand to stake me for the rest of the game. Remember that motorcycle game when you loaned me a hundred to stay in the game? My luck turned a couple of hands later, and we cleaned your old Sarge out of his motorcycle. Of course, I didn't have any money to pay you back with, just a motorcycle. But we had six fun months riding before I took it to the pawnshop and sold it off for that twelve hundred we split."

"I'll take your marker anytime," said Brick, passing his money to Monroe.

"Hutton's chair will probably be available soon," said Rocky. "That's his routine. He gets his entertainment from the game and Cy and Uncle Blue. When he's had his fill of camaraderie, he leaves, win or lose."

Monroe returned to the house, and Brick reminisced with Rocky about old Ocean Drive days and Rocky's DJ work before hearing a knock on the camper door. Rocky opened it to see Vann Hutton standing there.

"It'll be best," Hutton said, "not to mention my being here to Marina. She'll tell Lisa, and I'll have to explain more than I'd like."

"You're out on the town while the girls are at the High Point Furniture Show?" Brick asked. "Don't worry, your secret's safe with me."

"So I calculated," said Hutton, lighting a cigarette, then sipping his Scotch.

"Since we're sharing secrets, I don't mind telling you that Marina tells Lisa how fond she is of you. Lisa's pleased! But don't expect my mother-in-law to be overjoyed once she ever learns about your developing relationship.

"I was captivated by Lisa. It was that foreign, French thing. I believe every red-blooded Southern boy who ever aspired to a more worldly sophistication has probably fantasized how exotic it could be to have the cultivating experience that a French female might offer. You may be captivated by the same allure.

"I was Lisa's tutor, you know. She would look at me like she was absorbing everything I said with a pitiful blind faith. Maybe it was her father's unexpected death in that shipping accident that gave her the left-alone look, or maybe I was ensnared in my own ideation of her as a motivated student who was coming to realize her gifted potential.

"Then one spring day before heading out for a big Ocean Drive weekend, I finished a tutoring session with her, and looked deeply into her eyes. Something made me kiss her. She kissed back and that was that. I spent six months in the National Guard at Fort Campbell, where I thought of her every minute. When I got back, we couldn't keep our hands off each other, so we married. She graduated shortly after our marriage, and her mother came down for the graduation. That was the first time I'd met her mother or Marina, but I sensed her mother was distressed. No matter how hard she tried to hide it, Mme. Émilie de Lamartine LaGraves was pure stiff-upper-lip Francophile to the bone.

"The next time we met was after our first child was born, and Lisa was working in our firm. By then Mrs. Émilie couldn't say anything. Fortunately, my mother had adopted Lisa like the daughter she had never had. Mother was still living then, and her glow was a magnetic force field that kept all dark, unnecessary peevishness at bay when Madame Émilie was in town.

"Monsieur Frédéric LaGraves had spoken and thought in both English and French or Québécois, as well as in a smattering of Dutch and German because of his maritime work. But Madame was always French-only, pretending only the barest of English comprehension. Oh, she understands English, if circumstances force her, like needing to buy a roll of toilet paper.

"Lisa says her mother became bitter about her husband's death. She depended on his broader outlook to enjoy the world. He was fifty-two at the time, and she forty-six. Now twelve years later she's developed all sorts of arthritic-related problems, which make her pessimistic even though her husband's insurance left her financially secure.

"Luckily, Lisa and Marina still have hometown friends who look in on her. The Parquettes, Henri and Jacques, at the furniture stores, are the main ones. Then there's always the late Captain's first mate, André de Vaux, who Mrs. Émilie dislikes because she believes him to be a smuggler. She's probably right about that.

"He's spent the night at our house and been to this poker game twice. Monroe says he wouldn't be surprised if André's occasionally mixed up in several shady things to supplement his income. André suffered a severe hand laceration in the accident that killed Captain LaGraves, and now he's disabled enough to keep him from going to sea again. Unfortunately, he didn't pay extra for extended insurance benefits like the Captain, and he's probably tempted into occasional shady dealings.

"Mrs. Émilie's sister Joan is much more outgoing. She's a well-off widow, too. After her husband died, she moved to Montréal to be nearer Mrs. Émilie, but she also has a place in Florida. So Lisa and Marina rely on the Parquettes and old André to check on Mrs. LaGraves.

"Aunt Joan married a lumber lobbyist from Ottawa. They had no children, and she traveled with him all over Canada and the U.S. to homebuilder conventions. As a lobbyist, Jean Marc reported to his Board of Directors quarterly. These meetings always took place in Florida or Bermuda or some other faraway place. Once they met in Monte Carlo, another time in Florence. Such travels made Aunt Joan an excellent cook and her husband a wine expert par excellence, so Lisa says about her late uncle. While Mrs. Émilie is a good cook, it's Aunt Joan who gives Lisa and Marina their flair for cooking.

"Now I don't know what your chaplain cousin Wesley would say about all of this in terms of a cross-cultural relationship, but remember this from me: When you marry, you marry the whole family, and in this case that would mean Mrs. Émilie and her grudging disposition. Of course, it might not be much different from what you are going through now with your cousin and those missing cows. Cy says his brother John T's old lumber-company contacts, like Mrs. Iris' deputy-husband, Carley Ray, suspect Marsh sold the missing cows on the sly and pocketed the cash for himself—no income taxes, and the missing cattle can be written off as a loss! Slick! There were no obvious signs of breaking into the lock on the back gate. Somebody had a key, Carley Ray believes. As they say, when you make your bed with somebody, you have to lay in it, and take the good with the bad, plus all the uncertainty that goes with it."

"Mrs. Iris, Austin, and I can tell that Uncle Malcolm is befuddled about the missing cows, but we don't mention it," noted Brick.

"Well," continued Hutton, "in all your relationships you should reflect on your builder experiences. Remember, some things won't fit together without a spacer adapter and some things just won't fit at all. All relationships and endeavors can be dicey, like yours with Marsh. Any personal association can fail if there's no spacer to keep the relationship in balance.

"Likewise, know there's often more complications with a charming French woman than you can find room in bed for. But if you can deal with the undercurrent of what Mrs. Émilie infects her daughters with, you might find harmony and success. The only thing about it all, though, is that it shocks your soul once you realize that family isn't always a sanctuary for you, especially when you really need it."

"I'll keep that in mind," Brick noted. "Do you and Cy play here a lot with Monroe?"

"Cy does," Hutton answered. "I come with him occasionally. I met Cy and Monroe through Rocky's Uncle Blue, who was a plumber before he lost his leg to diabetes. Dad and I always kept running into Blue on jobs. When we had to estimate plumbing costs on projects, we'd take our plans to him for a cost number. Later Cy started doing framing and finish carpentry estimates for me. When Blue lost his leg and started running this poker game to help his financial cushion, many of his former construction friends started patronizing this game. At first it was a small, nickel-and-dime game. Now it's big-time serious.

"Cy's a good builder, but poker, alcohol, and occasional drugs sidetrack him. When he got into trouble on those Chapel Hill houses that you and Marsh finished, he was on drugs, and you couldn't steer him right with any advice. But according to Cy, it was Marsh's showing up with some high-quality pot that got him off track. Hell, whatever, they both got jammed up bad!

"I know Cy's customer-stealing annoys you. That's a part of any business game. But I've started on something now that should keep him out of your hair until you finish Sunrise Acres.

"I've designed plans for a chain of family-fare motels. The investors expect to cash in on the Interstate 95 family-travel boom to all those Florida vacation attractions since Disney World opened up last October. They're gonna be just basic, no-frills sleeping units. Family Dollar Motels is their proposed name. I helped Cy get the building contracts on three of them. He's starting on the first one next month just above the Virginia–North Carolina line, and we hope he'll start construction on the second site in South Carolina by September.

"The second site is near the Darlington Racetrack. It should be a guaranteed success with race-fan traffic and Disney traffic. In fact, we're already talking about increasing that site's size because of its double-dip appeal. Really, Disney and this stock-car racing thing are about as American as Mom and apple pie. The third one is south of Savannah. I suppose the thrill of starting it all is why Cy's betting freely tonight."

"That's good news for Sunrise Acres," Brick remarked. "We've lost sales to Cy, and those lost-sale delays, plus our delayed culvert-pipe installation, ran up the interest cost on our construction loans. Those extra-interest costs get your attention on small starter homes that don't offer much profit opportunity in the first place."

"True," Hutton replied. "In fact, the small-profit potential with starter homes is the very reason Cy passed on Sunrise Acres in the first place. He thought the Sunrise profit spreads were too small to survive the natural weather delays that slow all construction schedules. Cy has many faults, but he's not stupid.

"That's why they started the Chapel Hill project as Marsh mustered out of the Army. Those larger houses offered more profit opportunity. Malcolm could agree to sponsor the Chapel Hill project because Cy already had considerable building experience that could be passed onto Marsh. But with the zero building experience that you and Marsh had, a simple, no-frills starter-house project is what your partnership needed first.

"I know Malcolm needs to get rid of that dairy farm. It's a tax burden he can re-package by developing it as Sunrise Acres. But maybe the specter of cancer makes Malcolm push too fast on educating you and Marsh. Currently you've got excellent sales despite Cy's occasional customer steals, and those good sales can hide lots of business sins lurking under the surface. I still wish Malcolm had waited to find a site with sanitary sewer available. I've seen good septic tank treatment soil profiles change to poor treatment soils from lot to lot on other big tracts. I think I've addressed the poor septic treatment soil situation by laying out larger lots for septic line repair work in a couple of questionable places, but you can never tell. Have you had any septic trouble yet in that rocky area where the snakes hibernated?"

"None," Brick replied.

Suddenly there was a rapping on the door. Rocky opened it and Monroe said, "Let's go, Brick! I've won big, and it's time to leave before my luck changes."

The two left for Monroe's house, where Monroe told Ginger he thought he'd won big money. After paying back Brick his two hundred dollars, Monroe and Ginger counted. The winnings totaled over five thousand dollars. When Marsh and Dad heard of it the next week, they were gleeful that Cy had lost but thankful that he was headed into a new construction project that wouldn't compete with Sunrise Acres.

III

The following Wednesday, Junebug closed Miss Peaches' house and joined Brick, Marsh, and Sue Anne at the Greensboro golf tournament to follow Stan Cannon. After Saturday's round, they met Stan at a local steakhouse. Marina and the Huttons came from the High Point Furniture Mart to join them. With the Hutton group was Henri Parquette, the LaGraves girls' childhood friend. Thanks to Parquette's connection with High Point's furniture designer network, Lisa, ten years earlier, and later Marina, had been able to secure scholarships to N.C. State's School of Architecture and Interior Design.

As Stan had not been able to converse with Brick, Marsh, or Junebug during the tournament, much of the dinner conversation buzzed with Stan's questions about what PSR Club friends were doing since he had last been home. From this, Stan learned that Brewer and Nicole were spending a good-bye weekend with General Eisner, who was returning to Vietnam in his capacity as advisor to a munitions firm. Monroe and Ginger were now down with a flu that they had contracted from their baby, who had been ill the previous weekend. As for Dutch Lazlo, Stan said he was still in Florida, where he last saw him at a tournament.

"Speaking of the Dutchman," said Stan, "he was with a group of suspicious-looking characters in Miami. He was strung out on God knows what, doing one over-the-edge thing after another. I can't speak against him because his family's business supported me initially. Their endorsement money was never big-time like brand-name golf apparel, but it kept my expenses paid my first two years on tour.

"So much for my golfing life! As for you folks, Vann, I remember meeting you at last spring's PSR Club fundraiser. You and your Lisa looked like old-pro beach dancers that night. Brick and Monroe say you go back to the postwar beach-boogie beginning."

"Yes, but today's dance halls are nicer," replied Vann. "The original beach-dancing parlors, like OD's Roberts Pavilion, were only summertime operations, serving up cold beer and loud jukebox music. I worked there one summer before Hurricane Hazel blew it away. Those old bath-house venues offered the bare necessities. Knowledgeable college girls rarely consumed beer in them because the bad-smelling facilities rarely functioned. But for those of us born of parents just out of the Depression and World War

II, these spots were Meccas for a more promising, universal rhythm of life and hope. They reflected where the Depression-war baby generations had come from, yet also pointed to the growing electronic age of prosperity shadowed by numerous nuclear Armageddon scenarios.

"I know that sounds strange, but that was the rhythm that satisfied our bodies and souls from the late forties to early sixties. It was the era of backyard bomb shelters and all that end-of-the-world talk. Dad designed two shelters before I met Lisa. I still recall during the October 1962 Cuban Missile Crisis of wanting to be at the beach rather than in Raleigh as we all waited for the holocaust to begin. I thought that if I had to die in a man-made, mass community suicide over which I had no control, I'd rather slide out on a good note at the beach, with a dance step I could execute perfectly thanks to the dance floor's sandy surface."

"Vann, that's so prophetic that General Eisner might have said it," smiled Stan. "Brick tells me you've been touring the furniture mart."

"Yes," replied Hutton, "I wouldn't have come this year were it not for the need to scout out some inexpensive furniture for this motel project we're designing."

"Brick," Marina interjected, "Henri will be with us at the tournament tomorrow. He has three motorcycles, and quite often goes on weekend treks with his pals: a pediatrician, a dentist, an attorney, and a city cop—an interesting group, although I've not met them all. I'm sure Henri and you can find lots to talk about as we follow Stan around."

"Yes," noted Henri. "Marina says you once had a motorcycle."

The group continued to talk for some time until Stan begged their leave for sleep before the next day's final round. At the end of Sunday's round, Stan found himself in fifth place, wishing he had made a better showing before his home gallery. Brick told Stan he might make a better showing at Augusta since he wouldn't be distracted by hometown fans. But Stan said, "I get extra energy from friends, and besides, please come if for nothing else than to keep Dutch in check. You can always expect him to appear at a main event like the Masters."

But all had conflicts and couldn't promise.

IV

With Cy Turner's departure from the area, all were encouraged that their approved customers would not bolt to buy from other building operations. Consequently, Mr. Malcolm argued for developing the rest of the property, including the back forty, with water lines and paved streets. He did not want to experience another winter of delays like those caused by the infamous uninstalled culvert.

Austin, however, opposed investing so much up-front money because the project was producing so little profit per house. An economic downturn, he said, would stall house sales unexpectedly even though construction-loan interest would still have to be paid, house sales or not. Mrs. Penny, this would mean that the lumber company would have to pay it, as it was Sunrise Acres' only loan endorser of financial substance.

But Mr. Malcolm insisted on charging ahead, arguing that paying for street paving now would be cheaper than doing so later. Inflation at the time was causing alarm, and the Nixon administration had instituted some price controls to stem it. The two men quit arguing when Mr. Malcolm accepted Austin's idea of a a back-forty promotional barbeque on the Saturday of Memorial Day weekend to boost prospective customer traffic. To this, Brick and Marsh readily agreed, saying they would seek their Aunt Dot's advice on how to conduct a drawing for free televisions and other prizes.

Consequently, Marsh made daily appearances at the site to check on the Macks and discuss with Brick the latest advice from their Aunt Dot for managing a prize drawing. Brick also continued supervision corrections on Hogbear's notepads.

The most annoyed I ever saw Brick get over repairs was that Friday in May when he and Marsh were about to leave for Ocean Drive to see their friend Langdon Salt-Dog Butler. Brick's annoyance resulted from a request concerning Miss Peaches' bathroom sink repeatedly falling off the wall.

Peaches' niece came to make the repair request to Dad. Five-year-old Erica often lived with Peaches, who had no children. Erica said, "Mr. Deacon, that sink's fell again. It's my Aunt Peaches' boyfriend, Earl. Can you get it fixed again?"

"How many times has this happened, Deacon?" Brick growled. "I don't know what's causing it but tell Mingo to go fix it this time—correctly, please!"

Looking at Marsh in bewilderment, Little Erica tiptoed out the door as the cousins continued preparing to leave for Langdon Butler's last OD weekend. Langdon was in the process of moving to the Outer Banks for his new job of selling boating equipment and repair parts to the commercial fishing industry. His Fayetteville-area friends were coming to Ocean Drive under the pretense of helping him with last-minute packing. In truth, however, Langdon had already moved most of it. So Langdon's last OD weekend became an excuse for a beach party. In addition, Sue Anne and Lonah Slueter had a photo shoot of bathing-suit contest entrants the same weekend.

Langdon's place was in the heart of Ocean Drive, near the beach-dancing spots. Marsh, Brick, Brewer, and Monroe had rented a four-bedroom cottage within sight of

Langdon's. But all the action was to be at Langdon's because he had rented a free-play jukebox, which was to be supplied with records that Brewer and Nicole were bringing again from the Sampsons Landing Hunt Club jukebox.

Leaving the office, Marsh said, "I'm glad we're departing without seeing Cecil X. Now we'll have a chance to stop by that Little River Seafood House and pick up fresh seafood, just off the boat, without hurting Cecil's feelings."

"Don't worry 'bout Cecil, Marsh," said Dad. "Friday is his big fish-sale day. His wife's come back, and they're trying to work out their differences. He pretty much stays home when he's not working his fish routes or doing something for his mosque."

v

On arrival, the group purchased shrimp and breakfast items before settling into a shrimp cocktail dinner with plenty of beer to wash things down. About eight, Langdon returned from northeastern North Carolina.

After being reassured that the beach music records were there, Langdon raised his beer and offered his "Wild Bill Hickok and Holliday Doc" toast. Then he added, "Well, I'm glad we're able to have one last blast of a Wild West weekend here at OD. You all will have to come to Nags Head if you want to see me in the future."

"Brewer and I dread that," commented Nicole. "It's a long drive from Sampsons Landing to Nags Head."

"True," responded Langdon, "but life moves on. Say, have you heard from your dad lately?"

"No," Nicole sighed. "This is his third Vietnam trip in two years as a civilian. He only went once in the service. He says little, except that he'd love to see it done with. His civilian stays are short, thankfully. Brewer and I will clean his house before he returns in late June."

"Well, we always enjoy his bird-hunting company," said Langdon, "and I hope to hunt with him again this fall.

"But back to Nags Head: Can you all come up there in a couple of weeks? It'll be Memorial Day weekend. There's fast-lane activity at an in-crowd dance spot, but the area's slower pace is not an entrenched boogie-woogie lifestyle like here."

Sue Anne spoke up, "We'd love to, but that's the weekend of the promotional barbeque for the back-forty houses that Marsh and Brick are breaking ground on."

"That's right," put in Marsh. "Why don't all of you come there instead? Sue Anne and Marina will be there, and you'll get a chance to see what we're doing and meet a cast of real characters. Of course, you won't get to meet the black albino pot supplier, Chalky Newton. That reminds me, I've got a new bag off Chalky. It's as good as Dutch's Monkey Island stuff."

"Always glad to try some with select friends, just to be sociable, as Brick says," Langdon offered. "Even though my new focus is on my Nags Head future, an occasional blast from the past may help smooth my transition to those harder realities of responsible adult life.

"So, Brick, business must be good if you and Marsh are starting a forty-house tract?"

"Yes," said Brick. "But starter-house profit margins are always small. So you have to be mistake-free to be profitable."

"Brick's had some annoying days lately," put in Marsh.

"What Marsh is referring to is that this woman's sink keeps falling off the bathroom wall; three times now, just this week. The owner's niece says it's her aunt's boyfriend, but we can't figure it out, and the repairs are getting expensive. The guy must be drinking a home-made liquor that makes him hang onto the sink when he throws up. If it happens again, we're going to write him instructions on how to vomit in the damn commode!"

Suddenly, amid the laughter, there was a knock on the door and in walked Lonah Slueter. Like the other girls, she was dressed in shorts, but Lonah's were shorter.

"Hello, there!" Lonah said, easing into the room, leaving the men stunned. Even Brick cast glances at her from the corner of his eye.

"Where's Dutch?" Ginger asked.

Lonah said, "He's with his Puerto Rican friends doing last-minute outfitting on his boat. They're entering that fishing tournament up at Wrightsville this summer, and they want to get in some practice. Dutch says they'll be out all day tomorrow and Sunday.

"By the way, Sue Anne, maybe the girls might like to go with us tomorrow to help supervise the photo shoot at Blossom's Studio?"

Later, all went to Langdon's place and loaded the records on the jukebox. Like most of the surrounding houses, Langdon's was built on stilts to protect it from hurricane flooding. The upstairs living area was accessible by a large upper porch deck that faced the ocean across the street. They talked, drank, and danced until three in the morning.

For the next morning's hangover breakfast, Brick and Brewer had a beer, a multi-vitamin, and a raw egg. Monroe staggered in as Brick and Brewer downed their hangover cure. "Are you two having the alcoholic's breakfast of champions?"

"Trying to regain our health after last night's abuse," Brick croaked.

"Yes, Dr. Hill," Brewer put in. "Those eggs we bought yesterday won't get cooked by our women today. We might as well use them to soak up alcohol. The vitamins might re-nourish our livers. Of course, I don't recommend that you try this hangover recipe at home for a respectable family drunk. You could get salmonella from a lack of alcohol in an empty morning stomach. No, this cure is just for Wild West drunks like last night's."

"Brewer, not being a professional drunk like you and Brick," replied Monroe, "I wouldn't know about such. I just know I feel worse'n hell. Have you just got some damn aspirin?"

"Brewer, give the wimp a baby aspirin," laughed Brick. "And here's to 'Wild Bill and Holliday Doc,' gentlemen! Oh God, this 'Holliday Doc' feels like a crock."

This conversation roused the girls, who soon left for the swimsuit photo shoot before the men removed to sunbathe on the front deck, staring, zombie-like, at the ocean. A radio played The O'Kaysions' 1968 hit "I'm a Girl Watcher" and other beach music appropriate for a morning of barely breathing.

Around noon the smell of hotdogs and hamburgers drifted in on a breeze. Comments were made about lunch, but no one moved a muscle to go buy anything. Eventually Langdon came up the stairs to opine, "Man, oh man, this is a rough-looking crew."

Ultimately, Langdon and Brewer volunteered to visit the nearby hamburger-hotdog emporium and bring back everybody's order.

After lunch the ladies returned, minus Lonah, who remained at the photo studio. Each girl had a negligee that Lonah had purloined from Lazlo's studio stock. By mid-afternoon all had showered and dressed in Bermuda shorts for a stroll over to several nearby beer-hall dance spots, where they saw a host of friends.

Brick had not been to any of these famous dance halls since his Army days, but relished the opportunity to see old acquaintances and introduce Marina. At each spot, they promoted Langdon's going-away party to their Cape Fear, Coastal Plains friends of both Carolinas. The party was set to kick into gear after the lounges closed around midnight.

The group lingered at the last dance spot until dusk before returning to the rental cottage. Soon the girls agreed on going out to dinner, saying they'd rather save the refrigerator's contents for breakfast. At this point, Langdon suggested a ten-minute trip over the state line to a Calabash restaurant. No one took up the idea at first, but the mood changed when Marsh turned the radio to the local beach-music station, and the smell of hemp wafted through the house. One of Marsh's joints made its way around twice before the group departed for dinner.

VI

After a fresh-catch seafood meal, they returned to the cottage, where all partook of another round of pot before walking over to Langdon's around ten-thirty. His rented jukebox began competing with the melodies coming from nearby dance halls.

As the night wore on, couples and singles drifted to Langdon's as a result of the after-noon's party-announcement campaign. Some danced, others talked, and all indulged themselves in some sort of bring-your-own libation. No fights broke out, but a healthy amount of intemperance ensued. Men urinated in the darker corners outside between parked cars. Police kept an observant eye on the gathering but never interfered.

While the police eyeballed the reasonably tame crowd on the upper-deck porch, they could not observe what occurred inside. Had they seen that, there's no telling how many might have gone to jail—perhaps all! The combination of alcohol plus marijuana, along with the jukebox's rhythm-and-blues sounds, aroused shameless dancing and other acts of immodesty.

Chief among the flashy dancers was Lonah and Sue Anne's photographer-friend, Blossom. He and one of the swimsuit contestants he had been photographing stripped off their swimsuit cover wear to dance seductively to Ike and Tina Turner's "Rock Me Baby." The girl's swimwear looked more like a Lazlo negligee. This, in turn, excited Lang-don to bite the female on her buttocks every time she danced by his position in the crowded circle.

Such risqué behavior got the better of Brewer and Monroe, who dropped their Ber-muda shorts and stripped off their shirts to join in the suggestive carnality. Of course, this got the attention of Nicole and Ginger, who were about to retrieve and reprimand their spouses, when a tall, blond, drunken man dropped his shorts, revealing that he had on briefs, often called tank-style underwear. The sight of this generated roars of ridicul-ing laughter and cat-calls of "Superman underwear" that ended the activity before a shirtless Marsh could get into the act.

"What do you think you're doing, Marsh?" Sue Anne snarled. "Last night it was Lonah you were gazing upon, and now this!"

Marsh smiled sheepishly. "Don't worry, dear—I wasn't about to embarrass you. I don't have on Superman underwear; I got boxers."

"If you don't straighten up," Sue Anne shot back, "I'll box your damn Superman ears!"

This ruckus cleared out half the crowd in minutes though Langdon encouraged all to return for Sunday's final edition. The female partner of the risqué dancing couple put on her blouse-style cover-up and Blossom his long-cut Panama shirt, and they joined Langdon on the deck for a beer in the warm night's breeze before departing into the dark, never to be seen again.

Sunday, the girls prepared breakfast, complemented by an assortment of Bloody Marys, Screwdrivers, and beer. Then they went to Langdon's to assist him in moving out his last heavy belongings into a covered trailer. All that was left now was the jukebox, to be picked up by the rental company at sundown but playing on wide-open volume until then. While Langdon's party continued unabated, it was less raunchy than on the previous evening.

The farewell afternoon party started slowly. Most lingered on the upper deck, listened to the music, and watched Langdon greet and reflect on old times with well-wishers.

Amid this scene, a series of danceable beach-music tunes played and most flowed inside to dance to The Coasters, The Clovers, The Checkers, The Intruders, The Drifters, Garnet Mimms and the Enchanters, The Showmen, The Tams, Harold Melvin and the Blue Notes, Ernie K-Doe, Willie Tee, The Embers, The Intrigues, The Artistics, Major Lance, Fats Domino, Maurice Williams and the Zodiacs, Al Wilson, and Sam and Dave.

Sue Anne and Marsh danced until about halfway through The Tams' "What Kind of Fool Do You Think I Am." Then, claiming it was too hot in the crowded room, they joined Brick and Marina outside. Soon Monroe, Ginger, Brewer, and Nicole emerged, also.

Marina smirked, "I still wish I could get my feet to glide the way all of yours do. I'm afraid that Brick and I are just not compatible dancers. I'm sure he wanted to be in there dancing like he does with Becky Rollins!"

"Marina, our DJ poker buddy, Rocky, would understand your dance frustrations," Monroe said. "He'd say you first need to appreciate the different types of rock music. All rock and roll is fundamentally the music of blacks about their colored-town culture and is loosely called race music, or Chitlin Circuit music. There's rock and roll you can listen to or twist around to by yourself or with another, but at a distance. This would be high-energy tunes by Little Richard, Jerry Lee Lewis, Ray Charles, and the like. Then there's the four-four rhythm-and-blues shuffle or beach music tunes you can actually dance to, toe-to-toe, holding another person's hand. Since many dance floors are small, confining you to dance in a narrow slot to miss other dancers, the turns and twirls are more refined. Some call that 'dancing-in-the-slot'!

"Most pop rock and roll has been sanitized of its race music roots into those bobby-sox, bubble-gum tunes that do well on music charts with the teenyboppers you see doing some silly hully-gully dance on TV. That's not real hardcore rhythm-and-blues beach boogie music like last night's "Rock Me Baby" by Ike and Tina Turner. That tune's line of 'roll me like a wagon wheel' expresses a KMA raw edge craving for physical love inside the black neighborhoods where the opportunities for greater personal fulfillment amid family inclusiveness are often bleak.

"KMA?" laughed Marina, puzzled.

"You know, that 'kiss-my-ass' attitude like the Carl Perkins line in 'Don't You Step on My Blue Suede Shoes.' That tune is a bopper dance tune and not a beach music tune, but both genres must express a KMA attitude to be the real deal. Recall Vann's wish to be at the beach shagging his life away during the Cuban Missile Crisis when all thought the world would end. All that nuclear apprehension made folks look life in the eye with a KMA attitude and say, 'Go to hell!' It was like, we may not have a long future here, but we're going to face our end while being cool about our fate. That same don't-break-a-sweat attitude found its way into beach-music dancing because the cool-cat males wanted an opportunity to make love with a groovy partner. Rocky and the DJs say the four-four shuffling rhythm-and-blues notes give these tunes an edge that better reflects the realities of adult romance and the despair of love lost. However, if a man doesn't get to first base, he projects a 'so-what-and-better-luck-next-time' demeanor. So, beach music and its lifestyle are definitely not bobby-sox, bubble-gum stuff. It does reflect Elvis Presley's iconic 'Heartbreak Hotel' and suggests dancing the blues away. Joe Turner's 'flip-flop-and-fly-I-don't-care-if-I-die' line shows the male KMA attitude. For a sense of female despair, consider that line in The Enchanters' 'Quiet Place' describing a woman's longing for her missing Johnny Dollar or The Shirelles' 'Baby It's You' with its 'cheat, cheat, cheat' refrain.

"These KMA attitudes have not been hard for war babies and baby boomers like us to conceptualize here in the U.S. because we are just one step removed from the Depression and World War II eras of our parents, and we are facing an even crazier world poised to go to hell in some nuclear big bang. Even the Yankee and West Coast boppers, who have never smoothed out the boogie-woogie dance steps like Southern beach-music danc-ers do, dance with a KMA attitude. For our generation, it's been like eat-drink-and-be-merry all over the country, for tomorrow you'll die anyway. And I've heard from troop-ers trading at our pawnshop that the KMA attitude is most evident in Europe where US-NATO forces are stationed. Just imagine the tensions that postwar Germans and Frenchmen our age feel at critical points like Berlin's Checkpoint Charlie."

"Forget Monroe's analysis, Marina," Brick interrupted. "People don't dance forever. My grandparents finally gave up the Virginia Reel. You'll be O.K. just the way you are."

Then The Isley Brothers' party anthem "Shout!" came on. Many of the dancers moved off the floor to watch Langdon and a few others jump and oscillate around the room in a circular, warlike dance of mindless social rejoicing. In the middle of this romping, Lonah Slueter climbed the steps toward Brick and Marsh. She appeared dazed and cried as she began talking.

"It's Dutch," she moaned through the blare of The Isley Brothers' classic. "He called to say he's in jail! He doesn't know where to turn for help. His parents were in New York for several days and are en route home. They can't be reached. He's in the Brunswick County Jail."

"That's in North Carolina," said Brick, looking at Marsh confused. "Langdon's phone has been disconnected, but I'll find a pay phone and call Junebug for him. Stay here and catch your breath."

With that, Langdon's weekend spree ended.

VII

"Melody, your story is beginning to remind me of that first year or two that Billy and I were married after World War II. With the hardships of the war over, everyone was ready for a fun time—a party time, like the Charleston Ragtime era after World War I. But those times permanently intoxicated some—and they suffered."

"I can imagine, Mrs. Penny."

Chapter Ten

Drugs, Barbeque Promotions, and Vietnam MIAs

I

ABOUT MONDAY NOON, DAD, BRICK, AND MARSH were watching Jeff Mack repair a motor grader when Mr. Malcolm and Austin arrived. Mr. Malcolm barked, "What can you gentlemen tell me about Dutch's arrest?"

"Dad!" answered Marsh, looking at Brick. "How do you even know about this? We're waiting on Junebug to call with the inside story."

"Holden Rollins called about deductible rates for our insurance policy renewals," Mr. Malcolm began.

"He says the Pineland Springs rumor is that Dutch was caught smuggling drugs into the country on his boat. Were you two with him this weekend? I've got building projects everywhere, which takes lots of money—the bank's damn money! Crap like that'll get the bank antsy enough to foreclose on everything. I feared problems with Cy Turner's Chapel Hill screw-up, but with only three houses involved, no red flags were raised. Our accountants warned, however, that loan clauses about illegal activity could have provoked banker demands of immediate full loan repayments. So, tell me what you know!"

Brick explained that Dutch hadn't joined their weekend because he was fishing with Puerto Rican-Florida friends in preparation for a Wrightsville Beach fishing tournament later that summer. All they knew about his troubles came from Lonah, who didn't know why Dutch was jailed. Even Junebug had not yet told them.

Seeming satisfied the cousins weren't involved with Dutch, Mr. Malcolm looked at Jeff Mack. "Are you going to get this back forty ready so we can finish building this year? I don't want another winter like last year with that damn culvert pipe!"

"We're doing our best, Dad," interjected Marsh. "Look, it's lunchtime. Maybe you could invite Junebug to lunch so we can find out about Dutch."

"Lawyer confidentiality may prevent him from telling much," admonished his father. "But I also want to satisfy myself that you two won't be remotely implicated."

At the construction trailer Mr. Malcolm called Willinghams' law office. After the conversation, he said, "I'm satisfied you two are in the clear on this, but it appears to my old attorney's mind that Dutch is in deep trouble.

"The Willinghams referred Dutch to Wilmington attorneys experienced in drug smuggling. All they know is that Dutch's group made a blind floating pick-up of dope from an ocean barge going from Puerto Rico to Wilmington. The barge had been under surveillance since it left Puerto Rico. When Dutch's boat entered the Intracoastal Waterway, federal authorities stopped it north of Calabash and confiscated a big haul.

"Thank God you two aren't involved! Years back, just before Becky Rollins' debutante presentation, Duncan Lazlo said he wished Dutch had sisters like the MacKoy cousins and the Rollins brothers because a sister might have been a calming influence on Dutch. A young woman's charm represents a family's good qualities better than all the good manly deeds."

Then they adjourned for lunch with my dad. The conversation centered on the Memorial Day weekend back-forty promotion. Austin asked questions about the probabilities of converting the attendees into bona-fide homebuyers, sparking more opinions.

II

On Saturday, Dad, Cousin Mingo, and Hogbear started barbecuing six pigs about 2 a.m. Marsh and Donald came after cow-feeding to give them a break from scattering coals under the roasting pigs. After cooking, the meat was finely chopped by Mingo, Ollie, and Cotton Roberts.

Besides these cooks, Riley Carlisle and Bobby Jack Johnson prepared baked beans and boiled potatoes while Jeff Mack and my friend Desmond cooked hush puppies. Near the 1 p.m. mealtime, Brick and Marina arrived with soft drinks, tea, and coleslaw from Uncle Henry's Grill.

My job that day, Mrs. Penny, was to serve the drinks. Marina helped me, while Sue Anne helped Marsh and Brick serve the barbeque. Dad stood by the serving line, passing out numbered tickets to be used in the prize drawing.

Before the meal, a crowd of about seventy assembled by the serving tables at the end of the paved street that was to continue into the back forty. This location was ideal because there were both completed and uncompleted houses here. People could eat here, and at the same time scrutinize the construction stages. Before serving, Brick welcomed everyone, giving an overview of the homes and their costs. Dad announced how the food serving and the prize drawings would proceed, then introduced the Farm Home Administrator, Will O'Cain, who spoke about the merits of home ownership versus renting. Then Dr. Chester O'Malley, an instructor at the local community college and a part-time minister, returned thanks after promoting his community-college class on family budget skills for new homeowners.

This is the only time Brick's parents or Mrs. Colleen ever came to Sunrise Acres. Mr. Lee appeared impressed with what Brick was doing and listened intently to Mr. Malcolm. Austin said little as he helped Diane monitor their rambunctious boys.

As the MacKoys and I entered the food line, Junebug and Kay arrived. I happened to be standing beside Marina, who asked about Martha Sarah. I had babysat Martha Sarah three times since Super Sunday, but Marina had not seen the baby since. She did recall Kay's remarks about wanting to see Martha Sarah's first reactions to the sights and sounds of the ocean at Duck.

Kay replied, "Yes! We've been by car, and plan to take her by plane for the Fourth of July. I believe June has said something to Brick about coming, too, since the Fourth will be a long weekend. I hope both of you can make it."

"We hope to," answered Marina as we followed the line by the prize display tables.

While the prize drawings had been created to induce prospective buyers to fill out homebuyers' applications, less expensive prizes were available for existing homeowners who brought prospective customers with them. There were blue theater-style tickets for homeowners and red tickets for prospective buyers who signed Farm Home Loan applications and made an appointment with Dad and Brick for completing the applications later.

Being the last ones served, it was convenient for us to eat near my drink-serving station. I was standing between Marina and Kay when Junebug said, "Brick, this back forty will increase my office workload. Mrs. Ethel Sharpe has been with us since your Uncle Malcolm's days. It's all she can do to keep up now, and she'll probably retire or work less after Dad reduces his workload next year. I'll need some part-time help to keep up with all this."

Brick looked at Junebug, me, and Marsh. Nonchalantly he said, "Why don't you hire Melody? She's already typed up the forms and knows the paper trail. If you worked her part-time, along with her part-time work here, it'd help us both to keep a reliable person around."

When Junebug said, "Speed Thinker, I like that idea," I about fell down. The opportunity delighted me not just because it would give me extra income, but because it would look good on my résumé after next year's college graduation.

"Come and see me next week, Melody," said Junebug, nodding at me, then Dad. "We'll see if it's something you think you can handle."

After eating, the MacKoys, the Winships, and the Willinghams left for a back-forty tour. Dad thanked Brick for my job offer as Brick and Marsh left with their family and friends. Brick said, "We need a good person here and there to keep things flowing. Melody's most capable. Maybe Providence has put her in the right place at the right time for the benefit of us all."

III

Still joyous, Desmond and I joined Dad and Cousin Mingo, who were with Cotton Roberts, Will O'Cain, and Dr. O'Malley. Mr. O'Cain was voicing his concerns about the current inflation rate. "If the Nixon administration lifted their voluntary price controls from building materials now, it would send Sunrise Acres' house costs beyond the income level of the average starter-home buyer. Rising lumber prices could stop this project dead!"

Cotton Roberts seemed ready to comment when Cecil X and Shasta arrived. They spoke briefly and left. As they walked away, Mr. O'Cain said, "Deacon, they are back together again, but I wonder if their reunion will last."

Dad said nothing but Dr. O'Malley asked, "What's their problem?"

"I've talked with them together and separately about their marriage," O'Cain said. "She's tired of making their house payments alone. It's a Black Muslim thing.

"They were attracted to it in college—Black Pride, you know? Upon graduation, she got an accounting job quickly, but he didn't. After a few minimum-wage odd jobs, he started selling fish for the Muslims. Of course, all Muslim entrepreneurs are expected to donate heavily from their profits back to the cause. So Cecil rarely has enough money to pay his family-budget share.

"Shasta has an accountant's sense to see that it's all sacrifice and no payday down the road. She's developed cold feet about the Muslim view of Black Pride, while Cecil's still committed even though he can hardly pay his delivery truck's wear-and-tear. If the price of gas went up much, he'd go bankrupt. She left him, but they're back together. Being married for better or worse means many things, but it's often money that turns it good or bad.

"When Shasta left Cecil, she consulted with her auntie and brought the auntie to one of our private sessions. The woman is an old-timey, dyed-in-the-wool Baptist who loves Jesus but is scared to death of Muslim teachings. The combination of money woes and her auntie's influence has created a divide between Cecil and Shasta."

"His confusion is unfortunate," remarked O'Malley, staring at Desmond and then me.

"It's unfortunate because Cecil appears likable and smart. We need smart, likable blacks in the right places to lead by example, and particularly now that things aren't quite like they were when you spent that weekend with me in D.C. on the way to Michigan."

"Melody," said Mr. O'Cain, looking at me and Cotton, "you don't know what Dr. O'Malley's referring to like your dad does. But I'll tell you the story behind it. And, if Cotton listens, he may learn about what it's like growing up not being white, despite having a brain and a soul that long for more opportunity.

"Deacon and I graduated from high school in 1948. Your dad, of course, went into the family masonry business. But I went to college like Dr. O'Malley had done several years before. Chester's mama and mine were friends. My mama pushed me to be like Chester, a teacher, who later became a Washington, D.C., public-school principal.

"After college, I didn't know where I was going to get the money for a doctorate, but I did know that my college degree came with an opportunity to accept a second lieuten- ant's Army commission because I had participated in the College Reserve Officer Train- ing Corps program, or ROTC.

"Up until the late sixties it was mandatory that all undergraduate U.S. male citizens attending a land-grant college participate in ROTC. My right to accept a commission also meant that most of my college expenses would be paid after my tour of duty. So I became one of the few black Army officers of that day because the military offered the best path forward. Right after the shooting ended, I went to Korea as the commander of an integrated artillery unit.

"After Korea, I decided to get out of the Army, hoping for a civilian government job. I knew my officer's record would help me land a federal job, even in the Jim Crow 1950s. There were jobs available for blacks with the Farm Home Administration then, but they were all in the cold North and not the South just yet. In spite of disliking its weather, I knew nothing would be as cold as Korea. So I mustered out as a Captain, taking my chances that federal jobs would open up some day in the sunny South after Jim Crow faded with Father Time. My first job was in Lansing, Michigan, the state capital a good bit north of Detroit.

"When I mustered out at Fort Bragg, it would have been quicker to drive through western North Carolina, West Virginia, and Ohio to get to Michigan. But I didn't want my wife, with child at the time, or myself to get threatening looks at gas stations along the way. So, I gassed up my car in Fayetteville, and left around nine p.m. for a six-hour trip up to D.C. I knew we could get to Fredericksburg, Virginia, and be close enough to D.C. to fill up again without being hassled. Another reason for going that way was that I had always had an invitation to stay with Dr. O'Malley.

"We arrived on a Wednesday and stayed through the weekend. It was the summer of 1960, and Chester was principal by then of an integrated school. The perfect host, he fed us and took us to all the sights: the Capitol, the White House, the Smithsonian, the Washington Monument, the Lincoln and Jefferson Memorials, and Arlington Cemetery, located at General Robert E. Lee's wife's plantation home.

"Chester and I still talk about that weekend. Really, you couldn't walk around our capital without feeling the sheer greatness and potential of the whole country from coast to coast, and what the spiritual hope was for every citizen. Unfettered God-given opportunity seemed to exude from every alabaster pore like a cool breath of freedom. We both sensed an aura of possibility now that the Korean War was over. Caesar, at his peak of power, never saw such glorious opportunity in Rome for all the mankind of his day that any latent nobility in his breast may have wanted to serve.

"At Chester's home, over hamburgers or ribs and beer, we'd talk about the promise of the better times coming in Dixie where we wanted to be. We expressed hopes that someday we could return to where we were born and bred—and our forefathers buried. Here is holy ground where we must let our enslaved forefathers know that we are finally as free as the air we breathe.

"Anyway, I went to Lansing knowing my Army time would apply toward my retirement. I had a desk job and waited for a field-office opening. That's when I, too, was teased by the ideas of Black Pride and self-help as espoused in Black Muslim introductory literature. Detroit was a Muslim enclave and their literature was freely available. Oddly, the self-reliance and thrift dialogue of the Muslim brochures sounded like it was written by a bunch of white Republicans!"

All smiled and Cotton Roberts chuckled at this remark, before O'Cain continued: "My Farm Home Administration work was teaching me that thrift and self-help are good habits for achieving success and happiness. Consequently, I decided to study the Muslim movement more by going to a Detroit rally.

"All I found there was corrosive language, and I knew the movement wasn't for me. You see, I had led an interracial company in Korea. There, black and white had to depend on one another to be at the ready along the tense DMZ between North and South. So it wasn't in me to come home and adopt a hostile tone. I felt this even though the critical mass of racial opinion in the South was still balanced in old Jim Crow's favor.

"No, while the Jim Crow Southern bureaucracy disgusted me, I knew I could only help change things for the better down here from the position I found myself in up north. Black Pride comes from a job well executed, and not from any energy generated by the hatred of whites like I had heard at the rally. Hate is strong, but always short-lived and undirected like scatter-shot, even if justified. Only Love is eternal, says the Good Book. Thus my Muslim flirtation ended more quickly than it began.

"When opportunities opened here after 1966, I came home where I had always dreamed of being. Now it appears that one of my successes may be working with the white Mac-Koys on Sunrise Acres. When Chester came home last year to the community college after twenty-five years of teaching in D.C., I'm sure he realized some of his dreams, too. Maybe we'll both get a chance to do a little good for the families we've known so long."

IV

Brick returned for the prize drawings while people gathered near the tables. Among the first arrivals were the Lambs, along with Miss Peaches, her friend Earl, and niece, Erica.

When Erica saw Dad, she ran ahead, and blurted out, "Aunt Peaches' sink is staying up good now, Mr. Deacon, after Mingo put that big board under it."

"What board?" Brick asked Dad as he looked at Marsh.

"That sink don't fall no more, Mr. Brick," Erica smiled.

"Hush, child!" said Celestine Lamb. "We must not tell all of your Aunt Peaches' secrets."

No more was said about the sink as the prize drawing began, but Brick and Marsh looked puzzled. The less expensive items for the Sunrise Acres homeowners were announced first. All the numbered ticket halves were in a coffee can, and Erica drew one and then another for Will O'Cain or Dr. O'Malley to announce. Enough prizes were there for every homeowner to win something if they had brought a prospective buyer. Henry and Bertha Moore, as well as Peaches, won a small black-and-white TV. Donald and Bessie Mae won a super-size industrial floor mat, while Allen and Celestine won a kitchen carving set and a painting. One of Allen and Celestine's guests won a color TV. The process took thirty minutes, generating much enthusiasm.

When it ended, Brick and Marsh said good-bye to their families. That's when Bertha Moore said to Mrs. Colleen, "I know you must be proud of your Marsh. He always speaks to me anywhere he sees me. I believe a man always gets good manners from his mother. I know you must be grateful."

"Oh, I am," replied Mrs. Colleen with a startled smile, "and you are—?"

"Bertha Moore," replied Bertha. "This is my husband, Henry. We and my sister and her husband were the first home buyers."

"Well, I thank you for saying nice things about my son," noted Mrs. Colleen as she began to depart with her family. "And I hope you'll always be happy here."

I was still thinking about the passive Bertha's eager remarks to Mrs. Colleen, when Brick and Marsh offered to help take the color TV to Allen's guest's car. Sue Anne and Marina also delivered prizes. They transported Bertha and Henry's small TV along with Celestine's wall picture, then helped her hang it.

Erica and other children then began wandering around the back forty. When Peaches and Earl discovered that Erica was missing, they left to look for her.

Brick, holding the TV for Allen's guest, looked over at Marsh before asking Dad, "So what about Peaches' sink, Deacon? Did the plumber not nail the sink-hangers into the wall studs?"

"Didn't miss no wall stud," Allen dryly put in. "The stud, Earl, is the one who kept breaking the sink off the wall. You see, he was screwing Peaches while she sat on the sink. They couldn't do it in the bedroom because Erica kept coming in and interrupting. But the child would never bother them in a locked bathroom."

Immediately Brick and Marsh laughed so hard that Brick nearly dropped the TV he was balancing on his car's door.

"That mystery's solved!" exclaimed Marsh, as Brick repositioned the TV.

Then there was a scream and someone shouted, "Snake!" from the back forty. The voice sounded like Erica's. Several adult voices also shouted, "Snake!"

"Better go shoot another snake, Brick!" Marsh exclaimed.

"Can't," answered Brick. "I'll drop this TV. Get my gun, and you do it. Don't worry if you miss the first shot because I fully loaded it for snakes after shooting those three together last week. Mack's grading work has put them on the move again."

Marsh retrieved the pistol. I followed along with Ollie, who had been picking up scattered barbeque trash.

When we got to the drainage swale where Erica, Peaches, Earl, and others were standing, Earl pointed toward the snake. A nice, big, juicy cottonmouth was all coiled up, making mini-strikes at any movement.

Marsh advanced to within four or five feet of the snake and fired. A bug-eyed Ollie said, "You blew his head off clean as if it 'a been chopped with a bush axe! I reckon you coulda killed three snakes with three straight shots like Mr. Brick did the other day."

"You MacKoy boys musta had good Army training," said Earl, staring at the headless snake. "Marsh, I sure don't want you shooting at me anymore than Brick."

"Yeah, it was that military training, I suppose," said Marsh with a wink as he looked at Dad. "Deacon, let's give Brick a hand now before he drops that color TV in the street."

Upon securing the TV in the guest's auto, the cousins left to find Sue Anne and

Marina in Allen's kitchen. Marina had already helped Celestine pick out a spot to hang her picture, and she was now sketching gazebo styles for Bessie Mae, who had expressed an interest in them again.

"You know," said Bessie Mae, looking over the different sketches, "when we was talking about gazebos that day we met last fall, I thought they all looked like the one over at Fayetteville State. Can you draw me up one like that?"

"When I get spare time, I will, and it will look more professional than these sketches," answered Marina. "It'll be a gift from me to you. If you and Donald help Deacon keep on selling houses with your referrals, maybe Brick and Marsh will start another project that'll give me some new work to do."

With this, Brick reminded Marsh of the scheduled Pineland Springs dinner meeting that night with Brewer and Nicole Melvin, and they left.

v

The balance of this weekend's events came to me by Brick the next week, as well as by Donald's cousin Thomas, the PSR Club's bartender.

Marsh and Sue Anne rarely spent weekends at the PSR Club because Austin and Diane stayed there when Mr. Malcolm and Mrs. Colleen didn't. This weekend, however, produced conflicting schedules. So Marsh and Sue Anne were able to go. At the same time, Nicole Melvin went this weekend to spruce up her father's bungalow for his scheduled return home later in June.

The cousins arrived at the PSR Club for dinner with Brewer and Nicole. Sunday was to be a men's golf day while the women were to lounge by the General's pool and prepare a cold-cut-style lunch. On Monday Nicole would finish any remaining house-cleaning chores.

As Donald's cousin Thomas served drinks, they spoke of Nicole's father's return from Vietnam before the conversation moved to Dutch Lazlo's incarceration, and his not being able to arrange bail. All agreed that Lonah Slueter would never find another sugar daddy like the Dutchman.

Brick said Stan Cannon had called, saying he had read that Dutch's bust was the biggest to date in the U.S. Brewer noted, "PSR Club gossip says Dutch's lingerie business was losing money, but his family was prepared to back him more. His fast-buck scheme depresses me. Let's change the subject. How did today's Sunrise Acres promotional go?"

"A great turnout," answered Brick, "and Marsh killed a snake!"

"Like when we were kids at Sampsons Landing?" asked Brewer.

"No, better," said Marsh, "even though I wasn't going around singing Little Richard's 'I'm Ready-Ready-Teddy to Rock and Roll' like naked Brick. No, I just walked up, raised Brick's old forty-five, and shot. The full load of scatter-shot hit that snake's head perfectly. I must have looked like John Wayne because nobody knows about the scatter-shot trick except for Brick and me."

"Yeah," laughed Brick, "and I see no use in telling our little macho secret. It just may keep any hotheads at bay that might want to get an attitude around us someday. I said nothing about the ammunition to Bobby Jack, Ollie, or that Earl friend of Peaches, who was standing around when I shot three snakes last week. Nobody could have hit any of them on the first pistol shot with single lead balls or the hollow points I used, except Wild Bill Hickok.

"It's like Carbine Williams said at a cabin bird hunt once about shooting snakes. My first shot with scatter-shot set the whole thing up because the three snakes were so close together. The spray of the pellets made the snakes strike at anything whizzing near their heads. The hollow point fragments found their marks because the snakes struck at them. If they hadn't been striking at the fragment spray, I'd still be standing there trying to shoot them today.

"Girls, Carbine was the famous gun designer from Godwin, near the Sampson-Cumberland County line. His floating chamber made the WWII M-1 carbine an automatic rifle. He invented it in prison serving time for a deputy sheriff's death during a liquor still raid. He made the snake shot loads for me."

Marsh then revealed the answer to Peaches' falling sink mystery. Hearing the laughter, the cousins' Aunt Dot came up along with Mr. and Mrs. Holden Rollins. Their aunt inquired about the promotion, and the cousins related their satisfaction before she and the Rollinses left.

VI

Sunday morning Brick and Marsh met at the club at 9:00 a.m. with the idea of finishing golf by 1:30 p.m. for lunch with the girls, but by 9:30 Brewer had not shown. Finally, at 10:00, Brewer arrived on the General's cart, but without clubs.

"Something's happened to the General. His company sent two men to Sampsons Landing. When my farm help told them we were here, they called from my office. The details are unclear but don't sound good. You two play. I need to get back to Nicole. She's upset, as you can imagine."

"No!" Marsh said. "We'll get there as soon as we can rouse our women."

Marsh picked up Sue Anne and went immediately to Eisner's while Brick drove to his parents' home in town to fetch Marina. Brick told his mom and dad about Eisner and woke Marina. When the couple got to the General's home, a concerned but composed Nicole met them.

No additional news had come, but the first report said the General had been in a helicopter flying over an area near the borders of Laos, Cambodia, and Vietnam. Although nothing had been confirmed, the fact that the chopper had been missing for over twenty-four hours had prompted the General's civilian employer to notify Nicole.

At 1:30 p.m., Aunt Dot and Brick's mother arrived with chicken salad, deviled eggs, sliced tomatoes, apple cider vinegar–soaked cucumbers, and iced tea. Aunt Dot said she knew no one had the energy to prepare lunch under such circumstances.

Brick's mother added, "I wish that Wesley could be here for you, Nicole. Your dad is so fond of him, as I know you've been since Wesley conducted your wedding service."

Nicole replied, "Yes, it seems like it's time for Wesley's tour to end. When's he due home?"

"Next month was his due date," replied Mrs. Loraine, "but he's taking an extended tour. Something about an orphanage he's become attached to. Wesley has a soft spot for that type of thing, being an orphan himself.

"Wesley's written that he's seen your father several times recently. Perhaps I can give Wes a call to see if he can find out more. If we call tonight around 9:00 p.m., it'll be 8:00 a.m. in Vietnam. I can at least leave word if I can't talk to him."

Somberly, the group filled their lunch plates and gathered around the TV to watch Stan Cannon place third. Brewer then said he had to return to his animal-feeding operations.

"A good idea, Brewer," Mrs. Dot chimed in, "and for Brick and Marsh to be getting along too. It'll be late tonight before Loraine contacts Wesley, if we're lucky. He won't be able to tell us anything more until he's had time to check things out."

Then all left except for Mrs. Loraine and Mrs. Dot. That night when Wesley was contacted, he said he'd seen the General the previous weekend when he had taken him to the orphanage his outreach ministry was working with. He had picked the General up at his encampment and would begin his inquiry there.

VII

The next morning Brick's mother called the construction-office phone to say that Wesley had contacted Eisner's colleagues.

Radio traffic informed them that his chopper had been hit by ground fire in the border area of Laos, Cambodia, and Vietnam. The dense foliage made locating the chopper difficult, and the three-border location complicated rescue protocols. Still, U.S. Special

Forces units had been sent into a South Vietnamese village believed to be near the chopper's last radio communiqué, and they assured Wesley of full notification.

Why a civilian munitions consultant had been on such a helicopter flight remained unclear, but authorities said that it was not uncommon for munitions company personnel to occasionally liaison with combat troops.

Later that week, while I was discussing my part-time position at Junebug's office, Brick told Junebug and me that Wesley had phoned again. The search-and-rescue group had run into Viet Cong encamped near the crash site and had suffered casualties. In addition, the rescue units had traveled far enough to believe that the enemy encampment and any crash-site debris were most likely located outside of South Vietnam in neighboring Cambodia or Laos. A forceful effort, with coordinated air strikes or artillery bombardment upon multi-country enemy positions would require authorization from higher up the command chain. In addition, President Nixon's Vietnamization Plan to reduce U.S. troop levels by turning over more ground fighting to the South Vietnamese had left few U.S. combat forces still present in 1972. These complexities complicated a swift rescue.

Brick paused for a moment. On another note, Wesley had admitted that his interest in the orphanage had become not totally religious in nature. He had met a woman there whom he loved. Junebug smiled.

The previous weekend, Wesley had taken Eisner to the orphanage to introduce him to the woman, Lee Çu Nadeau. Her father had been a French medical missionary and her mother a Vietnamese nurse who had worked in local hospitals. After the French defeat, Lee Çu's parents had sent her to France in the summer of 1958 for her education, as there was much political uncertainty in Vietnam. In 1961, her parents were killed when the Viet Cong raided their village at the beginning of the Kennedy era before the U.S. build-up.

Lee Çu returned to Vietnam as a nurse after the Kennedy assassination. Wesley said they were both taken with each other immediately because the orphanage director had introduced them as orphans. The last thing Wesley told Eisner was that this was the first great emotional connection he had felt for another person, beyond strong friendships, since the death of his parents, and that his feelings for her were growing daily.

Wesley said he and Lee Çu expected to marry soon before U.S. combat forces were to be withdrawn, leaving only supply troops to aid the South Vietnamese. After the marriage, his schedule would allow the couple to safely remain in Vietnam long enough to determine Eisner's fate before returning home. He said a rain front was expected any day, and that would further frustrate attempts to pinpoint the General's debris field. Wesley concluded, "We'll have to wait to learn about Eisner, but it seems that his death is a foregone conclusion to U.S. personnel there."

Chapter Eleven

Triple Nickels Stop Trouble, a Baffling
Airplane Mystery, and Poker Turmoil

I

NEAR A FRIDAY NOON IN MID-JUNE OF 1972, Marsh was away making bull-breeding arrangements with Brewer's friend near Fayetteville. Mr. Malcolm was in Pineland Springs. I had finished typing the back-forty promotion applications and was explaining the paper trail to Junebug and Brick to reassure both of my ability to do law-office work.

My two employers were expecting to leave for lunch with Austin and Hutton, due to arrive anytime since Hutton wanted to check on construction progress while his wife visited Diane.

The day's clear weather benefitted the utility installers, whose work needed to be completed before back-forty road grading could start. On this day the water, electrical, phone, and natural-gas crews were all bunched up where the road turned.

Junebug and I remained on the office stoop as Dad and Brick walked to Brick's car parked near the two houses where all the crews were. Riley Carlisle, Mingo, Hogbear, and Bobby Jack Johnson were inspecting window frames needing to be re-leveled before Riley could paint. Bobby Jack was fuming about Riley's criticisms of his framing crew.

The several crews at these two houses had turned their radios to the same station in a stereophonic vibration of rock and roll for those workers sandwiched between the two houses.

The local noon weather report commented that from Wilmington to Raleigh, it was ninety-nine degrees. In the Fayetteville/Sandhills area, it was over a hundred. Locals knew that the Sandhills both absorbed and reflected the sun's rays to make our area the state's warmest, summer and winter. When the announcer said that Fort Bragg outdoor training had been suspended due to heat, we knew the temperature was officially steaming.

Before the music resumed, Dad and Brick leaned against Brick's car, wiping their brows. I continued talking with Junebug and occasionally glancing down the long, black-topped street to see if Austin's car was coming. The heat rising off the black asphalt was so intense that watery mirages appeared above the street.

When Austin's car entered the subdivision, the synchronized radios began the hard-driving beat of Mitch Ryder and the Detroit Wheels' "Devil with the Blue Dress On." Simultaneously, I saw a man between Austin's car and us running out of a house, down the driveway, and through the asphalt street mirages in our direction. He appeared to have a broom. I didn't think about it due to the mirages. The runner dipped out of sight into the valley created by the stream running through the infamous culvert. But when he came up the hill, unobscured, there was no mistaking that Peaches' Earl was running with a long gun!

Then others noticed him. Earl, looking unperturbed, ran toward the area between the two houses. He looked as if he was only hurrying into the nearby woods to check on a rabbit-box trap. Then he stopped dead in one motion and hollered at Mingo, who was following Bobby Jack to the next house.

When Earl aimed the gun at Mingo, Bobby Jack and all the other workers scattered like chickens from a snake. As the dust settled, only Earl and Mingo stood facing each other while the radio music roared on. Austin and Hutton gawked at the unfolding calamity as their car eased up. Riley Carlisle, with his head stuck out a window and his jaw hanging open, looked like a man awaiting the guillotine. Falling backwards, Bobby Jack began blindly groping about his clothing for his Saturday-night pocket pistol.

"Mingo Montana," snarled Earl, "you Jody-son-of-a-bitch, you leave my woman alone!"

"I ain't been messing with your woman!" blared Mingo, stumbling backward against a pallet of bricks.

"Bullshit! I keep seeing them MT-initialed tools laying 'round her place," roared back Earl as he lowered the double-barreled shotgun toward Mingo's waistline. "You been doing more than just going down there a'fixin up Peaches' sink. You been makin' it fall off the wall, too!"

"The hell I have!" shouted Mingo, the white of his eyes ablaze in fear.

Suddenly there was a gunshot, and my father bellowed, "Drop it, Earl, or you'll be seeing Jesus right now, no matter what happens to Mingo!"

Dad, unseen by anyone, had taken Brick's .45 from the front seat of his car and fired into the air. Earl's back was to Brick's car, so he couldn't see who had fired. Brick, like the rest of us, had been so focused on the scene that he also didn't realize what Dad had done until afterward. But after Dad's shot, Brick stepped quickly between Dad, Earl, and Mingo.

As Brick closed on Earl, with Dad following, the crunch of their shoes on clay and gravel alerted Earl to someone coming up on his back. Mingo's eyes darted in the direction of Brick's approach. The others, staring and dumbstruck, seemed ready to flee from some even greater looming danger.

That's when Earl's rage melted, and he asked Mingo, "Is that the one shot them three snakes?"

Mingo, with his hands still up in the air, nodded, "Brick's right behind you now."

"It ain't loaded," Earl said, his voice trembling. "I just want Mingo to stay in his place."

"O.K.," said Brick, stepping up behind Earl. "It'll be O.K. Just hand your shotgun back to me. Easy does it and nothing will happen to anybody."

Earl held the shotgun out to his side for Brick to take and disassemble. Everyone sighed with relief through the beat of the reverberating music.

"All right, Earl," Brick said, "I'll drive you home on my way to lunch. And Junebug! You can ride with Austin and Vann, while I take Earl to Peaches' house."

II

All left for lunch. By twelve-thirty the gossip in every Wisdom Station restaurant was that there had nearly been a killing at Sunrise Acres. In small communities, news travels fast and bad news even faster. Brick talked with Dad about this point after lunch. He said that Austin and Junebug expressed concern about Brick and Marsh's safety in a working environment where such things could happen. Vann Hutton also noted that Dad's apartment complex bankruptcy resulted from unsavory public visitors just appearing on the project like Earl had.

Brick told them, "Look, we can't control the public, but if we sense danger, we try to keep those people at a distance. You take Chalky; he's the very one who gave Deacon the sales lead on Henry and Bertha Moore, and also Allen and Celestine. Deacon pays Chalky for sales leads, but it's been necessary to tell the albino to stay away from Sunrise. Why?

"Because Bertha Moore, who wouldn't harm a fly, has said she'd kill Chalky because she's under some impression that he's responsible for her son's death that took place in a prison that Chalky's never been in! While that's just the threat of this befuddled woman's thinking, we've asked Deacon to deal with the albino elsewhere as a precaution. Of course, you can never cover all the bases since anyone is free to travel our public streets.

"I just hope this incident doesn't hurt the chances for Sunrise Acres to attract future sales. That concerns me most."

"You can't control gossip," grunted Austin. "What can you do about that?"

"I'll get Carley Ray, all dressed up in his deputy's uniform, to tell Earl what could legally happen to him if anyone were to file a complaint against him for endangering the public safety. I hope he'll move on when he considers the unpleasant legal possibilities."

After Brick finished relating these concerns, Dad mused, "While you're hunting Carley Ray, I'll see about getting Celestine to have Peaches get rid of Earl. If we can't skin a snake one way with Carley Ray, we'll do it another."

At sunset, Brick and Carley Ray arrived at Peaches' house. To Brick's surprise, most of the Earl Problem was about to vanish without Carley Ray having to say much.

While Brick had been finding and apprising Carley Ray about Earl, Dad had seen Celestine. Not only did Dad get Celestine to persuade Peaches that Earl's departure would be better for Earl, but Dad raised the ire of two old Triple-Nickel Buffalo Soldiers enough to confront Earl.

You see, Mrs. Penny, Earl became friends with Allen and Henry because of Peaches' relationship with Celestine and Bertha. In this way Earl had learned about Allen and Henry's 555th Black Airborne Battalion or Triple Nickel Army duty. This group had expected to see combat in Europe beside white soldiers, but they were sent on a secret mission to fight forest fires in Oregon started by Japanese balloon bombs.

The Japs had figured out how to get bomb-rigged balloons to follow the jet stream to the U.S. West Coast. Most fell into forests, starting large forest fires, but one plowed into a power line supplying the Hanford, Washington, nuclear facility that was furnishing material for the future Nagasaki bomb. These balloon bombs also killed six people, and Allen and Henry were a part of that fire-fighting effort.

The old Triple Nickels were dissolved by President Truman's 1948 desegregation order of the armed services, and Allen and Henry were assigned to the 505th Airborne Infantry Regiment, attached to Fort Bragg's 82nd Airborne Division. However, when Korea heated up, the 2nd Ranger Infantry Company was activated as an elite, all-black airborne unit at Fort Benning, and volunteers from Bragg's 505th and other airborne units were accepted. Allen and Henry made the cut because they were sharp and striking, or in Army talk, "strack" troopers.

This unit saw immediate Korean action defending a medical station being attacked by Communist guerrilla fighters. When the battle was over, all looked at the Communist dead, and the old battle cry of "Buffalo, Buffalo" started swelling from a low, African-like moaning into a loud cry. That was the old battle cry of the Indian-fighting, black Buffalo Soldiers of the Old West who had chased the Apache, the Comanche, and others.

After this encounter, the 2nd Rangers became the only all-black airborne unit to jump behind enemy lines. That was at Munsan-ni, Korea, in 1951. Allen received his disabling head wound there, but he recovered enough to stay on active duty until 1967, when he and Henry retired. Earl loved these stories, and once Allen and Henry even took him to a Triple Nickel Reunion at Fort Bragg. So Earl had a great respect for Allen and Henry, and Dad knew it.

According to Dad, Peaches had told Earl he was no longer welcome at her house. And Allen, with Henry looking on, was in the middle of lecturing Earl when Brick and Carley Ray came up under Peaches' carport.

"Earl, let me tell you," Allen admonished, "me and Henry have jumped out of airplanes into burning forest fires and taken all kinds of enemy gunfire. We ain't got nothing to prove to you or any man, white or black, about anything. If you leave us alone, we'll leave you alone. But if you hurt our friend Peaches or our community's reputation, you've not left us alone.

"We don't want our neighborhood's reputation hurt by stunts like you did that threaten the safety of our children or the value of our property. So you've meddled in our concerns, whether you realize it or not. And now it's time for you to go someplace else like Mingo's brother Juan who we all know about. If you don't, I'll get a lawyer, and run you off myself, if Will O'Cain down at the Farm Home office don't do it first. I can do that, can't I, Deputy?"

"Any man has a right to hire a lawyer, and you'd have good reason," answered Carley Ray. "I'd really hate to face Will O'Cain and some federal government attorney he'd get to indict me over something like they say you've done, Earl. I mean, maybe the FBI and everything, because these are federal-guaranteed loans."

"They're right, Earl," said Henry Moore, looking dead straight at Earl like some disgusted football coach, not moving a muscle. "If you don't move on like Mingo's brother Juan had to several years ago, we're going to come after you with the law."

"If you move on like Juan," added Carley Ray, "nobody's going to press after you because our county is too poor to go fetch you from another jurisdiction. Lord, we can't even afford a rescue squad. So, it'll be cheaper for us to let your kind be somebody else's problem. You don't have to go to Montana, but I'd leave now, if I were you."

"This is bullshit, just pure-damn bullshit!" grimaced Earl. "But I ain't staying where I ain't welcomed, and I ain't going to fight two old Triple Nickels I respect more than myself. You two done showed me too much about—well, that don't matter much after what's happened…."

Earl was nowhere to be seen the next morning or ever again. Later, Celestine said she'd heard he was over around Greensboro.

For the rest of the month nothing happened as stimulating as that gunplay, and the cousins were quiet, too. Even Stan Cannon's high U.S. Open finish that qualified him for another Masters elicited oddly restrained joy. At Sunrise Acres, cousin Mingo's motorcycle was often parked at Peaches' house on weekends, but not a word about it. Mingo and Peaches remained close through that summer, but they faded to a relationship of nods, waves, and kindly conversation, which has lasted to this day even after each married others. In spite of their initial attraction to each other, Celestine always said the two were just too different to live together on a day-in and day-out basis, without imposing on the distinctness of the other's free soul.

III

On Friday before the Tuesday Fourth of July of 1972, Brick and Marina left for Junebug's family cottage at Duck, North Carolina. Their early departure allowed for stops at Mattamuskeet and the Lost Colony site. Contrary to the original plans, Brick and Marina arrived a day before the Willinghams due to Junebug's belated involvement in a court matter.

Brick's plans suited Marsh, as Sue Anne was to judge a July Fourth bathing-suit contest at Ocean Drive. Thus Marsh was around for the Friday work schedule, while Brick returned to be on hand for the Wednesday, July fifth, that Marsh took off.

After their Mattamuskeet and Lost Colony visits, the couple met Langdon Butler at his new Nags Head quarters and went to a nearby nightclub. They agreed to meet back at the club on Monday afternoon, when the dance floor would be in full swing.

The couple then drove to Duck, where they found Willingham's cottage surrounded by sand dunes just beyond the end of the state paved road.

Brick never was the kiss-and-tell sort, and I didn't find out all that happened that weekend until years later. But by way of Junebug and Marsh, I did learn of an amusing incident that stuck with me over the years until I learned the truth and consequences of all that took place.

According to Junebug, he and Kay left Wisdom Station's private airport Saturday morning with Martha Sarah. For the infant's first flight, June chose to fly low to eliminate the air pressure in her eardrums.

June's routine was to fly into the Kitty Hawk airport beside the Wright Brothers First Flight memorial, where he kept an old Jeep parked. He had acquired the Jeep in exchange for legal work before I ever worked for the Willinghams. It allowed him the luxury of an Outer Banks vehicle. This transportation was an open-top rust bucket with wood bench seats that could survive a rain. Other Outer Banks cottage owners had similar transportation back then.

To announce his family's arrival, Junebug flew over the cottage before landing at the airport. To do this, he had to fly in on a tight northwest tangent to avoid entering the protected air space of nearby Coast Guard property. This required a long turn to the south over the Atlantic, preventing a quick return flight back over the house. On his first pass June said that he thought he saw two naked bodies lying on his sundeck. As he flew away from the house, the back of the small plane's cabin blocked the view of his isolated, easily identified property. By the time he made a long turn over the ocean for a return fly-by, there was only one body, Brick's. Wrapped in a beach towel, he waved up at them. When the Willinghams arrived to find their guests attired in skin-tone bathing suits, Junebug smirked before saying, "Caught you, didn't we?"

Looking at Marina, Brick said, "It's just her faded, yellow string bikini and my khaki trunks. Is the sun playing tricks on your eyes, my host?"

"So that's your story?" Junebug laughed.

"It should stand up in court. My word and the glare of the sun against yours; that's probable truth, Counselor," Brick parried.

Kay later told me that she thought it wise to end this mocking legalistic conversation. "What have you two been able to see so far?"

Brick then recounted their stops at Mattamuskeet, the Lost Colony, and the couple's conversation about the similarity between the failures of these two human endeavors. He concluded, "In fact, the waterfowl calls that so haunted Rachel Carson during her Mattamuskeet stay seemed to Marina and me to be like a message from nature mocking mankind's one-dimensional efforts to be the master of his destiny and soul.

"And then—the Lost Colony. When you're there, you can see how a few rows of corn or field peas might have made it possible for Sir Walter Raleigh's colonists to remain around their Roanoke Island compound. Yet, they vanished into the vast unknown of Carolina's mainland and thus into the long history of failed human endeavors. Little things make the difference between success and failure, and a good row of field peas might have eliminated failure."

"Yes," Junebug commented, "the colonists and the failed Mattamuskeet farmers were like the British poet Henley we studied at Coosa. When Henley faced the amputation of his diseased foot, he had no image of hope except the transcending thoughts expressed in that poem written in his hospital bed. If he couldn't be the master of his fate, he could at least be the captain of his soul in the midst of his despair. His work on that poem restored his courage to face the future.

"The same is true of those Lost Colonists as they moved into the woods to forage for food like Stone-Age hunter-gatherers. All they could control was their own spiritual outlook to guide them not to be savages. Nothing else in the world must have had any clarity or logic about it for them. Their only possession was their human hope—courage, really—that they would be able to meet the surprises of tomorrow and survive, somehow.

"A similar fate of failure might await you and Marsh if you are forced to face any more surprises like Earl trying to gun-scare Mingo. That next gunman may be loaded for bear, not scare, and the reputation for safety you need for Sunrise Acres to maintain good sales—along with all your hopes—would vanish."

With the review of the previous day's travels ended, nothing more was said of the flyover surprise. But as I say, Mrs. Penny, I always remembered this story and wondered what had been omitted.

Martha Sarah occupied the women's attention while Junebug and Brick surf-fished on the isolated beach and crabbed in the Sound. Their catches provided the bulk of dinner for the two evenings they were together, other than sweet corn and a few other items from the local general store.

Each evening, Brick and Marina walked the beach, while Kay fed Martha Sarah and lay her down for the evening. Their late-evening dinners gave way to ten o'clock bed-times. The sound of the waves came through the screens of the open-windowed cottage, producing a hypnotic rhythm of deep sleep even for Martha Sarah. The babe slept through both nights from 8:00 p.m. till 6:00 a.m., when her first bottle of the day sent her back into dreamland.

IV

On Monday, July third, Brick and Marina departed for the Boulevard Beach Cove Club, where they had left Langdon on Friday.

Flanked by two women, Langdon called to them from a back corner. Becky Rollins and Wendy Granger had arrived that day with Fayetteville friends of Langdon's.

Greeting them, Brick remembered Langdon's interest in Wendy at the previous fall's post-football game fraternity party. Langdon seemed happy that his first encounter with Wendy was running smoothly. Becky mentioned that she would soon be leaving for France.

"Yes, Brick," Wendy remarked, "life is splitting us up. Becky's off to France, and you'll be amused to know that I'll be working in your neck of the woods with Dr. Chester O'Malley as a home-extension specialist with the community college. I'm hoping the job will allow me to start on my master's after Christmas."

"Interesting," Brick replied. "Our Sunrise Acres homeowners would no doubt like all the free homemaking tips you can offer. Please visit."

Like Brick, Marina, and Langdon, many of the bar's patrons were dressed in Bermuda shorts, while others wore bathing suits with cover-ups. Becky and Wendy were of the latter group and shod in string sandals.

Soon happy hour blossomed with young adults dancing inside or out on a lattice-enclosed wood-floor patio. Although he was new to this seaside community, Langdon was in his element, conversing with everyone. A gregarious guy, no one was ever a stranger to him.

When Otis Redding's 1968 hit "Sitting on the Dock of the Bay" ended, and the more danceable "Thank You, John," by Willie Tee, came on, Langdon eased onto the dance floor with Wendy. Part way through the Willie Tee tune, Brick asked Becky to dance and continued to dance with her through a second danceable tune by Tyrone Davis, "Can I Change My Mind?" Brick and Becky matched their toe-to-toe steps to the rhythm. At each turn, the slit in Becky's bathing suit cover-up exposed the full side of her left leg up to her hip without any sign of her high-cut swimsuit.

While I had only met Becky once, I could imagine that her striking long legs and flowing blond hair, along with her perfectly executed dance steps, could enhance one's impression of her dancing without panties. During this time Marina sat alone, and Brick later said it occurred to him that Marina was making an effort not to appear miffed. For the balance of the evening, Marina continued to make small talk with both Becky and Wendy because Langdon's persona encouraged everyone's engagement.

One conversation that Marina took special note of was Becky's adventure with Brick, Marsh, and Diane in Myrtle Beach the summer of 1955 after Hurricane Hazel, when Becky was six. It was the week that Mr. Malcolm and Mr. Lee were selling Becky's dad on becoming a PSR Club partner.

The debutante, Diane, would drive Marsh and Brick every afternoon to an arcade recently constructed after Hurricane Hazel's destruction. Becky was eager to see it, too. To be invited along, Becky played up a baby-sister relationship with Diane, and thus Diane took Becky along on the Friday-afternoon arcade run, much to Brick and Marsh's dismay. Becky had an uneasy feeling that she had overstepped her welcome as they rode along, looking in amazement at all the houses still left in the canals from the hurricane damage of the previous fall.

When they played the arcade's miniature bowling machines, Becky recalled, "I did everything wrong. Finally, Brick and Diane showed me how to play. By then we only had enough money left to play one last game. So Diane said that she and Marsh would play Brick and me for the prize of bragging rights, as we were penniless. At the end, I made two strikes in a row, and felt like superwoman because Brick had stuck with me like a good sport.

"Going back to our hotel, we had to stop at the red light by the old hurricane-damaged arcade. Back in those days cars had no air conditioners. So, all the windows were rolled down in the summer's heat. There, a group of muscle-bound, football-player types were making cat-calls at all the girls driving by. When two of them saw the radiant debutante, Diane, they made a heavy pass. They boldly stuck their heads through our rolled-down car windows and started with their 'come-on-baby' sweet-talk. Marsh squirted them both in the eyes with his water pistol! Fortunately, the traffic light changed then, and Diane sped away. It was like committing the perfect crime: robbing a bank and getting away, clean as a whistle! It was thrilling for a tot like me, and I don't think I've ever had as much fun since."

After Becky's tale, Langdon danced with Wendy several more times. However, Brick did not dance again with Becky, who attracted two stray dance partners. The club's crowd remained thick until midnight closing. Afterward the group stopped by an all-night breakfast joint. From there, Wendy and Becky departed with Fayetteville friends, while Brick and Marina spent the night at Langdon's.

The next day Brick and Marina drove south to Ocracoke Island by way of the Hatteras-Ocracoke Ferry. Brick told Marsh that neither a stop by the Cape Hatteras Lighthouse nor the Hatteras-Ocracoke ferry ride budged Marina from her silence. Finally when they stopped at the Ocracoke Lighthouse, he asked her, "Marina, what's the matter?"

"You know very well what's wrong!" she snapped. "Leaving me alone to dance with Becky made me feel foolish. I know it's emotionally childish, and that I shouldn't expect you not to dance with someone who knows how to dance like you do, but I can't help it. Besides, she's a pretty girl, with a tot's crush on you, long legs and all. So why shouldn't that give me the right to be a little jealous after our weekend together? Abandoning me without warning was cruddy, and you know it."

"Marina," Brick pleaded, "Becky's a beautiful girl and a fabulous dancer, but she's a college kid going to France for a year or two. Her circumstances can't make you paranoid."

"I understand that," Marina countered, "but it was crappy to leave me alone without even asking me if you could dance with her. If you had asked, I would have felt better. I still would not have liked it, but I would have felt less discarded."

"I'm sorry," Brick said. "It won't happen again, I promise. It's our last day here and just the two of us again. Let's enjoy it before we go back to our real working world."

Brick pulled her close to him, looked into her eyes, and smiled, while he shook his head at her in amusement. She smiled back, and an ocean breeze blew her hair as he kissed her.

From here they stopped for a bowl of clam chowder before touring the British cemetery, where four Royal Navy sailors are interred after being torpedoed just off the island during World War II. Before returning to the mainland by way of the Cedar Island Ferry, they toured several novelty shops overlooking the harbor, where local legends say that Blackbeard the pirate was killed in 1718.

V

My first knowledge of this weekend occurred as Marsh bounced into the Sunrise Acres office with paperwork from Junebug and reported on June's flyover of the two naked bodies. Brick, of course, denied Junebug's version, but personally related the rest, including his dancing with Becky Rollins. Brick did admit to Marsh and me that he had been inconsiderate of Marina's feelings: "I wish Marina would make more effort to learn the beach boogie because I've always felt that the music's rhythm teaches your feet how to dance. The free-styling moves are basic forward and back steps. The man does all the work and the woman just has to look good, which Marina has down pat. But Mademoiselle Rollins did cut some kind of a sharp-looking figure on the dance floor with her two stray-dog Fayetteville friends. I can surely see how her beauty would be intimidating to another woman, no matter the other woman's own radiance."

"You cradle-robbing devil-dog!" laughed Marsh, slapping Brick's back.

"Changing the subject, Marsh," Brick said, clearing his throat, "did you or Sue Anne hear anything on Dutch during the holidays? Becky said that the word around Fayetteville is that he is now giving cooperative testimony to authorities. So the prosecutor's office has allowed him out of jail under a steep bond. She said he's secluded with his family and attorneys."

"Lonah said the same thing at Ocean Drive," Marsh replied. "But she says her Dutch information is now second-hand because she no longer has Lazlo family ties. She says she'll probably never see the Dutchman again."

"There's always been a social divide there," said Brick.

"True, but what a fine-looking floozy Lonah is now, no matter how fat she gets in the future, according to Monroe's theories on older women," nodded Marsh with an off-yonder gaze. Brick shook his head as he smiled at Marsh and then at me.

VI

For the balance of that summer Brick continued managing Sunrise Acres while Marsh came as needed for closings. Marsh concentrated on his cattle-breeding program with

Brewer's friend who owned several bulls. The man lived south of Fayetteville between Sampsons Landing and Pineland Springs, which allowed Brewer and Marsh to see one another occasionally. During this period, the one thing I do recall is that Nicole Melvin was finally notified that her father was now "presumed dead."

Thus Nicole, with the help of Mrs. Loraine and Mrs. Rollins, arranged for a memorial service to be held in mid-August. The two cousins, their parents, and Sue Anne attended the service held at the Pineland Springs Resort Club. Most of the club's shareholding partners attended on a Friday evening.

Brick's mother, in weekly contact with her chaplain-nephew, Wesley, asked that he send a letter with appropriate remarks for the occasion. Holden Rollins, who had always been closer to the General than anyone, read Wesley's remarks.

Wesley's letter cited the General's love of military and diplomatic history dating back to Greek and Roman times. He also credited the General for being a community leader, as well as his personal mentor, then compared him to the philosopher Aristotle and the fictional mentor Abbé Faria, of *The Count of Monte Cristo*, by Alexander Dumas.

When Mr. Rollins finished reading Wesley's remarks, he said, "Nicole, I am honored to have had a part in memorializing your father and our friend. When I think of the General's love of that Shaker hymn, 'Simple Gifts,' I can only imagine Aaron Copland directing the combined London and New York Philharmonic Orchestras with the Mormon Tabernacle Choir providing the vocals as your mother watches him ascend towards Gabriel. Obviously, none of us can arrange that, but I would like to think that God has."

The attendees received MIA bracelets with the General's name inscribed before moving to the club's bar for a cocktail party featuring the General's favorite libations of vodka martinis and rye sazeracs. There Nicole raised her sazerac and addressed the group: "The wearing of these bracelets means that Dad will always be in the hearts of those who loved and admired him until his bones return for the final closure—being placed beside my mother's."

Among the gathering was Becky Rollins, who said this was her last weekend home before departing for France. She remained with Brick, Marsh, and Sue Anne as the MacKoy and Rollins family members expressed their regrets to Nicole and Brewer. At the evening's end, Nicole, Marsh, and Brick gave Becky farewell hugs of good luck in her studies, but none ever mentioned this to Marina.

VII

The first Saturday of September, Brick, Marsh, Brewer, Monroe, Junebug, and Cotton Roberts all hunted on dove season's opening day at the Sampsons Landing Hunt Club, while I left for my senior year in college. The next weekend I returned home to my part-time jobs at the law office and at Sunrise Acres, where all was quiet.

What was not peaceful, however, was a poker-game surprise in which Monroe Hill, Vann Hutton, and Cy Turner were robbed on a Friday night before the Saturday football game that Brick and Marsh were to attend with their usual crowd.

Sue Anne found out about it before leaving for the Raleigh night game when Ginger called to request that Sue Anne double her tailgate order of fried chicken. Ginger said she had not cooked because she had to take clothes to Monroe and others in Johnston County since they'd been robbed in a poker game there and left naked. When Sue Anne and Marsh arrived at the stadium parking lot, Brewer, Nicole, Langdon Butler, and Wendy Granger greeted them but Brick and Marina were glum.

"We understand that Monroe was robbed at a poker game," Marsh said.

"Yes, we all know about it," Marina lamented. "Vann was there, too, along with everybody's favorite person, Cy Turner, and Lisa is livid! She and Vann argued so badly that I took the two girls up to my garage apartment and didn't return them until Brick came."

"This fuss will pass, Marina," Brick observed. "Everybody says Vann is mostly just a spectator at these games. When Monroe arrives, we'll find out what happened."

As all went back for tailgate seconds, Monroe and Ginger arrived. Brick asked, "Monroe, did Rocky fall asleep this time, or did his Uncle Blue's walkie-talkie system malfunction?"

"No," responded Monroe, "the Johnston County game site didn't have Rocky and Uncle Blue's walkie-talkies. If we'd had that equipment, maybe the perfect crime wouldn't have happened.

"I'd heard about this Johnston County game, and Cy's having big paydays with his bag of money and his buy-the-poker-pot strategy. Well, I calculated that I could go there and have a double payday like I did that night at Blue's.

"The word at Blue's game was that Cy had fifteen to twenty thousand from his poker winnings and construction-skimming. I went with five thousand, hoping to get myself to a big winning hand. Now I feel lucky we didn't get killed!

"We started playing about seven o'clock last night. Near ten-thirty, the game got interesting when I won a big hand and was maybe four thousand ahead. We all took a break then, and that's when the door busted off the hinges, and in came four sons-of-bitches with ski masks, carrying sawed-off, double-barrel shotguns.

"They made us strip naked, and took everything we had; money, clothes, shoes, socks, drawers. They said they'd shoot us if we came out before sunup. We waited after an hour or more of silence before going outside. They had let the air out of our tires and cut car-battery cables as well as the phone and power lines to the house. We were stranded in the middle of some Johnston County woods with deer flies eating up our naked butts.

"Hutton and I found two towels and two pairs of golf shoes in his station wagon. We put that on and walked through the woods at daybreak to a farmhouse, where we saw an old colored man feeding his hogs. He let us use his phone to call Ginger. She came about nine o'clock to get us after our neighbor awoke to tend our baby. I came home, took a bath, and went to bed. As tired as I was, I could barely sleep for the itching deer-fly bites and mental images of those bastards storming in with shotguns! I still nearly piss all over myself recalling it.

"I sure hate losing over nine grand, but Cy says he lost over twenty. Hutton lost nearly as much as Cy. I was surprised about Hutton, but not Cy."

Marina's eyes grew wide at these amounts before Brick remarked, "I wonder if Cy was pulling from his construction funds for the stake like you say he always brags that he does?"

"Well, he and Hutton were having a serious conversation about how this would affect things they're working on together. They mentioned the Family Dollar Motel deal, and a potential cash-flow squeeze. Of course, I don't know enough about their business to make much sense from the snippets of conversation I overheard.

"I'm just glad I'm alive! Please give me a beer, Mr. Salt-Dog. And here's to Holliday Doc and Wild Bill Hickok. Hell, I don't know how those Wild West characters survived it all!"

Langdon handed beers to the Hills, and the conversation changed from poker robbery to October football and the state fair. But Brick announced, "I'll miss all that this year. I'm going with Marina, Lisa, and her two girls to their annual Canadian Thanksgiving."

VIII

After the game, Brick and Marina returned to Wisdom Station with Sue Anne and Marsh, and all four came to Sunrise Acres on Sunday. Marina seemed uneasy, although I did not know yet about her sister and brother-in-law's quarrel over the robbery.

Brick said he enjoyed unhurried Sunrise Acres weekends because he had the leisure time to make correction notes. Marina's architectural eye aided Brick's efforts whenever she came along.

After that day's inspection tour, I overheard Marina say to Brick: "You know, I've used up my little notepads that you've given me. Do you have any more? They're so handy."

"They are!" Sue Anne commented. "Marsh has given me a few, too."

"Sure." Brick reached in the desk drawer and handed a couple to each. About that time, Cousin Mingo and Miss Peaches walked in.

"So, where's little Erica today?" I asked Peaches.

"Erica be with her daddy today, Melody," replied Peaches. "I'm busy telling Mingo Man where I want him to build me one of them gazebos like Miss Marina sketched for Bessie Mae. But I want mine to be different somehow, so everybody knows it's mine. I saw one the other day, when I went to Fayetteville. It had a little chicken house on top. I want one like that. Can you draw me one like that, Miss Marina?"

Marina looked at Brick, then Dad, who remarked, "She asked me about that earlier. I believe she wants a cupola with a rooster weathervane on top. I think she can order one from a catalogue I've seen in Cotton Roberts' office."

"Can you draw Mingo what I want so he can go down to order it?" Peaches asked Marina.

"Do you have any white paper, Brick?" Marina asked, whereupon Brick handed her several sheets of paper and his car keys, and Marina, Sue Anne, and Peaches left for Bessie Mae's house. I went with them, but Cousin Mingo stayed with the men, talking about the Macks' paving schedule since the roadbed grading had been finished.

Bessie Mae was alone, with Donald off to a church meeting. Bessie Mae said she'd be very happy to share her gazebo sketches in exchange for our company. It was just us girls. Of course, seeing Marina work and explain as she drew made it memorable.

Chapter Twelve

A Visit for Canada's October Thanksgiving

I

MRS. PENNY, THE CANADIAN TRIP began on the Friday before Canada's Thanksgiving holiday on a Monday in October 1972. Brick, Marina, and Lisa, along with Lisa's two daughters—Alyssa, nine, and Sylvia, six—left Raleigh for New York's connecting flight to Montréal.

Lisa's girls treated their Aunt Marina like a wise older sister, necessitating a seating change, leaving Brick next to Lisa, who described what Brick could expect in Canada. "Like the U.S., Canadian Thanksgivings are family affairs, but Canadians celebrate it less. Aunt Joan will meet us at the airport and do Thanksgiving with us before beginning her Florida winter stay next weekend.

"Aunt Joan lives in Montréal but lived in Ottawa before her husband's death from a benign brain tumor. Uncle Jean Marc would probably be alive today had doctors discovered his tumor earlier. They never had children, and Marina and I loved going to their home because they would spoil us. I suppose Marina's Aunt Joan imitation compels her to sit with my girls now, and not you. But that will change when she has her own. When you lose a parent suddenly, like we did so young, you feel like an incomplete ghost of your former, more secure self. Children restore that sensation of being one with the universe. Mine did for me, anyway, and I assure Marina that hers will, too.

"Like Mother, Aunt Joan received excellent insurance and pension benefits. She sold the Ottawa home and bought a Montréal co-op to be closer to Mother. Later, she purchased a South Florida condominium on the Gulf near her Ottawa friends."

"Yes," Brick said. "Vann says he enjoyed your uncle's lumber-lobbying stories. They provided a conversational link for Vann's architectural mind."

"You'll enjoy Aunt Joan," Lisa continued, "and our corner of Québec. However, I under-stand you and Marina will also spend time in Montréal. It's the world's second-largest French city, after Paris, and sits on Montréal Island in the middle of the St. Lawrence River. This location made it a great inland seaport because oceangoing ships couldn't get by the rapids. When the St. Lawrence Seaway's system of locks was finished in 1959, ocean-going ships could navigate from the shores of Minnesota and Wisconsin to the Atlantic."

"I didn't know that," Brick commented as the plane broke through the clouds, reveal-ing the Canadian landscape. Upon arrival, the garbled French and English being spoken startled Brick. He felt intimidated by the others' ease, including Lisa's daughters, who slipped with a nonchalant grace between the two languages as if they were trying on a different pair of shoes, but were, like many women, uncertain of which to choose.

Fortunately, Marina and Lisa sensed Brick's bafflement and introduced him to their aunt, with apologies for carrying on in polyglot acrobatics. Brick shook Aunt Joan's hand, saying, "It's O.K., I'm a deaf mute; pay me no mind."

"Oh, no," Joan smiled. "You are our most special guest, and I will pay you as much attention as Marina allows. I've heard so much about you."

"I hope it's been good," Brick smiled.

"Most assuredly," Aunt Joan said as Brick realized that the beaming, nicely attired woman reminded him of his spirited Aunt Dot.

Leaving the airport, heading east, they were sometimes within sight of the St. Law-rence. Although the sky was graying, Brick could see outcroppings of small, rocky islands in the river. In other places, barges laden with timber or ocean-bound ships full of grain from America's Great Plains or western Ontario and Manitoba moved down river.

The early fall-winter colors blinded Brick, with evergreen firs mixed among shades of yellow, maroon, brown, and those silvery limbs of the already bare-naked trees patiently awaiting spring's resurrection. At dusk, they arrived at the LaGraves' house, just outside the Pointe de Beaver township.

II

Following an ascending gravel driveway, they came upon a white, cedar shake, story-and-a-half house high above the St. Lawrence. The younger Sylvia squealed, "Look at the ships, Mommy! Wouldn't it be fun to be pulled on a rubber raft behind one of those?"

Before Lisa could comment, the older Alyssa said, "It's too cold. Soon it'll be almost frozen and only oceangoing ships can travel it. Better say no more, you know how sad it makes Grandmother."

"I forgot," Sylvia apologized.

Aunt Joan blew the car horn as she stopped beside a late-model foreign auto. A courtesy light came on as all exited the car when the house front door opened.

"Bonjour, Bonjour!" Madame Émilie exclaimed, walking across the porch and slowly descending the steps, holding onto the handrail. She beamed at them all as if she didn't know whom to hug first, her daughters or her granddaughters. Like her daughters and sister, she was a woman of medium height. Her hair was dark like the other women's, but unlike the others, her hair was streaked with three gray blazes, spaced evenly across her forehead.

"Mama," said Marina after welcomes subsided, "this is Brick, about whom we've told you."

"Bonjour, Monsieur Brick, enchanté," she gleamed. "Parlez-vous Français?"

"Brick non comprends, Grandmère," little Alyssa answered for everyone. All laughed at Alyssa's observation as Brick responded, "Nice to meet you."

"Let's move inside, Mama," Lisa pleaded. "It's chilly now that the sun has set."

Walking into the house, Brick said, "It's clear that your foyer was designed to welcome a sailor home from the sea because of your anchor-style chandelier, with hurricane lamps on the four arms. Nice!"

After storing the luggage, Brick came downstairs to again hear a mixture of English and French, but not as at the airport. Here English was spoken, mostly, he supposed, for his benefit. Even Madame Émilie generally spoke English while he was in her presence, except for nuanced things like setting the table a certain way or in food preparation. At these points Madame would fall back to her deeper comfort level with sprinkled French phrases. The English answers of her daughters or sister generally gave Brick a clue as to what was being said without translation.

Inside, and out of her topcoat, Brick could better see Madame's features. The gray blazes through her hair made her a most striking figure in spite of the fact that her hair was pulled back into a chignon. This contrast of schoolmarm style versus striking beauty was also apparent in a photograph of her as a younger woman, except that her younger beauty was stronger, thus overcoming the aura of primness projected by the chignon. Her bosom, too, seemed capable of bearing only her own cares, and though Madame's waistline was all but gone, she was not overweight. She walked a little pigeon-toed and would totter from side to side when traversing an open space where there was no support. After a couple of these tottering incidents, Lisa asked if her inner-ear stability had worsened.

Madame replied, "Non, the cooler weather may have done something. But we will have pea soup tonight and that will take the chill off my inner ear."

"Her inner-ear motion sickness will vanish in Florida come January," Aunt Joan commented. "This year I'll teach her how to bet on the greyhounds at the dog track. Once she wins a big purse, she'll want to move there, and leave these winters to the polar bears."

"Pay no attention to Aunt Joan's bad habits," Madame mocked in rebuttal. "We must never go to Florida for gambling but for the sun."

"Oh," interrupted Sylvia, "but we must go soon to see the new Disney World they've built. We could stay in one of those new Family Dollar Motels Daddy's working on."

"Disney will be fine, child," replied the grandmother.

"Now, my beef stew with onions, carrots, and mushrooms has simmered for four hours. The rice is ready, too. It's a variation on your veal stew, Joan."

"Beef is good, Émilie," her sister smiled. "It will do well with the Côtes du Rhône red I've brought along. It's always a good wintertime, hearty-meal wine.

"Marina, open the bottle and fill the glasses so the wine can breathe."

This Marina did while Madame and the others made the final preparations. Brick said the pea soup had a flavor of bacon seasoning, and the beef stew reminded him of his mother's. There was also a serving of salt-pork-flavored cabbage.

Aunt Joan initiated most of the dinner conversation as Madame's attention focused on her granddaughters. Joan's queries produced answers from Marina or Lisa that outlined the events to follow for the next two days. Lisa and her children would remain in Pointe de Beaver with Aunt Joan and Madame. Meanwhile, Marina would take Brick into Montréal for excursions with Henri, whom Brick had met at the Greensboro golf tournament.

Learning this, Aunt Joan noted: "Brick, Marina's keeping you to herself. But a Montréal trip will be entertaining. I do enjoy my life there.

"You should know that we are currently undergoing a resurgence of Francophone pride that sometimes becomes dangerous. You see, many French have felt culturally repressed by English rule since we lost the French and Indian War to the British over 200 years ago. I'm sure that sounds silly to outsiders, but cultural repression does foster resentments that can become violent.

"The October 1970 FLQ—or Front de Libération du Québec—kidnap and murder of our Province Labor Minister, Pierre Laporte, is an example of the tensions between the Francophones and Anglophones gone too far.

"Prime Minister Trudeau, a Québécois himself, was forced to send ten thousand troops into Montréal to assure the order of modern life. Many Francophones, including myself at times, have sentiments of desiring separation from the rest of Anglo Canada because it would be culturally and emotionally more simple to deal with. But such sentiments will not pay the bills, as separatism is a luxury we can't afford. My husband's exposure to the lumber industry taught me that, as did Émilie's late husband's work on the St. Lawrence. So we are practical most of the time, I hope and pray.

"Really, we French are an unpretentious stock. Our cool weather is perfect for dairy farming and cheese-making, as the milk won't spoil quickly. I am sure that you will agree that one does not see high pretensions exhibited by farmers anywhere, and such agrarian demeanor pervades Québec. So, just a little area history for you."

"Helpful history—thank you! North Carolina also has mostly small farms, and not much boasting of aristocratic heirships from that population, either," Brick rejoined. "I don't believe I've ever met a Carolina soul who didn't see value coming from our collective unpretentious beginnings. And, after all, we lost a war, too: the War Between the States—seems we have much in common!"

After dinner Brick scanned several magazines written in French. He later told Marsh that he felt like a first-grader again, looking at magazine photographs, yearning to know what the captions said.

III

The next morning Marina and Brick used Madame's car to travel to Montréal for an overnight stay with Henri, whose furniture store was near the Boulevard Saint-Laurent and Rue Nôtre-Dame.

In the store, a clerk said that Henri was away delivering, but that his father, Jacques, was at the office desk in the rear. There, they saw two men bidding their good-byes, one saying, "See you next week, Amos."

"Monsieur Jacques!" Marina exclaimed, side-stepping the departing Amos before embracing the man at the desk. "Meet my friend Brick MacKoy. He met Henri last spring during the High Point Furniture Mart and Greensboro golf tournament."

"Yes!" Jacques responded, "Henri mentioned your friend and Mr. Cannon, the golfer."

"I expect Henri's return anytime as he knows it's time for my usual lunch before I return to Pointe de Beaver for the weekend. I help Henri on busy Fridays and Saturdays, but business slows after the Saturday-morning rush.

"Alors! Here comes Henri! What took you so long, Henri?"

"It was a difficult delivery up three flights of stairs," Henri said. "Marina, Brick, bonjour!

"Papa, the woman now realizes she needs the matching end tables you suggested. I must order them before I forget, and make another delivery, too. I know you are eager for lunch before the trip home."

"I'm only starved," Jacques joked.

"Well, go, go!" Henri said, waving his father off. "I must price the end tables and call her back.

"Marina and Brick may wish to go with you rather than wait for me."

"Good," said Jacques. "This is O.K. with you and your friend, Marina?"

"Oui, oui," Marina responded.

"Bon," said Henri. "Save room for tonight's dinner!"

"Bien sûr!" Marina promised.

Outside Jacques asked if this was Brick's first Montréal visit, and Brick answered yes. Then Jacques noted, "Montréal is a mixture of many cultures, with Jews like old Amos, Greeks, Asians, Caribbean, African, and, of course, the larger core of French and Anglos.

"We are not unlike the historical Jews because our individual societies are self-contained and culturally preserved intact for the most part. Nothing demonstrates that more than the Rue St. Laurent we are approaching. It is the main street that divides the city and is thus called the 'Main.' To the west are the Anglos and to the east, the Francophones. The immigrants of the other cultures also came up this street from the docks and turned east or west into the neighborhoods of their most comfortable language and culture.

"During the day, we speak mostly English for business, but now with a resurgence of French pride, we also speak much French. Whatever the case, when we go home at night, we speak our native tongue, be it French, English, Greek, Yiddish, or the like.

"Aye, the restaurant! I desire a big meal, but as Henri suggests, you two may not.

"Henri opened the Montréal branch when the Old City renovation began around his graduation from Montréal University. The renovation efforts have been good for our business, and we now have customers from Outremont and the other suburban communities of Westmount and Mount Royal.

"I like wine," Jacques said as their waiter seated them. "I'll order a bottle, and you are welcome to try some if it pleases you. Last week I had osso buco with a red Rhône, but today a Bordeaux will match better with sweetbreads."

"Mother and Aunt Joan had a red Rhône last night with beef stew," noted Marina, pondering the menu. "That was a good match, too."

"Matching food with wine isn't easy when the wine comes from one place and the food another. Here I am ordering wine from France for an old French recipe prepared in

Québec. Legend says the combination is supposed to be better if the wine and the food come from the same soil."

"That's what my cousin's husband says," Brick commented. "Austin and Cousin Diane worked in France for over a year. That's the main thing they remember about the experience."

"It's no different with people, either," Jacques returned. "I noticed that you looked amused when I said that the French live on one side of the city's main street and the Anglos on the other. For many here, it's like wine and food; one can't force the matching of different cultures beyond the comfort zone of an individual's adaptability."

"Amused, but not shocked," Brick replied. "In fact, I thought of Chinatown and Harlem in New York City and segregated communities in the American South."

"Yes, similarities, certainly," said Jacques. "We may not have had a history of overt discrimination like the South, but it's here nevertheless, with a history of legal sanction. Take old Amos you saw in our store. His Jewish family was not allowed to attend our government-funded Catholic schools because of their religion. So, we, too, are segregated by our different cultural views of the world, even if it's less noticeable to the casual visitor.

"Today we have East Indians migrating here. Most return to India to find mates from their caste and cultural social order. While this is anathema to Western courtship and marriage views, it helps those of Indian culture identify the type of person one can best tolerate through the many struggles that any marriage encounters. Like pairing food with wine, the caste system can assist in pairing one of its members with a satisfying mate.

"To be sure, there are more marriages between the English and the French, but eventually one member of those unions gives way to the customs of the other, and the couple does its best to think, sleep, and dream in that language.

"Language, culture, and custom determine the outcome of things. One can trace Canada's history, for example, by studying the Hudson Bay Company annals. In its early days, it was a fur-trading operation. At the end of the Seven Years' War in 1763, the English Hudson Bay Company thought it had won an exclusive franchise on the fur trade. But the French fur traders had been trading with the Indians long before the peace settlement terms gave the Hudson Bay Company exclusive rights, and they continued trading. Without a government license, however, this was illegal.

"For years, the French traders outsmarted the Hudson Bay group because they had taught the Indians the French language and trading customs. The French traders also knew the locations of the best beaver streams due to their long history of Indian trading. The simple, secret weapons of language and culture were what the French used to their economic advantage. Years of heated competition and bloodshed between the French and English trading groups followed, until they merged into the one surviving Hudson Bay Company that exists today."

The waiter interrupted to deliver their food and refill their wine glasses. Afterward, Jacques continued, "We French settled here first. Then came the English conquerors after the French and Indian or Seven Years' War. Afterward, all business was conducted in English, and the English, for the most part, managed everything. Working for Anglos placed many French on a second-class level. That pit-of-your-stomach disappointment over French culture's being relegated to a second-class state is the reason for today's Québécois Revolution.

"But as we try to reassert our French spirit, our day-to-day business transactions with the U.S. and the rest of the world constantly change the cultural paradigms we use. We can't stop the flow of time long enough to analyze the problem, plan where our French culture should direct us, then act upon that plan towards the future. That's because all the cross-cultural exposures here in Québec influence our French culture and language to evolve naturally into some new pattern.

"Thus, much of our Québécois Revolution is only an intellectual amusement in treasuring a past that the present-day commercial world and its future are outrunning. Nevertheless, a shared culture is an opiate that tames people into a functioning society. Fortunately, the Good Book says, 'In my Father's house are many mansions.' I suspect that statement's implication for tolerance will absolve us of many sins since we don't know what we are doing, anyway, to paraphrase our good and Holy Christ.... But I hope the wine is satisfactory. That, too, must be considered!"

"Very good! Recently, I have wished that I was more of a wine connoisseur, capable of judging what wine would match what food, like you and Marina do," Brick answered.

"Marina, changing the subject, do you remember our American Thanksgiving trip to Fayetteville's Market House last year? Is Montréal's restoration program what prompted you to observe that one is needed in Fayetteville?"

"Bien sûr!" she exclaimed. "I think the number of mansard roofs in Fayetteville is what inspired my recognition of similarity."

The three continued discussing the restoration of Fayetteville and Montréal for the balance of the meal. Leaving the restaurant, Jacques accompanied them for a block before departing for Pointe de Beaver.

As Brick and Marina walked along, a horse-drawn carriage happened by, and Marina suggested they take it. They toured the Old Town for over an hour in this fashion before returning to Henri's store.

IV

Back at the store Brick and Marina meandered around until Henri announced he could leave. Henri noted they must stop at a "Société des Alcools" outlet to purchase their own bottles of wine for dinner at a restaurant near his flat.

Marina explained to Brick, "Yes, like North Carolina, Québec has a BYOB, bring-your-own-bottle, custom, too. Some restaurants allow you to bring your own wine, and they open it, charging a corkage fee, of course."

At the Société des Alcools, Henri suggested white Burgundies for the seafood restaurant they would go to, and added: "I'll purchase some vodka, too. My attorney friend is coming. I need to return a favor by entertaining him. We met through the Old Town Renovation Commission that his law firm advises. He has a motorcycle, and we ride together. So, we have a lot in common. I hope it's O.K. that he'll join us for dinner?"

"The more the merrier," Marina nodded. "What's his name?"

"Arnaud Brouillet," Henri answered, studying a vodka bottle. "He lives near your aunt. I told Joan that I'd introduce them, but their schedules have never been accommodating."

Henri's residence was one of several triplexes beside a small park. The neighborhood was changing from its blue-collar roots to one of academics, young professionals, and the well-heeled, like Aunt Joan. The bottom floor was his storage, laundry, and workshop area. The workshop was mostly for his three motorcycles and a scooter; however, he did some furniture repair work there, too. The middle floor was his kitchen, dining, and living areas, while the third floor was the sleeping area, with two bedrooms split by the staircase and a bath.

Mixing drinks, Henri explained that his renovation efforts had been on the interior. When Henri handed Brick his drink, Brick noted, "I wouldn't apologize for the exterior. It's mostly masonry except for the third-floor mansard roof area. As long as your roof doesn't leak, you can wait. Then you can blend your final exterior colors with your neighbors', who renovated earlier."

"Yes," Henri replied. "Arnaud advised that as we rode bikes. Speaking of motorcycles, come—see mine!"

"Sure!" said Brick before they walked down to the utility-floor level. There under separate covers were two shiny motorcycles and a well-waxed, pea-green scooter. A third bike, partially refurbished, sat uncovered. It was an Indian, like Mingo's. They spoke about this bike until their drinks ran low. As they evaluated their empty glasses, the doorbell rang.

"That's Arnaud," Henri noted, waving his glass toward the stairs. "Marina, let him in, and bring a glass with the vodka and tonic bottles on your way back. I have ice here in the freezer."

Shortly, Marina escorted Arnaud to the workshop, announcing, "Here he is!" before going over to Brick. Arnaud's gaze followed her every move until his eyes lifted to meet Brick's. His hair was dark brown, and his skin tone, like Marina's, had that everlasting Mediterranean tan. His eyes were black, and complexion smooth.

"Good timing, Arnaud!" Henri said. "We're ready to refresh our drinks. I believe you enjoy vodka?"

"Vodka is fine," replied Arnaud while shaking Brick's hand.

Handing Arnaud his drink, Henri said, "Arnaud, I've told them what a success you are, with a well-furnished pad. It would impress Marina, who's an architect and interior designer."

"Henri carries on too much," Arnaud smiled. "I don't believe it would impress an expert with Mademoiselle's credentials. No, I can't afford three motor bikes and a scooter. Whatever small amount of money I have must go on my flat."

"And your four-door sports sedan," laughed Henri. "I hope you are driving it because we'll need a big car for our dinner transportation."

"Yes," responded Arnaud.

"So, you're an attorney?" Marina asked.

"Yes, a junior partner with our firm," Arnaud replied. "I represent businesses like Henri's. The firm represents a lot of governmental interests, too. I am its advisor to the local advisory task force on bilingualism and biculturalism set up to ease tensions after the FLQ crisis. In fact, I was on the payroll clock until just now with a Québécois discussion group downtown.

"Like any group designed to air complaints and the possible solutions, I wondered if I would have been better off at one of the Renovation Commission hearings, which our firm also counsels. At the Renovation meetings I at least get to meet nice people, who often employ me later to handle renovation real estate transactions, just as Henri has."

Henri joked, "And he charges me extra because he craves a second motorcycle."

"Oh, I'd love to restore an Indian like Henri's," Arnaud noted. "Whenever he finishes, it will give me an inferiority complex riding my Japanese bike beside him. I already feel that way now riding beside his Harley."

They downed another round while discussing Henri's restorations before departing for a nearby restaurant.

v

At the restaurant, all reviewed the menu as the wine steward filled the glasses. Eventually Henri said, "Well, Marina, I hope you and Brick did eat lightly with Papa today."

"Yes," Marina replied, "and we enjoyed Jacques' comments about his Jewish friend, Amos, and various cultural problems."

"Aye, old Amos," mused Henri. "His conversations with Papa remind me of the conversations your father and Papa used to have at our Pointe de Beaver headquarters about the 'Zombies' of World War II. Amos, though, always speaks about the Zombies of World War I because he expected to be drafted into the Canadian Army when he became eighteen. The war ended in 1918, however, before Amos was old enough.

"Brick, you probably do not know what the term 'Zombies' means here. I am sorry to say that many French Canadians opposed the military draft and Canadian participation in both World Wars because they saw no reason to get involved in British affairs. But other Francophones favored participation because they knew they would be helping France stave off defeat in World War I and save it from Hitler in World War II. The ones who opposed participation in both wars were called Zombies because they were presumed to walk around in a Zombie-like mental vacuum, sealed off from the violent realities of their day. The mayor of Montréal urged French Canadians to defy the World War II draft and was imprisoned for this. His actions still promote distrust between Francophones and Anglophones.

"Marina's father and mine favored fighting to save France and the world from Hitler's kind. Her father was Navy and mine Army.

"I remember once in the early fifties, an old Zombie died, and our fathers were talking about it. The old Zombie was said to have been opposed to our World War II participation because so much of France had capitulated to Hitler's French Vichy puppet government. The Zombie therefore didn't care about helping the feeble French Resistance. With today's hindsight, this is hard to believe. But the moodiness of people on political issues is like the mood swings of people on any emotional issue. Indeed, emotions can produce actions that are stranger than fiction, whether it be over love or war."

Brick was saved from having to remark on the ticklish Zombie subject because a quartet began playing tunes that encouraged dancing. He ventured, "Those danceable tunes could pass muster in a beach-music club on the Carolina Coast."

"Yes, Carolina beach music!" Henri exclaimed. "It's on the radio when I go to the High Point Furniture Mart and reminds me of our Montréal clubs when I hear it.

"Swing-style dance music started here during Prohibition because Montréal was North America's only major city legally serving alcohol. From that beginning, swing, jazz, rock and roll, all have had their heydays. A few spots like this one blend the music into a danceable energy. But bar and club fashions come and go every few years, like changes in the weather.

"You know, they have the Myrtle Beach Canadian-American Days, called the Can-Am Days. I've been several times. The clubs there have a better Southern rhythm-and-blues selection than here, although Canadians like that style of music. You know, The Diamonds from Toronto made the song 'Little Darlin'' more popular, worldwide, than its composer's dance band from Charlotte ever did. Maurice Williams and the Gladiolas' version is just now getting appreciation outside the American Southland. My disc jockey friends say the tune is, today, perhaps the all-time most-requested song because it was performed so well by both the Diamonds and The Gladiolas, later called the Zodiacs.

"Marina says you are a good dancer, Brick. Why don't you two demonstrate the Carolina way for us?"

"Oh, no," Marina interrupted. "Brick's a good dancer, but I'm not his beach-dancing partner. Now, if she were here, you could see the real thing. All the men and women say she has a superior, poised, and mystical look, you know: long blond hair, electric-blue eyes, and lanky, sexy legs that men just drool over.

"But, alas, she's in France, so you can't admire their dancing tonight. Of course, I'm just teasing Brick. She's truly a nice girl, who's had a crush on him since she was a tot. She just looks like she doesn't wear undies."

Brick shook his head and smiled before Henri said, "I imagine that Brick is like our fathers who hailed from Marseilles. Such Mediterranean seaport peoples are more outgoing because of their exposure to a wider world."

"Yes," Marina said, tilting her wineglass, "I thought of Father today as Brick and I talked to yours. Our fathers enjoyed the world, but I'm not sure about the mothers and grandmothers who stayed home and lacked that exposure. But enough about us—we'll bore Arnaud.

"And so, Arnaud, you spoke of today's Québécois Advisory Council meeting. What's your view on our predicament?"

At that moment, their waiter came with bread and whipped butter. Arnaud looked into his wineglass until the waiter left. Then he said, "Excuse my delay. I have learned not to voice my opinions just anywhere because it remains an emotional subject, and our generation is still experiencing some difficulty in coming to appreciate society's need for tolerance that Canadians have always exhibited. Every generation apparently has to go through the process of learning how to express its feelings skillfully on matters of legal fairness.

"Often I reflect on what old Jacques has to say about the numerous cultures of Hindus, Buddhists, and Muslims that must peacefully co-exist for India's greater community good. Of course, most of the Muslims left to live in Pakistan after India won its independence because they didn't trust the non-violent Gandhi's Hindu majority. So it's still a flammable cultural crossroads there. Such reflections make me thankful for our much smaller Canadian conflict."

No one replied to Arnaud's remarks because the house band took up the slow dance tune "Smoke Gets in Your Eyes," and Henri asked Marina to dance.

As the two danced, Brick remarked to Arnaud, "Your answer to Marina's question seems practical. It's a shame that it's still such an emotional issue that you felt the need to refrain from expressing it in front of the waiter."

Arnaud took his eyes off Marina and Henri on the dance floor, looked at him, and replied, "You can never tell where a person might be on this issue. True, the issue has been around for a long time, and will never go away, even if all French intermarried with Anglophiles tomorrow. However, there would still be offspring from such unions whose souls would either be mostly French or mostly English. I think that's why Switzerland is still divided into German, Italian, and French sections.

"Here, many Québécois feel more like French peasants than members of some secure, middle-class nobility, who may be more immune to feeling emotional hurt when forced to turn the other cheek. The art of treating others as you would like to be treated is not an art of fun, but one of obligation to humanity for the common good. It's just that you'd like to see the river of life occasionally flow in your direction.

"How long have you known Marina?"

"About a year," Brick answered.

"Are you engaged?" Arnaud asked.

"No," Brick replied.

"She's a beautiful woman," Arnaud stated.

Brick said he looked into Arnaud's eyes, realizing that Arnaud was smitten by Marina, and raised his wineglass, replying, "With that, Sir, I agree—beaucoup et d'accord!"

Through the evening, the group conversed on many topics, and each man slow-danced with Marina. At the end, Arnaud drove Marina, Brick, and Henri back to Henri's, and promised to meet them the next morning at a local café known for its homemade Greek pastries and specialty coffees.

VI

The next morning Marina, Henri, and Brick discussed the best transportation to the nearby Outremont café to meet Arnaud. Marina agreed with Henri that a motorcycle ride would be fun if she could ride the pea-green scooter with Brick. Thus that was Brick and Marina's transportation for the remainder of the visit.

At the café, Henri dismounted as Arnaud called out, "Salut! Park beside my bike and come. I have a table with a view!"

Following Arnaud, they came to a table facing a picture window. Henri and Brick ordered coffee, Marina a cappuccino, and Arnaud an espresso. All ordered pastries. There was little conversation until Brick asked, "What's that huge domed structure in the distance? It caught my eye yesterday and this morning."

"That's St. Joseph's Oratory," Marina answered. "Its massiveness makes it visible nearly everywhere. It's the one Catholic church that Father would take us to after Henri and Lisa were singled out by old Father Auguste in a Sunday homily for being lax on the memorization of their religious studies. Unlike Henri's father, mine was so furious over Father Auguste's public reprimand of his child that he took Lisa and me out of our church. The church was truly backward and medieval in my childhood years.

"Mother wept, as she preferred tolerating the incident for the social benefits our church offered. Father, on the other hand, thought of it as some latter-day Inquisition mentality. We wound up going to Dad's First Mate's church.

"Dad's old First Mate, André de Vaux, is Protestant. The few times we went to St. Joseph's were either with Henri's family or to meet Aunt Joan and Uncle Jean Marc when they came down from Ottawa for Easter in Montréal. Father Auguste died when I was at N.C. State, and Mother returned to the local church.

"St. Joseph's always overwhelmed me, but my parents seemed to regain a sense of peace there. The stories about discarded crutches and other miracles of healing were also mysteriously interesting to me at that age. I think that's why I'm so attracted to Brick's friend Brewer's story about the Ghost Dogs of the Bentonville Battleground. It's another event that proves to me that there's an afterlife of some kind.

"Henri's father never criticized Father Auguste's methods like mine did, but many often heard Jacques say he was nearly ready to leave the local parish, too."

"Oh, yes," Henri laughed. "But that was the fifties, and Father Auguste is dead. The reforms of the Vatican II Council combined with the instruments of modern mass communication, like television, have modernized the church's spiritual outlook. The resurgence of pride in our Québécois heritage and the church reforms are all loosely referred to now as Québec's Quiet Revolution."

"Yes," Marina mused with a far-off look, "Lisa and I often speak of Québec's modernization. Mother sends us Sunday newspapers and magazines from here, and we read about this 'Quiet Revolution' overturning Québec's medieval Catholic mentalities. We just wish Father were still alive so he could feel justified for taking us out of Father Auguste's backward religiosity and into the modern world. As it's turning out now, Lisa and I feel they could have regained their peacefulness had it not been for Father's accident. But, of course, this cathedral's massiveness does have an impersonal quality about it."

"Well, it also depends on who you know," Henri remarked. "Arnaud has a priest friend at St. Joseph's from his days of Jesuit education. Father Marcel is an interesting soul—he has spent many hours in meditation on a variety of medieval and modern spiritual subjects. You'd enjoy this priest. Papa and your Aunt Joan do, and I believe your parents would have, also."

"This is true, Marina," Arnaud put in. "Father Marcel has a way of making you forget St. Joseph's massiveness. He's anything but impersonal!

"Brick, you'll be interested to know that St. Joseph's has over three million visitors a year that pay homage to Joseph, Christ's earthly father. Two hundred and seventy-eight steps lead to its entrance. Some pilgrims climb those steps on their knees as an act of penance, even though the stairs are not holy or 'Scalae Santae' like those in Rome's Basilica of St. John Lateran. Those in Rome are said to be holy because they're asserted to be the actual steps that Christ climbed on his knees to Pontius Pilate's Praetorium in Jerusalem the night before his crucifixion. Repeating this act of devotion here at St. Joseph's—or on Rome's true holy steps—is believed to purify the soul, gaining divine pardon for the climber's sins.

"A tiny particle of clothing thought to be St. Joseph's is kept inside. This holy relic, along with oil kept in a basin beneath the Saint's statue, are said to be the source of great healings that take place there. The number of crutches and braces found scattered about are a testament to these healings and cures. Three million visitors annually—it's a number that only the Lourdes and Fátima shrines can approximate.

"But as Father Marcel says, most of the visitors do not experience spectacular healings. Most merely light a candle in the Votive Chapel of private devotions to request a blessing or pardon."

"Those spectacular stories are always interesting, like the Ghost Dogs," Marina said. "But buying oil at the gift shop reminds me of our old, medieval-style church of the

1950s, before the Quiet Revolution's changes. That was a church of just tithe and give, you poor, to support an old feudal, spiritual bureaucracy that would give back nothing, yet heap public and private recriminations upon the pitiful, believing tither."

"Cousin Wesley says the church is always run by sinners and always will be," Brick noted. "Mistakes will always be made here on this earth in the name of God for as long as the earth turns. I doubt if it much matters where or how the believer gets his oil, but just that he believes. Those spectacular, spiritual occurrences are possible if one is in the right frame of mind.

"As you say, it's like the Bentonville story. The coon hunters in that story were in a fearful state of mind about it being after midnight and Sunday, rather than still Saturday. They were afraid of committing the sin of Sunday hunting, and that mind-set psychologically and spiritually determined beforehand what occurred afterward, with no one being aware of the connection potentials between this world and the eternal hereafter."

"Yes," Marina replied as she turned away from her outside viewing to look at him. "It is a fantastic story. Although it is not explicitly a religious story, it does testify to the immortality of the personal soul and its regrets."

"What is this story, Brick?" Arnaud asked before Brick then told the story of the coon hunters, who saw ghosts of Confederate and Union soldiers after taking an axe cut at a tree up which a coon had scurried on a foggy night.

"What strong regret and sorrow there among those lively ghosts of a lost cause propelled to be seen by living men! It makes me think that the nexus between this world and the next is as thin as a slice of fog," Brick said.

"Changing the subject, though, how does the word 'Oratory' fit into the cathedral's name?"

"It means prayer," Arnaud said. "St. Joseph is the great guardian saint of Canada. As a carpenter, he was a model to the workmen who built the country. Perhaps that's why Marina, as a child, was attracted to the place. She was already in the process of becoming an architect, even though she likely didn't realize it then.

"As the husband of the Virgin Mary, St. Joseph is looked upon as the protector of that virgin, pure of heart, that all men see in women as the foundation-stone of the family unit. St. Joseph is also a comforter of the afflicted and a patron to the dying.

"Father Marcel says that the Meditative Gardens around St. Joseph's are places for private, restful reflection. From Wednesday through Saturday, music pours forth to accompany those meditations, year-round, from the cathedral's fifty-six-bell carillon. Would you like a tour? Father Marcel is on duty now. Perhaps we can meet him."

"Sure! Why not," Brick answered, looking at Marina, who blinked at him in approval.

In a show of thanks for Henri's hospitality, Brick paid the restaurant bill after waving off Henri and Arnaud's protests. The group then motorcycled over to St. Joseph's and toured the gardens and chapel.

Just before leaving, Henri and Arnaud recognized Father Marcel. Short of stature and reserved in demeanor, he had an air of spiritual peace that impressed Marina, as she told the others just before she and Brick bid Henri and Arnaud "Au revoir" to head back to Pointe de Beaver.

VII

Arriving home after dark, Marina assisted the others in preparing vegetable side dishes for the midday Monday Thanksgiving meal. Around eight, she slipped Brick servings of scalloped tomatoes and turnips. Amid the conversation, Marina related details of the Montréal visit.

"Aunt Joan, Henri's attorney friend, Arnaud Brouillet, lives near you. Henri says that he has wanted to introduce you two, but it's never been convenient. Arnaud might be a good advisor for your estate."

"Yes," Aunt Joan replied. "I hope to meet him before I leave for Florida. Perhaps he can prepare your mother's estate as well."

The next morning Marina handed Brick a cup of coffee as he entered the kitchen where she was lounging with Lisa, who asked, "Are you all packed for the return flight? We are."

"Yes," he answered. "Where are the rest?"

"They've taken my girls to the grocery," Lisa returned. "They always want original Québec Maple Syrup to take home."

Brick sipped his coffee and announced that he'd go outside to gaze down the hill upon the St. Lawrence one last time. Outside he saw no vessels, but soon Marina joined him. He put his arms around her waist and they lingered. She noted, "River traffic basically stops after November because the ice on the Great Lakes slows the shipping. Our yard has a beautiful river view in the late spring and early summer with all the colors of the wildflowers beyond the lawn seeming to run down to the river."

Reentering the house, Brick looked at the pictures in the den until the voices of Alyssa and Sylvia announced that their trip for maple syrup was a success. As they went off to repack their luggage, Lisa served up white wine and announced that dinner was ready. She then offered up a "Happy Thanksgiving" toast, raising her glass to all.

The dining room table was dressed in Thanksgiving formality with a linen tablecloth and napkins, upon which lay Madame Émilie's best silverware. Crystal glasses of water had floating lime slices that nearly matched a centerpiece holly wreath, with mistletoe inserts. An ice bucket near the front of the table held a second bottle of wine.

Madame presided at the head of the table, while Joan faced her at the opposite end. Lisa sat to her mother's right, between her two children. This allowed her to serve the two girls and steady the passing of the serving dishes from her mother to her aunt. Marina and Brick sat to Madame's left, with Marina nearest her mother. Madame offered a short Thanksgiving prayer in French, followed by all reciting the Lord's Prayer in English.

"Let the feast begin," Madame announced, passing the silver platter of roast pork to Lisa. Awaiting the platter, each diner picked up the nearest side dish and served themselves before passing it on to the right. In a colorful circle went the scalloped tomatoes, turnips, scalloped potatoes, pole beans, fried apples, cranberry sauce, rice, and a pork roux. Intoxicatingly yeasty rolls, topped with creamy butter, disappeared into the mouths of Alyssa and Sylvia, both of whom asked for more bread before the bread tray could make a full trip around the table. Their grandmother looked at them, cheerfully rolling her eyes, and said, "Don't worry, there's more."

Aunt Joan remarked, "Lisa has adapted our scalloped potato recipe with some onion and bell pepper, sautéed with a hint of garlic under all this cheese. Tastes as good as it smells, too."

"So does your pork roast," Lisa countered in compliment. "The cherries enhance the blend of cranberries and fried apples, and the roux is smooth—no lumps and very tasty on the rice."

"And the scalloped tomatoes, too," Marina added. "Their sweet flavor blends with the stronger flavor of the turnips. Do the turnips remind you of your mother's, Brick?"

"Yes, very good turnips," Brick said.

"Well, I'm glad because I cooked them!" Marina replied with satisfaction.

"But in North Carolina," Brick laughed, "it would be sweet tea with turnips. I can truly say that I've never had wine with turnips before, but this wine pleases my country-boy palate."

"It's a Chenin Blanc," Aunt Joan remarked, raising her glass to him. "It goes well with pork, and perhaps, by mere coincidence, with our leafy vegetable that is seasoned with some of the same meat. It makes a happy marriage, like two people who complement each other."

The meal ended with the young girls' cries for pumpkin pie, redolent with ginger, on the sideboard. This was eventually served to the girls while the adults sipped coffee or finished their wine. Lisa and Marina then cleared the table and packed the leftovers in the refrigerator while their mother sat somberly in the living room with Joan.

Brick then began transporting everyone's luggage to Aunt Joan's car for the ride back to the airport. As he was lugging his bag and Marina's along, he heard a male voice say, "Aye, can I help you?"

Brick turned to see a man walking up who said, "You must be Brick. I'm André. Just came by to say hello to the girls before you leave. I don't lift much anymore since the accident that took Captain Frédéric's life, but I think I can still handle luggage with one hand, at least."

"Oh, André," Brick remarked, "I've heard your name many times."

"And I yours," André returned. "Not only from Madame, but also from Vann and your friend, Monroe Hill. The Doctor, they sometimes call him. A real character at the poker tables, so I observed more than once. You and he won a motorcycle in a game, I'm told."

"I'll never live that down!" Brick laughed as he reached out to shake André's hand. "So you were working with Captain LaGraves when the accident occurred?"

"We were on a mission from Montréal to haul a crane barge in for its usual winter repairs from channel dredging operations on the Richelieu River. A second tug accompanied us so we could sandwich the barge between two tugs for safe transportation in the wicked undertow currents where the Richelieu meets the St. Lawrence. We were the lead towing tug while the rear tug acted as the stabilizer vessel.

"I was below and didn't see how it began. But there was a sudden lurch that slammed me to the floor. Then the rear tug let out a series of five short horn blasts, signaling that great danger was near. I feared we were approaching the larger St. Lawrence River channel and must be about to collide with an ocean-sized vessel. I quickly headed up top.

"There, I could see that the barge we were transporting had come loose from both tugs as we entered the swift currents. The rear tug was still blowing danger signals, but our tug wasn't, and seemed to be rudderless. When I climbed into the pilothouse, Captain LaGraves was on the floor. There wasn't an eyelash out of place or a mark or even a spot of water on him or the floor, but his olive Mediterranean complexion was ghost-grey. I wanted to feel for his pulse, but instinct told me our tug needed steering in the currents made more turbulent by the recent November rains. Apparently, he and the rear stabilizer tug had begun their preplanned, radio-coordinated sequence of slowing each tug's speed with reverse-gear engagements as we entered the swirling waters at the confluence of the two rivers because the tug's gear was in neutral, and the propeller disengaged. That's why the vessel felt rudderless. We were floating at the mercy of the currents."

André glanced toward the house, then he continued. "As I was trying to reestablish control of our vessel, the loose barge slammed into our side. The crane on that barge came unanchored, and its lifting boom, which had been lowered to near deck level for transportation safety, ripped into the base of the pilot house. I was thrown into the cold, fast-flowing waters. That's when my left arm and hand were injured. The barge and our tug just kept moving with the currents until the two hit a sandbar beyond the shipping channel. The weight of the crane barge turned our tug on its side. Captain LaGraves, driven beneath the undertow, vanished into the mainstream of the St. Lawrence.

"His body was never found. The propellers on the big seaway ships must have cut him into shreds for the fishes, we all figure. Not a stitch of his clothing was ever found either. I managed to follow the current to the edge of the shipping lane where I grabbed onto a channel marker pole. The trailing tug rescued me. It was a freak accident, but then all accidents involving professional watermen, who deal with the same dangers daily, have a freakish element about them."

"I've known of the accident since I met the family, but I never knew how it happened," Brick commented. "The surprise of it still haunts them. Too bad you were injured, but thank goodness you're alive."

"The Accident Review Board agreed that I was lucky," André mused. "If I had been knocked out, I would have gone down the channel with the Captain. I had insurance, but not as good as the Captain's. Of course, he had a bigger paycheck, and a family to consider. So he had all the death and work disability benefits one could buy. I had only the basic package. I can't work the ships anymore because I can't lift enough weight with my left hand to meet the maritime-employment physical requirements. You've got to be able to grip ninety pounds with your dominant hand and eighty with the weaker one to qualify for employment as a seaman. I can't do that now, but I get along since it's only me to look after. Odd jobs help out."

Then they went into the house where André gave Alyssa and Sylvia small boxes of chocolates and talked with the family until all said their good-byes. Émilie promised Lisa and Marina she would visit them at Christmas in North Carolina before going to Florida to be with Joan during January and February. This Christmas promise eased the parting.

At the airport, Aunt Joan bid her good-byes, and promised to call after she settled into her Florida quarters.

Little was said on the return trip's first leg to New York, where there was an hour-and-a-half layover before the connecting flight to Raleigh-Durham. They stopped by the airport lounge where the adults had Bloody Marys and Alyssa and Sylvia each had a fountain soda. Here, Brick mentioned his conversation with André.

"André means well," Lisa remarked. "I wish Mother wouldn't be so hard on him. He was devoted to Daddy because Dad got him employment on the Seaway after World War II. They became acquainted serving on Liberty-style Navy freighters.

"André comes from the Richelieu River area. It borders the U.S. along the Vermont and New York state line that runs down the middle of much of Lake Champlain. Years ago, when most freight boats were not as big, there was lots of commercial shipping from the St. Lawrence to the Richelieu to Lake Champlain, and then south to New York by way of canals. This backwater traffic dwindled after World War I and was almost non-existent by the end of World War II. André's family eventually ran fuel tankers, about the only shipping activity left in that area. When the war ended, André knew he had to move to a better shipping environment, and Daddy found a place for him for which André was always grateful. I think André always looked up to Daddy because of their age difference: about fifteen years. They were like the oldest and youngest brothers of a big family, in my mind!

"Mother's frustration when she sees André comes from the fact that some of his family were associated with the smuggling of untaxed items between Canada and the U.S. during Prohibition, when a lot of illegal, cross-border trade went on. André's father's uncle was jailed for this. Lately cigarette smuggling has been the problem. Much of that comes out of North Carolina and Virginia up I-95. The border between Canada and the U.S. is long, and many isolated areas are not populated enough to have a heavy law-enforcement presence. That makes smuggling easy to conceal. Of course, we don't know that André does anything like that, but Mother always speculates that his extra income comes from such activity.

"But what really irritated Mother is the fact that André's Protestant church was so convenient for Father to take us to after the incident with Father Auguste. She felt like André was interfering in the raising of her brood, even though it was Father's choice. You see, the Richelieu border area has had a sizeable Protestant population because of the American Revolution, when so many Loyalists fled there to avoid civil war like the Flora McDonald–inspired North Carolina loyalists experienced at Moores Creek and other places. Some of André's forebears came from that Revolutionary War flight to safety. I think the fact that we attended his church made this lonely old bachelor feel more attached to our family than ever. After that, he became like our uncle. At any rate, he has always been very good to me and Marina and would do anything for Mother that we or she might ask."

Vann Hutton was at the airport when their ten-thirty flight arrived. This allowed Brick to go straight to Pineland Springs, where he piled into the bed of his youth and slept like a baby.

Chapter Thirteen

Impediments Amass on Every Street

I

BECAUSE OF HIS LATE-NIGHT FLIGHT from Montréal, Brick returned to work at noon on Tuesday. There he found Mingo filing the point of a spindle paper holder and asked, "Mingo, are you sharpening up our spindle because Deacon's found lots of new customer applications to stick on it?"

"Just sharpening it to clean my fingernails before I wash my hands for lunch—lost my pocketknife," Mingo answered. "Deacon's bringing sandwiches from Uncle Henry's."

"Well," Brick observed, "he's arriving now, with Marsh and Uncle Malcolm following."

Brick reported on his trip while Dad and Mingo ate. After Brick's report, Mr. Malcolm said, "Glad you had some time off. Now let's discuss our progress and how we can finish up Sunrise Acres.

"We've built and sold sixty houses since starting and could be through and ready to move on to more profitable building opportunities except for the culvert fiasco slowing us down. But now our utilities are installed and the road paved. Consequently, our construction schedule shouldn't be as badly slowed by this year's winter weather.

"So far, you've built ten back-forty units with thirty left to do, but lumber's inflation rate is increasing. Historically, timber prices drop when winter weather slows construction. If we can start the remaining thirty houses on our paved streets, with lower winter-priced lumber, we can beat the clock on the higher lumber prices that'll return next spring. Can you build these last thirty units so we can sell out by spring, and move on to more profitable building ventures?"

"Possibly, if Bobby Jack Johnson can round up Ollie and start two framing crews again," Brick answered. "If we can't find more labor at our contracted price, twenty-five is all we can build by February. It's true that our paved road will allow more winter work, but you still can't do outside construction on rainy days."

Mr. Malcolm said, "That's why we paved and installed the utilities: not to be totally stalled by winter weather like last year with the missing culvert. So you must hurry, Brick! Finish here and you can go to Fayetteville or Raleigh where better profit opportunities exist in exclusive home locations. Location, location, location is the builder's profit motto."

Spying Mingo using the spindle paper holder on his fingernails, Mr. Malcolm grumbled, "From now on, Deacon, I want to see that spindle holder full of applications. That's what it's for, not nail-cleaning. Besides, it looks so sharp that it's a danger to some customer's rambunctious kid. Put it in the desk drawer or throw it away."

The following Friday I arrived at Junebug's office to do his secretarial work just as Dad, Brick, and Marsh entered with two customers to execute their sale papers. After Dad left with the customers, Marsh asked, "What's the latest on Dutch? I see Lonah occasionally. She lives near Brewer's old farmer friend who breeds my cows. Lonah says she's heard little."

"Courthouse gossip says he may come home Thanksgiving for the holidays," Junebug answered. "He's a cooperative witness in Florida. In addition to his fishing buddies captured with him, they've picked up some Miami locals who also point to Puerto Rico."

Then their conversation turned to the upcoming presidential election between Richard Nixon and George McGovern. Junebug noted, "It seems that Nixon's a shoo-in. After the election, maybe he and Kissinger can end this war. Peace should be good for the economy, helping you get out of Sunrise Acres and into more profitable building."

The following day, I worked my other half-day in the law office before reporting to Sunrise Acres. When I walked in, Brick and Peaches were looking over a set of gazebo plans. I knew Peaches was excited when she exclaimed, "This is just like what I told Miss Marina I wanted before you went to Canada! But I can't afford it today. Erica's with me full-time now. Please tell Miss Marina thanks for the effort."

II

Before Nixon's 1972 landslide win, Brick began his final construction phase after Will O'Cain approved the thirty-house submittal. Brick and Marsh were upbeat about Nixon's win and hoped a Vietnam peace treaty would speed their prospects for completing Sunrise Acres. Of course, no one saw Watergate or the gas shortage lurking.

Brick had five houses scheduled for closing on the Friday after Thanksgiving. When I came into the Sunrise Acres office to begin my college holiday that Wednesday, Thanksgiving Eve afternoon, Brick was cheerful as he and Junebug discussed by phone a time for the Friday closings to take place.

Seconds after Brick hung up, the phone rang and he answered. After a pause, his face paled. Saying little during the call, he hung up and said, "Dang! It's Marina and Lisa's mother. She's had a fall on ice, and has broken several bones in both wrists and ankles. Marina and Lisa are trying to get a Montréal flight. That poor woman will be totally helpless."

As usual the MacKoys had their Thanksgiving feast in Pineland Springs. Bessie Mae said the MacKoys, except for Marsh and Sue Anne, attended the Ecumenical Thanksgiving Church Service, held that year at Donald's church.

Friday we met for the house closings at Junebug's office. Brick was businesslike, saying little. I assumed he was distracted by Marina's crisis. Marsh, however, seemed nervous. I still recall thinking how odd his dark mood was despite closing five houses in one day.

That night Sue Anne called. She wanted me to help her move some things, and said she'd pay me. I told her I would, thinking she probably had new furniture. When I arrived, I saw a rental truck and Bessie Mae on the doorstep.

Sue Anne said she was leaving Marsh because she'd caught him at Lonah Slueter's place, embracing her as he was leaving. Lonah was standing in the doorway nearly nude.

The living room couch, two end tables, and the loveseat were hers. Her other items were already packed. She handed us ten dollars each before we could say anything, and we moved her items into the rental truck.

Afterward she thanked us and wished us well before spending over an hour recounting some happy times of her marriage to Marsh and their relationships with Brick, Marina, and other friends.

This is when I learned much of what I've already told you about: the football tailgate parties, the Monkey Island trip, the ski trip, the Ocean Drive trip, and the marijuana and alcohol that accompanied some of it. She did not, however, speculate about Brick and Marina's passionate relationship if she, unlike me in that long-ago time, had any knowledge or suspicions of such. As private as Brick and Marsh always were about personal things, I still feel Sue Anne would have continued to respect that secrecy, even though she was furious.

Nevertheless, Sue Anne did not hold back about Marsh. "In hindsight, Marsh must have been fantasizing about Lonah even before my introduction to Marsh by Lonah and Dutch. We gravitated to each other immediately, even though both Marsh and Dutch were high on pot. Apparently Marsh has had some lingering desire to have Lonah. He had just returned from Vietnam, was at loose ends, and was therefore willing to do about anything short of going to jail. I was available, and Lonah wasn't back then.

"Truly, I was attracted to him because I could tell he wasn't a prickhead know-it-all or one of those effeminate types, like the males I see around the beauty contest backstage. I could tell that he came from money and knew the need to make his own. Perhaps I felt that because he was with Dutch, who I already knew had money.

"I sensed Marsh was a cowboy-rounder type who needed and wanted to settle down. So I invested my soul in him for a chance at a decent, respectable future. When you're an only child from a home broken by your father's abandonment, you grasp at a prospect for a more secure future, no matter the risk. Of course, everything's pretty much a risk anyway. Really, I wanted children with him, but now I feel stabbed in the back, and I won't tolerate his confused outlook anymore.

"We women invest our spirits to make a future with a man, and I hope you don't get let down like me, Melody. I thank you two for your help tonight—you're both a blessing to me."

III

The next morning at Sunrise Acres, I found Brick reviewing applications for me to type. He said he had heard that Bessie Mae and I had assisted Sue Anne's move the night before.

"Yes," I said. "Afterward I went to Bessie Mae and Donald's to talk about it. Donald and his Aunt Wixie seem more upset about Marsh's marital failure than the MacKoy family."

Brick replied, "Our families go back many generations together, so it's understandable."

"Donald's mentioned the Negrohead Road many times relating to you MacKoys and his family coming from Sampsons Landing," I remarked. "But it's all been in bits and pieces I've never understood."

Brick replied, "My MacKoys settled in the Cape Fear's Sampsons Landing area of the old Negrohead Road between the mid-1740s Scottish defeat at the Battle of Culloden and the 1775 American Revolution. The road ran from Wilmington to Campbellton Landing, later renamed Fayetteville to honor Revolutionary War French General Lafayette.

"The MacKoys married into the Brickman family of blacksmiths who made turpentine tooling and also traded the product. They were opposed to the English king's colonial tax policies and spied on Flora MacDonald's husband's Loyalist troops as they marched down the Negrohead Road to defeat at Moores Creek. How the road got its name during the Colonial era, no one really knows today, but it was a secondary back trail that no longer exists, except as a reference in old deeds.

"After the Revolution, my namesake forefather, Brickman Micajah MacKoy, married the only child of a Butler slave-holding family farming Sampsons Landing lowland rice fields. The Butlers were Methodist because John Wesley's disciple, Bishop Francis Asbury, traveled the Negrohead Road area east of Fayetteville converting folks. The MacKoys converted from Scottish Presbyterian to Methodist then because they had never truly accepted Presbyterian predestination theology.

"In the 1840s, about the time of my great-grandfather Everett's birth, the MacKoys freed their slaves because their turpentine business was more lucrative than rice farming and didn't require the expense of indentured help. Most of the younger freed slaves moved to Fayetteville to become brick masons or harness makers, but the older ones, like Donald's great-great-grandfather Old John, remained to tend the MacKoy turpentine and rice plantation on a share-crop basis because they were too old to learn a new trade.

"Prior to the freeing of Old John's family, however, an incident on a nearby large plantation called Island Fields frightened both masters and slaves all along the Negrohead Road.

"Island Fields had ten square miles of land with ample swamp bog fertilizer that could be blended with scarce animal manures for plant nutrition. When the likes of Micajah Autry left the sandy Carolina coastal plain for western, clay-based lands that better held fertilizers, a Wilmington agricultural, maritime shipping, and warehouse operation bought many plantations with swamp bog deposits to assure the continuation of their profitable shipping enterprise.

"Being a maritime agricultural shipper with no farm-management skills, they brought in an expert, Harvie Alleywine, who had run swampland operations in Louisiana and in Virginia's Dismal Swamp. His survey suggested that Island Fields needed fifty more slaves to maximize the plantation's potential, and this was approved.

"One slave purchase in next-door Duplin County, however, was troublesome: a swamp-bog mining team-leader named Wadeus.

"The Island Fields Plantation got its name because it was several large islands surrounded by swamp creek runs and bays in the Sampsons Landing–Negrohead Road area. This snake and alligator environment also made a good prison-like boundary for slaves, as it was difficult to make an escape from unless a slave knew the locale and could swim. Wadeus could swim and knew the area because he had worked as the swamp-mud mining leader on two other plantations in the Sampson-Duplin Counties region.

"Due to his responsibilities, Wadeus was granted the rare slave status of carrying a gun to protect himself and his crew in the swamps. His slave name was Wadeus because he was said to wade above the dangers of the waters. Wadeus, nevertheless, had no state-registered certificate, as required by slave laws, that would legally allow him to take his weapon beyond Island Fields.

"In August of 1831, the Nat Turner slave rebellion took place near the North Carolina border in Virginia's Dismal Swamp area of Southampton County. Sixty to seventy whites were killed, including Turner's master. Eventually Turner and thirty-some other slaves were captured in their Dismal Swamp hideout, tried, and hanged. This incident upset whites in the swampy areas of eastern North Carolina, where runaway slaves had often hid out with the apparent assistance of free blacks and remnant Indian bands. Many complained to the governor for military help in controlling the runaway slaves for fear of a similar Nat Turner rebellion here.

"Wadeus, having knowledge of the area, would occasionally slip out at night to visit free blacks or other slaves to find out what was going on and found out about the slave rebellion talk. One night he didn't return.

"At the time Wadeus disappeared, a mob broke into the Duplin County jail, seizing two blacks rumored to be Nat Turner–type rebellion leaders. These two men were beheaded, and their heads stuck on poles to serve as a warning to slaves that rebellion wouldn't be tolerated. Such mob action took place several times, including the arrest of fifteen blacks in Wilmington. Of the Wilmington fifteen, six were beheaded, and their heads stuck on poles along the old Negrohead Road.

"These beheadings and the fate of Wadeus, however, were not acknowledged at the isolated Island Fields Plantation, even though the county sheriff told Alleywine that a Negro called Wadeus had been caught with a non-permitted gun. The sheriff said the armed Negro was thus suspected to be a part of a slave rebellion plot, beheaded on the spot, and his head placed on a pole somewhere between Moores Creek and Fayetteville.

"Alleywine and his partners thought that keeping Wadeus' death quiet would prevent slave unrest that would stall Island Fields' success, but in less than a year they had bigger problems. In 1832 a powerful summer storm came. Today we would call it a hurricane, but hurricanes were not named, logged, or recorded until this century. This storm destroyed the Island Fields crops at the height of the harvest season and washed away the plantation's rice fields. Additionally, the timber surrounding the swamp-mud mining zone wound up as debris in these backwater bays. This made both farming and swamp-mud mining impossible for the next season and perhaps longer.

"After six weeks of starving by both master and slave, the Wilmington group told Alleywine to shut down and sell the remaining slaves. The investors then made deals with local white farmers to be tenants of the land, eventually selling all of it before the Civil War. My forebears, Monroe's, and Brewer's bought portions of the Island Fields, and our hunting cabin is located on one of its corners. Some say our hunting cabin is an old Island Fields' slave house.

"Over the years, the history of the Negrohead Road slave rebellion was largely lost to the collective memory of the general public because slave-owners were certainly not going around shouting about it. However, some blacks and whites of the area did remember, as Marsh, Brewer, Monroe, and I can attest to. Donald's family members recollect this terrible event, too.

"Now, the main reason Donald's family has always remained close to us MacKoys is a Civil War event. This event resurrected fears of another beheading in Old John's mind even though our family had freed him and his family twenty years before.

"The tale says a Yankee soldier came through Sampsons Landing scavenging during Sherman's march from Fayetteville through Averasboro and Bentonville to Goldsboro. This Yankee forager was on foot. Our great-great-grandfather, Cager MacKoy, the First, had, with Old John's help, hidden many of the family possessions in the swamp near the homestead. Even so, stories of Sherman's troops living off confiscated cured hams, salt fish and corn were abundant. Also word of their killing over 35,000 animals had spread like wildfire from Tennessee, Georgia, and South Carolina ahead of the Yankees' arrival in North Carolina. When locals heard of 3,500 animals being slaughtered in Fayetteville, people hid even more.

"Cager and Old John hid everything except a horse that was blind in its right eye. They feared the animal couldn't be left in the swamp because its blind eye made it so skittish that the horse might give away the hiding place. He would jump suddenly at anything that appeared to his good eye and always jumped away from a tree stump in the road beside the MacKoy home. Due to this skittishness, he was used only for pulling the buggy and plow since the buggy-plow harness had bridle blinders. Even with blinders, the animal had to be led around this mid-road stump to keep him from running away with the buggy. The horse was named Puller because all it did was pull a buggy or plow.

"Anyway, the Yankee trooper saw nothing but old Puller and the clothes on Cager and Old John. The soldier ordered the two men to strip naked, took their clothes, mounted Puller bareback style, and rode off in a March downpour. Naked Cager and naked Old John just looked at each other in silence.

"When Puller got to the stump, he jumped violently to his left, whereupon the Yankee was thrown to the right, head-first into the stump, dying instantly. Cager's wife, Rebecca, observing the whole drama from the porch, ran with two of her husband's nightshirts to cover up the men. Then they took Puller and the soldier into the swamp, where the horse was tied off with a black hood over its head and the soldier buried, fearing Sherman's marauding troops would think that they had killed the Yankee horsethief for the Rebel cause. The three then swore an oath of secrecy.

"After the Appomattox and Durham Confederate surrenders, occupying troops came inquiring about a missing Yankee. At this point Old John feared being caught, having his head cut off like Wadeus' and stuck on a pole. Old John reasoned that any connection of a white death to a black man wouldn't likely be seen in its true light as an accident and especially by a horde of thieving, white Yankee mule killers any more than by white Southerners of the 1830 Nat Turner era.

"When Old John would tell his children and grandchildren the Puller story, he always ended by saying that he was thankful the MacKoys had not blamed the whole incident on an old black man to save themselves. He often remarked, 'You just have to trust those other human peoples life throws you together with to be in brotherhood, no matter the circumstances.'

"So, you see, although Old John's reasoning was wrong by our post-war idealized standards of today's justice, the Wadeus beheading and Puller stories have been the connecting link for our families over the years."

Then I mused before saying, "My American Indian history courses speak of numerous treaties broken by the white man. My own people have no recorded history of broken promises because we were dispersed into the greater population before the time of Indian reservations that required treaty agreements. But I did go to school with blacks and know of their general distrust of whites. Their distrust made me better sense why there was a cultural divide and inconstancy of understanding between my own Indian forebears and the European whites, too, even if not recorded.

"Things like those beheadings cause great distrust, and in tumultuous Civil War times, I can appreciate how Old John thought that white Yankees would kill him. The circumstances forced him to trust the whites who had freed him and those whites to trust the man they had freed twenty years before because that trust was the only hope they saw in that hour. In the end, all kept their vow of secrecy for fear of a Reconstruction legalistic interpretation that might have hanged them all. Yes, an unusual wartime predicament created the unusual understanding for you MacKoys and Donald's people that's endured."

We said no more about Marsh and Sue Anne's separation after that.

IV

The next week Donald had stopped by the Sunrise Acres office when Marina called Brick to report on her mother. Brick listened to Marina detailing her mother's condition, then sighed and told Marina the story of Sue Anne's leaving Marsh. At one point Brick said, "Yes, it puts a big knot in my stomach, too. We'll both feel better if you just do the best you can for your mother and call me every afternoon if possible."

Hanging up the phone, Brick said, "Donald, Marina's mother's still in the hospital and Lisa is returning home tomorrow. Marina must stay in Canada through Christmas and New Year's to give her mother the care she'll need when she's discharged, as Marina's the only one available. Lisa says she and her daughters, along with Aunt Joan, will return during Christmas to give Marina relief.

"I hated telling Marina about Marsh and Sue Anne. I know it hurts her almost as much as it does us, but it had to be done."

"Yes," Donald commented. "I been knowing you MacKoys forever and you all put lots of stock in family. Good or bad, it's the only thing that lasts on this earth. My Mamma and Daddy won't right 'cause they left me as a throw-away child. But they was all I had, and all I ever wanted love from till I met Bessie Mae.

"Mr. Marsh's good heart means well 'cause I've seen him do good things. Like when you and him were talking to that Thornbo man about house painting and Marsh really put that man in his place. Yes, Mr. Marsh's got good intentions, and I know they must be bothering his conscience about now."

The next Friday Brick and Marsh were at the law office for another house closing when I arrived from school. After Dad and the new homeowners left, Junebug gave me the paperwork to prepare for courthouse filing, and I left.

When I reentered with the completed forms, I knocked, but made the mistake of opening the door a crack, too, and heard Marsh say, "Sue Anne's right about my always wanting a roll in the hay with Lonah ever since that first day Dutch introduced us. I just kept on seeing her at that country store near her house and the breeding farm. Sue Anne saw us embracing at Lonah's front door, and just imagined what had gone on inside."

I realized that I shouldn't enter, but I didn't want to draw attention by closing the door, either. So I stood motionless, one hand on the doorknob.

"Well, what's done is ugly," commented Junebug. "The question is how ugly can it be from here forward until your separation details for a divorce are worked out.

"Marsh, as I see it, Sue Anne has taken her items without your objection. So, the retained earnings of your one-third of Sunrise Acres and your 50 percent of the cattle are at issue. As I understand it, you have about $20,000 of retained earnings tied up in the paved roads and utilities of Sunrise Acres, and according to the market price of cattle, about the same. Of course, both values are like the daily price of gas or construction-grade lumber—uncertain due to volatility.

"For an uncomplicated divorce, you should offer her a settlement that would entice her to forgo any litigation process since she has no actual proof of extramarital relations, just good suspicions. If she's due $20,000 in general, her attorney will likely get a third of that. Thus she would clear maybe $13,000. To avoid trial, I'd offer her $15,000. Then pray she's the type who either wants to forgive you or simply leave you to get on with the rest of her life. If you like, I can make that offer. My charges to you will be modest, but you'll have to put $15,000 in my trust account so I can make her a genuine offer."

"OK, I'll be penniless," said Marsh, "but if that'll end it clean, do it to show her I'm willing to do the right thing."

At this point I could hear the movement of chairs, and good-byes, and I opened the door as if I had just appeared. Junebug gave me a stern look as I set the paperwork on his desk.

As the cousins were leaving, Junebug remarked, "Brick, I understand Madame LaGraves is in a real dilemma."

Brick replied, "Madame has broken ankles and hands. She's not able to bathe, walk, or blow her nose. How would you like changing a fifty-five-year-old woman's diapers?"

The cousins left, and Junebug glanced over the house-sale papers. "Melody, everyone who comes into a lawyer's office is entitled to confidential advice. That includes Marsh and Brick, who we both tend to think of more as friends than clients.

"Your uncertain entry allowed you to overhear some legal conversation on Marsh and Sue Anne's situation that must remain secret. I know Sue Anne's given you her account of this story, and thus you might wish to give her some comfort by prematurely relaying the terms of the settlement I've proposed to Marsh. But don't. The timing and the details of that are for me to decide only, understand?"

"Yes, sir," I said, leaving quickly.

Wet weather soon stalled the building pace and produced frustration evident at the lumber company Christmas barbeque when Brick and Marsh arrived at our table with their food. They talked to Cotton Roberts and Austin at the next table about the rocky, rattlesnake-infested lot where the old dairy barn had been located.

"So what's the health department say about that flooding septic treatment bed where the rocky snake pit was?" asked Cotton.

"The septic tank inspectors are glad Hutton laid out a bigger lot there," answered Marsh. "We'll have to double the size of the treatment bed with more seepage pipe to keep the sewage from oozing up to ground surface. The soil is just too poor on that lot to accept regular flows of sewer water, and so the system needs to use the lot's remaining land area."

"And it's something we'll have to pay for out of warranty money because the sale of that house is less than a year old," said Brick.

Then Austin saw his wife and children approaching the serving line with Mr. Malcolm and Mrs. Colleen and excused himself. I also excused myself, saying, "Mrs. Sharpe and her daughter are going away for the holidays. She's asked me to come in to go over things that I've never done. She says not to worry that I'm only familiar with real-estate transactions. She promises that all I'll have to do is to keep the radio tuned to that classical radio station while Junebug visits holiday drunk drivers in jail."

v

When I reported to the law office after Christmas, Junebug was adjusting the office radio back to the FM classical music station. He said he was going to breakfast at Uncle Henry's Grill and would return soon. Listening to Aaron Copland's arrangement of "Simple Gifts" renewed my sense of self-control in connection with the world's sanity once more.

But then Deputy Carley Ray Craft called, his tone urgent, and I took his phone number for Junebug. When Junebug returned, he took the number and went into his office, closing the door. When he emerged, looking as if he had seen a ghost, he asked, "Is Marsh or Brick at Sunrise Acres today?"

"I don't think so," I replied.

"Call around for them," he requested. "If no luck in Wisdom Station, try Brick at the PSR Club."

I could not locate Marsh, but the PSR Club golf shop attendant said he would have Brick call after his first nine holes. When Brick called, I passed the call through to Junebug's office. Ten minutes later Junebug emerged, saying, "Brick says that Marsh is at the beach and may return this afternoon. If your dad sees Marsh, ask him to have Marsh call me—pronto!"

Junebug then left for his holiday jail visits at the courthouse, and I didn't see him again that day.

That evening waiting for Dad to come home for supper, Grandfather and I were watching television. Dad came in and asked if the news had begun. "It's about to start," I said.

The lead story was about the discovery of a naked, mutilated body on the banks of the Cape Fear River between Fayetteville and Elizabethtown that had been identified as

Dutch Lazlo's, an heir to the Lazlo textile fortune of Pineland Springs. It noted that Dutch was charged in drug trafficking but was free on bond. The mutilation was not described.

When the story ended, Dad said, "I sure hope they get those who killed him, and I hope they don't get to Lonah, like Marsh worries they might."

"Dad, you've seen Marsh, and didn't give him my message to call Junebug? What's going on? I mean murder and—!"

"Marsh had been at the beach over Christmas with Lonah. When he brought her home this afternoon, they found her house surrounded by all kinds of police.

"Fishermen found Lazlo's naked body. He'd been shot in the back of the head. They cut his penis off, too, and stuck it up his fanny. It's some kinda 'don't-screw-with-us' gangster message to those cooperating with the investigation of the Puerto Rican dope business that Lazlo was involved in.

"According to Marsh, Lonah didn't know about the drug smuggling. But she knew many of the men by face and name, and the killers are after her, too. That's why the authorities were waiting at her house.

"By sheer luck, one of the federal cops spotted one of the hit men who Lazlo had previously identified from Miami police file photos. The cop and the suspect were both at a local country store near Lonah's, buying cigarettes. The officer overpowered the hit man, who had a concealed .22 caliber pistol. In the car, they found a photo in his luggage of Lazlo and Lonah together with some of their Puerto Rican cronies. Lonah and Dutch's addresses were on the back of the photo. The store's owner said that the apprehended man and another had been there the previous day wanting directions to Lonah's place. Other witnesses said that there were two men in the car and that the second man slipped away when he saw his accomplice being arrested.

"With one hit man still on the loose, the authorities said it's unsafe for Lonah to stay at her place. They're putting her under protection. That means resigning her job!

"Later Marsh called Brick, who told him what Junebug had said about Deputy Craft's phone call and Lonah's potential danger from the remaining hit man. That's why everybody's been trying to reach Marsh all day.

"When Marsh came by the Sunrise Acres office, he got me to follow him to his hay barn, where I helped him shut that big barn door so he could hide his car there. He drove a lumber company pickup truck home, and said he'd probably trade vehicles before the first of the New Year just to make himself more obscure until this blows over."

Mrs. Penny, I didn't sleep a wink that night for worry, and the next day's headlines were full of the Lazlo murder story, which included the medical examiner's mutilation details. That afternoon I stopped by Sunrise Acres to see Dad and found Brick on the phone with Stan Cannon, who was in California preparing for winter tournaments.

After much conversation about hit men, and one escaping by nearby I-95 to South Florida, Brick paused, then said, "Stan, my romance has hit the skids, too. Marina's mother's casts were removed yesterday, but x-rays showed that both of her wrists had been set wrong. So they were surgically broken and re-set by a specialist in Montréal, who says that because of the advancing arthritis, the casts should remain on twelve weeks, instead of eight. Her ankle casts were not scheduled to come off for another two weeks. She may have a similar ordeal to go through with them.

"Marina and her mother will be staying at Aunt Joan's Montréal flat throughout this second healing process so the orthopedic specialist can see Madame LaGraves weekly. Joan went back to Montréal during Christmas because of the accident but has returned to Florida. Of course, our friend Henri, whom you entertained at the Greensboro golf tournament, will be around to help."

VI

The cousins had an uneventful time that New Year's, but their friends did not. On Tuesday, Brick, Cousin Mingo, and Hogbear were inspecting a back-forty house when Marsh came in exclaiming, "Have you heard about Monroe and Hutton?!"

Brick had barely answered "No" before Marsh went on. "My own problems, Dutch's murder, and now this! Austin and Junebug have just told me the damnedest thing! Hutton, Monroe, and Cy Turner tried to steal a truckload of cigarettes Saturday night and got caught red-handed.

"Remember that poker game robbery? Well, Hutton and Cy lost more money than anyone suspected, and that restricted their business. To solve this problem, they went for a big score—stealing a truckload of cigarettes and smuggling them into Canada.

"Some poker buddy drives for a trucking company that occasionally hauls cigarettes. When Cy found this out, he talked the guy into turning a cigarette-loaded truck over to him for $6,000. Cy's idea was to make it look like the truck driver'd been robbed, when actually the driver was conspiring with Cy to steal the truck. Cy then got Hutton and Monroe to put up $2,000 each along with Cy's own $2,000 to make up the $6,000 needed to buy the truck driver's cooperation. All believed this would work because they'd met this smuggling friend of Hutton's, André, several times.

"They say a truckload of cigarettes is worth about $55,000 here, but over $75,000 in Canada because of their high cigarette taxes. A big profit on a $6,000 investment!

"However, the truck driver, who had all along been a mole, scoping out poker games for the poker-robbing bandits, alerted them. Cy made plans to divert the truck to a back road for the transfer. Here, the driver and his robbery buddies were planning to keep the cigarettes themselves, as well as the $6,000 pay-off money. Junebug says he's not surprised because shady activities like poker and cockfighting generally entice the more vicious ex-con elements back into crime sooner or later if big money is involved.

"What nobody knew is that the law had wire-tapped one of the suspected poker robbers, who has a prison record. The whole scam played right into the authorities' hands. They even discovered that the driver had been in on the Johnson County poker-game robbery and was waiting for the right time to hit Old Blue's game, too. So the sheriff just let the whole sequence of events play out while observing from the woods before they came out to handcuff everybody! Hutton, Monroe, and Cy are really screwed, big-time!

"Hutton's Raleigh attorney and Monroe's dad put up their bail. They'd do prison time if they had a criminal record or had been carrying firearms like the poker bandits. Likely they'll have to pull weekend jail time for public service restitution along with fines for being an expense to the legal system. The poker robbers and the truck driver will definitely do extended hard time."

"Damn!" Brick said. "Lisa's going to love hearing this story when she returns tonight from Canada. Marina says Lisa's still peeved about the poker robbery, but this cockeyed scheme should finish off their family harmony. I don't think I'll tell Marina this news. I'll let Lisa tell her."

Later we learned how furious Lisa was as Hutton's legal problems caused several clients to take their new project work elsewhere. No one wanted their projects sidetracked by time lost to Hutton's legal-defense meetings, and only those projects underway retained his services. As a result, cash-flow loss in Hutton's business set off consequences that affected the lives of several others outside his immediate family, including Marina.

VII

As I've said, Mrs. Penny, others related much of this story to me. But I admit that I found out the following secrets because of shameful prying.

I found a letter from Marina to Brick. Brick had hidden it in his desk drawer under home-buyer applications and forgot to take it with him when he left for that year's Super Bowl Sunday weekend. I spotted the letter while looking for the blank applications I needed to make my typed versions. I ignored it initially, but when Dad left to take a prospective-customer back to their apartment, I'm sorry to say that I read it. I've always remembered the wording of this loving letter, and how it captured the couple's dilemma:

My Darling Brick,

It's Sunday p.m., Mother's asleep, and I am missing you so much right now. I guess that's because we weren't on our routine phone call today. You were probably still golfing at our usual phone time, anyway, and I hope you had a good round but missed me, too.

I received your last Saturday's letter on Thursday. It made me miss you all the more. I've read it so many times that the envelope has begun to tear from taking your letter out. Your remembrance of my eyes at the beach, and our looking up at that imaginary figure of a non-judgmental God in the clouds makes me want to hold you close again—so much. I still get chills when the memory of that moment runs through me. My memories of it are a respite from the routine of attending to Mother.

Her call is like the interruption of Junebug and Kay's plane flying over our tender moment on the cottage deck, and it wakes me from my fondest reveries. I long for this snail's pace of existence to be over.

Thankfully, I may have something new to pass the time. Henri and Arnaud stopped by Friday. It was at a time when I had one of my light-headed spells, as you and your friends call them, and they gave me a break by entertaining Mother until I could recover. Arnaud has referred to Henri one of his clients connected with the Old Town Restoration. The gentleman and his wife have bought a huge flat nearby, and Henri wants me to help the couple realize their vision.

Henri says he feels he'll get lots of new referrals from this client's numerous financially well-off connections. He says he'll pay me! It won't be much, but anything will be great. I've had no money of my own since New Year's. I've had to take from Mother's resources a few times for personal necessities and feel guilty about it. A small check from Henri will be a relief to my self-esteem.

Speaking of money, I do not know if I would even have a job today if I were back in North Carolina. Between Vann's legal expenses, the poker robbery, and cigarette-investment monies, the firm's cash is drained. All this has caused him nearly to lose the balance of his contract on the Family Dollar Motel project, and did cause Cy to lose his contract outright. Lisa says Cy's filing for bankruptcy. I only hope that doesn't happen to Vann and Lisa.

Of course, new projects aren't coming to Vann, either. He and Lisa took out a second mortgage on their house last Friday to meet current expenses. She says they'll be able to pay it back in the spring once new work starts on projects they already had under contract and retained for payment draws. But they now have to produce the same amount of work with less employee expense to make the second-mortgage payoff. They can do that by working overtime themselves, but it means there would be no place for me if I were there. So I guess I'm meant to be here in Québec at this point in my life. That's the only logic I can see in all this nonsense. I don't like it, but I do the best I can because I must.

As bad as it is, though, at least I'm not in Vann's shoes. Lisa says she hopes they'll get off with a fine, a judicially approved confiscation of Vann, Cy, and Monroe's monies passed to the cigarette truck driver, and weekend jail time on community-service detail.

Lisa says that Monroe's father has put all of their business interests into Ginger's care and will not let Monroe near the petty cash or checkbook. It's too bad that Old Mr. Hutton won't do that, too. Lisa would run things ship-shape. But Mr. Hutton is just too old to do that to his son.

With all these losses, it makes our time together seem like a part of some faraway Disney World fantasy. Yesterday, we drove to Pointe de Beaver to check on things. Now that Mother's ankle casts are off, she can at least walk, even if she can't use her encased hands. It was good for her to get out of Aunt Joan's flat and see the world, and for me, too, because it's made me more patient. Not only did I enjoy the outing, I even enjoyed Mother because of her better attitude from just being out and about.

While we were checking the house, I had the opportunity to walk out into the yard where we snuggled and looked down at the St. Lawrence. It's now barren white all the way to the icy river. I imagined us there in May or June, with all the flowers in bloom, and me holding an arrangement of blue flowers for my eyes. It would be a beautiful spot for our wedding, and Father Marcel could perform the rites. I've come to appreciate his weekly visits with us, by the way, and I think I'll write down this future chore for him to perform in that little "things-to-do" fertilizer notepad you gave me!

I especially dream of such when I sleep in one of your old shirts. Your pure smell is still on them, and that makes me long for your tenderness.

My fondest love always,
Marina

I returned the letter to the desk drawer, feeling ashamed that I had read it and also relief that I hadn't been caught! Today, thirty years later, I am still bothered by my prying. But even so, the lovely letter raised my spirits considerably to read Marina's words for Brick. Even a love letter, though, can reflect the complications of life on this earth, Mrs. Penny.

Chapter Fourteen

Chaplain Wesley Returns

I

AFTER READING MARINA'S LETTER, Sunrise Acres' saga continued by exposing more of Cecil X and Shasta's troubles. Although it was the heady time of Nixon's second inaugural and the Vietnam treaty-signing that indicated financial health for housing, Cecil and Shasta's breakup foreshadowed troubles brewing for many starter homeowners.

Shasta's concerns about the Black Muslims were common knowledge. Her fears spiked on news reports of the murders of seven orthodox Sunni Black Muslims in Washington, D.C., the day before President Nixon's January 20, 1973, inauguration. This story surfaced late because of the press coverage on the inauguration and the Vietnam peace-signing a week later. Street-smart people believed a different sect of Black Muslims within the greater movement had carried out the massacre. To Shasta, these ideas of a jihad, or bloody holy war against people of other Muslim beliefs, was irreligious, like Christians taking the Lord's name in vain by killing each other in Northern Ireland. Such actions could never beget the true personal peace all seek. So she left Cecil and moved in with a female co-worker.

Now Cecil saw himself as a failed man. His depression deepened because he couldn't make his house payments alone. His once-prosperous fish business was now under economic strains that eventually bankrupted him.

The Muslims sold fish on consignment, and Cecil paid for his fish and delivery truck weekly. After expenses, he was expected to give back to the cause by renting the storefront mosque he headed. Rising gas prices put Cecil behind quickly on meeting delivery expenses. Gas increases plus lumber inflation also affected Sunrise Acres' sales volumes, and this was months before the October 1973 gas crisis.

Shasta told Mr. O'Cain, Dad, and me on the day we helped her move out that Cecil often gave as much as 60 percent of his profits back to the cause, which made neither business sense nor religious sense. She said Black Pride should make you feel better because you were living in the true saving light. It was not supposed to wear you down and make you feel poorer.

Cecil, however, seemed content to wade through the morass of multiple Muslim-sect misunderstandings and misinterpretations just as Methodists, Baptists, and other Protestants do until some higher understanding evolves. He finally left Sunrise Acres, seeming to be reconciled like a docile child to his circumstances, never being a militant soul anyway.

The Farm Home Administration took over Cecil and Shasta's foreclosed home to resell. There was no damage to the house, so Will O'Cain merely had it repainted and assigned ownership of the house to the next-in-line Sunrise Acres customer.

Rising lumber prices affected the last five houses of the thirty that the MacKoys had wanted to complete by the end of January. In spite of extra carpenters to speed the building schedule, the December and January weather had allowed only twenty-five of the thirty to be started. If the five remaining houses were started after huge lumber price increases, the MacKoys would lose money.

In late February of 1973, Dad was reading about the South Dakota Wounded Knee confrontation then underway, when Brick phoned him saying that Mr. Malcolm needed everyone in Cotton Roberts' drafting office to review a new house plan for the five un-built houses.

Mr. Malcolm reported that Mr. O'Cain couldn't appraise houses for more money to cover the higher lumber prices because wages had not inflated simultaneously with the price of goods. He added, "We must build a less expensive house to bring our construction costs down to be in line with the maximum that the government can loan."

"That's the trend now," Cotton Roberts chimed in. "All builders are wanting plan changes. Even country-club home builders are trimming back."

"Deacon, we're considering building a house without a carport and eliminating all the brick except on the front. What we want to know is, can you sell this new stripped-down version of a house plan?" asked Austin.

"There'll be resistance," Dad replied. "But they'll eventually buy if that's all that's available. If it's built so a carport can be constructed over the driveway later, I can tell customers they can add this feature when their paycheck increases to meet inflation."

"Good point, Deacon," said Mr. Malcolm. "Let's redraw these five plans for re-submittal."

II

When Dad, Brick, and Marsh presented the new plan to Mr. O'Cain, he noted that a review would take six weeks because his Raleigh headquarters was swamped with state-wide re-submittal plans since wages hadn't increased equally with the inflated cost of goods. "But I've got two more bad-news items for you," he added.

"First, the nationwide problem: the government is running out of money because of inflation, and President Nixon says he intends to fight inflation by impounding congressionally approved funds to reduce government expenditures. This includes all federal housing loans.

"According to Raleigh, all government-guaranteed loans will stop when our spending exceeds our division's prorated share of the federal budget. When that occurs, I'll have no mortgage money available until next year's federal budget, or the next, for these five houses or the ones you've finished but not yet sold.

"In addition, Raleigh says we'll need loan reserves to cover repossessions like Cecil's. Right now, there are ten Sunrise Acres homeowners who are behind on their house payments. Most of the loan monies I now have will be frozen so I can finance repossessed houses. There'll be little or no money to finance your new homes.

"Now, I've been discussing with our community college friend, Dr. Chester O'Malley, about having home economics classes for your Sunrise Acres residents. He has a white girl working with him, Wendy Granger, who says she knows you MacKoys. Chester says she can create a lesson plan that'll help our Sunrise families deal with inflation stress better. When I get more information on her lesson plan, I'll let you know.

"Your second problem relates to your septic tank troubles on that old snake-den lot. You got rid of the snakes, and thus far your drain-pipe extension seems to be working. However, the septic inspectors said you may have bigger septic problems on your last three lots in the back forty because they all back up to the river across from the General Electric plant.

"The septic inspectors are bringing in an N.C. State soils expert to analyze the ability of the soils on those lots to absorb and sanitize the septic sewer waters. If the lot soils are O.K., nothing changes. If the soils are unsuitable, I'll have to ban those three lots from the Farm Home loan program."

Brick said, "That'll kill us! We've invested $4,500 in paving and utilities on each of those lots. You and Raleigh approved all this when the health department did a general check of the area. You're changing the rules in the middle of the game. You've got to accept those lots."

"I don't have to accept anything that I perceive to be risky for the government's loan program," Will answered. "Nobody wants to buy a house with a commode they can't flush. Nobody! I'll let you know when the soil analyst will test the three lots."

Dad then followed the cousins back to see Mr. Malcolm, who called O'Cain to review these new developments. When Mr. Malcolm hung up, he said, "Well, this'll kill any profits we've forecasted. If he has to foreclose on any of these ten homes that are behind in their mortgage payments, it may take over a year to sell the unsold houses we've nearly finished. So there's no need to start the last five units until we have sold off most of what we've already built.

"Marshall, you and Brick stop paying yourselves. Then we'll still have enough money to make the interest payments on the loans, and pay for the travel wear and tear on your vehicles. If there's any profit left when this is over, we'll divide up what little is left then."

From then until Easter, nothing happened at Sunrise Acres except for Mingo's few warranty repairs. Bobby Jack Johnson and Riley Carlisle found work in Fayetteville and Raleigh that helped them along. Mingo worked with Bobby Jack on a framing crew, and Hogbear retired. Dad even returned to bricklaying with his brothers, but on the week-ends he was always at Sunrise Acres showing houses to potential customers. As for me, without any Sunrise activity I lost most of my hours at the law office.

Marsh tended his cows during this lull, and Lonah Slueter vanished, under government witness protection. The one thing I learned about Marsh, through occasional law-office work, was that Sue Anne had not yet signed their separation papers, which I thought odd.

Brick, however, was always around Sunrise Acres during the week, and his late after-noons revolved around almost-daily phone calls from Marina. From her calls we did learn that Henri and Arnaud's Old Town restoration connections were going to provide Marina with several renovation jobs due to begin around Easter. Her mother's progno-sis now looked brighter, and Aunt Joan's return from Florida was expected to provide Marina with much-needed nursing relief. Marina also hoped her new income stream could finance a North Carolina trip since Brick now had no paycheck.

Near the Easter break, the N.C. State soils specialist condemned the three riverfront lots because the river created a high water table in the soils so septic effluent could not be expected to be treated as needed. While the lots were not banned outright, the cost of constructing a septic system on such poor soils would be greater than the cost of the house. So those lots were abandoned. Thus, only two of the five houses without carports were ever built.

III

Dad and Brick discussed these financial reverses the Thursday Brick left Sunrise Acres for the Good Friday holiday. Brick said he was looking forward to seeing his cousin Wesley and meeting his bride, Lee Çu, since the couple had just returned to Fort Bragg from Vietnam.

Good Friday afternoon, Austin called Brick's dad to say that Mr. Malcolm had been taken to the hospital. Donald and Dad had found him wandering around the three condemned lots. Dad said he didn't seem to recognize them.

Dr. Street, the longtime family doctor, said that while Mr. Malcolm appeared to have suffered a stroke, he suspected this event might be connected to Mr. Malcolm's cancer medication and thus transferred him to Duke. Because his doctor was on Easter holiday, Mr. Malcolm's condition was uncertain, but at least he was stabilized.

Austin also asked Brick to locate Marsh, who was somewhere at the beach. Brick drove to Ocean Drive and found Marsh at a popular dance spot, talking with Sue Anne! Brick knew that neither had yet signed the couple's divorce instrument. It was after midnight when the cousins returned to Pineland Springs, alone.

The next day's events I learned from Kay, after she and Junebug had visited Brick's parents' Pineland Springs home to meet Wesley and Lee Çu. Aunt Dot and Brick's sister, Mary Lee, also joined in. To everyone's delight, Brick grilled steaks.

The dinner conversation initially centered on Mr. Malcolm's condition, but then changed to focus on Wesley, Lee Çu, and Wesley's views on General Eisner's MIA status.

Wesley noted, "I told Lee Çu that we'd see Nicole first after settling into our Fort Bragg quarters. We hosted her and Brewer last night at the Officers Club.

"Although there is nothing that I could add to the story, I did say that I, like many, believe that the General's munitions consulting was a CIA cover job. In Vietnam, he was often at their headquarters, and his private car was seen in the parking spot marked CIA Liaison Officer at the Bragg JFK Special Forces Center, too. Naturally, he and I never discussed this, but I often thought of him as a dark knight on missions that saved troopers' lives.

"I also told Nicole that the General's helicopter crash site is now marked, and eventually authorities will return to look for bone fragments and small, man-made items. That investigation may be years off since all U.S. combat troops departed just a few days ago on March 29. Investigating now amidst continuing hostilities in the region bordering Vietnam, Laos, and Cambodia will be impossible."

"I admired Eisner and his late wife, but please tell us about meeting Lee Çu," Aunt Dot asked Wesley.

Wesley smiled, saying, "In Vietnam, chaplains and medical teams visited villages, churches, and orphanages near encampments because such visits were considered ambassadorial work. The orphanage where Lee Çu worked as a nurse was nearby, and I was told of her background before our meeting. Consequently, I anticipated that she would be a person I could share some sympathetic talk with. I just didn't know that she would be a captivating beauty.

"I told Eisner that Lee Çu was the first person I had ever felt any complete connection with since the death of my parents. Our understanding of the orphans' spiritual complex simply made the world's nonsense go away every time we looked at each other. Mutual understanding flowed between us instantly. Her depth of loving acceptance surprised me because it was something I had never experienced.

"Yet, while I fell in love with her, my mind also cautioned me that 'The heart is deceitful above all things.' I had used this Biblical passage from Jeremiah 17:9 when advising young troopers against cross-cultural marriages. I naturally wondered if I was being emotionally intelligent about my own relationship with Lee Çu. Was my heart lying to me with innocent, wishful dreams that the realities of our different backgrounds would later destroy? Or would our common orphanhood override our cultural differences?

"Therefore, I prayed for a season on these issues, as ministers say. I prayed that I might not only save my own life for its highest intended purpose to pursue the fulfillment of my happiness, but also to not impose my influence upon on Lee Çu's highest opportunities for God-given fulfillment.

"After this prayerful reflection, I determined that while man's heart is deceived by half-truths, it is also that Tree-of-Life mechanism by which the Lord beckons us to action. I realized more rightly that the heart is a mysterious mechanism that filters life's experiences into and out of our rational intellect to motivate our energies of action, good and bad.

"I recalled the Jewish and Catholic Army doctors I had anguished over joining in matrimony. It was obvious that they each possessed above-average logical-emotive thinking abilities. Nevertheless, I worried about the nature of the emotional force that had brought them together. Such a union seemed to risk divorcing each from the heritage of their disparate family backgrounds that had rocked their cradles into adulthood. I saw this Catholic-Jewish couple as being in danger of cultural estrangement. Yet it was their right to embark on the journey. And what God had brought together, let no man put asunder, including a well-meaning chaplain!

"So I anguished after counseling them and prayed to God that he send one of his Archangels, like Raphael, Michael, or Gabriel, to guide them in marriage, as they are angels to Catholic, Jew, and Muslim alike. Truly, one can never divine the mysteries of marital bliss, no matter how many marriage-counseling seminars a chaplain attends!

"Ultimately, I suggested to Lee Çu that the common denominators of our orphan-hood and having lived with different cultures around the world could form a reliable enough foundation upon which we could grow together to build a lasting relationship. I proposed to her that we embark on marriage's journey with the Tree of Life guiding our mutual, spiritual empathies because this would be enough to guide us through life's future storms. That there would be storms to weather I had no doubt, I told her, but we would be together—no longer alone."

"Well, Nephew, we hope Lee Çu is adapting happily here to life in the United States," said Mrs. Loraine. "And I'm sure the Tree of Life will guide you both well."

IV

"Melody, I appreciate Wesley and Lee Çu being concerned about their differences. Billy and I never forgot each other when his unit pushed on after MacArthur's Philippines victory. Our native souls were different, but they spoke to each other from the depths of Mother Earth.

"Billy loved the openness around Clark Air Force Base as much as I did the arid gran-deur of his Four Corners home when we'd return there to see Pem's dad, Silver Hawk. The rhythm of our souls was also more closely intertwined by the many community-college courses we took on base. These included archaeology technician courses, which allowed us to work with archaeologists struggling to protect Philippine cultural history whenever a base construction project was underway. When I moved to the Four Corners with Billy, we did archaeology volunteer work at Indian sites before he died in '97. We were soul mates, but those courses recertified our unique togetherness daily."

Chapter Fifteen

The 1973 Gas Crisis Boils the Economy and Melody's New Job

I

After Easter, Mr. Malcolm's condition required extensive treatment, as his prostate cancer had spread. Radiation and chemotherapy treatments were prescribed so that he might have time to order his affairs. His end was in sight.

Mr. Malcolm's treatments weakened him, prolonging his hospital stay. While hospitalized he met with Junebug's father and the lumber company's accountant to discuss his will. At a second bedside meeting, Mrs. Colleen witnessed his signature and listened to the details, which were sealed until after Mr. Malcolm's return home.

During this time O'Cain repossessed a second Sunrise Acres house, but not much happened otherwise. Things, however, had gotten dangerous for Mingo's adopted brother, Juan Ingros, who was still hiding out in eastern Montana.

Juan's Pembroke College roommate had been Harry Bowmore, a Montana Crow. Many western tribes had participated in the Wounded Knee Sioux Reservation incident that took place next door in South Dakota that year, and Juan and Harry became involved, too.

Like the earlier news story on the Black Muslims massacre in Washington, D.C., the 1973 Wounded Knee events competed with the Vietnam Truce, Nixon's Second Inaugural, and the news coming forth daily on the aftermath of the Watergate burglary. Wounded Knee events and details covered in North Carolina newspapers were rare.

What we did know, however, was that Juan and his friends took a long weekend off from their Montana cattle-ranch work to visit the South Dakota Pine Ridge Sioux Reservation and see what all the fuss was about. Their winter workload was not demanding.

There they learned that many Indian and non-Indian sympathizers were backpacking supplies into the Wounded Knee compound nightly by back trails. This was dangerous work because shots were exchanged between the U.S. Government's Sioux police force and Wounded Knee-occupying Indians who were asserting their mistreatment and the graft of their resources.

Many backpackers were caught and charged with obstructing a Federal Law Enforcement operation. Most of these charges were eventually dropped following a lengthy legal process. Back in Montana after three backpacking runs, Juan and his friends had to lay low because the FBI had infiltrated the smuggling operation and had put out descriptions of those in hiding. Juan called Mingo from a pay phone to say that he feared his capture would reveal his true identity, then force his return to North Carolina for stabbing Chalky. He said he would continue to call home from time to time. Mingo, recalling how Hutton and Monroe were caught for cigarette smuggling by phone taps, advised Juan to call from different pay phones for fear that phones around the Montana Crow Reservation might be bugged.

After the Wounded Knee uprising ended in May 1973, Mr. Malcolm returned home. His weakness allowed Mrs. Colleen to drive him only weekly to his office and to Sunrise Acres. At either place, Austin, Marsh, or Brick would come and sit in the backseat to converse with him. He also went to the law office to see the elder Mr. Willingham about his will. Mr. Malcolm's accountants and attorneys hoped to be able to disclose the will by late July so the multifaceted components of the lumber company could continue to be managed profitably for the benefit of his family.

Upon becoming a full-time employee of Junebug's late that summer after college graduation, I learned about the will. When Ethel Sharpe announced her retirement date to be the last day of September 1973, Junebug brought me in for tutoring on the procedures I had not learned during my part-time employment there.

I was considering a home economics job offer in northeastern North Carolina prior to Junebug's offer. However, I gladly accepted his offer because it permitted me to remain in familiar family surroundings. I was not ready to be far away from my birthplace yet, Mrs. Penny.

II

During this time Marsh and Junebug said that Brick's interest in Marina was waning as she was dating others in Québec and he occasionally in North Carolina. Her main escort was Arnaud Brouillet, and Marina's new social life reduced her calls to the Sunrise Acres construction office from daily to occasionally. Marina did phone Brick, however, after Labor Day to say that she and Henri were planning to come to the High Point Fall Furniture Mart and that she would call later with their travel schedule. The early October trip was cancelled, though, with the beginning of the Arab-Israeli Yom Kippur War and the attendant gas crisis shortages in the U.S. and Canada.

The war's impact also forced Will O'Cain to foreclose on four more Sunrise Acres houses. Brick told Junebug, "These four foreclosures are pushing O'Cain to get Dr. O'Malley's community college family budget classes in place for our remaining homeowners. Deacon and I are meeting to discuss the class curriculum with Wendy Granger, the instructor. She'll hold classes at night so most of the residents can attend. I hope her classes help because O'Cain says there are others who may lose their homes. If we have more foreclosures, we'll not sell out the project in my lifetime.

"It's like the whole world is going to hell in a hand-basket, you know? Vice President Agnew resigns over bribes. Then, of course, there's Watergate, Watergate everywhere.

"So much for Lyndon Johnson's great American economy of guns and butter at the same time and Nixon's ending the Bretton Woods gold standard. Now we've got no gold, no war, no guns, and no damn butter, either—just pure confusion!

"These high gas prices not only cancelled Marina and Henri's High Point trip, they've also stopped all Disney World travel, killing Hutton's motel project. It's pushing him into bankruptcy like his buddy Cy, and now Hutton's a divorce candidate. And no, I haven't heard from Marina since her trip cancellation. In these uncertain times with its economic impact on her family situation, I wonder if I ever will again."

III

The tough economy also concerned Will O'Cain and his superiors. While only six houses of the more than eighty sold at Sunrise Acres had been foreclosed on, this still equaled a 7.5 percent foreclosure rate, alarming when compared to a normal foreclosure rate of less than 1 percent. Additionally, the fact that four foreclosures came in one month created more urgency for the family-budget counseling program.

With Dad, Brick, and Marsh, I attended the first meeting held at a nearby black Baptist church. Will O'Cain, Chester O'Malley, and Wendy sat in chairs behind the podium.

Dr. O'Malley began, "I have told Mr. O'Cain that programs like the one we've put together have helped first-time homebuyers all across the U.S. Raleigh has sent us an expert in this field. Please welcome Miss Wendy Granger with the N.C. State University Extension Service who'll be your primary counselor."

In outlining the program, Wendy said she'd first visit each Sunrise Acres household to review their individual budgets in hopes of providing a better focus for each specific family circumstance. She hoped to complete the individual family reviews by Thanksgiving. Then the family visits would continue along with a Thursday night class for everyone.

Because of the night schedule, Brick suggested to O'Cain and O'Malley that I assist Wendy since the work would take place after my day ended at the law office. My being with Wendy would help speed the process because I knew where everyone lived. In addition, two women out at night would provide more safety for both. O'Malley liked Brick's suggestion and said that the college could take care of my cost out of their discretionary funds.

Now I had two jobs! My combined income along with what I had saved from my first months of law-office work allowed me to make a down payment on my first car. Now I felt I had truly arrived as an adult.

Besides going with Wendy to meet families in their homes on Mondays and Tuesdays, there were also Thursday-night class sessions from six until eight for everyone. This meant that Wendy and I had late dinners. Wendy said she didn't want a late meal as it would make her Friday trips from Raleigh to see Langdon Butler on the Outer Banks overly tiring. I suggested the local pizza parlor beside Uncle Henry's Grill, and our Thursday-night dinners there for the next year and a half cemented our friendship.

My previous credit screening and paperwork for Brick, along with my college classes, had been background training for helping Wendy. Now, the work and our pizza-parlor talks gave me deeper insights into helping families keep their financial ships aright. With Brick and Dad, I had only seen the results of good or poor financial management. If people qualified for a house loan, that was great. But I always felt a sense of incompleteness when a prospect didn't qualify for a mortgage because I never knew the details behind their failure, just the bleak result. Now with Wendy, I felt like I could be a part of the solution to this problem by helping people catch their problems early enough to avoid becoming lost sheep.

IV

After finalizing Wendy's program routine during Thanksgiving week, Marsh's cow barn caught fire. There was nothing left of the hay-filled structure by the time the firefighters arrived. No one ever officially knew how the fire started but Dad later said Marsh thought it was carelessness on his and Chalky's part when they smoked marijuana that night. The more significant thing to me at the time, however, was Mr. Malcolm's failing health and the transfer of the lumber company's direction to his son-in-law, Austin.

Austin's seasoned maturity allowed him to take command of the operation with little notice. Even during Mr. Malcolm's waning days, Marsh never seemed interested in the lumber operation. Perhaps Marsh realized Austin already occupied that ground with managerial competence.

But I do know this: Austin, Diane, and Mrs. Colleen always attended Mr. Malcolm's law office visits to plan the post-mortem management of his estate. In fact, Marsh only attended one of the final meetings to contract four houses on the PSR Club lots left to Diane. Marsh would do this work for a construction-management fee that Diane would pay him after the sale of each house was complete.

Mr. Willingham and Mr. Malcolm knew that Diane had no construction knowledge, but that Marsh had acquired much from his Sunrise Acres participation. Thus Mr. Malcolm wanted Marsh to manage the building process for Diane and for Marsh's own personal improvement through the experience of helping his sister. Mr. Malcolm hoped this bond would help his adult children better face future opportunities and trials that life would bring them.

The other thing we learned of then was the formation of a new lumber company division that would specialize in railroad-tie production. This had been something both Austin and Mr. Malcolm had long wanted to do but had held off on due to the Sunrise Acres commitments. With Sunrise Acres being less demanding, entering the recession-proof market of railroad infrastructure's never-ending repair requirements became feasible. While Mr. Malcolm's body was tired, it was evident that his business acumen was as strong as ever.

Another service the law office provided was to produce a mortgage-free deed for Marsh's cow barn so he could forward it to Holden Rollins for an insurance claim. This Junebug gave to Marsh on New Year's Eve, explaining, "Marsh, I hope this gets you a few dollars after the insurance company subtracts their deductible from the barn's total value."

Marsh thanked June and then said, "You're right about Brick feeling left out in the cold now, although he's not surprised. But he'll come around if we can ever sell out Sunrise Acres."

When Marsh left, I asked Junebug, "What's bothering Brick?"

"It's the status of his now-ex-girlfriend, Marina," answered Junebug. "She got married on him Christmas Eve to that French Canadian attorney, Arnaud Brouillet.

"Brick says the shipping accident that killed Captain LaGraves affected both LaGraves girls with a great sense of loss. Lisa has often said that only the birth of her children filled that void and that Marina needed to get on with the rest of her life to have that deep experience, too.

"The world's economy being disrupted by today's high oil prices caused financial reverses for both Sunrise Acres and Hutton's business. Hutton is headed for divorce, and all that complicated things for Marina and Brick. Life goes on the best way it can, with people following the paths of least resistance to where they hope to find the satisfactions they're looking and praying for. Apparently, that's what Marina did. She called Brick before her wedding, and he told her he wished her well. But I'm sure he's not happy about the lack of her company, and that's what we're seeing in his lethargic behavior."

"Oh, I didn't know that," I said. "I'm somewhat shocked because they were a beautiful couple. But, oddly, my Indian instincts tell me it may be the best thing for them both.

"Marina might be happier married to a man of her own French heritage. Whites can't picture what's it's like living here in Wisdom Station, with most whites looking at an Indian as if you were black and most blacks looking at you as if you were a half-breed. But you always know where you're from, if you're an Indian with my family's stories of the many past generations before the Europeans came. That legacy's hard to part with, even though many Native Americans intermarry. Indian is what I'll always be because it's the only base from which I can relate comfortably to the world. Maybe being French has cultural limitations like that, too."

Mrs. Penny, while Marina's marriage to her own kind did seem natural to me, you must remember that I did not know the depth of Brick and Marina's relationship at this time, either. Only years later, when Kay told me the more intimate details, did I imagine any real pain on the part of either Brick or Marina. At this point in my life, I had yet to meet Pem to know such emotional intimacy. In 1973 I was just the lone Indian girl, occasionally realizing the incompleteness of my soul during spells of loneliness.

Truly I had only viewed them as a warm, friendly couple. And now the female member of that friendship had decided to go and live with her own kind, for her own reasons, possibly because there she felt more complete inside the core of her soul.

Chapter Sixteen

A Bronze Star Revealed

I COULDN'T DWELL LONG ON BRICK AND MARINA'S PARTING because I was still learning my two new jobs, and also Mr. Malcolm was hospitalized that New Year's of 1974. We were sure it was his end, but they kept him only three days to adjust his medications.

I didn't see Brick or Marsh after New Year's, but Dad and his brothers laid the foundations for two PSR Club houses Marsh was constructing for Diane. In the meantime, Brick and Dad consulted weekly on prospects needed to fill up the repossessed Sunrise Acres homes so building could resume for the project's completion. During this period, Dad, Brick, and Chester O'Malley went to Greensboro's North Carolina A&T University to ask their Extension Services for additional supplies for Wendy Granger's family-budget counseling. Dr. Frank Glover was their university contact, and he later came to two classes to observe our work before supplying additional materials.

Donald also mentioned that he saw Brick in late January at the Robert Burns Annual Memorial Supper at the PSR Club. Brick attended because of his father's induction as an officer of the local Scottish Clan Society. Brick's sister, Mary Lee, was a part of the entertainment, performing a Scottish Highland dance. The Burns Supper began with its traditional Toast to the Haggis. Yes, Mrs. Penny, that's a liver pudding meat! It ended with a hand-holding sing-along of Burns'"Auld Lang Syne."

At Mr. Lee MacKoy's table, along with his wife, two children, and sister Dot, were Holden and Rebecca Susan Rollins. They first spoke of Mr. Malcolm's health, and Mrs. Rollins complimented Mary Lee when she rejoined the group after her dance performance. She also mentioned that her daughter, Becky, had performed a similar dance when Mr. Rollins became a Scottish Clan Society officer, adding that Becky's stay in France had been extended. Amid this talk, Mr. Rollins asked Brick about Sunrise Acres.

Brick laughed. "We're promoting Wendy Granger's financial planning classes to stop foreclosures. Thus far, no more foreclosures. We're also helping Will O'Cain find customers for the repossessed houses since reselling those houses is the only way we can get back to finishing the project. It's a slow process, Mr. Holden.

"During last year's good sales, our Indian salesman went to factories and waited for a prospective customer's work shift to end so he could interview them. Now I do that by following up the leads we receive from black church leaders, mom-and-pop grocery stores, and barbershops. We leave Sunrise Acres literature at these places. If anyone is interested, we're notified to follow up. If this process results in a sale, the business owner or church leader gets a finder's fee for introducing the prospective homebuyer to us. Previously, our Indian salesman paid these finder's fees from his commission pay. Now we pay that to keep the process moving.

"In fact, I'm looking forward to paying a finder's fee to a Reverend Leon. That'll leave only two more repossessed houses to sell before we can sell ours and build the last two units."

II

The last Thursday in January, Dad and his brothers were finishing the second foundation on Diane's lots when Brick stopped to speak with Dad and Marsh. "O'Cain will close on that repo house tomorrow. Reverend Leon can meet us at the country store beside the General Electric plant to collect his finder's fee. Can you two meet there?"

"Maybe," answered Marsh. "I'm hoping to get a few hundred bucks of insurance money from Rollins tomorrow. I need that to square up with Chalky."

"Marsh, let's get in my car, out of this cold, while Deacon and his brothers clean up here," Brick said. "We can coordinate tomorrow's schedule after they finish."

The next day Brick told us that he remarked to Marsh, "Reverend Leon has found another prospect. If it pans out, we'll have only one more repossessed unit to sell. I'm glad Donald overheard our Thornbo conversation that day and spread the word. That leaped over the black-white cultural barrier and gave us the trust we need for sales.

"I'm also glad we've been able to arrange for Mingo to do part-time repair work on those repossessed houses. I've assured O'Cain that I'd routinely check Mingo's repairs just as we did while building those houses. I'll do some of that free Mingo-inspection work tomorrow after paying off the preacher. Donald's helping Mingo, and Mingo says Donald's skill level has improved beyond that of a sandpaper man.

"After meeting Reverend Leon and inspecting Mingo's work tomorrow, I'm coming back to the club's driving range to hit balls. Then Brewer and I may do some rabbit hunting Saturday. Wanna come?"

"No," Marsh answered. "After I get my insurance money, I'll see Dad. If he's stable, I'm meeting Sue Anne at the beach. We've discussed starting over again since you found us together at OD, when Dad's cancer returned. That's one reason she's never signed the divorce papers.

"I know that sounds crazy, but she and I are so much alike. Sue Anne's an only child from a dysfunctional home. Her father abandoned her and her mom to run off with a woman who ran a bar by the Norfolk shipyards, and he's never been heard of since Sue Anne was in grade school. Me, I'm just dysfunctional, period. We're both waifs like poor Ollie, looking for a secure landing spot. For better or worse, we have an emotional investment in one another, and need to give it another try.

"She appreciates that I was never like Dutch or Monroe and Vann because their circumstances are worse. When we were together, we talked about having kids. She would be a devoted mother, and at our age, it'll be the last chance we'll ever have. We want that opportunity. I just want to pay Chalky and get his drug bills off my agenda, so I'll have a future that offers less confusion and more hope."

"Good, Marsh. Marina and Nicole mentioned last spring that Sue Anne was having second thoughts," said Brick. "Our youthful KMA bullet-proof attitude never made anything better, and our Coosa School, slow intellect brain cells wouldn't kick into any realization that there's no future in being an eternal juvenile delinquent."

"Exactly," Marsh returned. "Our juvenile delinquent mindset never realized that Chalky's kind that would steal his mama's last Social Security penny couldn't talk any Aristotle or Socrates or be aware of what those philosophers imagined that mankind could be. I finally realized my mental disconnect about that when Chalky and I got careless smoking a joint the night my cow barn caught fire. Now you are the only one who knows how it started besides me and Chalky.

"I've thought about it a lot since the fire. Pot is a luxury of an emotional relief from life's grinding thoughts that crowd your brain faster than you can rationally assimilate them. It changes nothing and provides no solutions. But pot highs were fun for me in coping with the world's realities through a naïve brain until my next morning's moody hangover.

"Pot's like playing cowboys and Indians as a kid. One day, you just walk away from it. You don't walk away because your brain has some new insight from the Stoic philosophers.

You just walk away because it no longer provides anything interesting. The good insights I'm getting must be the result of attritional wear and tear on my ever-receding childhood brain."

"I like that thought, Marsh," Brick said, marveling at his cousin.

"Sex on the run is like that, too," Marsh laughed. "When it's no longer interesting, it's not worth screwing—Lonah.

"When I first saw her, I had just returned from Vietnam. The week before I came home, the Viet Cong overran our camp. We grabbed our weapons and shot back. The bullets sang by, and at some point, I threw a grenade. That stopped the enemy advance in our corner at the camp's supply depot, even though firing continued elsewhere in the compound.

"Then a second Viet Cong wave came in, but by then our helicopter gunships had been called in to mop up. The next morning the smoke cleared, and all we could see were enemy bodies piled up around us like cordwood. Those rotting corpses were nothing more than toothless peasants, who as Eisner used to say 'didn't know the definition of communism.'

"They must not have known the definition of the word STOP, either, because they just kept on coming right into our helicopter gunship fire. Looked like they had some primal, cultural urge not to be forced by our modern-world logic to think their way out of their existence. It was the peasant's version of the 'Don't-Tread-on-Me' Gadsden Flag idea. The illiterate peasants were brave, and you knew it was like Eisner always said: we were like the Muslim Moors, believing our new religion would conquer European culture before Charles Martel, his grandson, Charlemagne, and other El Cid types fully marshaled their forces to wear the Moors out. That's how it'll end in Vietnam, Eisner concluded—wearing out America's political spirit of false insight.

"I remember thinking that this must be Westmoreland's Light at the End of the Tunnel that McNamara and LBJ kept harping about. It dawned on me, however, that the Light-in-the-Tunnel amounted only to just keep killing the cavemen peasants until our crusading, European-borne intellectuality felt enough pity to have a belly full of it. When the battle was over, I wasn't in any mood to ask my country if I could do anything else for it! And I didn't give a damn who asked me, JFK or Jesus H. Christ!

"I was recommended for a Bronze Star, which came after I got home. I did go so far as to designate General Eisner as my preferred bestowal officer, but in the end, I just left the medal with him and Nicole because I trusted them to be quiet about it. You see, I had made buddies with this fellow, Rex, from Seattle. I don't remember his last name, but we smoked a lot of pot. He died in my arms during the firefight because the combat action kept us from moving him to the medical center. The last thing he said to me was: 'MacKoy, it's been good knowing you. I'll see you on the other side, someday.' All he got was the Purple Heart and a flag over his free casket. I still can't see how that's right, me being alive to hold a Bronze Star yet not even getting a scratch.

"I just wanted to forget it all, possibly the way Great-Granddad Everett and his brother, Cripple Cager, II, must have felt after the Civil War. Nobody gives a damn about the wars of lost causes except the poor suckers that fate stuck with the job of having to fight in them, and eventually they don't care about the cause, just the surviving—and that barely, most times.

"A week later, Rex's last words were still ringing in my ears when I saw Lonah with the Dutchman for the first time. She had that wet, prick-teasing, fuck-me look written all over her, and I wanted some of her to forget that battlefield-ringing hell still vibrating in me. Fortunately, Sue Anne came along moments after I met Lonah, and I never felt tempted to cheat on our departed Dutchman friend.

"Of course, his going to jail ended their relationship, and so I cheated on my wife with Lonah, which was much worse! Makes no sense at all, but that's the way it turned out because that's the way I felt; like life owed me a free fuck with no responsibilities to anyone, including Sue Anne after two years of marriage.

"That's the nice thing about these houses I'm building for Diane. Helping her makes me feel better about myself, like Junebug's dad said it would. It's even better than my battle-fatigue therapy sessions because it's about family, the only thing that lasts for you through the decades. I no longer feel like I have nowhere to go and nothing to do when I get there. My interest seems to be going to more normal places somewhere beyond the end of my dick and self."

"That's good," Brick interjected. "You should thank your dad for this opportunity to help your sister. It'll help him pass away on an easy tangent of hope to the Promised Land."

"I already have," Marsh replied. "Of course, I left out the juicy parts about my maturing insights on pot and sex! And I've never really told my parents about Vietnam—only Eisner and Nicole and now you, Brick. You see, Nicole arranged my first set of depression treatments with lithium through her hospital work. I trusted the Eisner father-and-daughter team to keep it a secret. I never gave lithium a chance because I continued seeing Cy Turner in Chapel Hill, but I'm back on it now for the cure from pot and the anxiety it promotes. Nicole always said I was living on thin ice because pot exacerbates phobias.

"I told Sue Anne the Vietnam things only because my therapy group and Nicole counseled that. Sue Anne did hint of some of this treatment routine to my folks, but not much because at the time I didn't see the importance of sharing it with family; they were non-combatants, after all. The only other people who know about the therapy sessions are Wesley and Henry's wife, Bertha, who I see sometimes in the hospital waiting room.

"I guess it's like being in Alcoholics Anonymous. Although Bertha and I are not in the same therapy group, what goes on there, stays there, and we trust each other not to tell. That's why she was friendly to Mother that day at the barbeque before I shot the snake. Wesley sometimes sits in on group sessions. I don't worry about a pastor ever telling anybody, either."

Brick looked out the car window. "Everyone suspected you'd seen combat, but I never knew the extent of your distress."

"Well, it's been going on ever since I returned from Vietnam. It's just that I've taken the treatment process more seriously since the barn fire. I'm glad I've had these last few weeks with Dad to reassure him that I'm finally getting my act together, and that I appreciate him.

"Truth is, I never liked Dad much until recently. I always loved my mother, I guess, because she was there to soothe my bruises. Dad, on the other hand, was always the aloof parent, away at his law office or at the lumber company doing those complex, adult things that a child's mind can't relate to. Sometimes after a bad day I couldn't understand his gruff moods because I didn't have the maturity to appreciate the adult obstacles that were vexing him. So, as a kid, I never trusted him because I could never read his moods.

"When I learned about sex, I hated Dad because he had defiled my precious, saintly mother to beget me. I told Wesley that I had it all figured out that I was born in 1944, and Dad was drafted and trained to ship out in 1943. So I was conceived in 1943 just before he shipped out. Since Dad didn't know if he was coming back or not, my conception was a desperation fuck. Him, reaching out to some great beyond in fucking desperation.

"So, you see, I was never a happy kid because I always felt like a child of desperation, fucking desperation. It was like I was always searching for the peace of the great love screw. Sometimes I even felt so bad as a kid, I would wonder if I wasn't remotely like my mother's epileptic nephew who died from a multitude of disability issues the year before we started Sunrise Acres. My migraine headaches have given me concerns about it to the degree that I asked my male nurses about mild childhood epilepsy causing my headaches.

"They asked me if I was sexually active. Of course, I said yes, and they said not to worry about it at my age because if I ever had been that way as an infant, it was age-corrected by now. It seems that normal sex glands are a sign of normal development. I told 'em that I was most comforted by their answer, but that I still didn't feel very secure that my good-working dick was going to fix my fucked-up brain. Now they've arranged for me to see a new doctor this time at the Veterans Hospital next to Duke Hospital in Durham.

"At the VA, I told doctors before Christmas about my migraines and my deceased epileptic Evabay cousin. They said that epilepsy has family patterns and that before the 1960s, mild childhood cases went undetected unless mild seizures were noticeable beyond the crib. While mine is now not identifiable, the fact that I do have migraines is an indication that I might have had mild childhood epilepsy. A normal sexual appetite is thought to be a marker that you are epilepsy free. They also said that migraine patients used to be given pot to smoke before it was outlawed in the early 1900s, and that this might explain my deeper craving for pot than most.

"I'm meeting with them again in two weeks. They said they might even schedule me for some hyperbaric oxygen treatments like they do for deep-sea divers who have the bends. Some believe Julius Caesar had epilepsy. I figure if he could get by with it back when they had no modern medicines, I ought to have a good chance of whipping my moody afflictions in this modern era. Maybe that's why I'm optimistic now.

"Of course, none of these revelations change the fact that I've never been the son Dad wanted. I should have been his answered prayer. As a kid, I always blamed him for dirty-fucking my mother against her will. But now, as a man, I know she was a co-conspirator, participating in mankind's fuck of desperation to imagine some future, peaceful Scottish vale of a Promised Land.

"It's all ironic, though, because Wesley says the ancient process of universal conceiving out of desperation will start all over again with Sue Anne and me, if we work things out this weekend. I just hope we can both come back Sunday night and tell Dad together that we've figured life out so he can die in peace. I owe him that much, and my mother, too, because she shared in all Dad's desperations about me. The happy insights I'm getting from extrapolating these thoughts out of my screwed-up life are better than any pot trip I ever had, believe me, Brick. Now, if I get a little funky in the brain, I've learned to invite poor Johnny Bell's image into my mind. Having to survive his last years with no legs and only a nub for his Jesse Root—hell, that thought alone makes me quit feeling sorry for myself!"

"Marsh," Brick said, "tell your dad about your dreams now and that you love him because he may not be here when you get back. I know because I should have told Marina that I loved her the last time we spoke on the phone, but I only told her that I wished her well.

"You see, she wanted to marry and come back here to do a historic restoration project in Fayetteville like the one in Montréal. But I told her about our shutdown and Nixon's impoundment that would stop all historical restoration projects faster than it did Sunrise

Acres. All this meant no income for her or me, and I said I wasn't going to be responsible for bringing kids into a world that neither of us could afford to feed. Not expressing my feelings like an adult was my lingering KMA attitude of resentment about our financial frustrations of the moment.

"Of course the Arab gas crisis doomed Hutton's business and marriage, which killed Marina's Green Card U.S. job certification. My despair isn't like an opiate-affected Edgar Allan Poe wanting to shoot somebody over a lost Lake Drummond Hotel lover, but I now appreciate the colored town desperations of adult love lamented in beach boogie songs. Rhythm and blues doesn't know a color line."

Then Dad knocked on Brick's car window, and that conversation ended so another could begin about the next day's schedule with Reverend Leon.

Later, when Brick related his talk with Marsh, he said that Marsh had an open, radiant gaze as the longer strands of his receding blond hairline blew across his forehead, in an aura of nobility. Brick said he was struck with the odd momentary thought that he hoped he'd always remember Marsh just that way—his best, most honest and caring self. Their talk even had the effect of bringing Brick momentarily out of his own state of regret over losing Marina.

Chapter Seventeen

Still No Rescue Squad

I

The next day, Dad, Brick, and Reverend Leon awaited Marsh's arrival at the country store by the General Electric plant. When Marsh didn't show, Brick paid the preacher his finder's fee and told Dad he was going to check on Mingo and Donald's repair work. Dad said he would be along after discussing Leon's new customer prospects.

Entering Sunrise Acres, Brick pondered Leon's additional prospects and also considered hitting golf balls at the driving range later that afternoon. These thoughts still elevated his spirits as he reached the back-forty intersection and the top-ten road. But he stopped immediately when he saw Donald running down the middle of the road and rolled down his car window.

"Mr. Brick! Mr. Brick! It's Mr. Marsh. I believe he's dead! He and Chalky had a fight and Mr. Marsh's got that sharp note-holding spindle stuck in his heart, and blood's everywhere! Chalky's out cold, too. Me and Mingo heard 'em hollering! I'm scared, and just had to run!"

"Get in! Where are they?" Brick exclaimed.

"The house we've been using for an office," Donald replied. "Mingo and I went to get sandpaper from his toolbox for using at the repo house. We heard 'em arguing."

Mrs. Penny, what I've said about Donald and Mingo going after sandpaper is what they told, and would tell today, I'm sure. But what they really went for was Mingo's brick hammer—my father told me the real story two years later.

I do know, however, that the driveway they pulled into was one of the last unsold homes with a carport since they had not yet built the houses without carports. This particular house was on a hill above the street, so no one could see to the back of the carport until they topped the driveway's hill. When Brick and Donald did top the hill, they could see Chalky's head partly out the kitchen storm door! Mrs. Penny, these thirty-year-old events came rushing back to me when Brick and I walked by that very house this past weekend at the reunion.

Brick trembled as he stepped over and around Chalky to go inside where Marsh lay. Marsh's left hand was turned like someone holding his left side in pain, but his hand was holding the spindle.

He also saw Mingo squatted where the kitchen cabinets met the kitchen stove. Mingo looked stunned, holding his brick hammer between his legs. His initials, MT, were visible as well as a smear of blood and hair embedded in those initials. But it was never made public that Brick found Mingo inside the house like this. A small-caliber pistol lay between Mingo and Marsh.

Brick looked over Marsh and then stepped back to look at Chalky. Donald remained under the carport, still fearful of going in. Brick fell limp into the chair behind the office desk that had apparently been shoved askew by the fight. With his head in his hands, he moaned, "I felt pulses in army basic training, but I can't bring myself to check Marsh's."

"We need to call an ambulance and Carley Ray."

"Don't you remember? We still got no rescue squad here," Donald said as he came inside, seeing Dad drive up.

"I—I forgot," Brick mumbled. "All we can do is call Carley Ray, and maybe Doc Street."

"No!" Mingo shouted out. "I'll be put back in jail immediately for breaking parole; or worse, get my privates cut off and stuck up my butt like your friend!"

"What?" Brick asked as Dad arrived and stepped around Chalky.

"It's not like it seems," Mingo said standing, still holding his brick hammer by its metal head end. "It was certainly about Marsh's not having money to pay for drugs. Donald and I heard 'em arguing about that, when we came to get my brick hammer. I've been keeping my toolbox here because I can't take it on my motorcycle. I needed the hammer to repair those cracked brick steps on the repo house. It was the last thing to fix for O'Cain."

"Then what?" Brick asked.

"When I came inside to get the brick hammer, they quit arguing," Mingo answered. "We could hear them arguing through the storm door because the glass panel behind the screen was raised. I told 'em what I had come for. Marsh said 'O.K.'

"Both sat against the edge of the desk and stayed silent while I went to the bathroom closet where my toolbox is hid.

"I got my hammer, and Donald and me pretended to go but slipped back near the door to hear what they were saying because they had been arguing before. I figured that Chalky might have a knife or gun because he wouldn't have been talking hateful to a bigger man like Marsh unless he had something to even up things for himself.

"I eased my brick hammer into its ring holster as Chalky said, 'Well, it's just you and me again. But it wouldn't matter if we'd talked in front of Mingo because he wouldn't give you any extra protection like your asshole, snake-shooting cousin. Mingo knows I can get plenty of people to say they've sold pot to Mingo. Anything that shows Mingo to be violating parole will get his Injun ass back in prison pronto, and he knows it.

"'So quit stalling for time, and get me my damn money, Marsh! And fuck all this bullshit about your unknown, high-deductible insurance with no payout. Damn it to hell, I've been screwed more than once by your fucked-up financial planning! Having those cows butchered for sale about got my ass caught. I'm here to tell you I ain't doing another cow stealing scam today!

"'You may have nothing to do but live off your daddy, and fuck somebody like your ex-sweetie Lonah, with your pot-hard dick, but I got to pay for this shit. I'll go out hard if I don't pay my suppliers, and I don't intend to wind up like your buddy, Dutch, with nothing between my legs. There's hit men for hire every day.

"'So give me my damn money, or I'll call your sick-ass daddy. Those Spic fuckers ain't goin' to have no reason to come after me!'

"That's when Marsh yelled, 'Get your hands off me, you freak! You'll get the money when I do, and you'll die before my daddy does if you ever call him about our dealings.'

"Then we heard struggling and a banging on the walls and desk. Donald and me didn't know what to do. Something hard dropped; probably that pistol. Then there was a hellish scream from Marsh. That's when I came to the door. Marsh was holding the side of his heart with his left hand, while his right hand was still gripped to Chalky's neck.

"I figure because Marsh is taller than Chalky, Marsh must have had a good-leveraged choke-hold on Chalky's neck. Then somehow, Chalky picked up that note holder on the desk and stabbed Marsh in his heart after the pistol fell on the floor. I guess it's Chalky's gun. I never saw it before. It musta' fell out of his pocket because they didn't mention it while fighting.

"That's when Marsh screamed, 'It's my heart, you've stabbed me in the heart!'

"I came in, pulled my brick hammer from its holster by the metal head, and slapped Chalky up beside his skull with the hammer's wood handle. Then Chalky spun around, looking dazed, as he staggered back to fall out the door, like you see him lying there.

"If he's dead, I must have caught him in his temple."

"Maybe the storm door killed Chalky when he fell into it," Brick sighed, wiping his wet eyes. "It's bloody and damaged badly enough to have killed him."

"I didn't mean to kill him," Mingo lamented. "I could see that Marsh was stabbed, and I didn't want him to have to tussle with Chalky anymore.

"I reckon I'll be dead with them soon 'cause I sure ain't going back to jail. Been there, not going back. They'll just have to kill me, that's all."

"That talk makes no sense," Brick mumbled, massaging his forehead with his hands again. "Were there any gunshots?"

"No shooting, but that don't matter. Not telling the whole truth is all that makes any sense to me," responded Mingo. "I've killed Chalky, and I didn't kill him in self-defense of me. I just killed him. You know how these district attorneys will be dealing with my prison record. They'd say I meant to kill Chalky because I was found guilty as an accomplice to Juan. It'd be a get-even-type killing to the courthouse boys and a slam-dunk for a third-degree murder conviction, or maybe even second-degree. Those prosecutor pricks know second-degree convictions don't come along every day.

"In prison, Chalky's drug friends would be waiting to kill me like they did Bertha's boy. It'd be a fight every damn day. If somehow I can be got off for accidentally hitting him too hard, his buddies will still be waiting to get me on the outside, and maybe finish me off like your buddy Dutch 'cause I ended their dope-money. I can't win either way this deal goes down. And I ain't going back to Montana with Juan, either. Besides, they'd really try to come get me over a killing. This isn't a minor stabbing where somebody just gets pricked a few times."

"I can't flee, either!" Donald blurted out. "And I sure don't want my privates cut off for accidentally witnessing this mess!"

"Yeah, they'd get you, too, Donald, no matter what happens to me," Mingo noted.

"But what'll we do?" Donald asked, looking around. "Peoples got to be told somehow so nobody comes after us!"

Donald stepped close to Brick and said, "This is sure more complicated than the two naked men standing in the rain seeing a Yankee get killed. We need to do something like that, but I don't know how."

"You mean your old Negrohead Road story, Donald?" Dad asked.

"Yes," Donald said. Then he told again how his forebear and Brick's stood naked in the rain, watching a Yankee ride away on a half-blind horse. When the Yank got killed by the skittish horse, the two men buried him, later denying ever having seen him. The cover-up disappeared with time because they had the courage to trust one another through their fears. "What can we do like that, Mr. Brick?"

"Well, we can't bury him," said Dad, looking at Mingo. "We oughta just say we found 'em like this since nobody's around, and there's a gun here. The only thing is Mingo's brick hammer. What do you think, Brick?"

"I've lost everything. Nothing makes any sense to me anymore," Brick mumbled. "Do whatever you want."

"Well, it's got to be simple," said Dad.

Then Brick looked up and cleared his throat. "Donald, did anybody see you and Mingo coming over here, or you running down the middle of the road, when I saw you?"

"No, not up this hill," answered Donald. "But everybody can see everything in an hour when school lets out, and then later, when folks start coming home from work."

"Right," Brick said, walking to the laundry room by the kitchen door where he rifled through several brown paper sacks with the lumber company's name on them, choosing one.

"Now," Brick said in a choking, hoarse voice, "if I was Mingo and Donald, wanting to avoid jail or crude castration, I'd say I just found Marsh and Chalky, like Deacon's suggesting. But understand, I'm not in your places. If anyone ever says that I've said anything about covering up, I'll call you all liars!

"For it to work, everybody has to take the secret to his grave like Donald's folks and mine did in the Civil War.

"If I were Mingo, I'd drop that brick hammer into this paper sack. Then I'd get Deacon to put his brick hammer into your toolbox, Mingo, and dispose of yours. By having Deacon switch brick hammers, there'll be a brick hammer in your toolbox that has no blood on it. Then I'd only tell the authorities that you overheard arguing and scuffling as you came here to the office. When you came around the corner of the carport, you saw Chalky fall out the door, and that neither of you went inside until after I came. Like I said, maybe the door killed him, and not the hammer blow. I think the investigation may focus on that gun, even though it apparently wasn't fired, instead of a possible head blow by Mingo's brick hammer. I never saw Marsh with a Saturday-night special like that, so it must be Chalky's.

"If you don't say anything to bring attention to the fact that you were in the house before Chalky fell out the door, nobody will ever be the wiser about investigating other avenues of thought. Heck, because of the gun, they'll probably never examine anything in your toolbox. But if they do, there'll be no bloodstains to find.

"Even better, on second thought, it would help more if you don't say you were coming for a brick hammer at all. Just say you were coming for the sandpaper Donald's always keeping in your toolbox. There'd still be no blood in your toolbox, and you wouldn't be giving them any probable-cause ideas about hard objects to investigate. Where's your nail hammer?"

"I left it back at the house we were working on," Mingo said.

"Good," Brick remarked. "That'll be another blood-free hammer left away from this scene for them to consider scanning under a microscope.

"That'd be my story, but we'll have to carry it to our graves. And I mean tell no one, not Bessie Mae or anybody. Mingo, you've got to make sure that you don't get caught up in a phone conversation with Juan once he learns about Chalky. You got to remember that all our phones might get tapped. That's how Monroe and Hutton were caught."

"I won't tell a soul, and I understand your fears of being unfairly mixed up in this," Dad said, picking up the paper sack and holding it for Mingo to place his brick hammer inside. Dad hid this in his car trunk while retrieving his own brick hammer to replace Mingo's.

This done, Brick placed a phone call to Dr. Street's office. He then called the sheriff's office and asked for Deputy Carley Ray Craft. The switchboard operator put him on hold. During the wait, Peaches Jones and her niece, Erica, came up for reasons never truly known, other than probably to see Mingo. About the time Brick began to talk to Deputy Craft, Peaches and Erica arrived at the storm door left open by Chalky's prostrate body and began screaming.

Deputy Craft, hearing the screams over the phone, asked Brick twice if there was still a struggle going on. Brick said, "No, but Peaches and her niece have just happened on the scene like we did." Before he could hang up the phone, Peaches and Erica left, running and screaming.

After the Carley Ray phone call, they went over their cover-up stories again. They knew that each would be questioned separately, and thus everybody had to stick to the simple story of Mingo and Donald coming upon two dead bodies after hearing some commotion coming from inside the house and out of sight. The fact that the argument was about drugs was to be left out to demonstrate that Donald and Mingo did not get close enough to the fight inside the house to witness anything more than Chalky falling through the doorway.

II

Twenty minutes later, Dr. Street and his nurse arrived. The doctor pronounced Marsh and Chalky dead before asking how the deaths took place. Brick responded that Donald and Mingo had approached the house to get some sandpaper and had heard arguing between Marsh and Chalky before seeing Chalky fall out the door. That was all they knew because they were too horrified to come any closer and stayed under the carport until after Brick arrived.

When Brick added that Deputy Carley Ray Craft was en route, Dr. Street said, "This seems to be an accidental killing resulting from a bad argument. Doesn't appear Carley Ray'll be able to add much to it. I really hate the thought of having to tell Malcolm and Colleen. Christ! Can't Malcolm die in peace without being told that his namesake heir is dead with no issue to carry on the family name? Damn, what a day!"

Then hollering began outside. After Peaches and Erica fled the death scene, they had run to Allen and Celestine Lamb's house where they found the couple talking to Celestine's sister, Bertha Moore. After telling them about Chalky and Marsh, Bertha insisted on going to the scene, and took out on her own with all following. Bertha was carrying a large shoulder bag.

As Dr. Street later told investigators, he, his nurse, Brick, Mingo, Donald, and Dad looked on from inside the house when Bertha Moore came up to Chalky and screamed, 'That's the white trashy-looking albino who had my boy, Ronald, killed in prison!' She spit on Chalky's face before taking a round-house swing with her huge handbag, slamming it against Chalky's head. The handbag's blow landed in the middle of Chalky's blood-clotted temple, and suddenly there was more blood everywhere. She swung again, landing a glancing blow across Chalky's right cheek, drawing even more blood.

Dr. Street then shouted, "Put a hold on her while I get a sedative!" Brick and Mingo ran outside to help Allen and Celestine steady Bertha, her bloody handbag smearing Brick and Mingo's clothing in her flailing around. Just then, Deputy Carley Ray arrived.

"I got two dead men here, Deputy," said Dr. Street, "and I'm trying to keep Bertha from killing that Chalky Newton again. I need to give her a sedative."

Deputy Craft stood there looking at Chalky and Marsh before he asked, "How did all this happen, Brick? Tell me again."

Still holding up Bertha with Mingo, Brick told how he came from Will O'Cain's office to meet with Reverend Leon and Dad at the country store before driving to the subdivision. As he entered Sunrise Acres, he saw Donald on the run toward his car. Donald exclaimed that Mingo and he had heard a loud argument and a scream as they approached the house to get sandpaper to use on a repair job at a nearby repo house. After they heard a scream, Chalky fell out the kitchen-carport doorway. Brick then drove to the house and found Mingo outside in a state of shock, before he himself went into some shock upon seeing his lifeless cousin inside the house. Minutes later, Deacon arrived. After he'd regained some composure, Brick said he entered the house and made a call to Doctor Street's office and then to the sheriff's office.

"Now, why is there a need to sedate Mrs. Bertha, Doc?" asked Craft.

"Shortly after I pronounced Marsh and Chalky dead," said Dr. Street, "Bertha came on the scene, and raged about the albino being responsible for killing her son, Ronald. She then spat on Chalky's face before taking a couple of swings at his head with her handbag. Her first blow hit Chalky right in the temple where he had already received a head wound. She hit him again in the face before her sister and brother-in-law could restrain her with Brick and Mingo's help. The blood on Chalky's cheek must have come from her first blow to the deceased's head because it was not there when I pronounced him dead. When Brick and Mingo helped Allen and Celestine restrain Bertha, they came to have bloodstains on them too, but well after I pronounced Marsh and Chalky dead."

"O.K., you can sedate her," remarked Craft. "I don't have to cuff her. I know why she did it. Our office has had numerous conversations with her about her theory that the albino had her son killed in prison. I'll call the coroner's office, Doc. He'll appreciate your staying here to certify that both men were dead before Bertha's arrival."

III

After the coroner went over Bertha's activities, she was charged with obstructing evidence, and three months later fined $300. One reason it took so long to hold the hearing was that the unfired pistol, which had only Chalky's fingerprints on it, could not be traced. At the hearing, the coroner testified that Dr. Street's pronouncement of death prior to Bertha's actions certified that Bertha's actions were not the cause of either death. While her actions muddled the investigation, they were considered to be of no real consequence.

Bertha's well-known state of anxiety was also a mitigating factor that the court gave temporary-insanity credence to when it was revealed that she had attended mental therapy sessions at Fort Bragg, as had Marsh, whom Bertha had come to cherish like a long-lost relative—possibly even a stand-in for her murdered son, Ronald.

Upon learning of Marsh's and Bertha's mental-health sessions, Dr. Street commented, in an aside, that he never considered Marsh to have been a childhood epileptic because he never suffered any identifiable convulsions medically associated with epilepsy. As for his fidgetiness and occasional migraine headaches being possibly related to some mild childhood epilepsy, such a diagnosis was beyond the science of the day, even in the modern space age, moon-walking seventies.

Besides Bertha's actions and Chalky's unfired pistol, the coroner's hearing identified the two issues that isolated the motive for the deaths to a bad argument gone wrong. First, the finding of blood and skin of each deceased man under the fingernails of the other, and the blood of each embedded in the fabric of the other's clothing isolated the struggle to only Chalky and Marsh. Additionally, the fact that Chalky's temple had hit the storm door's pneumatic-closing cylinder with enough force to knock the door off its lowest door hinge was said to have stunned Chalky into a free fall that severed his neck's spinal cord when he fell across the doorway's threshold four inches above the first doorstep. This last trauma was said to have caused immediate death. Additionally, Chalky's reputation as a dope peddler was confirmed by the drugs found in his car and enough in his bloodstream to make him euphoric and likely aggressive, feeling he could take on anyone and beat them.

The fact that illicit drugs were directly responsible for the death fight came to light accidentally the night of Marsh's wake when Deputy Craft struck up a conversation with Holden Rollins at the funeral home. Rollins said that he was likely the last person to see Marsh before his death, when Marsh came to his office that day to go over a fire insurance claim. Rollins said that while Marsh realized that Mr. Malcolm always carried a high-deductible insurance policy to keep his insurance premium costs down, he assumed that he would get at least a few hundred dollars. Rollins said Marsh appeared downcast when he left the insurance office with no monies because of the high deductible.

Also impacting Marsh's money shortages were the funds that Marsh had entrusted to Junebug for settling a divorce with Sue Anne. The divorce, of course, never happened, but Marsh was restricted from using those funds until he and Sue Anne were reconciled. With this information, Craft concluded that the fight was over a drug repayment plan to Chalky that came up short, and the investigation ended.

During this time, Marina called Sue Anne and Nicole upon learning from Lisa of Marsh's death. In her conversations with each, Marina expressed sorrow about Marsh and added that she now daily found herself thinking of Brick and the dreams they'd once had of a future together. Learning this, I began sensing Brick's loneliness every time I heard Brook Benton's "Rainy Night in Georgia" or Jimmy Ruffin's "What Becomes of the Brokenhearted."

Throughout the investigation, no questions were asked about Mingo's toolbox, although it was held for examination and not returned until after Bertha's hearing. After Deputy Craft's retirement, the case was forgotten. While Mingo's toolbox was impounded, he was forced to buy a few basic tools to perform his work. When the toolbox was eventually returned, Bertha noted to Wendy and me, during one of our family-budget classes, that all of his tools were initialed except for his brick hammer. At the time I thought nothing of her remark but would learn later that Bertha's remarks had not escaped Dad and Brick's attention.

IV

Mrs. Penny, even the sight of Mr. Malcolm's emaciated body as he was wheeled into the church sanctuary for Marsh's funeral could not do visible justice to his last tragic days. Witnessing this shell of a man and his shattered dreams brought many men to tears, and certainly me, too. Mr. Malcolm certainly forced his last public appearance.

The only thing that upstaged Mr. Malcolm's dire condition was the draping of the Bronze Star that Marsh had never acknowledged over the American flag covering his casket. At the graveside, the medal and flag were presented to Sue Anne, who transferred them to Mrs. Colleen. We all bowed our heads in respect, but I glimpsed both Sue Anne and Mrs. Colleen casting nods of thanks to Nicole, who sat with them.

Afterward Mr. Malcolm requested a last business conference at his home bedside. Attending were his wife, daughter, son-in-law, and Brick, along with Junebug, the elder Mr. Willingham, and Dr. Street. One purpose of the conference was to buy from Sue Anne the lumber company stock shares previously left to Marsh. The fact that she and Marsh had never divorced entitled Sue Anne to inherit Marsh's set-aside divorce funds, held in trust by Junebug, as well as over $250,000 in lumber company stock that Mr. Malcolm had left Marsh. These monies allowed Sue Anne to depart financially secure. Junebug and Brick later noted how ironic it was that Marsh had more than enough locked-up monies to pay off whatever small drug bills he had owed Chalky.

Then there was the matter of Diane's PSR Club building project and finishing Sunrise Acres. On both projects, the lumber company had co-signed for the construction loans. In connection with these loan obligations, it was a foregone conclusion that Sunrise Acres would not be profitable because loan interest payments were accumulating on zero sales. So the project needed finishing to end loan obligations.

Diane's PSR Club project also required completion to avoid being unprofitable. Fortunately, her project was not dependent on any government loan program being stalled by the Nixon impoundment program. Consequently, faster sales on her project demanded a skilled construction manager.

Mr. Malcolm told Brick that if he completed both projects, all Sunrise Acres' losses would be absorbed by the lumber company, and Brick's name would be removed from all Sunrise Acres' bank-loan obligations. As for the PSR Club project, Brick would be paid the construction management fee of six hundred dollars per house that had been scheduled to go to Marsh. Brick agreed to this because he saw no advantage in remaining a responsible party-loan co-signer on Sunrise Acres that could only, at best, break even.

By the lumber company's offering to be responsible to the bank for all the Sunrise Acres loans, it could in turn use all Sunrise Acres losses to reduce future lumber company income taxes. In the meantime, Brick was assured of at least some income from the management of Diane's project until the politically-charged economic conditions improved for Sunrise Acres completion.

Mr. Malcolm passed into the ages a week later, almost to the hour his son had, just before quitting time on Friday. He was buried the following Monday beside Marsh. Because the soil surrounding Marsh's casket had not set up, Mr. Malcolm's grave excavation exposed Marsh's casket side rails. The loose soil of the graves presented a wobble problem for the hoist that lowered Mr. Malcolm's casket and the two caskets' rails touched. Thus they were left with their casket rails touching for all eternity. The elder Mr. Willingham observed that whatever their differences in life, father and son had truly been joined in the hereafter, as Mr. Malcolm had wished, and Marsh had expressed hope for.

The hymns "Be Thou My Vision" and "Goin' Home" were played at both funerals, and Mr. Malcolm's Wisdom Station minister, as well as Wesley, spoke at each. Wesley said it was the hardest thing he'd ever done because Mr. Malcolm was family, with many of his dreams awash. The funerals reminded Wesley of losing his own parents when he was fourteen.

During the funerals, Brick was dressed in his best. However, his refined clothing did not hide his somber demeanor as a hunter-of-a-man, a seeker on a mission to see how he could make a difference in the world. Even though Brewer, Monroe, and Langdon were also pallbearers at Marsh's funeral, Brick seemed alone. His solitariness reminded me of Marsh's story about the man buying the lion, told during that ski trip when no one skied. Like Brick, the man had that Hollywood look of Stewart Granger, Clark Gable, or Gary Cooper—always appearing both manly and well heeled, with a font of money-making ideas, closely held, no matter how broke he might be, standing there in his last suit.

After Carley Ray Craft's retirement officially closed the case, I, of course, remained ignorant of what had really happened. When I did learn the truth of how Brick had helped alter the truth of Marsh's death, it stunned me. This revelation led me to reorder my life, taking me to the Southwest Four Corners to discover the peace of my own Native American traditions.

Chapter Eighteen

NCSU Champs and Edouard Manet's *Olympia*'s Glance

I

THROUGHOUT THE SAD WINTER OF 1974, one bright spot on the barren horizon ignited all of North Carolina: the heroic play of the N.C. State basketball team. This team answered seventeen years of prayers by Tobacco Road's basketball faithful who had not seen glory since the University of North Carolina Tar Heels' undefeated 1957 national collegiate championship season.

N.C. State was led by the greatest player, at that time, ever to set a tennis shoe on a basketball court, David Thompson. This young black player's high-jumping scoring ability kept us glued to the TV set each time he played.

After N.C. State had advanced to the national tournament's Final Four, the press made much of the fact that N.C. State would be playing the perennial national champions, UCLA, in the first game. In the final hours leading up to the game, basketball experts also lauded that year's Atlantic Coast Conference Championship game between N.C. State and the University of Maryland as the greatest college basketball game ever played. The game was so perfect that the losing Maryland coach, Lefty Driesell, congratulated the N.C. State team and gave them his best wishes for winning the upcoming national tournament. This kind gesture from an opposition coach powered the team and its followers into the semi-final game with UCLA.

Amid this hopeful frenzy, Brick went on a chilly March Saturday afternoon to the Sampsons Landing Hunt Club cabin to eat, drink, and watch the game with friends. Brewer Melvin and Monroe Hill, the latter now released from his year's weekend-jail sentence for attempted cigarette-smuggling, were there, and Junebug and Cotton Roberts came with Brick.

Langdon Butler and Wendy attended the game itself, held in Greensboro. Wendy had acquired tickets through N.C. State contacts for Langdon's birthday present. While the 1974 N.C. State–Maryland Atlantic Coast Conference Championship game is still recognized as the greatest game ever played, the N.C. State–UCLA game became legendary, requiring two overtimes.

Before the game, Junebug told me, the group ate barbeque sandwiches. Cotton Roberts also cooked French fries on the cabin's stove. At halftime, Brewer announced that there was enough barbeque left for each to have another sandwich: "Yeah, this last bottom-of-the-pan meat smells so good—almost like chitterlings, Monroe!"

"I'd rather eat weekend jail food," Monroe groused. "Remember Marina's chitterling-based andouille sausage at that Carolina tailgate party? That was something else!

"You all may have craved Marina's French sausage, but Hutton says Brick dodged an opportunity to be unhappy when Marina lost her green card. I should know, after hearing him complain about Lisa for fifty-two weekends in jail. Vann says the sex and cooking may be extraordinary, but you can't screw and eat your way into marital bliss if you have contrary expectations to hers when not in bed or eating.

"I don't blame Vann for our being caught—we each made up our own minds about cigarette smuggling, but his scheme fooled me. He said that Vermont and New Hampshire are homes to smuggling pros because the international line runs through the middle of some buildings in their border towns. Such obscurity makes smuggling hard to spot.

"He and that old coot, André, were going to handle everything in Québec, and probably would have except for those wiretaps. It went wrong on this end of I-95. But if we had pulled it off, Hutton would have had enough money stashed away to stay out of bankruptcy after his motel project failed during the Arab oil embargo.

"By the way, I understand from Hutton that Marina's already pregnant."

"Yes," Brick answered. "Cousin Diane and Lisa are close friends. Since you and Hutton were jail-birds last year, they became closer, and even corralled Junebug's Kay into their gossip network. Getting duplicate reports makes a man feel left out."

"Well," returned Monroe, "you aren't like me, at least. I have to take orders from my wife and father in my own damn business that I'm supposed to inherit. Dad's put the checkbook and keys in Ginger's hands. All my paychecks go to her, and she gives me just twenty-five dollars a week for walking-around money. I feel like a damn kid!"

"Brick, if you and Monroe think you've got problems, you should try being a dumb farmer, like me," Brewer laughed as Cotton Roberts came from the kitchen with the barbeque sandwiches. "Investing money and sweat in a crop and praying for rain at the right time instead of a flood followed by three months of drought is not for a pussy. When you think you've got it bad, just think of poor old Brewer, intoxicated by the lure of tending to one of the world's bread baskets, and being continually screwed by life's oldest, yet most alluring whore—a farm.

"Like Stan Cannon says, we're in adult life now. Yes sir, buddy! You can tell that old French commentator on American opportunity, Alexis de Tocqueville, that we're in the middle of real, fucking modern life today! And that means it's no longer as simple as just conquering vast lands occupied by a few noble savages. It's not like our childish cowboy movies, where you never had to reload your cap pistol while killing off a whole tribe of Indians before beginning to farm a thousand acres the next morning.

"No, now it takes real thinking using a slide-rule to figure out the devil in the details and mount all those goddamn angels on today's modern pinheads. Figuring out how to use fertilizers so you don't kill off Wayhab's shrimp and oysters a hundred miles downstream is a moving target. Today's farming management problems make me wonder if I won't wind up like those poor Evabay farmers, forced to survive on peas cooked without meat seasoning."

Junebug said Brick sat down with his sandwich, looked at Brewer, and said, "Yeah, this barbeque does have a little chitterlings smell! I'm sure I'll like it, though, since I'm so damned used to eating life's shitty stuff anyway."

Everyone laughed at this slapstick philosophy as they returned to the second half of the game, which provided enough excitement for all to forget their worldly troubles. N.C. State's victory over UCLA that day, as well as its victory over Marquette in the championship game the following Monday night, transported many North Carolinians from winter's gloom to spring's hope. In fact, the next week the weather cleared, and Brick began framing Diane's houses.

Mrs. Penny, Diane's house project kept Brick going while things were dead at Sunrise Acres. I say this because it took the rest of that spring and summer to sell the two remaining repossessed houses. No new houses sold off until after the resignation of President Nixon in early August of that year, when President Ford signed a bill rescinding Nixon's impoundment orders.

Austin and Brick continued supporting Wendy and me with the family budgeting classes, but once the repossessions halted, our classes grew stale. That's because we were reviewing the same materials with the same folks. Luckily, that fall, Wendy learned of a seminar to be conducted on family financial planning at N.C. State's continuing education center in Raleigh. When Wendy made Brick and Austin aware of it, they agreed to pay for my one-day's tuition expense if Junebug approved. Because the class was on a Friday, which was usually slow, Junebug didn't object. Weeks after the class, Junebug even told me that he thought what I had learned had helped with my law work, too.

II

This seminar was made more meaningful by A&T's Dr. Frank Glover, who presided over the morning session. Remember, Mrs. Penny? He was Chester O'Malley's friend, who observed our classes and furnished additional teaching materials.

Recognizing Wendy and me, Dr. Glover often called on us to relate to the class how we had dealt with situations at Sunrise Acres. He also explored what thoughts we had on using the new ideas he was introducing that day. On two occasions my answers to his questions required long explanations, and I was asked to stand so the large group could hear. On the second occasion, there was a back-and-forth exchange of ideas between other class members and me.

While my prominent class participation was made easier by my year's work with Wendy, it occurred to me at lunch that this was heady stuff. Me, the pudgy Indian girl of incomplete soul? Gosh, I had been teaching others! Big stuff, Mrs. Penny? Yes, indeed! I was proud of myself. As I mused in my pride at lunch, Dr. Glover joined us. "I haven't seen you ladies since I visited your Sunrise Acres classes. I hope that nice community is progressing."

"Dr. Glover, the Farmers Home Administration and Dr. O'Malley's community college's directors are pleased," commented Wendy. "And the subdivision developers are, too."

"They should be," responded Dr. Glover. "And Dr. O'Malley gives Melody as much credit for the success as he does the rest of us put together."

Smiling at me, Wendy winked. "Yes, Melody has made me look good. You can have all the class tools in the world, along with the best instruction on how to use those tools, but until you place those tools into the hands of a master surgeon, master painter, or master whatever, they are nothing. Melody has the master-teaching soul that releases that magic in a class."

When I heard this, it dovetailed into my private thoughts of self-praise so completely that I thought I'd levitate! Even today I'm still surprised that I could even hear what Dr. Glover had to say next. My grin was wide enough to close off my eardrums.

"Melody," Dr. Glover noted, "Dr. O'Malley thinks you're a natural-born teaching superstar. Wendy does too, and so do I. You demonstrated that today by the way you instructed us so freely. You must return to school for your master's degree because you'd be a real asset to the community-college system's extension-teaching program."

I replied, "It's no secret that I really enjoy helping Wendy because I feel I'm helping people help themselves. But I have a good job now that's paying off my new car, and I can't ask my father for more money during these hard times."

"I can arrange scholarship money for you," Dr. Glover replied. "I can also arrange enough part-time work for you that you'll be able to meet your car payments. It may take me a little time, but I can put something together when you're interested. Your law experience should allow me to find you part-time legal-secretary work while you attend school."

"Thanks, Dr. Glover. This educational opportunity you're offering is overwhelming!"

"Well, think about it, Melody. Knowing that you'll look at it seriously tells me that you'd be good at such work. Please promise to think about it."

"I will," I replied before we returned to class, where the words of Wendy and Dr. Glover returned to my mind continually.

When classes ended, Wendy and I walked to our cars. "I'm joyful one minute about teaching possibilities, Wendy, and perplexed the next about my responsibility to the Willinghams. I need to sit a spell in my car before driving home," I told her.

Wendy asked me to follow her to her apartment, nearby, so I could relax before making the hour's trip back to Wisdom Station. I told her that I didn't want to delay her long weekend trip to the Outer Banks to see Langdon. But she said that she and Langdon would be attending an East Carolina football game the next day in nearby Greenville. Thus she wouldn't leave until the next morning for the game. She insisted again, and I soon found myself following her.

III

Entering her apartment, Wendy explained, "My roommate is Becky Rollins, the insurance man's daughter. We've known each other since we were freshmen. She was in France for two years and returned last month, so we decided to rent this. Becky does part-time work at the state museum and will work there full time once she finishes her master's next semester."

"I know Mr. Rollins through my law-office work," I said, noticing the apartment's flow from the front door by the living-dining-kitchen area to a sliding-glass rear door that overlooked a patio. "I remember Becky being with you at the party after the football game."

I sat at the kitchen bar and thumbed through art pictures in a three-ring binder that lay on the counter while Wendy opened a Coke for me and a beer for herself. As I looked through the art prints, I turned to the one of that nude you've seen at our Four Corners home. I was captivated and immediately asked, "What is this painting? This woman appears so alone and mortal, but also aloof, as if to say I can handle what the world dishes out."

Wendy answered, "Becky will be home soon; ask her. Let's go out to the patio."

There we discussed the lesson points and how to apply them to Sunrise Acres' homeowners. Eventually the conversation returned to my future teaching possibilities. I went so deeply into this puzzle that I didn't hear the glass door open.

"Hello, hello!" said a female voice. It was Becky's, and her long blond hair and blue eyes fit my recollection, too. She was barefoot in cut-off bib-style jeans.

"Am I interrupting shop talk?" she inquired. "When I first arrived, you two seemed so deep in conversation that I went upstairs to change."

"Becky, this is the Melody Buckhorn I've told you about. The one that ought to be a teacher, you know?" exclaimed Wendy as Becky shook my hand and sat down. Her bare feet gave me a real down-home informal welcome, in spite of the pedicure.

Wendy then recapped the day's events, including my future prospects and my dilemma over choosing to remain where I was or to change careers.

"Yes," I said, "Wendy understands my insecurity about facing the unknown. I think I feel like that nude lady in your art notebook on the kitchen bar: a mortal female at the mercy of a man's world but determined to figure it out. Though I'm a Native American and she's European, we are both weighing the ways of the world."

"You mean my prints of *Olympia*, the French courtesan, by Edouard Manet?" Becky asked. "All women feel like her occasionally: a victim of circumstances, facing realities beyond any control we can use to change them to our feminine liking."

"That's probably what appeals to you. But I'm interested in your comment about how being an Indian influences your reaction to viewing it. You see, I am always an art teacher, and thus I look for art-viewing reactions that can help my students interpret their own responses. So what in your Indian background makes you gravitate to *Olympia*?"

"You must understand Wisdom Station's cultural backdrop," I began. "Our community has never recognized Indian cultural uniqueness. For us it's not like being a Cherokee on a preserved mountain reservation, where tourists have their photographs taken with the chief beside a teepee, and then privately dream of being like a noble savage, at one with nature. We're not only unlike the Cherokee, we're not even like my mother's Lumbee people.

"While the Lumbees do not have U.S. Government recognition, they do have our state government's recognition. The state also officially recognizes the Coharie tribe in Sampson and Harnett Counties. Their numbers are smaller than the Robeson County Lumbee, but still large enough to gain recognition.

"Before school integration, these three counties had separate school systems for whites, blacks, and Indians. But for Wisdom Station's few Indians, the tax base simply couldn't afford the luxury of a three-tiered discriminatory school system. Sometimes my family expressed the thought that it would be nice to have three school systems. Perhaps that way our Indian heritage would have had more recognition. Like blacks, however, we knew that separate schools really meant separate and unequal, and that system could not incorporate us into the greater world.

"There we Indians are, caught at the between-point of an evolving situation. We are black to many or we are a mulatto racial hodgepodge, at best, to most. One can sometimes feel black men saying with their eyes, 'Do you think you're too damn white to date me?' or some white mocking under his breath to another, 'Is that your half-sister? I believe she's near-white!'

"But you know who and what you are, and where you came from: the Lost Tribes, lost during the European discovery and settling of the New World. You steel yourself to the cultural heritage that your soul glimpses and feels from afar, a Promised-Land happy-hunting ground. And you use that feeling to rise above the reality you face daily to say: 'This is me; I know who I am and I know my worth, even if you don't.'

"That's what the nude in the picture says to me: look out for yourself by not denying yourself so you won't be unhappy. But it's hard learning these things. I'm not white; I'm not black; I'm an Indian of a less numerous culture. The Lumbees of Pembroke can express more of their Indian ways because of their greater numbers. But our few Wisdom Station Indians live in isolation, making us feel mighty alone. Often I feel like a faded chalk mark on a blackboard, lightly erased, but not washed off yet with a wet sponge. That faded mark is only a shadow of a former self that isn't fully known and thus can't be defined. In addition, I'm a college-educated Indian, which sets me apart even more because I can't be just anybody's squaw, following behind an unschooled brave, the two planting corn seed like some I know. It's hard realizing the world is somewhat closed to you, but you do, and that's what I see the nude doing in the picture. That's the look she gives me—be strong despite the limitations on your freedom!"

"That's the most heartfelt interpretation of any art that I've heard," said Becky. "It's also very interesting to me because I'm vaguely aware of the Lumbee and the other more scattered Indian tribes throughout our state. So I can understand how you connect with this painting in that way.

"You might be interested to know that the work does reflect the universal themes of female alienation that you've touched on. As I said, it is a painting of a French courtesan.

A courtesan was a woman who prostituted herself to upper-class, wealthy men connected to the French king's court. Such was a courtesan's only opportunity to get ahead and possess the finer things of that day.

"Courtesans were like all women, except more so. They knew too well that the charm of their sensuality would last only until their beauty began to fade. Consequently, they were ever on the hunt to build up all the power they could while their bodies could entice. Thus, it was one court intrigue after another, one lover after another, each courtesan scouting better opportunities of lasting wealth and perhaps a royal title of Marchioness, Countess, or the like.

"Manet did the painting in 1863, at the time of Emperor Napoleon III, who you'll remember took over Mexico. Thus, there was much court intrigue when Manet painted it. I like to think of the woman in the painting as being a part of that whole scene, with its false glamour. And as you say, steeling herself to withstand all the intrigues and political capriciousness so she'll first and foremost have some nest egg for her retirement. Her expressed desire not to be a victim of her societal environment is what appeals to all women and many a man viewing the painting today."

"You're probably right about those universal interpretations," I said. "But speaking for myself, I feel like I'm the first person ever to look at it, though the painting is over a hundred years old. Isn't that silly?"

"Silly?" asked Becky. "No! I think I thought the same thing when I first looked at it. When you looked at it, you saw it from the uniqueness of your own experiences, as an isolated Indian in a larger world. When I look at it, I see it as the blonde who doesn't want to be thought of as a dumb blonde! My brothers are smart. One's an insurance businessman, the other a doctor. So I do fear being thought of as the spoiled little sister, and I'm determined not to be regarded in that way.

"Sometimes when I've looked at it, I tremble with fear that my love of art has led me down a path that cannot possibly fill my soul with any complete sense of happiness. When I went to France, I was so thrilled that I was going to study what I loved with true masters, and I did in some cases. But it was funny that the more I studied, the more I realized I was only acculturating what others had produced. I began to see art as an adverb or adjective that highlights the soul of our lives, but not the verb and noun that do all the work. I feared, and still fear, that I can never be an art contributor because I've never been able to draw anything other than a stick figure. I also can't do a landscape, but I still get inspired by looking at forms that contrast and blend together. Finding patterns in art—and life—is a joy to me.

"When I realized this for the first time in France, I felt like my entire educational process had lied to me. I missed the ideas learned in my father's house, such as earn something by making a contribution of valuable service to our fellow man. Some nights I would lie weeping that I was nothing more than a feminine adverb or adjective like the many frivolous, art-obsessed people I saw around me. But I stayed on because I had nothing else to do. My parents visited me there twice and encouraged me to persevere through my doubts for some unknown, bright future. That gave me hope, but my daily reality still doesn't provide any vision of personal fulfillment.

"Melody, you and I have a commonality of insecurity, but from different starting points."

"I suppose," I said, setting down my empty Coke. "I'll think about being a person of self-determination tonight on my drive back home, and probably for some time to come. This has been stimulating and comforting as well to see that others are fighting their own battles of parsing out order from confusion, related to but different from mine.

"Thank you so much for sharing your experiences and thoughts, Becky, but I'd better go. The rush-hour traffic has eased off."

Walking back to the kitchen, Becky said, "Here, you really liked this print; please take it to remember our conversation on female empathy. I have others because it's a helpful teaching aid."

I took it, surprised by the offer. I muttered, "I would love to have one, thank you. I was going to ask where I might buy one when I get out on my own."

"No, no, I have other copies; take it!" Becky implored, as Wendy smiled. "Like I said, it'll remind us of our connection."

I took it home and placed it under clothing in my dresser drawer. To this day I've never told Dad that I have it. I even hide it when Dad and Mingo come to the Four Corners to visit and hunt with Pem. When I remind Pem of its significance, he smiles and says, "I know it's important to you, but to me, it's just a picture."

I never found a suitable frame for it until moving out west, though I began searching for a frame the next week and continued to do so through the Christmas holidays of that year. I knew the expression on the courtesan's face could inspire me to be strong and self-accepting every time I glanced at her—whether in my drawer or on the wall.

Chapter Nineteen

A Sunrise Gazebo, Epiphanies, and Vietnam's Collapse

I

DURING 1974'S CHRISTMAS SEASON, Austin and Brick decided to resume construction on Sunrise Acres' last two lots because President Ford had restored the government mortgage funds impounded by President Nixon. Sales, however, continued slowly.

In spite of the uncertain economy, there were opportunity niches, and one involved the lumber company, Mrs. Penny. The early 1970s housing boom built over two million homes annually, generating great lumber demands. Once the economy slowed housing starts to fewer than a million units annually, lumber needs fell, too.

But Austin had MacKoy Lumber's railroad-tie operation running by the fall of 1974. This market niche was immune to recession because railroads always needed new wooden rail ties to replace those worn by time and rot. By coupling railroad-tie sales with construction lumber's remaining sales, the lumber company's operational efficiencies of scale allowed Austin to produce both railroad ties and construction lumber at a profit equal to that of a boom-time housing-construction-based economy.

I remember the MacKoy Lumber success because I went with Junebug, Kay, and Martha Sarah to the lumber company's annual Christmas barbeque. I attended to Martha Sarah so Kay could enjoy the company of Diane and Mrs. Colleen. Austin welcomed us all: "We're rehashing this year's profitable business conditions that are unique just for us. After all, it's all attorney-client privilege here with this group, right?

"Diversify, diversify! Diversifying into railroad ties has saved us from the collapsing confusion of an overheated guns-and-butter economy sandbagged by high interest rates and oil prices. Next year looks great, too."

"If you've had that good a year in this dicey economy," Junebug said, "it should be a good time to absorb your Sunrise Acres losses to date, as Malcolm suggested. I'd also write off those three lots denied a septic tank permit. In a spooky economy like this, your lucky rabbit's foot of diversification may not hold.

"I suggest declaring a fair-market value on those lots by FHA's valuation system, and then donating them as a community park. That way you'd be rid of their property tax. Of course, you'll have to improve the area so it'll meet an IRS standard definition of a useful park."

"Improvements shouldn't cost much," Brick noted. "You could improve it for two thousand, tops, because the land is already cleared. We could build a gazebo, which would qualify as a recreation focal point to the IRS. Marina drew gazebo plans for Bessie Mae. Cotton Roberts and I could redraft them on a larger scale for a park."

"Interesting!" mused Austin. "Let's mention it to the accountants at the barbeque."

As we walked toward the barbeque tables, the men discussed the park and questioned Brick about Marina's gazebo plans. As Marina's name was mentioned, Diane whispered to Kay: "You know, Lisa said Marina had a baby girl on our Thanksgiving Day after a difficult pregnancy requiring a Caesarean. Her name is Danielle!"

"I did not know that!" Kay said. "Lisa has not been to see June lately, but what a pretty name! I suppose Lisa is traveling to Montréal for Christmas to see her niece."

Diane responded, "She was there for the birth because of Marina's difficulties.

"Gosh, Kay! I recall meeting Lisa and Vann at a conference in New Orleans. They were that beautiful couple who hypnotized everyone. It's so sad to see their marriage dissolve."

II

After the holidays, Brick started construction on the last houses and the park's gazebo. I knew little of Brick's work then, even though I visited the subdivision weekly with Wendy for our family-budget work. But that was at night.

I finally saw the construction progress on a Saturday afternoon in late February when I found Dad and Brick at the gazebo watching Riley Carlisle and Mingo as Riley finished his first coat of painting. Although the gazebo was still unfinished, its value for the community was evident. Mingo was adding a cupola to the roof's peak that focused my attention on the whole scene. It was a rooster weathervane, similar to what Miss Peaches described to Marina to distinguish Peaches' gazebo from Bessie Mae's.

"Where'd you get that weathervane?" I asked.

"Aunt Dot found it on an old barn between Southern Pines and Pinehurst," answered Brick. "Only paid fifteen dollars for it, but I like what it adds to the structure."

Dad said, "A basketball court will be on one end and a barbeque cooking area on the other. A few picnic tables under the gazebo will finish it."

"So, what'll you do when you finish Sunrise Acres?" I asked Brick.

"Not sure," he answered. "I'm considering two options. I might build houses in Raleigh on Uncle Malcolm's subdivision holdings. But the recession has slowed construction even in the pricey markets now. Of course, recessions don't last forever, so next year might be O.K. It'll take a year to get these Sunrise units sold, and a slow schedule here will give me the time to get plans ready for a building operation elsewhere.

"My dad, who's still a director with Amalgamated Industries, says there's a job in that company, with management stock options, for someone with my construction experience. These multi-industrial conglomerates are always strong on top-down, balance-sheet financial planning, but short on the bottom-up, ground-floor experience that's required to make a business function profitably, according to Dad. They're looking for someone like me, who knows how all the ground-floor pieces must fit into the accounting formulations back at the corporate ivory tower.

"I might do that. I've fought the muddy weather and what it'll do to construction schedules. One too many weather-delayed culvert pipe installations will give anyone a negative attitude. A change may do me good.

"Junebug's going with me next weekend to meet Amalgamated's management team that I worked with when Dad was selling out. They're flying into Pinehurst for two days of golf, then they're going to Sunday's Carolina 500 stock car race at Rockingham. I told them to take their golfing wind suits to the racetrack because it's always cold for that early March race. But, Lord, they've got an enclosed VIP booth, and the president has told Dad that I can just about write my own ticket. It looks promising."

Realizing Brick's future required his reflective thinking, I thought about my own. While I had a good job in my hometown, something about the opportunities that Wendy and Dr. Glover had mentioned just kept pulling on my insides. Really, I think I felt a lot like Brick that day.

I continued musing about this as Mingo dismounted the ladder to the gazebo roof and tried to replace his initialed nail hammer into his toolbox. He couldn't do this without emptying the box's contents and rearranging. As he did this, he took out his brick hammer. I noticed it wasn't initialed like his other tools, but I had no reason to think anything odd about it.

III

Monday, Junebug and I were reviewing Brick's Amalgamated contract offer, and we also discussed the race results I had listened to on the radio with my grandfather. It had been the typical Rockingham race, with numerous wrecks and lead changes. In the end, Cale Yarborough won, followed by David Pearson, then Richard Petty in third. The fact that three of the top drivers had finished one, two, and three made our conversation memorable. Before noon, Junebug called Brick to rehash the three-day weekend and Brick's new business opportunities. June suggested that Brick also have his accountant review the job offer. Then he went home for lunch.

When June returned, he looked worried. According to his third-hand version from Kay, who had heard it from Diane by way of Lisa, Marina and Arnaud had gone to her mother's that Sunday. They wanted to ski after being isolated in their Montréal flat all winter with Danielle. A public ski slope near Pointe de Beaver gave them the opportunity to ski and gave fifteen-week-old Danielle some bonding time with her grandmother.

Marina had skied only once since returning to Québec, and that had been on the couple's honeymoon in western Canada. This Sunday they skied and took a snack break before returning to the slopes. On the last run, Marina insisted on skiing the advanced slope, which had abrupt turns and elevation variations. At mid-run, Arnaud reported that Marina bent over suddenly, and from this unstable position she careened to the left through a row of trees, landing in a parallel ski run.

After Arnaud and three nearby skiers arrived, one skied for help. Her bloody left side had suffered severe bruising to her ribs and pelvic area, and she was incoherent on the ambulance trip to the hospital, where she lost consciousness.

"Marina has not yet recovered," June reported, "but Lisa is en route to see her."

That night Marina expired before Lisa arrived. An autopsy revealed that she had bled internally in her pelvic and abdominal areas, resulting in an embolism that cut off the blood supply to her lungs.

IV

Brick and Bessie Mae knew of Marina's unconsciousness but not her death. However, both said they had felt her passing from their hearts before it was confirmed.

At the time of her death, between six and six-thirty, Brick was leaving the subdivision for home. Fog covered his darkened windshield. When he turned on the ignition and the defroster, a strange left handprint-like impression was on the windshield.

While Brick thought of Marina's possible demise, he also quickly thought it to be nothing more than the dust-traced impression of an oak leaf that had blown upon his windshield. But then, he said, a flash of light flowed from the depths of his unconscious mind out through his eyes and into the great ever-after. In that split-second vision, he could see Marina escaping into eternity. He sat there briefly, wondering if she had indeed died, while looking at the hand impression fade from the heat of the car's defroster.

Again, he dismissed all this as a fluke. Then driving out of the back forty, Brick saw Bessie Mae in the road by her driveway, frantically waving a dishtowel at his passing vehicle.

"Come, Mr. Brick, and see!" exclaimed Bessie Mae as Brick got out of his car to investigate. "A few minutes ago, I started hearing this scratching-knocking sound all around the windows and doors of my house like somebody wanting to come in from the cold. I assumed it was Donald, home from work.

"When I looked out the kitchen door—no car. Then I heard that scratching sound at my front door and went to open it. No one! That's when I saw this odd left handprint on my storm-door glass. I went back and opened the kitchen storm door to recheck for Donald's car and saw a left handprint on that storm-door glass pane, too. It must be a sign Mrs. Marina has died."

Brick followed Bessie Mae to both storm doors, but nothing was there—evidently, the heat of the house had evaporated the prints.

"I tell you, Mr. Brick, it was there!" Bessie Mae said. "I've been thinking about that poor woman and her child and husband all afternoon. I said to myself, Mrs. Marina is bad-off, like blood disease cases I've heard about at Duke that can cause anything to happen."

Then Brick told Bessie Mae what he had seen, and they talked about his car's defroster, and the heat from inside her house evaporating the handprints. As Brick turned to leave, he said to Bessie Mae, "Perhaps it is a sign from the beyond like the Bentonville and other battlefield ghost stories we've heard. We'll know soon because I expect Lisa will call Diane. If I hear anything from Diane before morning, I'll call you."

Lisa did notify Diane that night, and Diane did Brick, who phoned Bessie Mae. The next morning the foggy left handprint story was all over the subdivision and the lumber company, along with the retelling of Bentonville Blue ghost dog tales and other battlefield ghost legacies.

v

On the first Saturday in May 1975, just after the fall of South Vietnam to the Communists earlier that week, Lisa visited Diane and Kay in Wisdom Station and related the facts surrounding Marina's death.

Marina had experienced heavy bleeding at the end of her first trimester, but clotting medications remedied the situation. Then in the thirty-ninth week of gestation, the condition returned, causing Marina's hospitalization. Plasma and anti-hemophilic agents were administered to control bleeding, and her doctors began considering the pros and cons of a natural birth versus a Caesarean for the health of the mother and unborn child. Lisa was asked to come, as it was believed that blood transfusions between sisters would offer extra safety over hospital-stored blood if a Caesarean became necessary.

Blood tests showed that Lisa's and Marina's type-O blood matched, but with one variation. Marina's heavy bleeding condition was due to her blood platelets not clumping together for adequate clotting—not unusual for a small percentage of pregnancies in the last weeks. Lisa's blood showed the same condition, though she hadn't been pregnant in several years. This revelation stumped her doctors, who ordered more tests, saying that any test will produce variations among the different persons conducting them, even though their testing procedures and protocols are the same.

When the third battery of tests came back with the same results, a blood disorder specialist was consulted. His report stated that Marina likely had a rare blood condition called Von Willebrand disease. The specialist said it was difficult to diagnose because in-depth research was just beginning on this disease, even though some doctors had known of it since the late 1920s. While little was understood about the malady, it is thought to be prevalent in nearly 1 percent of the global population and could have come from either parent.

His report additionally stated that the estrogen therapy Marina had been on since puberty had controlled as well as probably masked her condition. The specialist said that Lisa likely had a milder version of the same disease because she did not require a Caesarean until her second child's birth, nor had she ever suffered from anemia. Lisa's condition could be a milder form simply because she was conceived when her parents were younger and more robust.

The disclosure that either parent might have been a contributor to both daughters' long-term health seemed to bring some closure to Madame LaGraves' grief about her husband's death. While Madame continued to grieve for her lost ones, her sister Joan said there was a grace about her not seen in years. Madame would often say that she was thankful that Marina's sudden fatigue did not occur while the couple motorcycled, because it could have caused an accident that killed both of Danielle's parents.

Marina did require a Caesarean and was warned that a hysterectomy might be required for her long-term health. She pleaded that this be avoided if possible since that procedure would preclude her having future children. While a hysterectomy was avoided, a D and C procedure was performed two days later to remove leftover placenta tissue. Antibiotics for infection, plasma with clotting agents for bleeding, and pain medications were administered intravenously.

At this point, apparently, the combination of anemia and the pain medications caused Marina to have hallucinations about her possible death and her father's. She insisted on dictating letters of motherly advice for Danielle that Lisa transcribed. Later Marina wondered why she had done this, musing, "Lisa, you must have thought I was crazy. But I'll keep them for their motherly sentiments, to give to Danielle when she's of age. In fact, I made up a lullaby that I'll add to them."

The sisters laughed at this, but Marina's premonition bore truth from eternity as the autopsy noted that her skiing accident evidently had perfectly retriggered hyper-coagulation issues to produce an embolism that starved her lungs of oxygen.

Then Diane related Brick's and Bessie Mae's separate visions of the fading hand. Hearing this, Lisa insisted on hearing Brick's account directly. She went to Sunrise Acres on her way home and found Brick about three-thirty in the afternoon.

They went to the completed Marina-designed gazebo to talk. Lisa showed Brick Marina's wedding pictures and a photo of her daughter. Then they went to Bessie Mae's house, where Lisa tearfully struggled as Bessie Mae related her own vaporous handprint sightings, as well as the sounds of someone knocking as if wanting to come in. Lisa then showed Bessie Mae the wedding photos, including a close-up photo of Marina's ring that displayed her slender fingers. This made Bessie Mae exclaim, "Those are like the slender fingers of the foggy handprints, but without the little finger. It probably faded out from the heat."

Quivering, Lisa responded, "You only saw four fingers because the little finger had been shredded by her fall through the trees, requiring amputation—surely a sign from heaven."

Bessie Mae said she looked at Brick and saw him to be as ghostly as she felt.

Mrs. Penny, Bessie Mae said these from-the-beyond spiritual messages of the missing finger and the possible connection of Marina's death to her father's bothered her for some time. Then one day during a lunch break she relayed the Von Willebrand related events of the LaGraves family to a Duke vascular surgeon. He said that in spite of modern medicine's sophistication a blood disease can cause all sorts of unexplained and unanticipated medical events to occur.

After Lisa left, Brick went to the Pineland Springs home of his parents, who were away.

The next day, Brick returned to Sunrise Acres as he did most Sundays. But he said little. Like most Americans, we were immersed all week in the television news programs covering the fall of Saigon. It was depressing to see the same re-runs of helicopters lifting off from the top of the U.S. Embassy there. The images of defeat and failure rolled again and again: Vietnamese pleading for salvation by helicopter—and the looks of abandonment on the faces of allies left behind.

Brick's face expressed sorrow as did those of the Triple Nickel veterans Allen Lamb and Henry Moore, who viewed the news with us. But something else was going on in Brick's mind that I did not learn the details of until Kay visited me out west years later.

As we viewed Vietnam's abandonment drama, Brick told me about Marina's having had a death premonition after which she dictated several letters of guidance to her daughter. These letters were to be opened by Danielle at the appropriate ages marked on the sealed envelopes. Lisa said they were letters of motherly advice on such issues as how to take care at sixteen to drive safely, and at eighteen to be moderate with alcohol consumption and the like. Our knowledge of these letters was tinged with sadness because they demonstrated Marina's deep faith and abiding love.

However, Lisa had told Brick other things that had already brought back the appearance of Marina's ghost to him along with those of the old ghost dog, Bentonville Blue. Junebug and Wesley learned of this additional revelation before the year's end in December 1975, but I did not, Mrs. Penny, until Kay's Four Corners visit years later.

Chapter Twenty

Closing Out, a Wedding Announcement, and Confessions

> And the Voice Responded: Truly, a persevering Wisdom,
>   forged in patient Love, must follow Knowledge about,
> cleaning up after the many invalid insights that
>   Knowledge often begets.
> —*"Preamble to the Beginning," Chaplain Wesley Wyatt, U.S. Army*
>   *The Coosa Valley Boarding School for Boys*

I

MRS. PENNY, BRICK'S MALAISE CONTINUED after Lisa's visit until the first two of the remaining unsold houses received buyer loans. As all the houses were now constructed, Brick accepted the Amalgamated job in June 1975, but continued spending his weekends at Sunrise Acres until all the houses were sold.

Bobby Jack Johnson, Riley Carlisle, and Jeff Mack moved onto other projects. Mingo hired on at a kitchen cabinet firm but checked with Brick every Saturday about warranty repairs, which rarely took long.

But whatever Mingo's schedule, Bertha Moore sought him out to insist that he have Saturday lunch with her and Henry. Sometimes Dad went, and once Brick did. This started about the time Bertha commented to Wendy and me that all of Mingo's tools were initialed except his brick hammer.

I placed no significance on these lunches because I didn't yet know the truth about the Marsh-Chalky death scene. Dad later told me that Bertha had taken an adopted-son liking to Mingo. Mingo humored her because he feared that Bertha might have, by pure accident, almost caught onto the truth of what might have caused Chalky's death.

One Saturday after the coroner's office returned Mingo's toolbox, Henry and Bertha hired Mingo to install an extra bathroom towel rack. Mingo left his toolbox under their carport to prevent scratching anything in their home. After Bertha told him where to place the rack, she sat down outside on the carport partition wall beside his opened toolbox. When Mingo finished, he returned to put his tools away. That's when he saw Bertha Mae holding the brick hammer my father had furnished to Mingo as the weapon-substitute.

Bertha broke into tears. "I had lots of time to think about those police questions between the day of the killings and my own hearing for hitting that dead Chalky. Henry says he wished he had been there to keep me away, but I'm glad I went 'cause I just know he had our son killed. All them remarks about some hard object hitting Chalky in the temple. I felt relief when they finally blamed it on Chalky's broke neck after falling into that door-closing cylinder. I know you're glad to finally have your toolbox back so you can initial your new brick hammer to be like all your other tools."

"Yes, ma'am," Mingo said, a chill running down his spine. "I lost my old brick hammer around Christmas, and never got the time to initial my new one before all that confusion started."

II

The loans for the last houses closed the Friday after Thanksgiving at the Willingham Law Offices, with Austin and Diane also present. Austin treated everyone to a celebration lunch at Uncle Henry's before Brick, Dad, and Mingo departed to clean out a rented mobile office for its return. The main lunch-hour topic, however, was the pending wedding of my mentor, Wendy Granger, to Langdon Butler.

Brick asked, "Melody, are you going to any of the wedding parties?"

"Only the wedding," I said. "I'll miss the Kitty Hawk party you and your friends are giving them. June and Kay want me to remain here to help Mr. and Mrs. Willingham with Martha Sarah. Of course, Mr. Willingham and I must keep the office open."

"Well, I'm looking forward to the Boulevard Beach Cove party," Brick said. "Brewer and Monroe have hired Rocky as disc jockey. We're all ushering in the wedding, and Wesley is doing the service. Wendy's always liked how Wesley did Brewer and Nicole's wedding, and Langdon was moved by Wesley's words at Marsh's funeral."

That night, when Dad came home, he said that Henry, Bertha, Allen, Celestine, and Miss Peaches all came to say farewell to Brick as Dad and Mingo helped Brick clean out the mobile rental office. What Dad did not tell me then was that Brick commented as Bertha walked away with the others: "Well, this is the end for us. I like my Amalgamated job, and don't expect to come back here unless Bertha should publicly hint about Chalky's death.

"She may have a spooky insight about what happened, but she's also aware that she knows nothing for sure. So, I don't believe her word could ever prove a thing. The fact that she's under psychiatric care over her life's sorrows means that no official would likely believe her. Besides, with Carley Ray being retired, I doubt if there's a lawman around that she'd feel comfortable approaching. We've got to continue staying quiet and hope she does too. If she does talk, she'll have to produce a killing instrument. I hope you threw that hammer into some deep river where no one could ever find it, Deacon."

"I never did that," Dad replied. "I put it in my smokehouse right after the killings to get it out of my car. Every time I got ready to go fishing and sink it, somebody would come up wanting to tag along. So, the hammer's just stayed there, out of sight between two rafters."

"Damn!" Brick exclaimed. "Give that thing to me. I'll get rid of it somewhere between here and the Atlantic Ocean so no one will ever find it."

All three drove over to our house, where Dad retrieved the hammer from the smoke-house and gave it to Brick for disposal.

III

Two weekends later Brick drove to Junebug's Duck cottage on a stormy Friday evening before Saturday's Boulevard Beach Cove wedding party for Wendy and Langdon. Brick arrived late due to visiting the Lake Mattamuskeet Hunting Preserve.

Brick and Wesley sipped red wine while Junebug nursed a scotch and grilled steaks on the cottage deck between rain squalls. Kay and Wesley's wife, Lee Çu, were attending a bridal shower for Wendy near Kitty Hawk.

Junebug entered and put the steaks in the stove warmer. "Glad I finished grilling before hard rains return. It's time for steak and your red wine, Wes."

Wesley noted, "It's a hearty Rhône, June, like good Episcopalians favor. Lee Çu picked it out. Her French exposure, you know."

As they ate, a nor'easter gusted up. Junebug said, "That's just a stiff breeze. It's about that same time of year of the Wright Brothers' first flight back in December of 1903. They came here believing our local December winds would help launch their craft."

Brick finished first, and refilled his wine glass before walking to the big window over-looking the rain-soaked cottage deck and the Atlantic's turbulent, white-capped waves. He asked, "May I help you clear the table?"

"No," Junebug said. "Relax! You deserve a break after several rough years. And, knowing you, I expect you still blame yourself for your losses. Nationwide and even worldwide, these years have brought a lot of economic difficulty for individuals to fight. It financially sacked you, along with some of your customers, and caused you to lose the girl, too. But, of course, Marina died, so you would have lost her anyway. This'll sound hard, but be thankful that you're not the father of a child with a dead mother."

"Yes," Wesley put in. "The Bible often speaks of the troubles of widows and orphans, but never of widowers. There seems to be no guide for that loss.

"As for your housing foreclosure setbacks, we chaplains often deal with soldiers losing their VA home loans. It's common for all beginning families on a budget. Be thankful you still have your shirt, and your Amalgamated opportunities to capitalize on."

"Yes, surviving to the next opportunity," Brick said wistfully. "I thought of that at Mattamuskeet today. Uncle Malcolm, Marsh, Marina—gone; and Hutton's mentally castrated by it all.

"I thought of Hutton today because we had talked about the Mattamuskeet farm failures. Seems mankind is always out-thinking itself, believing the next bite out of the apple from the Tree of Knowledge will provide the ultimate solution for him. But solutions to complex environmental problems come only with time, and trial and error, while man cries, 'Am I killing the tadpole or is the tadpole killing me?'

"Life is a struggle no matter one's education or the help that family can give for dealing with it all. But I know I'll make it because Marina entered the good eternity from right here on that deck, even though she died in Canada. In spite of our loving miscalculations, she found the courage to struggle into heaven's gate when at death's judgment door.

"Junebug, you probably still wonder about your thoughts of seeing nudes laying on yonder deck. On your return flyover, Marina was inside, and I was alone, wrapped in a beach towel. But you had guessed right.

"They say you must get things off your chest by 'sharing.' Marina shared our story with her sister before she passed. Lisa told me when she came by Sunrise Acres last spring to see the gazebo. But I've not shared my story of Marina with anyone.

"I know I can share with you two, and not be a kiss-and-tell man because I know my story will go no further than here—with my lawyer and my minister! So, I now invoke all my off-the-record privileges.

"After Marina and I arrived here that Friday night for the long Fourth of July weekend, we tried to sleep, but the Atlantic's roaring waves wouldn't let us. I'll just say we gave into the romance of the ocean breeze.

"The next morning we went out onto the deck. I only had a towel wrap and she was in the black, sheer silk sleeping top that Lonah had given her from Lazlo's negligee photo-shoot. Remember when we were at Ocean Drive, the weekend of Dutch's arrest? Anyway, we sat on the edge of that same lounge chair you see drenched now. We knew we only had a little time before your arrival with Kay and Martha Sarah. I looked at her and said, 'Now I see what Junebug means about the deck's privacy from prying eyes.'

"She smiled as we arose, and I pulled that lounge chair mattress off onto the deck. I could see our shadowed outlines as we embraced to surrender into the sweetness of the moment. Afterwards, we knew that we had seen the great deep of the universe together.

"We looked into each other's eyes until we nodded to sleep, like Sunday church folks who find inspiration and peace from the first part of a sermon but can no longer remain awake.

"When we woke, we looked through the lattice screen and saw a lone cloud floating in from the ocean. You know how it is with clouds. You can imagine seeing a horse or whatever in them, but this cloud had the face of a man.

"Lying there, Marina said, 'That cloud looks like a man with one eye upon us. I can't tell if he's smiling, but he does not appear judgmental. It makes me wonder if that's what God is like: simply observing. That may sound as silly as the Bentonville ghost story or the legends of St. Joseph's Oratory. But both stories suggest that we're always on the edge of eternity, and in that way I believe both stories are true, don't you?'

"I agreed with her and we continued looking until the cloud faded away. As Marina had said, it was a non-judgmental gazing cloud, and it reminded me of the *Mona Lisa*. You can't tell what the *Mona Lisa* is thinking either, as she sits, nearly smiles, and observes."

IV

"You probably wonder how this connects with the Bentonville ghost stories and the miraculous healing legends of St. Joseph's Oratory, but Marina was always drawn to such glimpses into eternity by her father's unexpected death when she was barely a teen. She coped with the loss through holding onto some seemingly certified promise of a hereafter. I never paid much attention to it until we went to St. Joseph's with Henri and Arnaud.

"At St. Joseph's, Father Marcel told us of the many discarded crutches and leg braces left there by pilgrims who had experienced some degree of healing. There are also stairs that pilgrims climb on their knees hoping to gain forgiveness. St. Joseph's stairs are like the Holy Stairs now in Rome that are said to be the actual stairs Christ climbed to Pontius Pilate on the night before his crucifixion. Many pilgrims climb St. Joseph's imitative of those in Rome because it's said that the repentant thought in the sinner's heart is what truly counts toward forgiveness.

"When Lisa visited me last spring at Sunrise Acres, she told me how Marina's exposure to St. Joseph's miracles and the Bentonville ghost stories affected her views of eternity at the end.

"Lisa said that when Marina decided to accept Arnaud's marriage proposal, she confessed her relationship with me to Father Marcel, who counseled her. While Father Marcel did not suggest a climb of repentance, Marina nevertheless did so the night before her wedding rehearsal. The Greensleeves Christmas carol, 'What Child Is This?' ringing from the Oratory's fifty-six-bell carillon added a surreal sense of divine pardon for her sins, both past and future, as she climbed, bloodying her knees. She wore thick gauze bandages at her wedding to prevent blood from leaking into her stockings and onto her white wedding gown. Too bad no one recognized her blood disorder then.

"Marina confessed to Lisa that her memories of our times together were obliterated after her stair climb…until Danielle's birth. Then Marina feared calling my name from a deep recess in her mind, as if she wished that Danielle were my child, while also being thankful that she was not. Because she had given life without me, she prayed that my persona would never haunt her again. But she also found herself hoping that I was as proud of her at that moment as she was proud of herself. So she prayed for the same joys for me someday with another, hoping the thought would help her forget me.

"After Danielle's birth, she remained hospitalized due to post-partum surgery, and the combination of pain medications and blood loss–related anemia gave her greater hallucinations about me and her own portending death. She feared moaning out my name in her sleep and making Arnaud needlessly jealous over an old lover, miles away, that she would likely never see again. That's when she confessed her deepest feelings and fears about me to Lisa…":

"Lisa, Brick's being a builder and my being an architect seemed like Heaven's match. Mother's anxieties over cross-cultural marriages were nothing compared to the conspiracy of events that the greater world produced to wreck my dreams.

"I wasn't like an ambitious, hungry lioness on the prowl. Why did I indulge in such physical fulfillment with Brick? I'm scared that my carnal desires eclipsed that greater love of my own self-worth and dignity.

"I pray that I will not be judged by Arnaud! He has given me Danielle and a good life in our own language. And I pray I've been a good, robust salmon come home to spawn. But, Lisa, these hallucinations of Brick and me! When I awake

I realize they're just dreams. It's like looking at a split-screen television. One side shows my chaste married life and the other shows me lost in an opera of lust that makes me feel immoral.

"In both visions, I stand naked as I was born before Christ, totally defenseless against my exposed sins. One vision shows my desire for Brick, now that I have all I ever wanted except him. The other, a vision of Jesus suffering for my soul, while I pray at the cross for a blessed eternal relationship with my child and her father.

"Will my prayers blanch the stains of my childish dalliances? I never realized that Christ suffered so much for me, personally. He has as much passion for suffering through my dalliances as I have for Brick in the other vision. Christ's tears are of blood, and He accepts me, which totally obliterates Brick in the other vision. But then I backslide into another tender vision, and the two repeat—cycling on and on, driving me to grievousness.

"I'm forced to ask myself if I desire Brick more than I do God? Is that not crazy? Have I placed myself in a precarious spiritual position of desiring Brick more at death's door than God beyond it? I pray that the miracle of St. Joseph's stairs will fall upon me that I might be in paradise with my daughter and husband where nothing will be evident of my former self...."

"Then when Bessie Mae and I learned from Lisa that our fog-induced prints of Marina's left hand accurately captured that she only had four fingers after the accident, it unnerved us both. At that point Bentonville ghost stories rushed into my mind with a force of spiritual believability I had never known."

V

"Arriving at my parents' home after Lisa's Sunrise Acres visit, I read a note from my mother to feed Mary Lee's Chihuahua, Flip. My parents had gone for the weekend, and Mary Lee was at school," Brick continued.

"I was tired, needing a restful evening. As I stirred my double bourbon and ginger ale, cut with water, the tinkling ice cubes awoke Flip from his spot on the couch in the adjacent den. Soon the dog was pawing on my leg for food and affection. Looking in the fridge for leftovers to please him, I saw that my mother had left me a porterhouse and a salad.

"I lit the patio's charcoal grill and went to the den to watch the news while the coals burned off. Because the U.S. had abandoned Vietnam that week, that story dominated. After the news, I mixed myself another drink before preparing dinner.

"Watching the steak sizzle, my thoughts of our country's failure in Vietnam intertwined with my thoughts of Marina's last hours as Lisa had related them to me at the gazebo earlier that afternoon. It was an emotional cocktail, and my mind was the blender. It was all so final. JFK's words, 'We shall pay any price, bear any burden, meet any hardship, oppose any foe...to assure the survival and success of liberty,' seemed as hollow in the sight of our abandonment as the abandoned dreams that Marina and I'd had. Both situations were a comedy of well-intentioned ambitions too weak to handle the enigma of complex difficulty. As I ate, I realized my mind's free-flowing juxtaposition of these two events would be an irrational connection to most sensible people. But both were about absurdity and incompleteness.

"Unlike the Bentonville Battleground ghosts who were searching for a ripped seam in the fabric of eternity, I hoped that Marina's ghostly hand was a sign that she was free of such spiritual confusion. I prayed that she had secured her atonement at St. Joseph's, and agonized over her soul's being stuck somewhere in limbo.

"After a shower, I saw that *How the West Was Won* was the Saturday night movie on TV. It being a favorite, I wanted to see it again for the umpteenth time! As the movie's music intro roared, I mixed another drink and gave the dog a steak scrap. Then we both found our spots on the couch. With only the light from the TV, I found myself nodding off, in spite of wanting to see the film. But I was exhausted after months of coaxing and cajoling the Sunrise Acres project into its final stage.

"Between nods I remembered that Marina had seen this movie with her father just before his tugboat accident. Besides the movie's main musical score, this film features several adaptations of 'Greensleeves.' So Lisa's story of Marina climbing the stairs of St. Joseph's while the cathedral's carillon played that melody wafted through me deeper with each snoozing breath. I fell into a sleepy fog.

"When I awoke, only the TV test pattern remained. The dog had awakened me from the strangest dream. He seemed to have tugged at my bathrobe from midair to pull me back down upon the couch, as if I had been levitating! I arose groggily and let Flip outside before sitting at the kitchen table to await his scratching for reentry. Only the full moon's light flowed through the windows as I pondered my dream.

"In this dream, I had my head between my legs as I sat in a small johnboat floating aimlessly backward through a fog. Feeling helpless, I saw I had no paddle for controlling the boat. It was dark, and the water was as tar-black as any swampy stream in the Carolina Coastal Plain. To my rear, I saw the half-naked ghost riders of my youth galloping away from Sampsons Landing's colored swimming hole with Bentonville Blue following. I saw one of Donald's elder cousins laughing, 'Get your white asses out of here!'

"The boat continued drifting backward through the darkness, but the immediate fog around the boat slowly changed into a steady glow of white, lightning-bright vapors, so bright that I could not look directly at that fog for fear of being blinded. I kept my head down to protect my eyesight. I saw only glimpses of my surroundings from beneath the edges of my thighs, which acted like blinders on a mule's bridle and saved my sight. The light was otherwise not threatening, but especially warm and pleasant to the core of my bones.

"From beneath my thighs I suddenly saw bright angels' feet below wings like those of the Greek God Hermes. Their feet were tapping about upon the surface of the waters that had turned a crystal blue. Next, I saw Bentonville Blue on the bank of the stream as a hidden heavenly choir hummed 'Let Us Gather at the River.' Momentarily a voice reverberated from the fog. Like the light, it was not threatening but said in a matter-of-fact way: 'Be Humble—Be Humble—Be Humble.'

"Then Flip awoke me with his tugging on my bathrobe. I was at first afraid to open my eyes for fear of seeing a vapor too bright. I had not yet realized that I had been dreaming.

"In the kitchen, I thought about the dream's words 'Be Humble' until Flip scratched on the kitchen door to reenter. Then I went back and lay down upon the couch, drifting in and out of consciousness as if on a drugged trip to some other level of awareness. I hadn't done any drugs since a year before Marsh was killed, but that's what it felt like.

"The next morning, I felt rested in spite of my disconcerting dream, and that day at Sunrise Acres, I felt fine. But the effects of my dream continued to work on my mind through most of the next week like Dutch's opium-laced hash, hard to shake off.

"I pondered the dream's message, 'Be Humble.' I had never felt the need of humility or appreciated being 'humble' as a desirable personal trait in my entire life in any way. The whole idea of 'humility' was as totally foreign to me as something from another universe! So you can understand why I spent so much time wondering about this particular thought. I still have no clue to the thought's genesis, unless it came from the taking of the communion elements or my infant christening shortly after my circumcision. The whole experience felt like a phone call from a long-lost friend. It made me wonder if Marina and the Almighty, Himself, had together called me on a spiritual telephone via the dream.

"That dream, along with the foggy handprints Bessie Mae and I saw, made me ask whether I'd been visited in a dream like Jesus' father, Joseph. I don't know and can't prove anything, but I, dumbfounded, believe it to be the truth for me.

"I now believe that the seductive purity of God's love did obliterate any lust that Marina's memory had conjured up, and the vaporized hand is an assuring sign of that. Like the good thief on the cross, Marina had squirmed humble prayers to return to that eternal power-source that said, 'Let there be light.' Perhaps that was the impetus or impulse that led me to my own dream of humility. Whatever the case, I believe that a lack of humility is the only thing that stands between us and our safe return to the everlasting light. 'Be ye as a little child' is the only way.

"My 'little child' thought came from a lullaby Lisa said that Marina had concocted for singing Danielle to sleep. Marina had sung it to Lisa, and Lisa sang it for me. It was a mother's prayerful lullaby that her child would climb life's spiral hill of new understanding at each age in life to reach the best possible fulfillment of self.

"Then today I stopped by Lake Mattamuskeet as Marina and I did on our Fourth of July weekend trip here. There I thought about us, and the many things done in this state from the Lost Colony forward that failed but did not end man's larger journey. And I asked, WHY do some of us get to go on while others don't? That old saying of 'Only the good die young' makes me wonder if it's not just the assholes like me who survive. I know I should feel guilty about it all, but I don't. Yet it makes me feel guilty or at least confused that I don't feel guilty! Truly, I'm thankful—beyond my understanding—that I'm still standing and moving forward, appreciating humility and charity for myself and for others."

Chapter Twenty-One

Junebug and Chaplain Wesley's Wisdom Poem

I

WHEN BRICK FINISHED HIS TALE, Junebug said, "Speed, that's quite a story."

"There's more," Brick said wryly, before telling June and Wesley the full history of his and Marina's affair from Monkey Island forward. Kay related Brick's confession to me years later during her visit to the Four Corners.

After Brick's unburdening, Junebug said, "Oh, Speed, you intellectual lightning bolt! You've had a transcendental brain pain—the highest of epiphanies! Yet you're feeling guilty about not feeling guilty for your moment of personal salvation. Shame on you for feeling guilty about not feeling guilty! Be thankful, damn it!

"Remember our old Speed Doctor's Latin verb conjugation drills: Amo, Amas, Amat; I Love, You Love; He, She, It Loves? It's Love, Speed! Love of one's own self-worth. Remember that Christ said, 'Love your neighbor as yourself.' Something's in play there about loving and forgiving oneself first, before one can truly appreciate how to love others. Really, in the divine comedy of human errors we continue to make the same dumb mistakes from age to age. Those age-old Sunday-school Bible lessons must be learned anew by each generation.

"You're right that you should be humbly thankful, but don't equate your guilt to being an asshole; just a lucky horse's ass. I felt guilty when my first wife and I divorced. We both had good intentions, but our egos realized after the sex hit its repetitive dead end that we weren't enough like each other to endure together. Our egos hadn't yet matured to control our basic psychological instincts. It still hurt, though, that I had interfered with another's worldly journey by hoping to remold her ways to mine. At least you didn't do that.

"Lawyers see all kinds of troubles, Brick. There's not much dignity in being a lawyer because it's generally just you, a law book, and a judge trying to repair the screwed-up lives of society's dregs. So I know assholes when I see 'em. Most of the time I can smell 'em coming, even if they've had a bath; that hard-headed, bloody-minded redneck glint in their eyes gives 'em away every time, even if they've still got all their teeth.

"So I can assure you that you're not an asshole in comparison with the greater spectrum of men because you've spent too much energy giving hope to others by furnishing them the opportunity to turn a bunch of houses into a community of homes. Assholes never try to create opportunities for others. They don't have the positive energy to follow through when the going gets tough because anything worthwhile always has its tough spots to overcome. Marina also wanted to be a part of that positive flow. So you can't blame either of you for being attracted to that vision's glory, and through that into miscalculating about how each other would fit smoothly with your own ways, tastes, and beliefs."

"It's comforting to hear I may fall into the greater perspective of not being a real, certified asshole, Junebug, just a near-miss. I like the way you rationalize the outcome because, like Marina, I indeed do have a dog in my soul's fight to make it back inside heaven's gate."

"In the greater perspective, we're all near-miss assholes, Speed," Junebug replied. "Think about it like a lawyer. All moral failures are a little like second-degree murderers. Second-degree murder is not moral, and it's so truly blamable that there are hard consequences for the murderer, right? However, the second-degree murderer is seen in modern times as being untainted enough to be redeemable for future use in society. That's because the second-degree murderer did his horrible crime out of some presumably correctable, emotional ignorance on the spur of the moment. The guilty have always been found to be less guilty for hasty, unpremeditated crimes than for those that proceed from a premeditated deliberation implying a spiteful, sinister soul.

"It was like that with my first wife. We unintentionally injured each other's ability to love freely. While I'm thankful we're only injured lovers, and not second-degree murderers, there's no real spiritual difference between the two."

II

Wesley added, "Brick, God gave man freedom of thought, knowing that some thoughts would be unintentionally bad thoughts, some unintentionally good; some deliberately good and some deliberately bad. Actions may or may not follow from our thoughts—some being healthy and some being temptations. Like us, I think God wants to be freely loved without our feeling obligated to Him. I believe He'd like to be liked and appreciated for His ever-creative, interesting magnitude just as we would like to be admired for our healthy creativity.

"Of course, giving man freedom of thought means that God must sometimes suffer being freely rejected, even though our rejection of Him is prompted by our own naïve, free-thinking spirit. The great perilous consequence of having freedom of choice is that our free choices often lack foresight for avoiding our own self-induced deceptions—that hubris comes with the territory of being human.

"Brick, from our Army days, we know that the word 'hubris' is a nice way of saying that one is egotistically full of himself—or full of crap, as the saintly soldiers say.

"My hubris came from hating God for allowing my parents to die when I was young. I studied much about the world's unfairness, like Hitler's killing the Jews, while considering my own worldly predicament, but my study yielded no insight until my first year at Duke Divinity.

"Near that year's end we had a retreat on the world's unfairness with graduating Baptist divinity students from old Wake Forest College. This was before the college moved from Wake Forest township to Winston-Salem. Our retreat bus stopped in Wake Forest to pick up our Baptist brothers before motoring to the nearby Oxford Orphanage. The orphans were the focus of our retreat about unfairness. My Biblical teachers and counselors had often advised that I must spiritually age through numerous life experiences to comprehend the greater answers on unfairness. However, I was often impatient, causing my anger to elevate. The orphanage trip began like that but became the scene of my epiphany.

"After the orphanage tour, several of us Methodist seminary students joined some Baptist seminary students at an outlawed beer party on the banks of the Neuse River headwaters. Seminary students, even in the late forties and early fifties, were known for swilling a few beers while enjoying their Camels or Lucky Strikes before taking up the cloth formally and denying worldly pleasures.

"We Methodists laughingly said we were all Episcopalians on the inside, having enjoyed Methodist outlaw functions in Durham, and it reassured me to learn that Baptists were about as bad as Methodists at the art of double-speak on the subject of alcohol. That thought caused me to imbibe an extra beer or two, which didn't help me deal with my flooding emotions.

"With my fourth beer and a Lucky Strike, I slipped off to relieve myself by the shallow Neuse headwaters. Between cigarette puffs and beer sips, the angry tears poured as I realized again that I was as alone in the world as the orphans I had seen. I felt like a club-carrying Neanderthal man-child walking around a caldera and gazing up at the moon to ask—no, demand—the big 'WHY?—WHY ME?'

"'Honor thy Mother and Father and you shall inherit the Earth,' one of the Ten Commandments teaches. It's the only commandment that promises any kind of reward if we obey it—'Inherit the Earth!' They had told us that the next day's discussion would be centered around the thought that we are to honor our parents even if they abuse us and perhaps willfully abandon us to an orphanage, as some of the children we had seen that day had been. What kind of God sits by and allows unjustified things to happen to children—the most defenseless of His creation? That was my hate-tinged question.

"So, I asked myself, as my saintly Army troopers often ask after losing a limb, is God an uncaring son-of-a-bitch or a bastard? Well, I answered 'no' to those questions because God has no parents. So, I asked, if it's impossible for God to be a bastard or SOB, is He possibly an asshole? After all, it is arguable that He had been one to me and other orphans, just as He allowed Hitler to kill all those Jews. But then I had to ask myself what kind of a Soul would create a world of torture? The pain of it all would surely burn out its Creator with misery. So there I sat asking those stupid sophomoric questions of Who, What, When, Where, and Why that my soldiers say 'have no real friggin' answers.' They're just questions we all pitifully ask while trying to understand our confused place in existence.

"Sensing the helplessness of finding answers to these 'why and how' questions, it occurred to me that if I felt helpless, perhaps God does sometimes, too, because He made Himself helpless to control our free-will decisions in the beginning. I became deeply focused on the problem of God's helplessness.

"Suddenly, I felt sorry for God, as He never gets any relief from observing all the miserable actions of His world. The poor sucker can't quit being God even if He wants to. He's stuck with the job of being God forever and ever because He's the First Realizer; He's the First Questioner, the First Answerer, and a victim or prisoner of His Love's never-ending centrifugal force. Truly, then I realized for the first time that God's not an asshole, but just the big, suffering parent of us all. This idea became even more real to me as I recalled Christ's directive to visit prisoners and the confused sick and poor because it would be like also visiting Him as His spirit would always be with the afflicted. My mind connected Christ's being with the afflicted to God's being with the babes slaughtered by Pharaoh at Moses' birth and also by Herod at Jesus' birth, and thus likely with the Jews slaughtered in WWII. My epiphany and revelation—He had always been with me, shepherding me to more spiritually mature realizations.

"Immediately a peace fell over me that must have been like John Wesley's peace experience at Aldersgate because it seemed to pass beyond all logical understanding. I had heard of this peace but had never connected with it to discover a higher understanding.

"I then reflected that Christ's coming into the world showed the Father's appreciation for our worldly sufferings by having His son suffer an unjust kangaroo trial. Thus, what we have in common with the Father is suffering, the suffering of great wrongs. I realized that night that suffering is the great common denominator connecting us all to one another through Him.

"My epiphany made me realize further that God must have seen a brightly lighted spiritual Promised Land inside Himself before He felt forced by His own inspiration to say, 'Let there be light.' He realized that He must create a realm of mental understanding so resplendent in light that the gravity of darkness He found Himself to be in would never be able to shut the light down. And to do this He realized that He needed to release mankind from His interior self into the universe to assist in changing darkness into an eternal light without end.

"Since I imagined God realizing this, I perceived Him thereby to be the First Realizer, counseling Himself toward the foundation of our present eon before he said, 'Let there be light.' I imagined that He counseled with His various spiritual parts like charity, love, wisdom, truth, patience, and knowledge. From this counsel He realized that knowledge could produce many incorrect and even dangerous assumptions, but also that only free inquiry could allow knowledge to function fully. Thus, a charitable forgiveness from His eternal Love must be prepared to persevere in loving patience with mankind for cleaning up man's many invalid insights that a freely inquiring knowledge can beget, as wisdom always comes later after reflections on the miscues of our first impressions. Forgiveness is life's natural self-correcting process that readies us for eternity. That forgiveness process causes Yahweh of the Burning Bush to burn because He knows that's His necessary job if the life of His expanding eternity and our lives in it is to continue.

"Then another urge to evacuate my bladder ended my wonderment. That night I slept well, a reborn soul, because I felt I had realized God's own primary Realization—Himself!"

"Wesley," Junebug asked, "how did your river experience evolve into your poem-essay, 'Preamble to the Beginning'?"

"That came later, after my failed ministry appointments and my return to the Coosa School as a teacher," Wesley answered.

"Returning to Coosa where I had been raised helped me reset my spiritual gyroscope after confronting my inadequacies as a minister. We all grow by trial and error, and come to realize, as an Existentialist does, that each of us—simply by existing in this world—becomes responsible for determining the essence of our personal existence. It's evident that Marina felt the same way when she foresaw her deathbed except that she wanted to determine her essence for eternity and was disappointed that her essence was, to the last, quite torn between carnal desires and her desire for oneness with God.

"However, unlike Marina, I got to live to share my insights with others, where such testimony is appropriate. Thus my 'Preamble to the Beginning' was written for sharing to help readers to a new realization of insight that we all learn through experiences of failure and spiritual disgrace."

III

Then Junebug recalled, "Brick, I studied Wesley's 'Preamble' poem about the purposes of suffering to understand myself better after my first marriage dissolved in divorce.

"Naturally, like any pre-law student, I cross-examined my depressed self. I used Wesley's poem as a self-examination guide. As I thought about Wesley's perception that God suffered through the dark eons, and that suffering is the common denominator between the Father's experience and our own personal, worldly sufferings, I became increasingly steady with my thoughts and temperament. From this common denominator of suffering, I wondered if I had any of Lincoln's positive angles of thought in common with the Godhead. The First Realizer did, after all, come out of His darkness to say, 'Let there be light.' Was there a potential life of light in my soul as in His, or does doubt reside throughout me? I asked myself. More so than at any earlier time in my life, I knew that the human soul is bombarded with all sorts of stimuli. The soul can react to this multitude of stimuli with a loving, faithful prayer for wisdom, or it can react with conventional half-truths that result in greater levels of confusion.

"While this realization made my heart humble, I also knew that it wouldn't be the last time I'd experience the spiritual crisis-and-restoration process. I had seen too many glum repeat offenders in Dad's law office to think otherwise. So I decided then to try being more prudent in my thinking about each new step in life. I began to appreciate that life is not a damn vacation, or a party, but a job to be entered upon in some spirit of a determined, prayerful hope not to fail. With this realization, I became a hell of a lot less cavalier. Christ and prayer cleanse your sins, but neither cures you of your propensity to sin tomorrow. Only death does that."

"Yes," Wesley put in, "we three have suffering in common, but different sufferings because they came to different minds out of different experiences.

"We understand your financial losses during a bad economic cycle, Brick. As for Marina, I've seen too many young soldiers marry foreign girls only to seek a divorce. Others, much like Marsh and Sue Anne, marry, remarry, or sidestep a divorce out of sheer loneliness. I counseled Marsh and Sue Anne about that because I easily imagined a train wreck for their relationship, had Marsh lived. A culture-clash divorce also worried Lee Çu and me greatly before we married. However, our common orphanhood bonded us and allowed us to discover life together more easily and thereby have time for realizing our better selves through each other's guidance."

IV

Then Wesley pulled a tattered copy of his poem from his coat and read it. At the conclusion, June asked for the copy, saying he'd have me retype it and provide copies for all.

Wesley agreed, then said, "Friends, it's late! I can't wait up any longer for Kay and Lee Çu to return from the bridal shower.

"So let us three say *Selah* or 'Pause' as we reflect on your life journey, Brick, and on ours. And to that I'll add *Shalom Aleichem*, or 'God's peace be with us all,' when we arise for a new day tomorrow."

The next week I retyped Wesley's "Preamble to the Beginning" and kept a copy for myself. I'll mail you a copy, Mrs. Penny, when I return home.

Chapter Twenty-Two

Return to Corolla, an Outer Banks Wedding Party, and a Wright Brothers Memorial Visit

I

THE NEXT MORNING, AT KAY AND LEE ÇU'S INVITATION, Langdon Butler stopped for coffee on his way to Corolla to deliver boat motor parts. They had seen Langdon the previous night when he chauffeured Wendy and her maid-of-honor roommate, Becky Rollins, to the wedding shower. After Langdon's morning visit, Brick joined him on the Corolla trip when Langdon promised they'd return before Brewer and Monroe arrived at his cottage for a sleepover.

Bumping along, their heads bounced to the beat of John Phillips' tune "Down the Beach" and the Eagles' "One of These Nights" on the radio. Both men marveled as they tracked this ancient telephone-line repair path, still unpaved by the highway department. Twice they stopped both to appreciate nature and to allow nature to appreciate them. At Corolla, Langdon stopped by the general store where Brick and Marina had snacked on johnny cakes, hoop cheese, and Nu-Grape sodas. Langdon asked the whereabouts of Wayhab, saying that he had a motor part for his skiff.

The clerk said Wayhab was at the Whalehead Club dock working on his boat.

"But I thought the Whalehead property was still for top-secret rocket design," Brick said.

"That's over," replied the clerk. "The place is for sale to anybody able to afford it. Wayhab is a guard. No entry restrictions now."

They found Wayhab wrestling with a skiff motor anchor bolt. His wife was holding a can of oil spray. Wayhab winced before coming up with the bolt, saying, "I tell you, Jharu, the salt air freezes up the metal, no matter how often oil is put on these bolts."

Langdon asked Wayhab if he remembered Brick. Brick smiled, "You toured me and a woman around the Whalehead grounds on New Year's Day back in 1972. We had hunted off the Monkey Island Club with Dutch."

"The Dutchman," Wayhab responded. "I advised him against smuggling. But the Monkey Island days you remember are about over. This may be its last season. If you walk to the end of the pier, you can see the lodge from here.

"I recollect you and the girl touring the Whalehead Club. Langdon said she died from skiing accident complications."

"Yes," Brick replied. "She and Dutch have departed, as well as my cousin, Marsh, who was accidentally killed—difficult years for me. But we all had a good time back then, thanks to you and Jharu."

Brick nodded at Langdon holding the packages for Wayhab and walked to the end of the dock so the two men could conduct their business. He stood at the end of the dock looking across the Currituck Sound at the Monkey Island Lodge.

After a few minutes, Wayhab left Langdon in Jharu's care for payment, and walked over to Brick.

"Aye, Missy was a pretty thing. I hope you aren't like that Indian brave at Lake Drummond that paddled his life away, looking for his dead Indian princess, or your Bentonville Battleground ghosts wanting a second chance in this world."

"No," Brick answered. "I know she's with the Father, waiting on her child and husband to come to her someday. Her sister related these insights to me, saying that Marina had prayed for such in a Catholic church of miracles up in Montréal. She had also prayed for me to find peace with another."

Wayhab noted, "It's good you both were oiled in deeper faith for protection like my bolts in the skiff, not froze together waiting through an eternity of purgatories for relief from regret."

"It wasn't meant to be," Brick concluded, turning to go to Langdon's truck for the return trip. "Take care, Wayhab—you and Jharu both. Good to see you again."

Mrs. Penny, that's the last time Brick ever saw Monkey Island. The North Carolina Nature Conservancy acquired it soon afterwards. Later, when Pem and I went there, the hunting lodge was barely visible. Kay says underbrush hides it completely now.

II

That night, June and Kay departed early to settle up costs with the other party hosts, while Brick rode later with Wesley and Lee Çu to the Boulevard Beach Cove Club.

Arriving, the rhythms of The Tymes' tune "Ms. Grace" beckoned from the establishment like the temptress call of an old memory, and Brick sensed a good time coming—he hadn't felt such elation in a long while.

Entering, Brick saw Brewer and Nicole Melvin dancing among Fayetteville friends with Monroe and Ginger Hill. Langdon was at the edge of the sandy-smooth dance floor, drink in hand, admiring his friends' footwork timed to the beat.

The danceability of "Ms. Grace" had enticed most of the guests to the floor, leaving the bar area clear for new arrivals, hungry for an array of heavy hors d'oeuvres from the land, sea, and garden. All said, the feast was as sumptuous as a similar presentation at Wendy's wedding party.

Brick, Wesley, and Lee Çu nibbled on toothpick items as they made their way to the end of the bar where the bartender was standing with Junebug, Kay, Wendy, and Becky Rollins. All were watching Langdon as he watched Brewer, Monroe, and their wives dance.

"A great layout, Junebug!" remarked Wesley.

"Extravagant!" Wendy exclaimed. "I only hope that my parents will have something half this generous at my Sampson's Landing reception."

"Well, we'll not match this feast at the apartment block party we're doing next weekend," sighed Becky.

"Now, Becky, with your function taking place in the Christmas party season, everyone will already be too gorged to notice a sparse table," beamed Kay.

"Mademoiselle Rollins, don't be intimidated trying to compete with all this," Brick interjected.

"Advice from a stranger isn't reassuring," smiled Becky. "I haven't seen you since I returned from France, over a year ago."

Brick returned, "Perhaps we've been too much on the run to encounter one another, worldly traveler. I've been occupied with finishing off Sunrise Acres and starting my Amalgamated job. Working weekdays in Charlotte, plus my weekend shifts at Sunrise Acres, took up every second this past year.

"However, I saw you at last year's midnight Christmas service. You were with your brother and another fellow kneeling at the communion rail."

"That was Artie, my museum co-worker," Becky replied. "His fiancée had returned home due to a family illness, and he had nothing to do. Consequently, I invited him home for Christmas. He and his love are married now.

"Both wanted to be here so we could tour the Wright Brothers Memorial tomorrow as an art appreciation review of the memorial's architecture. But they are expecting, and she didn't feel up to coming. I'll go alone since Wendy and Langdon are moving furniture tomorrow.

"And I saw you at last year's Christmas service, too. You and Mary Lee left the communion rail with your dad before we could speak."

Then the DJ, Rocky, invited Wendy and Langdon forward for the traditional solo dance. The anxious Wendy said she felt surreally protected by the applause as she and Langdon moved to the dance floor, where they slow danced to the Joe Cocker version of Billy Preston's song "You Are So Beautiful to Me."

As they danced, they gazed out at their friends. The only one not gazing at them was Brick. He was looking at Becky, and near the song's end, she glanced back at him with an accepting smile as their eyes met. When the tune ended, Langdon made remarks of appreciation, and then said, "Now, let's get this party started!"

The tempo immediately picked up as Rocky played The Trammps' newly released "Hold Back the Night." Two chords into the song, Brick took Becky's hand. Neither appeared to have a care in the world, as each danced seamlessly entwined with the other to the rhythm.

For the balance of the night they remained together in conversation, occasionally interrupted by Langdon and Wendy and their party guests. But generally, like the other guests, they danced to Rocky's beach music repertoire. The final tune of the night, however, was the slow dance tune "Lady Blue" by Leon Russell.

Everyone said that Brick's and Becky's eyes sparkled as they moved together, whether dancing or talking with others. It was apparent to all that they exuded magic.

At eleven, Wesley and Lee Çu bid their good-byes, asking Junebug and Kay to ferry Brick home. But Junebug and Kay came home that night minus Brick, who stayed at Langdon's with his overnight guests Monroe, Ginger, Brewer, and Nicole, in addition to Wendy and Becky. They stayed up till dawn, until Brick snoozed atop Langdon's breakfast bar, with an old poncho for cover and a couch pillow for a headrest.

Junebug said that Becky brought Brick back to the cottage around Sunday noon to retrieve his car and belongings. Although exhausted, Brick and Becky still emanated pleasure over their previous evening together.

III

Waiting for a rain band to pass, Becky told June, Kay, Lee Çu, and Wesley that she and Brick would make a stop at the Wright Brothers Memorial before heading home.

At the Memorial's welcome center, they purchased a booklet describing the lofty, triangular pylon and the Wright brothers' struggles to discover flight's exacting principles. Driving in, Becky perused the booklet for points of interest as another rain band came through. The winter showers had discouraged visitors, and only one other car was in the parking lot at the memorial's base.

"It says that construction work commemorating the Wrights' December 17, 1903, first flight began in 1929. The sixty-foot-high monument sits on a ninety-one-foot sand dune."

When the rain ceased, Brick gave Becky his golf umbrella and took the booklet. Trudging up to the monument, he said, "There's a stairway inside leading to an observation platform up top, where we can see the surrounding area."

On the observation deck, they saw the lone car next to Brick's departing. Mrs. Penny, Pem and I later stood on that very spot with a horde of tourists and I imagined Aaron Copland's "Fanfare for the Common Man" ringing down upon us. So, I now easily imagine Brick and Becky, alone, viewing the Atlantic to the east, the Roanoke Sound to the west, and the sand dunes north and south, but accompanied by a barely audible, soft-reed, wind-like scoring of Copland's piece.

Brick continued summarizing, "The brothers suffered through many refinements on the mysteries of flight before achieving any success. Enduring that trial by fire of running into dead ends must have been mentally draining and spiritually excruciating.

"They studied all flight's forefathers back to Leonardo da Vinci, and played with toy helicopters built by a Frenchman, Alphonse Penaud. Penaud's toy aircraft were powered by twisted rubber bands. The brothers also looked at dirigible balloons and gliders. One of their mentors was Dr. Langley of the Smithsonian. He had built power-driven airplane models, but all Langley's full-sized man-carrying efforts had failed.

"The difficulty with up-scaling model planes was that eight times the power was needed for airlift each time the engine size was only doubled. That was a tough mechanical engineering problem to solve. Designing a propeller with the right blade pitch and diameter for maximum lifting power by a small, twelve-horsepower motor was a key puzzle for them to solve. Even then, had not the right wind conditions existed, that first flight of just 120 feet in twelve seconds would not likely have occurred. But by 1905 the brothers had improved their understanding of airborne mysteries to make flights of up to twenty-four and a half miles.

"Surely, Providence shone on the Wrights the day they overcame all these difficulties. It seems ironic to me that this North Carolina endeavor succeeded within a few miles from where the Lost Colony and the numerous Mattamuskeet agricultural efforts all failed. This triumph over flight's mysteries is captured in the monument's inscription:

In commemoration of the conquest of the air by the brothers Wilbur and Orville Wright.
Conceived by genius. Achieved by dauntless resolution and unconquerable faith.

"Praying about solutions to the mysteries of flight like lift and drag and rudders and ailerons seems to be no different than trying to sort through the other mysteries of life. The winds of life are stormy, too."

"Yes, it is like that for life's spiritual side," Becky replied as she looked at Brick and then toward the Atlantic. "I feel like I've reached that point in life where I must pray over all my decisions if I'm to feather my way through the real world with more lift than drag. It's not college-party time every day in an adult life, as Langdon noted at that post-football game party in Chapel Hill way back when.

"It renews me to see this monument to a faith that never surrendered to mental road-blocks because my own life has been difficult lately. I always loved art and studied it with the expectation of being fulfilled. Then I graduated and went to France for more study. There, I saw that much of the Paris art scene lacked robustness because I met no men like my father or brothers or uncles. My family men had always seemed to selectively choose from a mass of information to produce services for others that earned my family an honorable income.

"In France, I realized that art study couldn't provide me with gratification like the act of creating art does. I collapsed into depressing relationships with people who only discussed art already created by others. I stayed there trying to find the right connections to satisfy me, but I was sick at heart with my career choice.

"I came home to finish my master's because I already had spent so much time in the field. I was happy to get employment at the museum, but I still feel imprisoned by my profession. I'd love to save up enough money with my inheritance to go back to Pineland Springs, and take over your Aunt Dot's antique and interior décor shop someday. I enjoyed working there because that's where I saw satisfied people who bought or rejected art according to their individual taste. That's where the proof of art's worth is for me.

"Wendy told me about your losses at Sunrise Acres, Brick. That must have been disappointing, too."

"What started out with the best of intentions ended up in the ditch because of world-wide financial ailments over which no individual has any control," Brick answered. "If it hadn't been for Wendy's work, we would have had more foreclosures."

"Once," Becky noted, "I met Wendy's co-worker, Melody, when she came to our apartment after a conference. Wendy said the two often speculated about your carrying the weight of Marsh's death and later Marina's in addition to the Sunrise Acres problems. I was always envious of Marina being available for you at the right place and time in your life. I could see that the two of you satisfied a need in one another."

"Trust me, Marina was envious of you," Brick smiled. "Your beauty was clear to her, and she was envious of those times we danced even though you had not even graduated from college into the world of hard knocks. She always wanted to be able to do the light-fantastic beach boogie like you! Her feet never got the hang of the beat, though. She saw that you had a mystique, a graceful style of superior poise and confidence that someone gains by dint of being in their natural environment. I remember her also remarking that age would not wither your qualities of personal presence, but only ennoble them over time.

"Marina and I did talk of marriage. But when she went back to Québec, I think she began to feel a comfort there amongst her French roots that she had probably seen in your comfort here. People belong with those who can make them the happiest with little effort because it's natural, like falling off a log. Like I say, she was envious of you, but also admiring, too."

"Well, I may have the hang of a dance beat, but I don't have much confidence that I'm making any progress at getting the rest of my life refined down to a comfortable rhythm. And that's the most important beat to get in step with!" Becky smiled timidly.

"Becky, you're wise enough to figure out the beat to the rest of it and feather your way through the daily maze of information and confusing stimuli. Life has certainly taught me that hope is confusing because your hopes are always balancing between a hope that has disappointed and the one in front of you that beckons with promise."

Then it began to rain, forcing them back through the doorway to the stairwell. Chilled, they descended the steps to the door at the memorial's base. There they huddled like two wet puppies as the rain poured. Brick took the umbrella and opened it. As they moved under the umbrella, they looked into each other's eyes again, and embraced in a long hug that turned into a kiss. Their lips parted but not their embrace, as each continued to hold the other closely.

Brick said, "Right now I want to take you off to the backside of some island that's so remote we couldn't be seen or heard of for thirty days."

Becky whispered back, "I wouldn't care because after thirty days I know we'd be pure friends, searching our way together for some new truth of lift and flight. When I saw you at the altar during the Christmas communion service, I felt like you were going somewhere I wanted to go. I've always sensed that my desire for a fulfilling life would be compatible with yours."

"I've sensed that about you, too," Brick replied. "Not many men and women can feel that way about each other. As you've implied, someone you can kneel down and pray with, and then wake up beside the next morning with your pajamas on, or off, will be a soul you can enjoy the journey with either way. We mustn't take us for granted and screw up that need to know ourselves better through knowing each other."

"I won't let us do that," Becky murmured.

"Nor I," Brick whispered.

IV

Wendy's wedding in Sampsons Landing was a beautiful high-noon affair with an abundance of flowers at the church and a huge feast afterward at the country club. There Brick and Becky hovered around each other as they ate, talking with the Willinghams and me. I recall Becky's asking me if I was still enjoying the print she had given me of Edouard Manet's *Olympia*. I told her that I was, but that I had given up hope on finding the right frame for it until I had a place of my own.

Brick and Becky married a little over a year later and eventually had three children. However, none of this took place until I found out the truth about Marsh's and Chalky's deaths. That revelation changed my life forever and resulted in my marriage, first, before my move to the West for a fresh start.

Chapter Twenty-Three

Melody's Old Carolina Mysteries Solved in the Four Corners

I

"BUT, MELODY, HOW DID YOU LEARN the details of Brick and Marina's intimate relationship?"

"Well, Mrs. Penny, you must first appreciate the back story on that question by recalling that no one ever told me anything that I could report. Remember, Marsh and Sue Anne were the only friends of Brick and Marina that I ever had any continuing conversations with. I never met Brewer and Nicole, nor Monroe and Ginger or Dutch and Lonah but that one time at the post-football game fraternity party I helped cater. Of course there were Junebug and Kay who were closed mouthed like Marsh and Sue Anne, except for June's mention of that fly-over incident which Kay promptly cut off. Thus I could not report on what I did not actually know. However, Kay did confide to me about Brick and Marina's intimacy several years ago when she spent a night with Pem and me at our Four Corners home while traveling to see Martha Sarah's new baby girl in San Francisco. While telling you the tale I did filter Kay's love encounter report into my narrative, but remember that her remarks about those intimacies were relayed long after they happened back in the seventies.

"Say, the sun's rising. Let's move to the gate. They'll start boarding our jet-age Butterfield and Overland Stage to Denver and Santa Fe about 6:30 a.m."

"Yes, Melody, we don't want to miss our boarding time. But continue your tale while pushing me."

"Sure, Mrs. Penny. Well, it was late February of 1976 after Wendy's Christmas wedding that my life took the turn that led me to meeting Pem and moving to the West."

II

I didn't see Brick after Wendy's wedding, but Junebug or Kay would tell me things about him and Becky. As time passed, the reports dwindled, and they became fond memories as June's law office events took my daily attention.

Anyway, I came home one Friday to find that Dad and Grandfather had brought some Florida mustard greens. Dad was washing the greens at our backyard hand pump. He knew I hated washing fresh greens and looked at me with his fatherly smile, implying "I've already done the washing part you hate." So I knew I had to cook 'em, even though I was tired.

I changed into my bib jeans and got a knife to trim seasoning meat hanging in our smokehouse near the hand pump. While I was walking to the smokehouse, Cousin Mingo rode up on his motorcycle. I waved to him before going inside.

I turned on the light but didn't attempt to close the heavy door fully. Looking over the hams I heard Dad greeting Mingo after the bike's engine stopped.

"Donald says Bertha Moore just died, sitting under her carport. That'll close off our loose ends, and it'll ease Brick's mind to know it, too," Mingo said.

"I'll phone him when nobody's around," Dad answered.

"OK! See you Monday, picking up Juan at the airport," replied Mingo. "I'm glad Junebug discovered that time and Chalky's death have solved Juan's legal problems here. There's still right many killings going on out west among the different Wounded Knee tribal factions, and Juan says it's safer to be here at home."

"Well," Dad returned, "remember how bad Juan hated Chalky for causing him to run off to Montana. So just know he's going to be asking questions about Chalky's death, and that means sticking with our story, like we told it to Carley Ray. It'll be like all your phone conversations with Juan, where you had to keep quiet about what went down. And now, it'll be every day for the rest of your life that you'll have to be on guard. But I know you'll manage since your neck is most on the line."

As Mingo left I couldn't cut the meat for pondering their conversation. What was it all about? My curiosity was high. I pushed the smokehouse door fully open and said, "Dad, I can't cut this tough meat for thinking about your conversation with Mingo."

Dad looked at me like a child caught stealing and said, "Your big ears and curiosity always pick up everything like some kind of radar. I've always been proud of your being one smart gal. Reckon I'll have to tell you the truth so you'll know why you've got to keep your mouth shut if you don't want to see us all go to jail."

Dad cut several thin meat slices while telling me what really happened concerning Chalky's and Marsh's deaths. He said he didn't know what had happened to Mingo's original hammer that had possibly killed Chalky because Brick got rid of it on the way to Wendy's wedding shower at Duck. When he finished, I said, "Well, you must notify Brick. But never tell him or Mingo or Donald that I know. They mustn't worry about my telling a thing."

That night after Granddad was sleeping, Dad called Brick and told him of Bertha Mae's passing. For the rest of that weekend I tried not to think about the disclosure. I was hoping to pass it off as the way the world unfolds sometimes, and I had to be a grown-up and accept it. However, the next week, just being in Junebug's law office gave me ethical willies. I kept thinking about legal protocol issues.

I worried more the next Friday night at a family reunion dinner for Juan. Thankfully, most of the evening was taken up with Juan's Western experiences and the Wounded Knee incident. Juan did ask lots of questions about Chalky's death, causing Dad and Mingo to exchange looks, but the evening ended without others learning the truth.

The next night I kept Martha Sarah while June and Kay went to a Duke Chapel concert. Looking at the child sleeping on a floor pallet of quilts, I realized I had become an after-the-fact, cover-up accomplice. My position in Junebug's law office would reflect badly on him if the truth were uncovered. Such a finding could possibly make Junebug look like an accomplice, too, and perhaps subject him to a probe by the authorities and bar examiners. Suddenly I was angry at Brick for allowing my family members to participate in activities that might endanger my own future. Couldn't he have thought of something better?

Of course, I couldn't tell Junebug because that would expose my family. Looking down upon Martha Sarah, I wondered if it wouldn't be better for me to find another job before ghosts started coming out of the woodwork. At least June and his family's reputation wouldn't be as likely to become entangled if I were working elsewhere.

While I continued hoping my fears would subside, they didn't. Then one day I saw Dr. Chester O'Malley at a department store. He said that he was shopping because he and his wife were going to visit Dr. Frank Glover and his wife for the weekend. At that point, a light bulb flickered on for me.

"Oh, yes, Dr. Glover was so nice to me at that credit-counseling seminar you arranged for Wendy and me to attend at N.C. State," I noted to Dr. O'Malley. "I can't believe that was almost two years ago now! He wanted me to return to school for a master's degree. I didn't think much about it then because I had just bought a car and needed my steady law-office job to pay for it. But that's behind me now, and I'm interested in pursuing the opportunity if Dr. Glover could still help me."

Dr. O'Malley replied, "I'll inquire on your behalf this weekend, if you like."

"Please do," I responded. "But don't say anything to Dad. I wouldn't want him to hear about this unless it's all worked out, so he won't feel like he has financial obligations."

The next week Dr. Glover called me and said he would mail me an application and the transcript release forms for my grades. Later, at an interview at his N.C. A&T campus office in Greensboro, I explained my financial situation, telling him that while I had paid off my car, I was lacking enough funds to pursue a graduate degree. When he said that he could secure me a part-time legal secretarial job that would supplement my tuition loans and grants, the deal was sealed.

Days later, I mustered the courage to tell Junebug my plans to seek a master's degree. I explained that I had enjoyed my credit-counseling work with Wendy and loved that energy you get when you see the results of helping people. I guess I was still too young and unwise about the ways of the world because I had feared a frown.

Junebug gave me a big smile, saying, "I'm happy you want to help people before they get into real trouble that requires attorneys and the courts to practically perform brain surgery on their lives to re-right their affairs. Besides, the government's retirement is better than anything I could offer you here."

Mrs. Penny, Junebug's words lifted a great burden from me! He asked that I continue working to train my replacement before the summer semester. My replacement was his Kay. So, the way it worked out is another reason, besides being her daughter's babysitter, that Kay and I have remained friends, even though we've lived in different parts of the country for many years since.

That night I told Dad, and he asked, "Why all this?"

I told him of my need to leave Junebug's office in case the Chalky cover-up ever became known, but that my desire to help others was really the driving force behind my decision. I added Junebug's remark about government retirement benefits. When I said that, he understood.

III

I met Pem in an economics class that summer. I didn't know he was from the Southwest Four Corners area because we never talked after class, our schedules taking us in different directions. Nevertheless, he had caught my eye, for he was not only an Indian in a sea of black-college campus faces, but his build reminded me of Cousin Mingo's, only Pem was thicker.

Although never a petite woman, as you can see, Mrs. Penny, I had lost my baby fat by then and had a healthy body size. So, I began dressing more in Indian fashion for the class with Pem. I tried not to be too noticeable, just changed minor things, like a brass concho belt one day and my miniature dream catcher earrings another. I hoped the dream catchers would allow good vibrations to flow between us. However, dream catchers or not, he never appeared to notice me, leaving each class quickly.

The first time we talked was at the second Saturday Robeson County Lumbee Homecoming Festival and Powwow's closing day in Pembroke, near my mother's homeplace. The second Saturday is the biggest day of this week-long celebration. I rode there with Dad and Grandfather, while Mingo, Juan, and their parents followed. There, my female cousins and I waited on the tribes to assemble for the Lumbee Homing Parade. Besides the Lumbee, the Coharie, the Waccamaw-Siouan, the Haliwa-Saponi, the Occaneechi Band of the Saponi Nation, the Meherrin, the Catawba, and the Southern Tuscarora, other eastern tribes were also assembling. The week-long homecoming is held over the two Saturdays nearest July Fourth to encourage visitors from near and far. Today over 35,000 people attend. This 1976 event had large attendance because the drama *Strike at the Wind,* by playwright Randolph Umberger, was presented for the first time the night before. There was much crowd conversation about it.

That's when Pem walked by and smiled directly at me, saying, "Miss Melody!" At that moment, the parade's first drumbeat thundered down, and my heart jumped into my throat with such emotion that I felt paralyzed. But I now remember thinking that my earrings must have sent good vibrations after all. I introduced him to my cousins, and we marveled at the parade's festiveness.

The Two-Step Dance followed. All knew it was the custom for the female to ask the man to dance this dance, and that the male would have to give the female five dollars if he refused. So I asked him and to my joy, he accepted—and that's how we began.

When the dance ended, I said, "Thank you for not refusing me in front of my family and friends. I've never seen you in Robeson County before, Mr. Dare-Hawk, but with a name like Pembroke Dare-Hawk you must be from nearby."

"No, Miss Melody," Pem replied, "I'm from the Southwest Four Corners area, but my forefathers came from this part of Carolina, and that's partly how I got named. Hawk is the name of my Navajo grandmother, and thus the name of my father. When my dad was in the Marines during World War II, he was given a Social Security number. He then told my mother before their marriage that they should start following the surname lineage rather than the customary Navajo tradition of following the female lineage. Both wanted to avoid future Social Security confusion.

"He added Dare to the name Hawk because his grandfather had told him about being from southeastern North Carolina, where variations of the Lost Colony's Virginia Dare name survive. He told my mother that Dare-Hawk would mean that 'We dare to hunt where the White Man preys; and thus may I return safely to you after the war.' I never knew my great-grandfather, Croatan Joe, but his stories about my family travels from North Carolina to the Southwest live to this day."

"Gosh," I said, flattered that he knew my name from our class. "What brought you to N.C. A&T?"

He replied, "I'm working on my agricultural engineering master's degree to better advise the Navajo on irrigation, drainage, crop rotation, and so forth. My family has fortunately been more educated than most, and we feel it a duty to bring a sense of hope to the untrained.

"Of course, agricultural advisory skills do not help Indian peoples combat their depression and alcoholism. Often I can't get to a bounty-of-the-harvest discussion for dealing with the issues of personal estrangement that Native Americans feel from the country's dominant European culture."

"I'm in the Home Extension Services master's degree program," I said. "We try to address those problems with all cultures. Why did you come to Greensboro's A&T? Don't Arizona or New Mexico colleges offer such courses?"

"They do," Pem returned. "But A&T is known worldwide for its hands-on agricultural-technical courses, which I need for proficiency in field work with ranchers and farmers. That proficiency level of A&T grads is especially highlighted by their female grads who checked and double-checked the answers to formulas that produced the atomic bomb and later put man on the moon. In those days before computers, it was that vision of colored girls with slide rules and pencils sending us into the atomic and space ages that appeals to everyone's desire for excellence. Besides, I've always wanted to investigate my family's North Carolina connections."

"My father first excited me to come here after his 1958 visit, when the local Lumbee Indians ran the Ku Klux Klan out of the area. The story spread across the nation, and inspired everyone's imagination, especially Indians.'"

"Why did your family move west?" I asked, hoping to keep his company.

"It involves the post-Civil War saga of the local Lumbee hero, Henry Berry Lowrie, and suggestions from Federal Reconstruction authorities that he move west. I saw the play last night. But my family's story starts before Lowrie's time, in East Texas with a Wichita-Caddo Indian, called Wichita Scout, who came from a Comanchero trading family. His family traded with the Comanche and Kiowa tribes who followed the buffalo from Mexico to Canada, then south again each year. These Comanchero traders knew Spanish, French, and many Indian dialects besides broken English.

"During the Civil War, young Wichita Scout's hate for white Texans caused him to join General Sherman's Union Army at Vicksburg. His Indian tracking ability gave him spy-like cunning, useful for scouting. General Sherman appreciated his scouting skills but couldn't remember his true Indian name. So he dubbed him 'Wichita Scout,' which stuck until his death.

"When Sherman crossed the North Carolina-South Carolina border headed north in March of 1865, Wichita Scout had already made advanced contact with many Scotland and Robeson County Indians. Henry Berry Lowrie's family had given refuge to Union soldiers escaping from the nearby Florence, South Carolina, Confederate prison. Henry's father and brother were killed by the Confederate Home Guard for helping the escaped Yankees just prior to Sherman's North Carolina invasion.

"Henry also reportedly killed a white planter who had accused him of stealing hogs for feeding the escaped Union Army prisoners. He was arrested for the white man's murder after the war, but he escaped to hide in the Carolinas' swampy border area. Lowrie's guerrilla band robbed to survive, but never killed. One interloper band member was an Indian named William Chavis, who made their bullets. My great-great-grandfather, Joseph Ingold, worked with him. Ingold was the father of Croatan Joe. Great-grandfather Croatan Joe was likely seven or eight then.

"During this postwar period, Wichita Scout scouted for the Second Military District Union troops in charge of the Carolinas Reconstruction program, and he found Henry Berry Lowrie in his swamp hideout. The Reconstruction authorities knew that they were sitting on a powder keg of Civil War animosities between defeated Confederate whites and Robeson-Scotland County Indians. They realized that any chance for their peaceful Union rule would be strengthened if Henry Berry Lowrie's gang left the area. Consequently, Wichita Scout suggested to Lowrie's group that they leave for Texas and the Comanchero trade that Wichita had known from childhood. Lowrie considered these western promises, but legend says he remained in his Carolina swamp country, likely striking at the wind as the play suggests, trying to understand the changes that time and events bring for greater individual fulfillment.

"William Chavis and my Ingold family, however, left the area in 1867 or early 1868 when Lowrie's band was labeled outlaws. I don't know if Chavis made it to the West or not because my family stories never mention him again. As for my people, my father could not find the name of Ingold in Pembroke when he visited here at the time of the 1958 Klan incident, and I have not been able to either."

Then Pem smiled and looked around, as if awaking from a dream. "Miss Melody, the smell of the powwow vendors' food makes me hungry. Come, I'll buy you lunch."

IV

While eating, Pem related how his forebears flourished inside the Comanchero trading society thanks to their bullet-making skills learned with Lowrie's band. Wichita Scout also taught Croatan Joe the many languages he knew. Pem's story is as amazing, Mrs. Penny, as the plot of a movie. But this life ended with the Comanche defeat at the Second Battle of Adobe Walls, Texas, in June of 1874. The defeat forced Wichita Scout and the Ingolds into Old Mexico, where Wichita Scout and Croatan Joe's parents died of ailments that today could probably be cured by penicillin.

With his language skills and weapons knowledge, Croatan Joe connected with a group of ex-Comanchero traders, who were supplying cattle and horses to the railroad constructors, mining settlements, and Indian reservations of the New Mexico and Arizona Territories just north of Old Mexico.

In the late 1870s, Croatan Joe's business led him into the Fort Sumner-Bosque Redondo area, populated then by the Mescalero Apache and a few Navajo. These Navajo had been force-marched from the Four Corners area to Fort Sumner during the Civil War by the Union Army scout and Indian agent Col. Kit Carson, on what has been called the Long Walk. This Union action was intended to prevent Indian alliances with the Confederacy. Most Navajo returned to the Four Corners' Canyon de Chelly area after the war, but some remained in Fort Sumner to intermarry with the Mescalero Apache. Through these remaining Navajo, Croatan Joe learned the Navajo language, aided by the lifelong friendship he cultivated with a Navajo called Ox Too-Tall. He also met Billy the Kid.

Once Croatan Joe saw Billy writing a letter to New Mexico's Territorial Governor, Lew Wallace, the *Ben Hur* author, about Billy's amnesty for participating in the Lincoln County Range War. When Billy asked Croatan Joe to proofread it, Joe replied that he could only read simple poster signs. Billy noted: "But you speak so many tongues and cipher, too; I thought you could read and write like a white!"

Shamed, Croatan Joe hung his head. "Only speak many tongues, count, and read poster signs. Not read papers or write; maybe someday." This admission made Joe determined that he and his heirs would be educated.

Croatan Joe left Fort Sumner for trading opportunities when the Apache Chief Victorio's band escaped their Arizona Reservation to return to their nomadic life along the Mexican-American border. But modern settlements had reduced the hunter-forager game supply, forcing Victorio's group to steal cattle, thereby attracting the wrath of both the Mexican and American Armies. Joe ultimately found Victorio's ally, the old Chief Nana, who said Victorio had been killed by Mexican troops. Thus Croatan Joe and Nana traded Joe's bullets for a few stolen cattle near the Mexican-American border in late 1880.

Afterwards, Joe and Ox crossed the border to dispose of their cattle at a New Mexican ranch recently established by two reliably shady cattlemen, Johnny Ringo and Ike Clanton, buying agents for Ike's father, Newman Clanton. Joe and Ox's cows were housed briefly on Ringo and Ike's ranch before being driven to Ike's father's spread near Tombstone, Arizona.

The new Ringo-Clanton ranch needed help, and Croatan Joe and Ox Too-Tall agreed to employment because Nana, Geronimo, and other Apache chiefs were being chased too hard by the military to be reliable trading partners.

In the summer of 1881, Ike's father was killed by Mexicans near the New Mexico-Arizona border with Old Mexico. Joe and Ox later went with Ike and his brother Phin to exhume the Senior Clanton's body for reburial in Tombstone's Boot Hill Cemetery. Here he was reinterred beside his youngest son, Billy, who had been killed during Tombstone's O.K. Corral gunfight in October of 1881 by members of the Wyatt Earp family of lawmen and their deputized friend, Dr. John Holliday, a dentist.

Then Croatan Joe and Ox moved north to Ox's Navajo relatives' home in the Canyon de Chelly after the June 1882 so-called suicide of Johnny Ringo on Turkey Creek in Arizona's Chiricahua Mountains. Though deemed a suicide, many said Ringo's body looked like he had been killed by another, but no one knows the truth of it. Croatan Joe surmised that the revenge war between the Clanton family and the Earp lawmen over the O.K. Corral gunfight had become too entangled, so it was best to move on. Also, Geronimo's Apache Indian band was returning to reservation life and thus was no longer accessible as a trading partner.

In the Four Corners area, Croatan Joe's trading skills landed him a peddler's job trading among the Navajo and Hopi. Finally, he found peace in legitimate work. When Joe left North Carolina in 1867 or 1868, he was six or seven. Now, he was about twenty-one.

Croatan Joe eventually married into the Muledeer family, adopting his wife's family name, according to Navajo custom. The marriage produced Pem's grandfather, Ingold Muledeer. To assure Ingold's education, he was sent to Pennsylvania's Carlisle Indian

School at about age twelve. After Ingold returned, he married into the Hawk family, which is where the Hawk part of Pem's name comes from.

Pem's grandfather's education at Carlisle resulted in a Navajo Tribal Council job at the same time that new mining processes had been developed for extracting coal and minerals. Pem's father's name became Silver Hawk because he was born on the day Pem's grandfather and a metallurgist discovered a silver vein on tribal lands.

Mrs. Penny, that's when Pem noted that your father was a Filipino graduate of the Carlisle School. He also told me about your Philippine home and your marrying his dad's childhood friend and Code-Talker teammate Billy Springs at the end of World War II. He didn't call you Penny, of course, but used your full name, Penelope Ruez, while telling me, "My parents and Billy Springs were students at the old Fort Collins, Colorado, Vocational College, which Southwest Indians attended. After the war, my father's Army benefits helped him complete his college education that landed him an Agricultural Department job. I have followed in his footsteps."

v

"Henry Berry Lowrie couldn't adapt to cultural changes, Pem. And, you know, we've just endured another culture clash in Vietnam with one society wanting to save another with the modern knowledge required to take advantage of today's opportunities. But the Vietnamese could not culturally or spiritually connect with our paradigms. Talk about modern enlightenment being unwelcome, that was America in Vietnam, many say."

"Progress is progress," noted Pem. "Whether by some nurturing governmental program or by the conquering and taking. Progress just comes upon us like the Horsemen of the Apocalypse on the chariot of time and in any form it can." Then he looked into my eyes. "Seems we see the world pretty much alike."

His gaze gave me the courage to say, "Come, meet my family. They'll appreciate your story, and maybe know of some Ingold families that'll connect your missing family links."

After that we met daily, and Pem spent Labor Day and Thanksgiving with us. We also went to the Sampson County September Coharie Powwow, but Pem couldn't find any Ingold family connections there, either. There was only the name of the Ingold community that had no Indian connection. Later he went on a black bear hunting trip with Dad, Mingo, and Juan in Croatan National Forest near the Cherry Point Marine Air Base on the North Carolina coast before returning to his Four Corners home for Christmas. During this hunting trip, my family learned of the strange link between Pem's family and ours.

Dad asked Pem to tell them anything else that might identify some clue to his long-ago Carolina connection, and Pem replied that the only other Croatan Joe family story was that of a black slave girl's daughter named Paleface-Black Dove. A Spanish seaman had raped the slave when the Spaniards invaded North Carolina's coast during the 1740s War of Jenkins' Ear. When Pem had finished his version of the story, Dad said, "Pem, you told this almost like my wife's Pembroke kin have related it for years! Few know this story outside her family."

Did this mean we were related somehow from long ago—and to a black at that? We don't know, but we did know then that we would be so far removed in kinship that it would not impact the future of our relationship. If we were kin to Paleface-Black Dove, did it matter that we had black blood? I think we both knew that we had no control over the past, only some control of our future. So we vowed that we would pray to have the courage of Black Dove's pregnant mother, who escaped the bare comforts of a slave dwelling, hoping to find a true freedom in the dangerous, unmapped swamps for her offspring and herself.

VI

After Christmas, we talked of marriage despite the difficulties of transferring my North Carolina tuition credits to Pem's western home. At Easter break, we flew to Santa Fe and traveled the southern Colorado-Utah-Arizona-northern New Mexico area inquiring about positions within the Land Grant College Extension system that could financially credit my tuition expenses. Responses didn't come quickly, but when we married in June, we had faith that all would work out.

I learned much of my Sunrise Acres story during our honeymoon trip, Mrs. Penny. Before our wedding, Junebug, Kay, Wendy, Langdon, Brick, and Becky had given us a party at June and Kay's home. Here, Pem found himself involved in hunting stories with Brick, Langdon, and Junebug. Pem also related his family history of moving from Carolina to the West, which captivated the men.

When Pem got to the Carlisle School part of his story, he noted, "The Carlisle educational regimen became controversial because strict educators believed that the students must speak only English if their minds were to understand the European way of viewing the world's realities. Students were punished if caught speaking in their native tongues.

"For many students this educational process created a sense of dislocation or alienation because the spiritual nature of the Indian language was not usefully relied upon to help absorb, assimilate, and organize English instruction into the Indian soul. Thus, much of the life-giving benefits of knowledge dispensed at Carlisle-type schools went for naught. My grandfather nevertheless realized that he must make the best of a new unfolding reality, or just be dragged along by the process of change, kicking and screaming like a child trying to hold onto a past that was nowhere fully available.

"Granddad said that Geronimo's last days exemplified the educational controversy's dilemma. He was the lead rider in President Teddy Roosevelt's 1905 Inaugural Parade.

"Traveling to the Inaugural, Geronimo stopped to speak to the students in Carlisle. He counseled them to absorb their educational studies because he did not wish for their generation to suffer the culture shock that his generation had suffered from coming into contact with the pervasive late-nineteenth- and early-twentieth-century white American culture.

"Geronimo, by now a Dutch Reformed Church member, had come to appreciate education. However, he died in 1909 after lying out drunk all night in a mud-hole, during a freezing February rain. So, Geronimo's Henry Berry Lowrie-like strike-at-the-wind behavior makes it clear that his noble soul had been estranged while trying to progress spiritually toward some higher Valhalla of Olympian, Judeo-Christian-European policy and industrial-entrepreneurial practice touted by education.

"Changing people through requiring a Western-civilization-centered education also involved sending Puerto Ricans and Filipinos to Carlisle-type schools after the Spanish-American War. Establishing the American-Philippine Protectorate era after 1901 was another culture-clashing time, and many Filipinos still resent America today for suppressing their native language and culture. Puerto Rican resentments even led to an attempt on President Truman's life during the early 1950s. Ironically, the Carlisle School closed at the end of World War I because too many agreed that a forced education repressed and brutalized the soul rather than inspiring, motivating, and ennobling it."

Brick looked at Junebug and then at the others. "As General Eisner often said, the experiences of Geronimo and Spain's El Cid predated Vietnam's cultural mis-assimilations long before Vietnam, as did Britain's failure in India and Afghanistan. Evidently Wesley's sayings about old Sunday school lessons having to be relearned by each new generation apply to our government's policies at home and abroad, too."

VII

That evening, Junebug said his wedding present would be the use of his cottage in Duck for our honeymoon. He knew we were cash-poor. Also, Wendy and Langdon promised us an extended tour of the Outer Banks and Corolla. On that trip, we met Wayhab and Jharu.

From Corolla's Whalehead Club dock, I could see Monkey Island, where Brick and Marsh had hunted with Dutch Lazlo. Here, Wayhab answered my questions about his hunting-guide days for the New Holland-Mattamuskeet Lodge, as well as at Lake Drummond, Virginia.

Wayhab's High-Tider, Jacobean English brogue made his stories about the Indian lovers of Lake Drummond and the agricultural disappointments of New Holland come alive, as if I were hearing them for the first time. Pem also enjoyed Wayhab's stories, but Pem did not know then that I was visualizing Brick throwing away Mingo's hammer at almost every spot Wayhab mentioned. I had not told Pem all I knew yet because Langdon and Wendy were with us.

Only a long conversation between Pem and Wayhab on Rachel Carson and the water-quality impacts on wildlife habitats blocked my craving to ask Wayhab if he had seen Brick throw a hammer off the end of the Whalehead Pier. Langdon's attention to Wayhab's hunter-fisher-naturalist stories and Pem's agricultural engineering insights were woven well into their long discussion.

Pem concluded, "Science must improve water quality so you'll never see your oysters and shrimp eradicated like our buffalo were in the West. Of course, the buffalo issue was a sin of commission, and not the ignorant-bliss sin of omission that intelligent people struggle with today over society's mistreatment of the natural world. Our friend Brick says today's scientific struggles always pose the question, 'Am I strangling the tadpole or is the tadpole strangling me?' It seems that the human population has met its sustainability match—ourselves."

Days later we passed Sunrise Acres' entrance, leaving Wisdom Station for our western home. A burden of fear lifted then because I had the hope of a new life without the troubled baggage of others to carry. Even though I had rightly worried over the cover-up surrounding Chalky's death, the true facts were never discovered.

I still wonder if I might have remained too satisfied to have ever left Junebug's law office had it not been for the cover-up. Each time I think of this, any lingering anger I had over Brick's participation in the Chalky conspiracy vanishes from my thankful soul because I met Pem as a result of it.

VIII

"Yes, Melody, when life gave me Billy after our separation during the war, I was most thankful. He returned to find me working in the American PX and shortened my name from Penelope to Penny, saying my necklaces and bracelets reminded him of those of a white woman he often saw as a child working in a dime store in Winslow, Arizona. Perhaps my jewelry appealed to Billy's Indian soul like your Indian jewelry appealed to Pem's. We seem much alike.

"We both worked at Clark Air Force Base civilian jobs until the 1991 Mount Pinatubo volcanic eruption made the base uninhabitable. That and the political unrest over America's presence in the Philippines made Billy want to return to his Four Corners home even though Silver Hawk had just passed. Billy knew that he was heading into his last days, too. Our daughter and son-in-law moved with us because they didn't want to face the Philippines' political instability, either.

"I'm happy that my daughter's family is nearby. It's costly raising their children, and your travel with me to Duke's Hyperbaric Center has saved them that expense. I truly appreciate your kindness of making this trip with me."

"Think nothing of it, Mrs. Penny, because it gave me a chance to return home for the Sunrise Acres barbeque reunion. In past years when I came home, I would see June and Kay as well as Martha Sarah, but never Brick and Becky, who lived in Pineland Springs. The last time I saw Junebug was at the 1991 barbeque. He had heart problems by then, but still I was shocked when Dad told me he died in his Cadillac while stopped at a traffic light in 1997."

IX

Then on Maundy Thursday in 1999, Kay stayed a night at our Four Corners home and told us more about June's ailments while on her way to San Francisco to welcome Martha Sarah's first child. Of course, she and Junebug had always dreamed of visiting the nearby Canyon de Chelly after their Grand Canyon tour when his Army duty ended. That was just before the Sunrise Acres project started. Kay told me the intimate details about Brick and Marina's relationship while we toured the Canyon at sun-up on Good Friday morning. I know that she would not have told me even then, had the Four Corners not been my home for over twenty-five years—it had been that long since I had last lived in Wisdom Station, North Carolina. Also June's passing and thus Kay's release from law office propriety in not sharing confidences likely made her feel safe about confiding something of a personal nature to me.

On the afternoon of her arrival we went out and viewed the Canyon from the Spider Rock Overlook before going to Maundy Thursday chapel services. There, as is often the practice at many Easter services, we sang Christmas carols selected to commemorate Christ's birth as well as His portending crucifixion. We sang the old standard "What Child Is This?" and the more recent ballad, "Mary, Did You Know?"

Early on Good Friday morning, we went to the Canyon de Chelly's south rim above the White House ruins, and negotiated the combination of wooden stairs and dirt pathways to the canyon's floor five hundred feet down.

Fronting the stark alabaster White House ruins, I mentioned the incompleteness of Brick and Marina's relationship that I had sensed in the aftermath of Marsh's death. The reports of Marina's phone calls to Sue Anne and Nicole inferred to me that she found herself thinking of Brick and the dreams they had once shared. That news haunted me and again made me recollect Junebug's fly-over story, and what might have been hidden in it. Now that I knew marital affections, I suspected a deep love affair between Brick and Marina even more. Kay then related Brick and Marina's romance as Brick had told it to Junebug and Wesley at the Duck cottage the night before Wendy's wedding party.

At her story's end, the sun's rays began bending around the horizon above to illuminate the night sky's clouds with purple light. Those purples turned a rusty red from the sun's reflection off the desert floor above as the sun continued rising. When the light rays began illuminating the sandstone canyon walls, I thought of Wesley's "Preamble to the Beginning" and the glimmerings of light that must have sparkled around God's voice as he said, "Let there be light."

After Kay related Marina's dilemma over being with her family in eternity or with Brick in a paradise of careless, youthful bliss, I told her that Marina's desire for a happy family life in eternity reminded me of those Navajo women who had died by fighting the Spanish. Many a Navajo woman died for the peace of their eternal family unity along the narrow ledges of the Canyon de Chelly's cliff dwellings when the Spanish attacked a few years before the 1810 Mexican Revolution against Spain. Isn't Marina's motherly lullaby of prayerful hope for Danielle spiritually like the sacrifice of the Navajo women being led by their children to die for the soul of their family unity? Truly, family survival was the balm of Marina's mothering soul, and I believe that Danielle drew Marina back into the cradle of God's accepting, reassuring love. I think Marina must have realized a sense of renewed faith in the eternal forgiveness of the Christ of the Burning Bush that is never consumed, but is always in a state of eternal resurrection through forgiveness for those of us who humbly seek it.

Then I saw a one-eighth moon appear over the canyon walls with a halo around it as Kay finished her story. We stood there quietly with "Greensleeves" and "Mary, Did You Know?" ringing in my ears before I pointed out the moon's halo to Kay. We agreed that it was like a sign of the Angel Marina looking down upon us amid the purple, Lent-colored rays of forgiveness suddenly bursting forth upon the bright white alabaster of the White House ruins. The halo seemed like a sign that Good Friday morning of Marina's stepping with the courage of blind faith into God's never-ending eternity that draws souls to the greater purpose of obliterating the dark in their lives with the light of love. Tears welled up in both of us at the realization that an accepting forgiveness is the only answer to the Neanderthals' eternal cry of why? Why? WHY?

Our epiphany was shared, but as I have said, Kay wouldn't have told me anything about Brick and Marina had June been living and I not moved out west—legal protocol would have prevented it. I thought then of telling her about Chalky's death, but thought it better not to.

I did not see Kay on this trip, but we exchange Christmas cards annually with detailed personal notes. I hope we'll see each other again. She's sixty-one now.

And yes, I will mail you a copy of Wesley's poem, Mrs. Penny. Its promise of forgiveness is what requires the Burning Bush to keep burning."

X

"Here come the flight attendants and gatekeepers, Melody. I guess our Overland Stagecoach, as you call it, is ready to transport us into the morning skies."

"Ladies, you must be the two who barely missed your connecting flight to Denver last night. We've heard of your mechanical delays back in North Carolina and are so sorry.

"I already have your boarding passes right through to Santa Fe, connecting in Denver. You are Melody Dare-Hawk and Penelope Ruez Springs, right?"

"Yes, ma'am!"

"We'll start boarding at 6:30 Central time in case you haven't set your watches back from Carolina's Eastern time. You may also want to note that it'll be Mountain time in Denver when you arrive there. Most travelers change their watches to the time zone they'll be arriving in once the flight lifts off. Here folks do that as they fly by the Arch to the West designed to recall America's promise—one full of challenge."

Chapter Twenty-Four

The Wrap-Up and Daybreak September 11, 2001

And then the Face of Knowledge re-entered the Face of Truth, and the Face of Truth re-entered the Face of Wisdom. As the Face of Wisdom re-entered the Face of Love, Love said to Wisdom: The First Realizer is the First Light. His love is more pure than my love, for His love subdued the inertness of the dark of doubt without blemish. It can shepherd us away from the temptation of false insights . . . .
—*"Preamble to the Beginning," Chaplain Wesley Wyatt, U.S. Army*
The Coosa Valley Boarding School for Boys, ca. 1954–55

I

"TELL THE STEWARDESS ONLY COFFEE, MELODY, so I'll remain awake after staying up all night learning what led you to the Four Corners. We don't want to miss our Santa Fe connection!

"But now tell me what you learned about your North Carolina friends at the reunion barbeque. On our flight to North Carolina, you were so eager to attend it."

"Exactly, Mrs. Penny—reuniting with my old friends, then telling you about my Sunrise Acres experiences has brought my life together after many years of wondering how all the pieces fit.

"Although Wendy propelled me to study for my master's degree and that led to meeting Pem, I believe Brick and Dad inspired my career path. I've not seen Wendy and Langdon since my honeymoon because they've remained on the Outer Banks, but we correspond. They have a boy and a girl."

II

I never saw Brick or Becky after my wedding, but I heard about them when Pem and I vacationed in North Carolina. Brick did find great success with Amalgamated Industries, and his division produced enough boot-strap equity for him to cash out with considerable funds.

With that money and his dad's additional backing, Brick bought out a Pineland Springs plumbing supply store as the recession of the early 1980s ended. Brick's Industrial Water and Electrical Supply Company thrived in the new construction boom, allowing him to put together a chain of stores serving the Southeastern Carolinas Coastal Plains.

Along with Juan, Cousin Mingo continued his kitchen cabinet installations. They have actually done work for Becky, who left the museum after more than twenty years and took over Mrs. Dot's Antique and Remodeling Shop after she passed.

Twelve years after Sunrise Acres was completed, Allen Lamb had a barbeque fundraiser for Bertha's widower, Henry Moore, who had lost his Triple-Nickel, parachute-jumping legs to diabetes. The fundraiser was Allen's inspiration for helping his old Army buddy supplement his veteran's health benefits. Henry died shortly after, but all had such an enjoyable time that the idea of a barbeque reunion was born.

The reunion is held every five years. Since the first Sunrise Acres houses were started in September of 1971, the first barbeque was held in 1991, the next in 1996 and now September of 2001, thirty years later. Allen died, but his Celestine and others have kept it going.

Pem and I attended the 1991 affair, but Brick did not. He and Becky attended the Myrtle Beach-Ocean Drive Fall SOS event. This SOS acronym stands for the Society of Stranders, alluding to the Myrtle Beach area's Grand Strand of beaches. It's a ten-day reunion of the fifties, sixties, and seventies generation that spent their college summer weekends beach-dancing. I can imagine the two-weekend SOS event easily appealing to Brick and Becky.

In 1996, our roles were reversed as Brick attended the reunion and I didn't. But we both attended this 2001 year, along with Becky. There was someone there from every family I ever knew through Sunrise Acres except Kay and Wendy.

Arriving at Saturday's reunion with Dad, I saw Cousin Mingo near Marina's gazebo standing between two barbeque cookers sprinkling oak and hickory coals under the cooking pork. Juan assisted Mingo, and both hugged me when I came up.

They asked when Pem was coming back to black-bear hunt in the Croatan National Forest, and I speculated when Pem's work schedule might allow for it. Then I saw Miss

Peaches and Erica, who now has a child. Next to arrive were Donald and Bessie Mae. Their two children were not with them, but I was told that the daughter is a nurse, and the son manages the local hamburger chain outlet.

Bessie Mae and Miss Peaches said that they, Celestine, and others had prepared side dishes. Donald added that Austin, Diane, and their twin boys, Kit and Nance, would be bringing cole slaw and iced tea from Uncle Henry's, compliments of the lumber company, where Donald still works as the delivery-truck dispatcher and loading foreman.

Then I asked about Cotton Roberts, the lumber company draftsman. Mingo said Cotton had moved the farthest away. "Cotton had sketched a plan for a gynecologist who taught and worked at the UNC-Chapel Hill Hospital. Shortly afterward, Cotton captured her heart and married her! When his wife took a position at Tulane Med School, in New Orleans, Cotton moved with her. He's now in heaven, restoring old New Orleans homes and commercial units."

When Austin and Diane arrived with their twin sons, Diane announced, "Lisa Hutton is coming with a special guest!" Just then a large black SUV rounded the curve at the junction of the top-ten and back-forty roads, and we watched the vehicle until it stopped.

III

It was Brick and Becky, as vibrant as ever. When Brick exhibited his hopeful smile that had always been his gift, I, too, felt buoyant again.

Dad, Mingo, and Donald were the first he spoke with after exchanging greetings with Austin, Diane, and their two sons. Then Brick said to Becky, "Well, it's our lost Melody from the West! Where's Pem?"

I explained Pem's Santa Fe conference, and my traveling with you, Mrs. Penny, for your Duke treatments.

"Melody," Brick said, "I remember Pem telling his family story during Junebug and Kay's wedding party for you. I marvel how his family migrated from Carolina to the West after the Civil War. At the 1996 reunion, people told me his tale had mesmerized everyone. I would have loved to have heard Pem tell it again."

"Dad, Mingo, and Juan retell it so much that everyone here knows it as well as I do," I replied. "They come to see us every other year to hunt mule deer with Pem. The off years, Pem and I come here for their black-bear hunts at Croatan. So Pem's Dare-Hawk family-migration story of Croatan Joe is retold often."

"You never had children?" he asked.

I replied, "That's true," before he, Becky, and I began walking toward the street and the houses beyond.

"Melody," Brick said, "I often think about what happened to the people here. You take Cecil Crisp or Cecil X; Donald says Cecil died in a prison uprising up North, apparently trying to be a chaplain to Black Muslim inmates. Cousin Wesley did a prison ministry briefly after leaving the Army. I've always liked to imagine Cecil X doing something similar to Wesley's calling. It's just unfortunate that Cecil was killed trying to counsel others."

"Yes," I said, "I had heard that. Cecil was a peculiar fellow. Another peculiar fellow I wondered about was Lisa's husband, Vann. I had heard that his death was odd."

Brick began, "Hutton passed just after the 1991 Sunrise Acres reunion. Becky and I went to the Ocean Drive SOS festivities that year with my friend Brewer Melvin and his second wife, Brandy. In fact, we are all leaving tomorrow for this year's SOS Fall Migration.

"Brewer and Nicole have divorced. Apparently rural life's tranquility was too much for Nicole. She later married a Fort Bragg Army doctor, and they now live in Hawaii.

"When Brewer, Brandy, Becky, and I walked into an OD dance club on a Friday afternoon, we saw Hutton on a barstool, listening to The Love Committee's 'Cheaters Never Win.' Some blue-haired dame came out of a dark-cornered ladies' room to hang on his arm.

"Hutton was living just over the North Carolina state line and managing house construction on a new golf-course development. Cy Turner was Hutton's interior trim crew chief. Cy's arthritis limits his work to the miter saw and telling others what to do.

"Cy's crew was a group of homosexuals he had become acquainted with through a lady-friend bar owner he had helped on a remodeling project. Cy didn't realize he was working with gays until after the project was underway, but they executed his instructions well.

"When that project ended, Cy brought his skilled trim crew to Hutton's golf course-housing project. That was when Hutton began rambling that gays were an odd lot because they were generally gifted in spite of their inability to live a normal family life. His comments made me remember your friend, Dizzy."

I replied, "I felt sorry for Desmond because he never could establish any emotional balance over urges that grieved him. He said everyone wants the assurance of feeling normal, and not just existing like a zombie. I liked his company because he reminded me of me, the unfulfilled Indian girl. I was always offended when people said I shouldn't befriend him.

"The Navajo recognize Desmond's kind as two-spirited souls, calling them Nadleeh. They play special roles in Indian religious ceremonies and were accepted as natural tragic figures until the arrival of European religions introduced different beliefs. When I think of my life of shared hope with Pem, I always regret that Desmond couldn't find the normalcy he wished for. I've heard he's waiting tables in Charleston. Lately, I've wondered if age might moderate his alienation to leave him with a sense of dignity and peace through an acceptance of himself in this life before he must depart for another."

"Melody, that reminds me of my disappointments in France that I told you about," noted Becky. "In my dissatisfaction with art, I came to understand that my unfulfilled feelings resulted from my spirit's not sensing its integration into the greater whole of the universe that I longed to contribute to and feel accepted by. Your friend seems similar."

"Those are good insights," Brick said. "But back to our SOS outing. The dance club began filling up as the DJ played The Sanford-Townsend Band's 'Smoke from a Distant Fire,' William Bell's 'Easy Coming Out / Hard Going In,' and then Gloria Hardiman's 'Baby, Meet Me with Your Black Drawers On.' Hutton danced two numbers with his blue-haired friend and still put down smooth steps. A few couples joined them, but everyone in the place, including Becky and I, took to the dance floor for Hardiman's 'Black Drawers On.' After that, Brewer and I turned to go to another spot, and there stood Monroe Hill talking to Hutton as The Futures' 'Party-Time Man' wailed through the cigarette haze.

"Like Hutton, Monroe had a gray-haired woman. Ginger had divorced him after Monroe's mother died of congestive heart failure because neither she nor Monroe's dad could control Monroe's gambling addiction after his mother's passing. His dad sold out the family's laundry-pawn shop operation and moved to South Florida's Gulf Coast with a woman he quickly married. Mr. Hill left Monroe fifteen thousand dollars, telling him to 'Make it with those funds or starve, Boy!'

"Monroe purchased a pushcart-style hot dog and popcorn stand from one of his elderly poker-playing buddies. He pushed this around downtown Raleigh during the week, doing well for several years. But he told us at SOS that he was selling out to move to South Florida to be near his dying dad.

"I saw Monroe again before he left Raleigh. He said Hutton had died two weeks after we saw him at SOS. Cy Turner found Hutton—it should have been the other way around! —slumped in a recliner chair with a death grip on a full martini and a wide-open stereo playing Steely Dan's 'Do It Again.' Cy said not a drop of the martini had spilled.

"As for Monroe, I saw him twice more at Fall SOS events before Brewer, Langdon, and I scattered his ashes this past May in the waters off Fort Jefferson by Dry Tortugas National Park in the Gulf of Mexico.

"After Monroe's dad passed of colon cancer, his widowed stepmother returned to

North Carolina, but Monroe remained there because he liked the place. His dad's house was in a little fishing village with access to the Gulf near Marco Island. It was paid for, but his dad didn't leave much else. At Langdon's suggestion, Monroe got a job as first mate on a pleasure boat. The operation transported snorkelers and sport fisherman to the Dry Tortugas, located about seventy miles off Florida's southwest coast. Of course, Monroe never met a stranger, and the pleasure-boat work fit his personality well.

"Two months before Monroe died, he notified Langdon that he too had colon cancer, like his dad. His immoderate lifestyle, reminiscent of his over-consumption of salt-cured country ham to raise his blood pressure to avoid the Vietnam draft, no doubt hastened the collapse of his health. Langdon called Brewer and me and we went to bid him farewell. Monroe wanted to die on his catamaran within sight of Fort Jefferson Island, where he had taken many tourists, but his doctors said such a request was impractical. However, his captain and friends promised him a farewell Gam, a meeting of ships at sea where crews exchange news. The Gam took place just off the public dock in front of Monroe's house when several commercial pleasure craft assembled to heave to-and-fro like they had done at sea.

"Near sundown, his doctor increased his morphine drip level to reduce pain before he passed. He was attired in a double hospital gown, one for the front and one for his backside, and transported out to the pier in a wheelchair-commode that allowed for the convenient evacuation of his bowels and bladder.

"There, three pleasure boats soon glided to a stop, and the seamen came to Monroe. It became like a mini business convention of competitors standing around a bar talking shop, except that this was for saying good-bye to a colleague.

"After half an hour, Monroe's labored breathing forced him to nap for thirty minutes. Even the rumbling motors of the departing boats and their diesel fumes did not awaken him. When the sun began fading, he awoke and took several sips of bottled water.

"Looking west, he said: 'This view reminds me of the solitude around waters of the Dry Tortugas and Carolina's Outer Banks and Ocracoke. Such views always made me feel near eternity's unending oblivion, and in wonder of the world and its Maker.'

"Then he laughed, 'My doctors said I'd likely crap while passing away. That idea made me at least thankful that I'd die with my privates attached, unlike Dutch. It also made me think of Hutton's last moments. He died clothed, holding a martini. But, I think of him as dying naked, on cocaine, and having a big schizophrenic desire for an erection he could no longer muster as he waited for the next blue-haired woman to enter his orbit of dance-hall doctor psychology—a hell of a way to look into the abyss of one's life. Like Dutch, Hutton had a great college-degree vocabulary, but no practical brain to go with it. Some can have a good time and leave it. Then some, like Hutton and me, focus on party-time all the time. I don't have any more brains than Hutton, but thankfully I at least got my friends about me.'

"Speaking those words, he evacuated his bowels and died. Two days later his captain took us out to scatter his ashes to the four winds during a soaking Gulf rain within sight of Fort Jefferson." Monroe, like we all, may have questioned his brain's more practical intuitions about happiness fulfillment. But like the Henley's poem line 'captain of my soul,' he showed us how to die believing in eternity's unending visions of hope.

"So the Monroe-Hutton-Marsh era is over except for you, Brewer, and Langdon. Of course, I hear that Stan Cannon did well in the golf world," I said after a pause.

"Yes," Brick replied as we stood looking at the house where Marsh and Chalky died. "Stan has had double-digit tournament wins, including several majors. Those accomplishments put him at peace."

"Chester O'Malley died peacefully in his sleep," I added. "Maybe the same will happen to Will O'Cain, who's in a Durham rest home. Dad says both Hogbear and his wife have died. I miss his little scratch pads. And whatever happened to the painter Riley Carlisle?"

"He painted at the lumber company's Raleigh subdivisions," Brick answered. "But he now has emphysema.

"And Hogbear's little fertilizer scratch pads! I haven't thought of them in years. I used those note sheets to get construction mistakes corrected. Too bad I didn't keep extras with me to prevent my own personal mistakes that I should have better anticipated."

"Changing the subject, Melody," Becky interjected, "did you ever find a frame for Manet's *Olympia* print?"

"Yes," I answered. "I'm amazed that you remember giving it to me! It's on my bathroom vanity wall."

There was silence as we turned to look back toward the gazebo before beginning our return stroll. As we passed back by the house where Marsh and Chalky died, Brick pointed it out to Becky, saying, "That's where it all ended for Marsh."

I wondered then what Brick would think if he knew what I know. But I felt satisfied keeping the secret to myself, though still wondering where Brick had disposed of Mingo's hammer, before we walked up to Austin and Diane.

IV

"Is this Lisa's car approaching?" asked Diane. A car with Québec license plates eased by, and a woman waved. It was Lisa. The female driver looked about thirty.

"Lisa!" Diane called. "It's been a few years! I hope you recognize my older version."

Lisa laughed as she waited for her driver to emerge. "I am envious of you! You haven't gained a pound."

"My pounds are the same, but redistributed to all the wrong places," answered Diane as the two embraced.

"You mentioned a special guest. Is this Alyssa or Sylvia?"

"No," answered Lisa. "I said 'special' guest because she has especially wanted to come here for some time. I knew from your notes that these reunions would be the best time for her to come to get a sense of this place and possibly some of the people her mother knew. This is our Danielle, Marina's daughter!"

"My, my!" said Diane. "She looks like her mother, indeed!"

"I knew it when I saw her," Brick said. "It's like seeing a ghost; the eyes, the hair, even her earrings bounce the same."

"That's because the earrings *are* the same. They are some of the few tangible items Mother left me, and I wanted to wear them here," smiled Danielle, as Donald and Bessie Mae came forward with disbelieving stares.

"This is Bessie Mae and her husband, Donald," said Lisa to Danielle. "And this gentleman is Brick MacKoy. Brick and Bessie Mae are the ones who felt your mother's presence when she passed.

"I have often told Danielle the stories I know of her mother's life," Lisa explained. "Prominent in my story are Bessie Mae's and Brick's visions of a left-hand imprint."

"My mother wrote me several letters before she died," put in Danielle. "Each letter was advice about the seasons of life that she had experienced in her few years. One letter mentions Sunrise Acres. Lately its words have become more significant to me, and I wanted to come here to better absorb her message—it's my only way of communicating with her—you understand."

Brick nodded and added, "When Bessie Mae and I felt your mother's spirit, we were touched by it because of having seen the same thing, but in different places. Our double witness certified an unusually strong message from your mom to us from the other side. This was disturbing, of course, but also warmly reassuring.

"Later, when your Aunt Lisa came to see this gazebo, she spoke of the amputated little finger matching the four fingers of the foggy handprints. We then knew we had witnessed a message from above. That experience has had a profound effect on us all to this day."

"Time to eat!" called Celestine. Going through the serving line, I thought of the epiphany that Kay and I had experienced at Canyon de Chelly only a few years earlier. It, too, was a part of Marina's legacy, but I knew that this vision of her soul coursing from the amorous to the humbly faithful had to stay with me alone if for nothing but to honor Brick and Marina's love as they had done.

As we ate, Diane asked, "Danielle, how many letters did your mother write?"

"Five," Danielle replied. "One was on youth and being full of hopeful expectation through play. In it there were cautions not to become too concerned with rejections by friends since life eventually separates us all for our different stations and tasks. She also warned me not to get too involved in cliques, but to always think for myself. Her letters are wonderful words of advice, and I feel her voice speaking to me through them.

"There was another on puberty. Mother said it was a sign from God that one had been chosen to be a vessel for the future of an improving humanity that strives to leave the world a better place than it's born into.

"Another letter was on getting a driver's license and the need to be careful. Mother also wrote an admonition to be prudent in the consumption of alcohol, whether driving or not.

"There was one on education and preparing for the future. Here she spoke like Father, suggesting that I seek the counsel of others whom life had shown me to be wise in the ways of the world because my formal training would be only the beginning of my education. My life after college, with its pains and joys, she said, would be my real educator."

"And then there's the letter you brought with you today," said Lisa. "I've read it and believe your mother wouldn't object if you passed it around among her friends or read it aloud. The letter may give us all some closure on our grief at our loss of Marina in this significant time and place. It's wise insight we can use, no matter our age. Why don't you finish eating first, and then decide what to do?"

Since Danielle and Lisa had been among the first served, they were among the first to finish eating. As conversations continued, Danielle opened a brown business envelope, and pulled out a letter along with a small, pocket-sized notepad with "V-C FERTIL-IZER" on its front cover. I immediately recognized it as one of Hogbear's notepads from years ago. Out of the corner of my eye I saw Brick focused on it. Consequently, he didn't see a tear form in my eye.

Danielle read the letter silently while holding the V-C notepad. Then she arose and strolled about.

v

Danielle returned after all had finished eating and said, "I've often read this letter, but never appreciated its instruction until my divorce last year. The envelope instructs me to open it upon my college graduation, or upon becoming a mother.

"I read it at graduation, and appreciated its intent, but did not feel its wisdom until after my painful divorce. Mother's letter gives no examples of divorce, but her message about disappointments still seems spiritually instructive. I hope reading it here will help me to know her better from afar, for she mentions Sunrise Acres as a place of joy and pain:

My Dear Danielle,

I am praying the future will allow me to see you read this someday, and occasionally discuss with you my own views about maturing through the joys and pains of life just as my mother did with me.

Currently, I fear this is unlikely, as I sense the presence of my daddy's holy ghost about me. Thus I pass on my thoughts about joy and pain to you by the hand of your Aunt Lisa. As she and I together do this, know that I am cuddling thee now, which is not only more pleasure than writing: it also inspires my thoughts Aunt Lisa pens.

I am praying that you will have been an obedient daughter to your father and to our Lord's Holy Spirit and will have arrived at that departure point into adulthood when you are graduated from college or are entering into motherhood.

At this point, life events will naturally require that you come out of the shadows of the scholastic and parental nursery you've been in. Life will demand that you learn to use your educational tools to manifest your own visions of happiness. Know that it will be a challenge to apply the knowledge you've gained to the actions you take. This, however, you must do, or face a mental withering of yourself into that of an educated but hollow shell.

Thus, there will always be the challenge to do, and by your doing, learn even more. And this "more" that you will learn from "doing" is called wisdom and insight, neither of which can be imparted to the soul by study alone, even of worthy ideas. Your notions derived from schooling must be placed into the crucible of activity where they will be tested by the fire of experience.

Unfortunately, the common-sense tools needed for managing oneself toward a happier existence cannot be offered in a college course titled HAPPY LIFE 101. This personal happiness is something you must create for yourself out of your own trial-and-error. Were such courses ever offered to college seniors, few students would be able to appreciate the course's content because most would not have yet had the opportunity to experience enough of the real world's disappointments and suffering to connect with the truths taught. Suffering renders wisdom via revelations that can't be learned by words alone. One can realize wisdom only through the private reflections of one's own soul. So keep your mind and heart always open for renewal amidst the greatest difficulties and disappointments. Be open and remember the words of the Bible: "When I was a child, I thought as a child; but when I became a man, I thought as a man."

As for myself, I was nurtured by the core Renaissance thought that sees humans as being in some designing control of our own destiny. Perhaps it was my girlish vision of my father charting his Canadian Merchant Marine vessel through the German submarine gauntlets of World War II, or later through the ever-changing currents of the St. Lawrence and the windy Great Lakes. Or perhaps my dad's conversations with our old family friend, Jacques, at his furniture store about the French adventurers out-maneuvering and out-trading the English Hudson's Bay Company fostered some competitive, pioneer-like spirit in me.

Looking for ways to make things better is the pioneering spirit of all of North America. Being imbued with that was why it was so easy for me to follow my sister to the U.S.—I saw more opportunity there to create my own destiny of self-worth. Americans had, after all, put a man on the moon. I visited a place once—in secrecy, I might add—where the moon-rocket fuels were tested. There I felt so much on the inside-knowing of it all. It was thrilling, and the tides of opportunity that lift all adventuring ships of dreams were strong for me that day.

On my secret moon-rocket tour were persons I had come in contact with through your Aunt Lisa's husband's business, where I was an intern architect. These people had a home-building project that embodied that pioneer spirit of improving opportunity for a better life.

This project was like myself and most young people, who are full of good intentions and exalted optimism but clueless to the need to be alert to those important rules for living a good life. The experience taught me about a need for a more sophisticated insight into what is practically achievable and what is not. To be sure, my disappointment came to me sweetly amid my naïve notions of possibility. But then all creative dreams of worldly improvement are envisioned innocently without realizing how many difficult mountain paths one must negotiate, spiral rising upon spiral to the peak before a dream's best aspirations can be realized.

The home-building project was Sunrise Acres. Even the name offered promise. Here I saw some of my dreams realized in part, but in the end the project was a financial failure for the builders as a result of insurmountable difficulties in the national economy at that time.

Sunrise Acres was a starter-home project of small, three-bedroom houses. Its customer base was mostly black, the result of several U.S. Government programs designed to promote ownership opportunity for this population segment.

Like most first-time homebuyers, these homeowners had little money saved for hard times. Thus, when a financial recession came along, as they naturally do, some lost their homes because they could not pay their mortgage. These repossessed units jeopardized the builder's opportunity to sell the remaining, unsold houses in a timely manner, so the project failed financially. In addition, the son of the project's principal partner died before the project's completion in a freakish incident never totally explained. I enjoyed the son, Marsh, and his wife immensely. His death ruined my worldly perceptions.

Nevertheless, it invigorated me to be a small part of this positive enterprise because the project made me feel that my life had some greater purpose and worth. My friends there all felt a similar connection to the pioneer-pilgrim experience of building a better opportunity for others as well as realizing a more perfect manifestation of themselves. After all, being a builder always makes one feel a little God-like. That's a narcotic feeling that invariably faces a humbling correction. I got the point of my never-ending need for humility from this experience of failure.

A Sunrise Acres friend used to give me little notepads like the one enclosed. He used them for writing down construction mistakes that needed correction so the houses could pass a final inspection. I always found these pads useful for making all sorts of to-do lists. We should each do the same with our personal mistakes, for there will be a final inspection on each of us, too. As you go through life, I encourage you to imagine listing your personal mistakes hereon and think of how to correct them until there's only a blank page left. Of course, we know realistically that there will never be a blank page left because newer manifestations of our improved thinking and acting will produce newer and more complex mistakes and blunders as we refine away the earlier dregs of our life's wine.

So where can happiness be, then? Can it be had by listing a life full of Corrections-To-Do? While this sounds trite, it is, however, what we all pretty much do in some way. Our self-correction process is often painful, especially if it involves something emotionally subjective and not mechanical behavior. But both our emotionally subjective and our rote behavioral errors are standard, stock essences of the full-life experience, and thus should not be viewed as tragic.

I say that because the process of being deceived by the heart's first impressions only serves to deepen one's understandings to a higher level of awareness that begets a wiser gut-instinct, and thus a deeper faith in one's next adventure.

Know, Danielle, that the beauty of Hope is that one's Hope is always at the ready to be renewed, with a wiser insight wrought from the pains of a recent disappointment. From those ashes, the wiser, rising Hopes will offer you better-balanced new promises for your every tomorrow.

After one has gone through enough disappointments to realize that disappointments are the way of the world, one becomes aware of the question of desirable ends, and realizes that the end is personal happiness within that pattern of loss and hope.

Thus, I encourage you always to order your desires to that end. As wiser people manage their spiritual journey along the spiritual spectrum between happiness and regret, they come to appreciate a need for relationships that are better capable of promoting their happiness. Seek always visions of virtue and friends of virtue, for a virtuous life is necessary for your deeper, lasting peace of mind—the peace all seek.

My first post-college, real-life failed dreams of grandeur were at Sunrise Acres. When you hit that first emotional brick wall of adult life that comes your way, I hope your Aunt Lisa can take you to Sunrise Acres where I met mine. There you can better realize what I am telling you now: Your failed efforts are fine. For me, they led to a more perfect destiny that resulted in you, as you were always in my visionary consciousness, even before I met your father. He renewed my dream of you even more perfectly. So you must not be afraid that your dreams will always disappoint; some dreams will, indeed, evaporate, whereas others will grow, change, and flourish from a heart made wiser by the failures.

This spirit of maturing through failures was on my mind when I made up a lullaby to sing for you alone. It goes:

Danielle, Danielle, you're the sweetest I've beheld.
You are my baby girl, the loveliest in the world.
Say you will, oh, say you will, always climb life's spiral hill,
until youuuuu arrive at the summit to realize!!
That your heart is made of gold, toooo make you brave and bold;
Toooo seeee yourself clearly, in eternity freely.

To be free from fear and free from want, free to choose and say don't.
Free to know that you are an everlasting star!

Say you will, oh, say you will, always climb life's spiral hill, until
Youuuu arrive at the summit to realize!

Therefore, my prayerful thoughts are of you and your inevitable future struggles against doubt and disappointment, as I consider my journey across the river. Always know that from there I will cheer you, and I encourage you to realize and realize again and again the golden purity of the heart that God gave you for standing at the ready to renew your hopes.

God's Speed, My Child; God's Love, My Child,
God's Courage to Endure into a More Perfect Love
That Will Divine the Ways of the World.

With all my love and prayers,
Your Mother

VI

When Danielle finished, Brick examined the notepad before standing to comment.

"Realize, realize, realize! Marina instructed Danielle in her letter and lullaby. Yes, we should realize that our hearts are made of a spiritual gold that can filter and process one's dreams like a dream catcher. My cousin Wesley, a retired Episcopal Army chaplain, and I have had many conversations over the years about reaching higher spiritual insights. He's now a halfway house administrator for alcoholics near the coast. His wife is his assistant. Wesley and Marina apparently had much in common in seeing our spirit's heart or soul being a force of realization for producing wiser understandings for each soul.

"Wesley once wrote about the first realizer, God. He named his work 'Preamble to the Beginning' because it is about what Wesley imagined God to be doing in the eon before God said, 'Let there be light.' Wesley thought of God as being in the center of a black hole. Because God realized His presence in the dark and knew that He was all that existed, Wesley called him the First Realizer. Even though the dark force around God was so strong that there was no light outside of God, that dark force was not strong enough to extinguish the light of God's love residing inside Him. Thus, when God compared the interesting force of beautiful light within Him to the dark nothingness outside Him, He realized that the force of love's light inside Him must be released to permeate that dark nothingness. And so, He said, 'Let there be light,' and we each came from within that light as it continues to spread through space and time.

"Were Wesley here today, he would agree with Marina's counsel that only a spotless, golden heart can negotiate life's path. Wash it daily with a shower of charitable forgiveness, Marina implies. Wesley would counsel the same. So, Danielle, you may not have had your mother long, but life could not have given you a better advisor for dealing with life's disappointments and our need to be reborn again daily.

"I am humbled to learn today that in her final days, Marina thought that Sunrise Acres manifested and assisted some of that happiness-pursuing spirit. Like all my family, Marina believed that all humans had a basic desire to pursue a God-given unalienable right to seek happiness in a way that does not obstruct the same search of others attempting the effort. To her architect's heart, a home was the best haven to venture out from to meet these challenges of building a personal Promised Land. She would often reflect that even the Chinese Communists honor the long-held Chinese sanctification of personal property ownership.

"Before Columbus and the Vikings, history and legends noted the movement of individuals like Abraham seeking a more fulfilled life. Our desires to realize our individual dreams are God embedded and that personal fulfillment desire is deep in man's nature. The tales Melody's husband, Pem, tells about trading among the ancient tribes relate that negotiated trades produced mutual respect between parties and individuals as far back as the Stone Age. That history of trading respect begot the Biblical idea of 'Do unto others as you would have them do unto you' long before Christ's statement of it recognized that civilizing core principle of mutual respect for all.

"The American spirit has endeavored to support an opportunity to pursue happiness. However, that happiness is defined differently by each individual. Thus, there is no equality about the happiness pursued or achieved, just some opportunity to pursue it. So as we journey through life to the fulfillment of what makes us most happy, may we reflect on the words of America's Hymn, 'America the Beautiful,' that pleads with its phrase 'God mend thine every flaw.' This is each new generation's challenge and each person's—to make the Promised-Land journey more unfettered for all as time marches on. Western Civilization democracies are not perfect governments, but they attempt to mimic the Master's forgiveness that renews our hopes. Any exceptionalism observed is our striving amid the disappointments of the moment for a new day, and that can only be accomplished by one individual at a time. Truly, the Promised Land is always a continual work in progress, only glimpsed as we go from age to age.

"Yes, Marina's letter reminds us about the process of living as individuals through hope to pain to hope again and again. That's why our Marina told her Danielle years ago in the letter to come here to glimpse a slant of light from her mother's aspiring soul that her daughter would never otherwise have the opportunity to know. Here Danielle can connect her mother's soul to the living word of the Tree of Life—the Bush that burns but is never consumed. That Bush is always in a state of eternal resurrection through eternal forgiveness. That forgiveness process always produces a more perfected personal happiness."

Brick paused and looked at Lisa, Danielle, Diane, and Becky before holding up the notepad and casting his gaze out to the rest of us. Then he said, "It's been a long time since I've seen one of these notepads. The autumn of life surely strips away the leaves of our youth in many ways. It tells me we're all getting grayer and it's prudent to conjecture that we may not have an opportunity for this particular group of people to meet again in five years. If a future meeting is not possible for me, I say to you as my Cousin Wesley does when bidding farewell: *Selah*, meaning pause; *Shalom*, meaning peace; then *Aleichem*, meaning come forth; *Elohim*, and imbue the peace of your Word upon our hearts, Amen and Amen and Amen."

Only birdsongs broke the silence as Brick bent down to give Lisa a hug and a thumbs-up. She smiled at him, and said, "Bless you and yours always."

Then he said to Danielle, "Your mother's spirit was not fully of this world, but of that greater eternity that we all hope to dwell in. Trust in the good counsel of her letter. It will help keep your heart fresh for every tomorrow's promise of newly unfolding opportunity. Trust from all said here today that her pure heavenly spirit will always be with you.... Peace be unto you."

Then Brick went among us shaking hands and bidding good-byes. As he and Becky walked to their car, I had a musical vision of Mr. Malcolm, Marsh, Marina, Junebug, Bentonville Blue, and others, now departed, looking down upon us from on high, while spirits hummed "Amazing Grace," "At the River," "Simple Gifts," or its Methodist version, "The Lord of the Dance."

When Brick drove away, my soul whispered, "Selah," because the experience of the day had closed finally and satisfyingly my young-adult years before my Four Corners life absorbed me fully.

VII

"Well, Mrs. Penny, we're arriving in Denver on schedule at 8:00 a.m., Mountain Time. Did you set your watch back, too?"

"Indeed. Our two-hour flight from St. Louis is about the maximum sitting time for my legs, Melody—but next stop, Santa Fe! It'll be good to get home again.

"Again, I enjoyed your story, Melody. I always knew we had a special connection because of coming to the Four Corners from elsewhere. After hearing your tale, I appreciate our shared dislocation from our family roots even better. I also sense it's meant a lot to you to reflect on your past."

"Most certainly, Mrs. Penny."

VIII

"The last person is off the plane, and here's your wheelchair, Mrs. Penny."

"Ladies, please re-check your Santa Fe connections at our flight desk inside. All flights in U.S. air space were cancelled half an hour ago at 9:45 a.m. Eastern Time or 7:45, local Mountain Time. I've just been told that there are only a few commercial or private flights still in the air and those must immediately land at the nearest airport.

"Two planes crashed into both towers of New York City's World Trade Center this morning and a third plane hit the Pentagon. The World Trade's south tower collapsed minutes ago and the collapse of the other is expected. All news networks are saying that their intelligence sources suspect Osama bin Laden, but President Bush, so far, has said only that it's an apparent terrorist attack."

"Melody! That's Shasta's thought of taking the Lord's name in vain again using violence. If it's bin Laden, the greatest cultural war of history could be unfolding! Our old Clark Air Force Base military security friends with CIA contacts all worried that bin Laden's post-Afghan campaigns against the Western world would also begin among the Philippine Muslim dissidents after the 1991 Mt. Pinatubo volcano eruption forced America's departure. But no bin Laden Philippine intrusion was ever detected. In World War II, my Billy and Silver Hawk would say, 'Pass the ammunition and let God do the judging. That's His job.' We'll have to do that now, but we'd better pass out Bibles at the same time and pray to avoid Armageddon!"

"Gosh, bin Laden, Mrs. Penny! That's possible. I remember President Clinton's 1998 attempted cruise missile strike against him.

"It's 8:20 now. I'll call Pem! He's always up and about by eight o'clock, even with a day off after his Santa Fe conference concluded. Maybe he can come fetch us, or we could catch the West Coast train."

THE END

Epilogue

January 1, 2002

Dear Mrs. Penny,

So much has happened since our North Carolina trip after what everyone is now calling the 9/11 attack, that I have nearly forgotten to mail you a copy of Chaplain Wesley's spiritual thesis, "Preamble to the Beginning." It's included here.

I apologize for not inquiring about your leg and confess that I have become so absorbed with our country's effort to capture or kill Osama bin Laden and his cohorts that I find myself excluding all other interests, even my friendship with you. Bin Laden can continue to deny direct responsibility for 9/11 while hiding in a cave if he wishes, but his culpability for inspiring the attacks threads through all the information collected so far. Apparently bin Laden has escaped our December NATO allied campaign to corner him and his Taliban-al-Qaeda fighters at Tora Bora.

I hope they get him soon. The nearly 3,000 killed in the 9/11 attacks is considerably more than the 2,400 killed at Pearl Harbor, leading to WW II. So you know we'll have to keep up the effort.

My absorption with these events comes from our conversations at the airport and on the trip home with Pem that we might be witnessing the greatest cultural war of history. However, unlike the Charles Martels and El Cids of old, who defended aggressively, but sought opportunities for political solutions, we may not have a chance to find understanding in today's nuclear age; one nuclear suitcase bomb and good-bye modern world, hello caveman!

But the Bush that Burns is always beckoning mankind to figure out some new and deeper insight to promote everlasting life. Therefore, I pray that the God of the Burning Bush will send his Angels recognized by Christian, Jew, and Muslim alike to guide us away from this abyss. The spirits of angels like Marina who have already rejected the dark for eternity's everlasting light will be our beacon, leading our prayerful hopes for a safe future like little babes do when their mere presence renews our souls.

I pondered these things we had discussed while re-reading Wesley's essay-poem before enclosing it. We must now pray for courage in a new vision of hope through goodwill and charity that only God sees. Like the sentiments of Wesley's thesis, only the better angels of mankind's spirit can aspire to God's charity since no human, no matter how well intentioned, will ever attain a perfect understanding of it amid the obscurities and absurdities that naturally evolve in this world.

AH, *SELAH* AND HUMBLY YOURS,

MELODY

Preamble to the Beginning

by Wesley Wyatt
The Coosa Valley Boarding School for Boys, ca. 1954–55
(Later, Chaplain Wesley Wyatt, U.S. Army)

And from the center of the deep the Voice said: Oh, what fate has rendered me forsaken?

Again, I am here talking to myself. All this dark continually compressing 'round me is like a friction forcing ME to realize ME! Why is there no other realizer to speak with, and make company with, inside this chaos of darkness with but few zips of light and insight?

This absolute-dark nothingness is empty. From nothing you can only get more nothing! Oh, I am tired of this Eon of Darkness. I wish to manifest an Eon of Light like the one I sense growing within myself, for the Dark, as Dark, offers no joy. I create my own conversation and musings, but the Dark offers absolute nothingness in response to my restless idea-making. I feel a compassion and passion for more.

This light I observe within me, however, is curious, for it is cheerful and implies all sorts of possibilities while the dark 'round me is empty. My only companion is myself and this squiggling light within. I shall remove this exciting light from me so as to have at least a reflection to look at while talking to myself, rather than feeling and seeing the light only in my bowels. Yes, I have suffered in nothingness long enough, and this Eon of Darkness must end.

Now, Little Light, you are separated from me for reflective conversation. Your small blinking tickles my curiosity still, as you did before I separated you from out of me. At times a pulsating glow illuminates your small figure even more. What is that and why does it now grow?

And the Small Blinking Light answered: 'Tis your greater glow that illuminates me with my ebbs and flows. You say that I blink, but you glow continuously.

And the Voice responded: Your squiggling and blinking amuse me as you zing away into the dark mass of nothingness 'round us, then return.

And the Light replied: Yes, the dark is vast, and talking between ourselves is almost like talking to one's own self, as I am the First Essence begot from you.

And the Voice responded: You rightly imply that if we continue to talk to ourselves, the conversation may tempt vanity. I know vanity because I feel that I have lived with vanity in this chaos of darkness while searching my depths, yet realizing nothing but myself.

So, to avoid vanity's temptation I will force this darkness off of us that we might be able to have a better view of our situation. Thus I command to come forth out of me a vertical post upon which I can lean as I force back this mass of the dark. Come forth also arms and hands and legs with feet that I can use to hold away the four corners of the dark.

And the Small Light noted: As you commanded, these things have come forth. That's astounding! How did you do that?

And the Voice replied: I felt that I could do what I willed.

And the Light said: Well, it's also a wonder! For as you commanded, hands and feet did indeed come forth and were joined to your face and mouth that have been doing the talking. Am I talking back to you with a face and mouth like yours?

And the Voice responded: Yes, but I realize your face to be smaller, yet splendid!

And the Light observed: The darkness recedes only at the four points where You push back with your feet and hands while leaning upon your post.

And the Voice said: As you say, this is not effective. If I push out here, but then move my limbs to push out there, the darkness collapses in again at the first push-point while I am pushing out at the second one.

Now I realize what I must do. I'll spin 'round and 'round on this post with my four limbs stretched out so the darkness cannot collapse against the greater total force of my spinning action. Having been so unrealized in the dark, I did not appreciate the trial and error needed for a more perfect realization. Now I see as well that not every truth is wrought from abstract intellectuality. The fiery furnace of activity proves, disproves, and improves abstract concepts, as I now more fully appreciate. So come now, Blinking Light, sit upon my head that we may observe together while I spin around my Back Post creating a gravitational force that pushes out this mass of darkness.

And the Blinking Light said: This is a much better view. As you spin 'round your Back Post with your arms and legs spread out against the darkness, it's forcing that darkness out into a disk that remains a repository of your light.

And the Voice said: Oh, spin on, now, light of mine, to be brighter and brighter while I torque around my spinning, shafted post amid light to observe this open area in amazement.

And the Blinking Light said: You have created this expansion of light as lovingly as your curiosity freed me from out of your own existence. Are there other essences within you besides me?

And the Voice said: Well, let's see what the light tells us about itself. Thus, I hereby command that this disk of light reveal the full nature of myself and my first essence, my Son of Light.

And from the deep of the light a reflective face appeared as the Voice had commanded, and it said: As your Son of Light has said within you, you created me lovingly out of the deep graciousness of your realizing curiosity that knows no depths or bounds. So call me Love, for I am that great part of your totality. Your soul's love is that part of you that realizes first, an amazement for what is, and then an awareness of the dark circumstances you find yourself to be in. Your love desires a way to break out of stifling, chaotic darkness because the centrifugal force of your love desires to be shared. Love, in fact, gets restless to be shared, and that fact squirms and tickles your delight, eager as it is to express your fuller being.

And the Voice replied: Yes, I well know, for in the Eon of Darkness I absorbed all the Knowledge of the dark and found it to be a stifling accumulation of bits and pieces of information. In the absence of Light and Love, Knowledge is only random, unordered, and lifeless information in the dustless dark.

And the Face of Love said: Truly you know Knowledge. It is the part of you that is

dark but that contributes to the light. Thus allow me to bring forth that other facet of your loving light, which is called the Perspective of your Truth—Wisdom.

And from the Face of Love a new face mutated, and it said: I thank you for calling me forth for this council on your realized being. I am called Truth and Wisdom and am that part of your realization that has in the Eon just past distilled perspective from the two sides that comprise Knowledge. My Wisdom weaves the dark side and the light side because its desire is to make sense of bits and pieces of the chaotic information of Knowledge that yet requires Your Perseverance in order to distill the Wisdom of Truth. The desire of your Love has made that persevering Faith possible, which in turn has produced me.

And the Voice replied: May we explore that point of thought more deeply? What say you of all this, Knowledge? Are you a chaos of raw facts or a golden fabric of enlightenment?

And from the Face of Truth and Wisdom mutated the Face of Knowledge, and it said: Truly, I am the storehouse of all information, thus called Knowledge. I am the first keeper, the library, if you will, and I don't appreciate being belittled by this conversation between Truth and Love. You and the Small Blinking Light are observing passively for your own curious amusement at realizing more and more variety while I must work continuously to catalogue your speeding realizations. I just don't have time for this gibberish conversation of Truth to define its Wisdom. I have work to do. Please allow me to attend to my duties of gaining more and more data because I am the driving power of all in bringing about more realizing revelations.

And the Face of Truth and Wisdom responded: All we've got is time! Bridle thy tongue, Knowledge! True, you are resplendent as your information bits of glowing red light sparkle and slither white against the background of your dark face, all highlighted by those white sparkles near your ears. But your duties are subservient to the greater goods of my Truth and nothing but the wise Truth, and thus to my master, Love, that makes up the Spinning Tree of our realization and existence. You are, indeed, the Tree of Knowledge, but only one component of the greater whole of this spinning Tree of Life. You cannot add one iota of loving Wisdom to any bits of Knowledge you gather, and catalogue.

And the Face of Love remarked: Let him go, for he glories chiefly in the power of accumulation.

Then the Voice said: Yes, let Knowledge go where it will, for unlimited freedom is the only state in which it can function.

And then the Face of Truth and Wisdom commented: Yes, Knowledge requires freedom to nourish us together. Knowledge freed up produces my eternal truths that burn forever and are not consumed. Other times free Knowledge produces a short-lived Truth that applies only to one context of circumstances. Then on other occasions free inquiry produces seemingly curious, incoherent, or even arcane bits of information that may or may not be useful in some future circumstance. Thus, may we have your persevering faith, oh, spinning post of light, in order that wise, loving judgment and a holistic perspective will reign in us continuously, not extinguishing thy glowing light in a blind fury, leaving us with nothing more than dark, oppressive, fear-borne bits and pieces of randomly hit-upon information.

And the Voice responded: Oh, to be sure, my loving Wise Truth. I have wrestled with this perplexity you describe while I plumbed the depths of Myself amidst the dark Eon of Nothingness. Truly, a persevering Wisdom, forged in patient Love, must follow Knowledge about, cleaning up after the many invalid insights that Knowledge often begets. But the light of patient Love cannot be stored like Knowledge in a library for later use because Love continually beckons to be free. It craves growth, gained only if it is being practiced continuously.

So, what do we do with this gracious love? It should not be confined or hidden. For an answer, the persevering faith of my Love answers to Me that the whole of Me should be put to work through the expansion of my Light even more than in its present disk-like state. For a busy, working Love, tested by trials and errors, shall flourish with expansion, and not be fretful. Yes, putting the Light of Love to work will expand my light, thus rolling back the depths of Darkness massed up around Me. The expansion of my Light will turn Darkness in upon itself for self-reflection, and the growing heat will create a bigger and brighter light that can be enjoyed by all within my Fullness. Such an action will end this continual suffering my disparate parts have experienced amidst the data points of dark chaos.

I do not know why fate has freed me to realize my existence. But I know that no matter what I do, I cannot now make myself un-exist. I have realized myself, and that realization has perceived stimuli. Knowledge is produced from these stimuli, inchoate though it yet be. The Knowledge I realize can be used for good or evil because much self-deception exists in raw data, and appearances can distract, then dissimulate. On the other hand, for the everlasting light to be extended, this dark must be overcome by the mass force of many, who are distilled and purified of Knowledge, and who do not fret that Love is the only everlasting stimulus because Love does not nurture chaos in the grand sweep of things. I cannot be selfish, hoarding Light and Love, while ignoring this timeless Truth within Me.

Thus, I shall create beings from each spark of light I see within Me. I shall create them in My likeness that they may freely ponder the circumstances of Knowledge as I have in this Eon so a greater critical mass may glean Truth and Love thereby down the ages. And it must be our duty to pray with hope that these newly created beings shall choose happiness through a growing faith in this pondering process, when they, like we, go about

the work of divining the Truth of Love. We must pray in hope of this because in the free processing of Knowledge, they will often misperceive partial Truths for whole Truths, and thus follow blindly chaotic bits and pieces of Knowledge untested by the loving wisdom of the ages. Always a free self-deception shall point the way to the need for pure hearts from which the sweet honey of eternal life may be consumed.

And now Truth imbues Me more fully with the mechanics of our work at hand, creating a new Eon of Everlasting Light.

And the face of Truth replied: You are the First Light because you are the first realizing Soul, as you have said. Your realization manifested yourself, then separated yourself from the dark that compressed around the magnetic energy of your spirit. The friction that erupted between the dark and your loving magnetic realization has produced the light of your Love in which my Truth resides. That harmony manifested yourself, your personality parts, traits, your depth *ad infinitum*. When you became tired of absorbing and suffering in the darkness of this Eon, you spoke because you wished to. Likewise, when you were in need of hands and feet, you spoke and they came forth. Thus, if you wish to expand your realization to a fuller reality, all you have to do is speak, and it will come forth.

And face of Knowledge reappeared from out of the face of Truth, and said: It's fundamental that $e=mc^2$.

But you must appreciate again that there will be a greater suffering if you create these greater numbers. E=mc² is not capable of unifying everything within your unending field of vision.

And the Voice replied: I appreciate what you say, Knowledge. But with greater numbers will come a greater opportunity for joy, because the everlasting darkness will be transformed into the everlasting light. The free right to the pursuit of Truth and the magnification of Love will give greater opportunity to pursue happiness and/or pain equally. Thus the need for a wise Love will be grasped by a greater mass of the faithful, then carried and cherished in continuing force to press the darkness away.

And the face of Knowledge said: What will you do when the poor subjects you have created, though with truly good intentions, are hopelessly lost in the pain of coursing through my library? Will you banish them even more deeply into my ever-growing shelves?

And the Voice said: Oh, no, Knowledge. Don't fret. I shall not banish my creation into an obscurity of confusing facts that will only produce absurd vexations of woe.

And the face of Knowledge replied: Then what will you do with me besides acknowledging me as you stand there in all-knowing aloofness with that silly vertical post at your back?

And the Voice chuckled: I do appreciate your question, but I cannot be aloof to the sufferings of my creation, for they will truly suffer through the revelations they will realize. In fact, that will be what they and I have in common—suffering through the continued necessity of finding Love amid clouds of obscure factoids.

No, I shall not be aloof, but I shall lean upon this spinning back post, and suffer with my Love for them to also locate a persevering faith by which they may divine the Truth out of your bits and pieces of dusty Knowledge that can confuse as well as edify.

As their realization-time will take a new Eon, I am sure that my arms will get tired. Thus I'll place a cross beam upon this back post so as to allow me a balance point to suffer longer with them, for them, and through them.

And the face of Knowledge observed: But you are too powerful to be seen. How will your creations realize that you and they have this common denominator of suffering? They will need a sign.

And the Voice replied: I will send them a sign of myself suffering here on this back post and cross-bar of my first greater realization.

For a sign of myself, I shall send my essence, my small blinking Son of Light to guide my beings through the maze of minutiae that you, Knowledge, discover and catalogue. I shall send my Son of Light because He is the first thing realized from me, and thus He knows my resolve and intentions innately. He will carry out my wishes without questions such as yours, as He is the first pure light cloned of my light, and therefore my essence. The words and actions of His Life are the symbol of my essential Love, and the cross-beam and post a sign of my loyalty to the beings of my creation.

And the face of Love said to the Voice: This is good. All your parts shall come together to obliterate the anguish of the dark. Thus, all created in our likeness of curiosity and desire shall be freed from Your embodiment to pursue both happiness and the pain of correction in their unique freedom. All points of light will come to know the whole Truth of Love and nothing but the Truth of Love, realized again and again by all. And the Father Light's forgiveness will allow for a renewal of Hope that keeps the process of Love and Truth refinement going forever in each soul created.

And the Blinking Son of Light said: Come ye, all parts of His Holy realizing spirit back into our Father Light that He may begin His new Eon of expanding Light. This Eon will perfect that Light into an eternity that knows no bounds. Thus may the obscurity of the dark become pushed back forever.

And then the Face of Knowledge reentered the Face of Truth, and the Face of Truth re-entered the Face of Wisdom. As the Face of Wisdom re-entered The Face of Love, Love said to Wisdom: The First Realizer is the First Light. His Love is more pure than my love, for His love subdued the inertness of the dark of doubt without blemish. It can shepherd us away from the temptation of false insights through the charity of His understanding forgiveness that keeps the process of our contribution to His expanding eternal light unfolding with growing opportunities. Such can fulfill the essences of our gifts within His visions of Hope. Guided thus, all, even I, shall want for nothing.

And when the Little Blinking Light completed the re-entry of all back into the whole of the First Realizer, its Voice said: "Let there be light."

And suddenly there was light reaching far beyond the point of the Voice, and e did indeed equal mc², and the present Eon, as we know it, began according to the Word of the Good Book.